THE TRUTH

Also by Peter James:

Dead Letter Drop
Atom Bomb Angel
Billionaire
Possession
Dreamer
Sweet Heart
Twilight
Prophecy
Host
Alchemist

THE TRUTH

PETER JAMES

ORION

Copyright © Peter James Really Scary Books Ltd 1997
All rights reserved

The right of Peter James to be identified as the author
of this work has been asserted by him in accordance with
the Copyright, Designs and Patents Act 1988.

First published in Great Britain in 1997 by
Orion
An imprint of Orion Books Ltd
Orion House, 5 Upper St Martin's Lane,
London WC2H 9EA

A CIP catalogue record for this book
is available from the British Library

ISBN 0 75281 019 7 (cased)
    0 75281 254 8 (trade paperback)

Typeset by Deltatype Ltd, Birkenhead, Merseyside
Printed in Great Britain by
Clays Ltd, St Ives plc

ACKNOWLEDGMENTS

I owe an enormous debt of gratitude to Robert Beard, FRCS, Felicity Beard, Andy Holyer, Bruce Katz and Sue Ansell, who never flagged or ceased to respond vigorously and with warm goodwill to my ceaseless barrage of questions in the researching of this novel.

And also to Richard Howorth, Dr Duncan Stewart, Barbara Haywood, Peter Rawlings and Dr A. M. Anton for their help.

Writing is only in part a solitary task, and as ever I owe a huge thank you to the invaluable creative input and tireless support of my UK agent, Jon Thurley and his brilliant right hand, Patricia Preece, as well as the very considerable creative contributions made by my new editor, Simon Spanton, my new copy editor, Hazel Orme, and my US agent, Brian Siberell at CAA.

And as always the book could not have happened without the forbearance of my wife, Georgina, and the tolerance of Bertie who only sometimes barked during my deepest moments of thought ...

Peter James
scary@pavilion.co.uk

*for Jon Thurley, who gave me the guidance,
the will, the hope, and above all else,
the belief.*

Prologue

Permaglow from the city lights makes it brighter than the three men like. They were hoping for darkness but all they get is a neon twilight.

One holds a briefcase and a photocopy of a fax, one a flashlight, one two shovels taped neatly together. They should not be here, and they are nervous; this is not at all how they imagined it would be, but that's the way it is. The one with the briefcase is smarter than his colleagues, and he understands: nothing is ever quite as we imagine it.

They have travelled a long way; being here scares them; the thought of what they are about to do scares them even more. But neither of these things scares them as much as the man who has hired them to do this job.

Two of them have never met this man, they have only heard stories about him; they are not the kind of stories they would want to tell their kids. The stories work on their minds even now as they search, fuelling them with a determination they have never felt before. They are riding emotional rapids on a flimsy raft, and the raft has a name: it is called *Fear of Failure*.

The beam of the flashlight strikes a gravestone, sweeps away the darkness as if it is a layer of ancient dust. Engraved words appear. A loved one, long dead; it's the wrong one. They move on across the flat ground, past a clump of trees and a small, landscaped mound.

Another headstone; also the wrong one. They stop, consult the blurred fax. They look around them, see marble obelisks, onyx cherubs, granite slabs, porphyry urns, chiselled endearments, quotations, poems. But these men are not readers of poetry, the words do not reach out through the darkness to them.

'We're in the wrong line, you assholes. Next line along. Look, it shows you clearly, you have to count three lines. We only counted two.'

They find the right line. Find the right gravestone.

Hannah Katherine Rosewell. 1892–1993.
Dearly beloved wife and mother.

The man checks the fax, reading the fuzzy words with difficulty, then studies the inscription on the headstone once more. He is being methodical. Finally he nods assent.

Carefully the other two cut the turf and roll it back as if it were a carpet. Then they start digging; the man with the fax watches, listens to the crunch of the blades, the traffic on Sunset beyond the locked wrought iron gates, watches for shadows that move, for a shape that was not there last time he looked. It is a warm night and the soil is dry, it has the texture of calcium, of old bones that have gone beyond brittle and crumbled.

A shovel pings as it strikes a stone, and an oath hisses through the humid darkness. After a while the men pause to drink from a canteen of water.

They work for almost three hours before the lid of the coffin is fully exposed. It's in good shape, there's still a gleam from the varnish, rosewood; this is a deluxe, a tree in a rainforest has given its life for this coffin.

The two men standing on the lid lay their shovels on the ground, then stretch their backs. Each is handed a nylon cord with a shackle, which they clip to the end handles, then they haul themselves up out of the grave, and stretch their backs again, gratefully. One licks a blister on his hand, then binds a handkerchief around his palm.

Even with all three working, it takes several minutes of clumsy, painful effort to haul the coffin up and onto the ground, but finally they succeed, and the one with the bandaged hand sits on it, momentarily exhausted by the effort. They drink more water, all three peering anxiously into the night around them. A small rodent scurries past and is absorbed by the darkness.

Now they have the coffin out, the urgency with which they have been working has deserted them. They stand back from it for some moments, looking at the brass handles, looking at each other, each thinking their own private thoughts about how a corpse might look after three years underground.

They go to work on the screws, remove each of them and pocket them carefully. Then they hesitate. The two who have dug the grave grip the lid and try to free it, but it's stuck tight. They try a little harder and there's a crack like a gunshot as the seal gives and the lid raises a few inches at one end.

2

Instantly they drop it again and stagger away.

'Yech, Jesus!' says the one with the bandaged hand.

The smell.

Nothing has prepared them for this smell. It's as if a septic tank has been vented beneath them.

They move further away, but the smell is everywhere, the whole night is thick with it. The one with the torch gags, then swallows back down a throatful of vomit. They shuffle further away still.

Finally the smell recedes enough for them to be able to move back towards the coffin. This time they prepare themselves, taking deep breaths before they heave that lid up and off.

Inside there is fine quilted satin, white, the colour of death. The old lady's hair is white also; it is thin and wispy, the same hue as the satin, but its sheen has gone; her face is brown, like scuffed leather, patches of bone show through: her teeth forming a rictus smile look like they have been freshly brushed. Her state of preservation owes as much to the quality of her coffin as it does to the dry Californian climate; in a more humid soil, in a cheaper coffin, she would look less good.

The smell isn't so bad now, it's being diluted by the fresh air that the corpse hasn't seen for three years. The one with the fax looks at his watch and knows they have a little under three hours of darkness remaining to them. He reads the instructions at the bottom of the fax although he has already memorised them, has been thinking about them day and night for the past week.

He opens the briefcase he has brought, removes scissors, a scalpel, a boning knife and a small cool-box. Working swiftly he snips a tuft of hair, excises a square of flesh from her chest, then amputates the index finger of the woman's right hand; no fluid leaks from the cut; the finger is dry, leathery, like an antique peg. He places each of his prizes into a separate compartment that has already been prepared in the cool-box, then checks the instructions on the fax once more, before mentally ticking them off.

They screw the lid back onto the coffin and begin the task of shovelling back the soil. It goes back in faster than it came out. But not that fast.

In the morning one of the security guards passes by; he notices nothing amiss; he has no reason to.

Chapter One

'It doesn't have a garage,' John said.

'I can live with that. How many houses in London *do* have garages?'

John nodded. She had a point, maybe it *was* no big deal.

'I love it, don't you?'

John looked absently at the For Sale sign, deep in thought, studied the particulars he had in his hand, looked up at the columned porch that was almost absurdly grand for the house, then at the red-brick walls clad in ivy and clematis, and back at the turret. It was the turret that was really getting to him, hooking him.

In his teens he'd dreamed of being an architect, and had he lived in the previous century, this was the kind of house he might have designed. It was individual, on three storeys, the only detached one in the street, beyond the end of the Victorian red-brick terrace, and it was the turret that made it, set if off, gave it an air both of importance and of eccentricity.

The estate agent, Darren Morris, whom John placed at a mental age of about twelve, jigged around at the edge of his peripheral vision, chewing a wad of gum with his mouth open which, combined with his forward-combed fringe, his stooped back and gangly limbs, made him appear almost Neanderthal; he looked like he wanted to be somewhere else – *needed* to be somewhere else – in a hurry, gave out the vibes that they'd been keeping him from a far more pressing engagement. John manoeuvred himself behind him, then, holding the particulars in his teeth, began mimicking a gorilla scratching its armpits.

Susan looked away quickly, but was unable to mask her grin. The estate agent turned round, but all he saw was John studying the house with intense concentration.

'South-facing garden,' Darren Morris said. This was the third, or maybe fourth time he had parted with this nugget of information. John ignored it, he was still gazing at the house, trying to keep the interior alive in his mind.

The sunlight through the bay window in the drawing room, that gorgeous combination of both airiness and warmth, and of space. Those wonderful high-ceilinged rooms. The deep hall that gave such a great welcoming feeling as you walked in. The dining room that could seat twelve, no problem (not that they had ever entertained that many at once, but who knows?). The small room next to it overlooking the garden that Susan had already bagged for her study. The cellar that he could one day rack out and fill with wine.

He looked up at the turret again. That room up there, with its views all around, would make the most sensational bedroom. And there were four more rooms on the first and second floors that would make a den for him and spare bedrooms, plus a loft they hadn't even gone up to.

'I really like the garden,' Susan said. 'It's a huge garden for London.'

John liked it too, the privacy of it, and the fact that on the other side of the fence was a beautiful park with tennis courts, and a pond, and acres of grass that were sparkling with frost this morning. The house needed money spent on it, that was the one serious consideration. The roof did not look good, or the wiring or plumbing, and God knows what other kinds of old-house problems lurked in here. He'd be hard pushed to find the asking price, without even beginning to think about repairs and renovation.

The turret got to him again – he couldn't stop looking at it, he was filled with a sudden deep urge to live in a house with a turret. But it wasn't just the turret. This was the first time he had walked into a house and thought, yes, I could spend the rest of my life here. It had grandeur, but it was Bohemian also, funky, elegant, it had *style*. This would be a great place to bring clients, he thought. This was a place that announced: *John Carter has arrived!*

But it had no garage.

Suddenly John, who had always wanted a house with a garage, saw no need for a garage. There was a small concreted area, enough for one car. Plenty of spaces in the tree-lined street. It was peaceful here, tranquil, there was no noise of London traffic. An oasis.

He thought about making love to Susan in the bedroom in the turret; he thought about making love to her outside in the private garden, in the sunshine, in the summer that was not far off. It was the last week of February, they could be in by then.

'I love it,' he said.

'And I love you,' Susan said, putting her arms around him, hugging him hard. 'I love you more than anything in the world.' Then she looked longingly beyond him at the house, hugging him even harder. She was staring at a piece of the England of her dreams. The house was conjuring up for her all kinds of images from books she had read: Austen, Hardy, Dickens, Trollope, Thackeray, Forster, Greene. One after another, descriptions of elegant London houses and country houses came into her mind.

She had often, in a Californian childhood largely buried in books, imagined herself in England, living the lives of the characters she read about, maybe hosting an elegant, witty dinner party, or calling on someone and being received by a butler, or just hurrying through London in the rain.

'And I love you too,' John replied.

The estate agent moved away and hovered by his car, then looked at his watch again and dug his hands in his pockets. Everyone went nuts over this house, everyone who saw it wanted to buy it but they never did, because of the horrific twenty-nine-page survey they would get listing all the problems. That combined with the asking price, which was much too high – and from which the vendors would not budge – made this place a sticker.

He looked at this couple, trying to size them up. Susan Carter was American, he guessed from her accent, late twenties, shoulder-length red hair cut modern, long camel coat over jeans and boots. She reminded him of an actress and he was trying to think who, *Gorillas in the Mist* was the film. Then he remembered: Sigourney Weaver. Yes, she seemed to have that same mixture of good looks and ballsiness. And maybe a hint of Scully in *The X-Files* also. Yup. As he looked at her again he could see even more of Scully coming through.

John Carter was English, a little older, early to mid thirties, he reckoned. Sharp dresser, tweed trenchcoat, Boss suit, buckled shoes, looked like a media type, advertising probably. Straight black hair, sleek, handsome face, an air of fresh-faced boyishness about him, but tough with it, there was a definite hard streak in this guy. He looked across at the Carter's black BMW M3. Spotlessly clean, gleaming, went with John Carter's Mr Immaculate image, he thought, but he was surprised there wasn't a personalised plate: the one on the car showed it to be four years old. Poser's car.

Still holding John and looking at the house, Susan asked, quietly, vapour streaming from her mouth, 'Can we afford it?'

'No, we can't possibly afford it.'

She leaned back, the morning sunlight striking her eyes, turning them lapis-lazuli blue. These were the eyes John fell in love with seven and a half years ago and had been in love with ever since. She grinned. 'So?'

They'd been told that the previous owners had moved overseas. The place was empty and must be costing them money – maybe they'd lower the asking price for a quick sale?

John grinned back. He was tantalising her, he was tantalising himself. It would be reckless to buy this place, but then again, all his life he has been reckless.

Chapter Two

The man of whom so many people were afraid presided over his vast office with an air of courtly ease.

His aristocratic face had become a little gaunt over the years, but his complexion still retained that unique pampered sheen of the well-born. His grey eyes, clear, sharp, full of observation and humour, required no glasses or contact lenses. His dark hair, elegantly streaked with grey, was swept with *élan* back from his temples.

He was dressed in a Savile Row suit, his tie was elegant, winged horses printed on green silk, his black shoes, out of sight beneath his desk, glinted like mirrors; his long, slender fingers, which were leafing through a computer printout, had been finely manicured. His whole manner exuded confidence. He might only have been in his mid fifties.

His name was Emil Sarotzini.

The name was a legend. People told stories about his fabled life with the post-war set – on the French Riviera, partying on the Dockers' yacht in Cannes, dining with Bardot in St Tropez, lunching with the Grimaldis in Monaco; and in the US, where he courted stars like Mansfield and Monroe, and where he was himself courted by the aristocratic circle of the Vanderbilts and Rockefellers and the Mellons. It was rumoured that Warhol had painted an entire collection for him, which Mr Sarotzini had forbidden ever to be shown to the public. And in England, it was whispered, he had been shielded by the Astors from the glare of the Profumo scandal.

Other stories about the man were more discomforting, and there were plenty that would chill people to the marrow. Some of these stories no insider ever dared to tell, because, it was rumoured, Mr Sarotzini had ears everywhere and disloyalty was not an option.

Rumours surrounded every aspect of his life, and none more so than his age, which was to some a matter of idle speculation and to others a disturbing enigma.

No one who worked here was innocent of Mr Sarotzini's reputation. It acted like a magnet: they were repulsed but they were attracted. Positive and negative. Intrigue, mystery and speculation had been Mr Sarotzini's ever-present shadows throughout his life. And few people he met failed to fall under his spell.

The man who was bringing him the information he was awaiting knew more about Mr Sarotzini than perhaps any other living person. And, for this reason, was even more afraid of him than anyone else.

Kündz opened the panelled double doors and entered the secretary's ante-room. She was the sentinel who held all the keys to access Mr Sarotzini, and precious few ever even reached this inner sanctum of her office. But she barely gave Kündz a glance.

Mr Sarotzini was visible through the open entrance beyond her, like an Egyptian god in his hypostyle hall. His office was mostly in darkness, one pool of brightness from a gold table lamp illuminating the neat stack of papers beside the leather blotter on his desk. There was a large window but the slats of the blinds were angled and narrowed against the glare of the mid-morning sunlight.

Kündz was six feet, six inches tall, with broad, quarterback shoulders, close-cropped hair and a blunt boxer's face. He was dressed in one of his habitual plain two-piece suits, today a navy one, his tie carefully adjusted, his shoes scrupulously polished. The suits were made for him by Mr Sarotzini's tailor, but in spite of the expensive cloth and the careful fittings, he never looked quite at ease in them. To the casual stranger he could have been a night-club bouncer, or perhaps a soldier on leave in borrowed civvies.

Before taking a step forward he swallowed, checked the knot of his tie, shot a glance down at his shoes, buttoned his jacket. He knew that, sartorially, he failed Mr Sarotzini. But in every other respect he prided himself on the way he learned from his mentor and carried out his wishes.

Mr Sarotzini had made him everything that he was, but Kündz was aware that he could just as easily strip it all away from him again, and this was part of the fear that fuelled his slavish devotion to the man.

'So?' Mr Sarotzini said, smiling expectantly as Kündz approached his desk. The smile relaxed Kündz and his love for this man was so intense that he wanted to reach across that huge desk and hug him, but this he could not do. Many years ago Mr Sarotzini had forbidden this kind of physical contact. Instead, Kündz handed him the envelope, and stood stiffly to attention.

9

'You may sit, Stefan,' Mr Sarotzini said, shaking out the contents and immediately becoming absorbed in them.

Kündz sat, tensely, on the edge of a chair that had once been owned by an Ottoman prince, whose name he could not remember. Although Mr Sarotzini's office was filled with treasures and antiquities, there was something about this room that mere money alone could not create, and that was the sense of power it exuded.

Kündz felt like the little girl, Alice, who had stepped into a world where everything was so much bigger. He sat dwarfed by the size of the furniture, by canvases the size of high-rise buildings that hung from the walls, by sculptures and busts and statuettes that leered down at him, by shelves of leather-bound volumes that sneered at anyone of lesser education than their owner. He looked up at Mr Sarotzini.

It was hard to read his expression.

The room smelt of stale cigar smoke, but the only ashtray, a cut-glass one on Mr Sarotzini's desk, was clean. Kündz knew that Mr Sarotzini, who was a man of habit, would have already smoked his first Montecristo of the day, but would not light his second for another hour.

Mr Sarotzini held the thin document, just six pages long, with fingers that were long and bony, softened by hair. He said nothing until he had finished reading, and then his face tightened with displeasure.

'What am I to do with this, Stefan?'

This threw Kündz. Yet he knew, from long experience, that the answers Mr Sarotzini required were not always the obvious ones. He took his time, as Mr Sarotzini had long taught him, not rushing into his answer. 'There are no restrictions,' he replied, finally.

Mr Sarotzini's face hardened into a near rage that made Kündz frightened and confused. 'This is a shopping list, Stefan, a grocery list. Look, it says, "Twelve bagels, two litres of skimmed milk, butter, dried apricots, salami." What have you given me this for?'

Kündz's mind swirled. This wasn't possible, surely, he couldn't – couldn't have made a mistake – no. Where could this list have come from? He thought quickly, thought of the man who had given him this document, a very great genetics scientist. Could this fool scientist have given him the wrong thing?

No, it was impossible. He'd checked and rechecked it.

Then the expression on Mr Sarotzini's face changed from rage into a quiet smile. 'It's all right, Stefan, don't look so worried. Relax. I'm only joking. You must learn to take jokes.'

Kündz stared back at him, bewildered, unsure what was coming next.

'This is good,' Mr Sarotzini said, tapping the document. 'It is very good.'

Kündz tried not to show his relief: he had learnt never to show weakness to Mr Sarotzini. And gratitude was weakness. He was expected to know that the document was good; a reaction was not required. With Mr Sarotzini he was on a learning curve that had no end, and he had lived with this almost all his life.

He looked down at the soft pile of a Persian rug to avoid giving anything away in his eyes, and took in the complex pattern; all Persian rugs told stories, but he did not know what this story was. He turned his thoughts to Claudie, focused on her, wondered if Claudie would let him tie her up tonight and whip her. He decided he would ask her, and if she said no he would do it anyway.

Her smell rose from his skin; he thought of her sprig of black pubic hair and his fear of Mr Sarotzini turned fleetingly into arousal for Claudie. Then the fear returned.

He looked up at the painting on the wall directly behind Mr Sarotzini: modern art, abstract, he did not understand this kind of art, he did not know whether it was a good painting or bad, he knew only that it must be of immense value, of great importance to the world of art, to be in this room. Then Mr Sarotzini skewered his thoughts with his voice. He spoke, as usual, in flawless German, although Kündz knew that German was not Mr Sarotzini's mother tongue.

'It has taken thirty years. This is how long we have been looking. Thirty years, Stefan. You understand the importance?'

Kündz understood, but remained silent.

'You have a weakness, Stefan?'

Kündz was surprised by the question. He stalled, knowing that with this man he could not lie. 'Everyone has a weakness. That is the Nineteenth Truth,' he replied.

Mr Sarotzini seemed pleased by this answer. He opened a drawer in his desk, took out an envelope and handed it to Kündz.

Inside it Kündz found photographs of a man and a woman. The man was in his mid thirties, with dark hair and striking, if boyish, good looks. The woman looked a few years younger; she had red hair that stopped just short of the shoulders; a pretty face; modern.

There was another photograph, showing her in a T-shirt with straps, and a short skirt. She had great legs, slender, a touch muscular maybe, and he realised they were arousing him; her breasts looked firm inside her T-shirt and they aroused him also. He wondered if she smelled as good as Claudie; he decided he would like to tie this woman up and whip her.

Perhaps with her pretty boy-faced husband trussed up and watching. Mr Sarotzini spoke again, interrupting his thoughts: 'Mr and Mrs Carter. John Carter and Susan Carter. They live in a house in South London, which they have only recently purchased. He has his own business, in multi-media, she works in publishing. They have no children. You will find me John Carter and Susan Carter's weak spots. All is clear?'

Kündz looked at the photographs again, his excitement deepening. In particular he looked at the one that showed Susan Carter's legs and breasts, and wondered if her pubic hair was also red. He hoped so.

Mr Sarotzini had given him Claudie as a gift for being good. Maybe if he continued to please Mr Sarotzini, he would give him this woman as well.

'All is clear,' Kündz said.

Chapter Three

As John Carter hurried up to the front entrance of the bank, he was suffering a bad attack of butterflies. He was perspiring and he could not remember when he last felt like this – probably not since those terrifying summonses to the headmaster's study when he was at school.

His shirt clung to his back, and his brain had locked up, hung itself, crashed. He pushed the door, which was clearly labelled PULL, but was too nervous even to feel embarrassed.

He crossed the foyer, feeling even more like a scared schoolboy, glanced at the queues at the tellers' desks, got his bearings, then walked over to the window marked ENQUIRIES.

Even the woman clerk made him feel uncomfortable as she looked at him through the glass partition, as if his name and description had been circulated to the entire staff here on some secret blacklist. *Watch out for this man.*

'I have an appointment with Mr Clake,' he said, his voice withering like a faltering sales pitch under the clerk's stony glare, and he worried from her frown of disapproval whether he had incorrectly pronounced the manager's name. 'That is how you pronounce it?'

She nodded stonily.

John was wearing his most conservative suit, plain navy lightweight, white cotton shirt, a quiet tie and black lace-up brogues – as well as his red and white polka-dot boxer shorts, which he wore when he needed luck. He'd discussed what to wear with Susan both last night and this morning, and had tried three different ties and four pairs of shoes before she felt that the image was right. He looked smart, she told him, without looking *showy*.

He thought about Mr Clake, wondering, for the umpteenth time, what kind of a man he was. He had been thinking about him for a full twenty-four hours now, ever since the phone call from Mr Clake's secretary yesterday. He thought about his car also, which was sitting on a double yellow line down the road from the bank; maybe he'd get lucky and wouldn't be clamped but it was an anxiety he could do without right now. He'd had no choice – there were no parking spaces and he was already fifteen minutes late.

John thought suddenly of a joke he'd heard. It was about a man who told his friend that his bank manager had a glass eye. His friend asked how he could tell which was the glass eye and which the real eye. 'That's easy,' the man replied. 'The glass eye is the one that looks warmer.'

The joke didn't seem funny any more. John pulled out his handkerchief and dabbed the moisture that was running from his forehead like a burst main, silently cursing evolution for sabotaging his body. Adrenaline was the problem. Fifty thousand years ago adrenaline had helped cavemen flee from the sabre-toothed tiger. But John didn't need it right now. He didn't need the glands pumping the stuff out, powering his muscles, switching up the rheostat of his heartbeat, dilating his pupils, converting his sweat glands into fire hydrants. He needed calming down, and evolution had not equipped him with anything to do that.

He mopped his forehead again; his neck was sticky, the sweating getting worse. Not *sweat*, he thought suddenly, no. *Horses* sweat, ladies glow, men *perspire*.

John's brain was swirling; he was finding it hard to hold onto his thoughts. He felt a brief stab of panic about his car. How long could it last on a double yellow line in Piccadilly? Ten minutes? Twenty?

'Would you like to come this way?'

He stooped to glance at his reflection in the glass, nursed back into place some stray hairs with his finger, straightened his tie, then took a deep breath. Control. All his working life he had been in control. He knew how to charm people: he was a master at manipulation and he had charmed the socks off his previous bank manager, Bill Williams. All he had to do was keep calm, be polite, friendly, show this Mr Clake just how good the future was looking.

He followed the assistant through a door. It was all bland blue carpet, dark wood, the same as it had always been, with just one difference. Mr Clake, instead of Bill Williams.

Bill Williams had been a sucker for technology and for seven years John had juiced him with it. They played virtual golf between their offices on their computers, and occasionally John took him out to his club at Richmond and they played real golf. John taught him how to surf the Net, and where to find the dirty pictures – the *totties*, Bill called them – and how to stack them up inside a sequence of files on a hard disk protected by a password.

John taught Bill Williams more than he ever needed to know about computers and, in return, Bill gave him all he needed from the bank, and more, far more, than enough rope to hang himself, Bill often joked.

And now Bill Williams was history. He had taken early retirement. Overnight. Bill had rung him just a week ago, sounding like a man bereaved, saying he would explain some time but was not at liberty to do so at the moment. He apologised, he was truly sorry, but everything would be fine, he assured John. They agreed to have a game of golf but made no date. The bank would continue to look after John, he was in good hands. But there was no conviction in Bill's voice.

And there was not much warmth in Mr Clake's handshake. Even less in his expression. He was as bald as an egg, his mouth was small and off-centre and he wore square glasses that did not suit him. 'Mr Carter, it's good of you to come at such short notice.'

He talked like a ventriloquist, his tiny skewed lips scarcely moving, as if he was gripping a pin between his teeth.

They sat down. Mr Clake leant forward across an open file containing several sheets of computer printout. Without reading them, John guessed it contained the financial entrails of his business. Beside them on the desk was a photograph that he presumed to be of Mr Clake's wife and children. John studied the wife's face. She looked pleasant – at least Clake was human, he thought, feeling a ray of hope.

'You're in the multimedia game,' Mr Clake informed him.

John nodded, and swallowed. Mr Clake's body language was making him tense as hell, and he did not like the way the man had said *multimedia*.

'Yes, technology.' Mr Clake drew a breath with a hiss and glanced down at the printout. 'Technology.' He smiled. It was like the flare of a distant match in a vast, freezing emptiness. John fleetingly thought about his car, wondering how long Mr Clake was going to detain him, but the car wasn't important. He brought his focus back to this meeting, ran over the answers he had prepared for any of the questions he figured might be lobbed at him.

'Not a computer man myself,' Mr Clake said, sitting tightly behind his desk. 'Don't go for all this technology. It has a place, of course, and I can understand why you see the potential.'

John looked at Mr Clake's dapper suit, at the man's smug face, and felt the anger rising inside him like a choking fog. How could anyone, in a modern bank, in Mr Clake's position, make such a crass remark?

Then he noticed an object on the bare expanse of desk that he had not previously seen. As he looked at it harder, he could barely believe his eyes. It was a Bible. Mr Clake had a Bible ostentatiously placed on his desk. What was this man, where was he coming from, John wondered.

'The five-year forecast,' Mr Clake said. 'Who produced it?'

Clake must be a born-again Christian, he decided. He could detect something devout now in the man's expression; something pious; something messianic. Maybe Mr Clake was on a crusade to save the world from technology?

John, his heart sinking further, struggled to keep his cool and maintain his warm, polite, courteous façade. He rummaged inside his briefcase, pulled out his laptop computer and powered it up.

Irritation showed on Mr Clake's face and John's apology that it would take a minute or so to boot up only served to annoy the bank manager further. John ransacked his brain for something to say to break the awkwardness of the silence, to try to find common ground between the two of them. 'Are you – a – golfer?' he said, lamely.

Clake responded with a single shake of his head.

'How long have you – been – with – the – bank?'

'Fourteen years. How long is this machine of yours going to take?'

'It's almost done.' John stared at the screen, willing it to be ready. Then, when the computer finally stabilised, John asked, 'The plan? The five-year plan or the five-year forecast?'

'The *forecast*, I said.' Mr Clake's reserves of courtesy appeared to be running out. John tapped two keys and his computer crashed.

Blushing, and sweating profusely, he was forced to reboot. It was all slipping away from him, everything he had worked for, he could sense it. The meeting was running dangerously out of control, and John was fast losing confidence in his ability to pull it back together.

His thoughts flashed to Susan, her happiness in the new house, and all that they stood to lose if Clake cut up rough. And his partner, Gareth, to whom he had given a stake in the business when he had started, eight years back, and their staff of sixty, many of whom had worked for him since leaving college.

He had been rash in taking on so many new employees just recently, in buying a lot of equipment, in moving to their new offices, in buying the house, but they were on such an incredible roll that he had been completely confident. Now, desperately, he needed to convey that confidence to Clake, but it was deserting him.

He gave Clake a nervous smile. 'Have you? Always? Been here, in London?' John heard his voice sounding like a tape being played at the wrong speed.

Mr Clake did not reply; he was studying something hard in the printout. He was not looking happy.

Chapter Four

'Where do you think I should put this?'

Harry, the painter, looked at Susan with his big, sad eyes. He had a droopy moustache that reminded her of a Mexican bandit in some Western she had once seen – perhaps *The Good, the Bad and the Ugly*, she wasn't sure, and anyhow, it didn't matter.

Her mind was all over the place and not where it ought to have been, which was on the manuscript she had brought home. She was finding it hard to concentrate on her work because she was worrying about John's meeting with the bank.

It was much easier to watch Harry, much easier to think about the colour scheme for the house, to look at the books of fabrics and wallpapers, to walk around the rooms, marking crosses on the walls to indicate where the power points should go and where the radiators should be fixed, than to plough her way through a chapter full of equations that explained gravity.

John had promised to ring her straight after the meeting and let her know how it had gone. It ought to be finished now and he hadn't rung. Maybe that was a good sign, she thought, but she knew she was kidding herself. If the meeting had gone well, he'd have rung her straight away. She was tempted to phone him but held back, not wanting to pressurise him.

She had been frightened by the state he had been in this morning. John was not a worrier, and it was his air of confidence, his calm way of handling problems, coupled with his terrific, unstoppable drive, that had most attracted her to him. He had always known exactly what he wanted and how to get it. He told her on their first date, shouting to be heard above the noise of a crowded bar in Westwood, that he was going to marry her, and when she had laughed, she had seen the hardening in his eyes, the determination in his face, and it had turned her on in a way she had never experienced before.

She'd had plenty of boyfriends, but no one had ever *wanted* her in the way she had seen John did. The following morning, there had been so many flowers in her office she could hardly get in the door.

She had always felt safe, secure with him: he had never made a promise he couldn't keep, or a commitment he couldn't meet. Nothing before had ever worried him. Within weeks she had left everything behind her in California and moved to London. He had become her world.

But this morning he had been a stranger, fumbling around, pulling out different shirts, ties, socks, trying them on, changing them, until in desperation she'd dictated to him what to put on and sent him on his way, and was left feeling, suddenly, very vulnerable.

She always thought they'd been open with each other, but it wasn't until somewhere around dawn this morning, after hours of sleepless tossing and turning, that he'd confessed he was a lot deeper into the bank than he'd previously told her. And he was more worried than he had previously let on about a lawsuit hanging over the company from a composer.

She'd had her suspicions that things had been harder in recent months than he was admitting but he had always convincingly brushed them aside. And, anyhow, he'd been through a few tough times in the past years and always come through. He'd find a way to come through now; that was the kind of man he was.

And if he didn't? Could her income support this place? It might just pay the mortgage, but not much else. British publishing houses were not renowned for the generosity of their salaries, and in any event, a dark cloud was hanging over her job right now: the threat of a takeover bid from an American media giant, which already owned one large publishing house in London.

And there was an even bigger problem than the house if their incomes dried up. How could her kid sister, Casey, be funded?

She stared out of the bay window at the garden for which she had so many plans. They both loved this house so much: was it possible that it could be taken away from them before they'd even had a chance to finish decorating it?

It wasn't just the house that was so wonderful: it was the neighbourhood too. She was enjoying exploring their new world. In the past couple of weeks since they'd moved in, she had discovered a bakery to die for two minutes' walk away, a specialist wine merchant that it was already hard to keep John away from, and a great little Thai restaurant whose owner kept bringing them dishes that he refused to charge them for because he had taken a shine to them.

She had sorted out the kitchen, repapered the shelves, put up a spice rack and the paper-towel holder, and was really pleased with her prowess with John's tool kit. She had written to her parents, enclosing photographs of the exterior and interior of the house (the interior labelled, clearly, BEFORE!!!) and she had written to Casey and sent her photographs as well, not that Casey could ever see them or read the letter but that did not matter. Susan kept Casey in the loop on everything.

Harry was taking his time thinking. He dipped his roller in the paint, then applied it to the wall again, up and down, steady vertical sweeps. In front of her eyes the living room was changing colour from sludgy beige to Dulux Not Quite White. She wanted this Not Quite White theme throughout the house with all the woodwork contrasting in satin black.

Afternoon sunlight spilled onto the bare oak floorboards; outside in the garden the cherry tree was in blossom. The house had large rooms and neither she nor John, who shared similar tastes on most things, wanted to clutter them. They had agreed to keep the feeling of space, airiness, light.

Harry pushed the roller up, against gravity, then down, with gravity, thinking about her question. She could see from his expression that he preferred the down strokes to the up strokes, and wondered if he was aware that gravity was helping him with the down strokes.

She was big on gravity right now, having spent the last ten days editing a book on it. Although adept at physics, gravity had always given her a hard time, but she took comfort in the fact that it had given Einstein a hard time also – although, as she confided in John, maybe not *quite* such a hard time as herself.

To make matters worse, its author, Fergus Donleavy, one of her favourite authors and her most successful acquisition for Magellan Lowry, was trying to be too clever in this book, or so both she and an independent reader thought.

'There, by the French windows,' Harry said finally. 'That's where you should put it.' Then he muttered something about good *feng shui* that Susan didn't quite catch.

She lugged the Victorian pot stand over to the French windows. Harry was right, it looked good there. They both stood, admiring the piece, which she'd bought last week in a bric-à-brac shop a few streets away. Then she made a cup of tea for Harry, coffee for herself, and went back to the small room next door which she had made her study. She sat at her desk, in front of an open window overlooking the garden, and turned her attention once more to the manuscript.

She forced her way through three equations before the warm air on her face, and the scents of the garden that it carried, distracted her. This weather reminded her of California, her childhood in Marina Del Rey, and her student days on the UCLA campus at Westwood. The memories were mixed, happiness tinged with sadness. The failure of her caring, loving parents to succeed at what they really wanted to do in life. The tragedy that had overtaken Casey, which continued to affect all their lives.

She sipped her coffee, looked at the blossom on the cherry tree, at the wooden seat and the small brick patio with the kettle barbecue and picnic bench, and dreamed for a moment of smoky outdoor evenings and chilled rosé wine. Then she turned her attention back to the manuscript, pushed back the sleeves of John's old shirt that she was wearing over her jeans, picked up her pencil, chewed it and concentrated.

Time is a curve, not a straight line. Linear time is an illusion; we exist in a space-time continuum; your wristwatch at the top of a mountain tells time more slowly than your wristwatch at the bottom. This has nothing to do with gravity, it is relativity; but they are interconnected.

This was one of the key points Fergus was making, but considering that this was meant to be a book for the layman, he had not explained it clearly. Even she was getting confused.

Some while later Harry knocked at the door and told her he would see her in the morning. She waved good-night without looking up from the manuscript, drank the last drops of cold coffee and marked an indent for a new paragraph. A blackbird hopped across the lawn, in and out of the line of shadows stencilled on the uncut grass by the trees in the park beyond, its head jerking like a clockwork toy. She watched it until, as if it sensed her gaze, it took off.

John had still not called. She picked up the phone, unable to contain her anxiety any longer, and the doorbell rang.

She went to the front door and opened it. A man in brown overalls stood there; parked behind him in the street was a van with British Telecom markings. 'I hope I'm not too late?' he enquired. 'I was delayed on another job. My office rang you?'

'No, I didn't get any call,' Susan replied, her mind more on John and the manuscript than this visitor. 'But that's no problem.'

The man looked relieved. He held a tool box in one hand and a jumble of wiring attached to a metering device in the other. He was a big man, built like a quarterback, with a blunt face and close-cropped hair. He didn't look English, more Eastern European, but his accent was North London and he talked in a way that made him sound, somehow, a little simple.

'If it's too late, I can come tomorrow.'

'No, it's fine. What actually are you doing?'

'I am here to test your lines. Four lines, plus an ISDN?'

'Yes,' Susan said. 'Come in.'

The man looked at her: she was even prettier in the flesh than in the photograph, he thought. He made a careful study of her eyebrows. Always the giveaway. They were red, like the hair on her head.

So now he knew that the pubic hair inside her jeans was also red. And that excited him.

Chapter Five

'What the fuck's this?'

'It's a telephone,' John Carter's secretary replied, calmly.

John regarded her as if she was plankton in a bucket. 'I *know* that, Stella, OK? I want to know why I have *this* telephone on my desk and not the one that was there when I went out this morning.'

Mr Clake was mostly to blame for John's mood but the traffic warden who had arranged for his car to be clamped had contributed to it, as had the news broken to him by his lawyer with whom he had spent most of the rest of the afternoon. But Clake had really trashed his day. Although right now John was more focused on the shiny grey BT CallMaster telephone, which had not been on his desk seven hours earlier.

'British Telecom replaced it. A man came – said there was no charge. He replaced all the CallMasters,' Stella told him. 'They're exactly the same as the previous ones,' she added, used to John's moods and normally able to calm him.

John picked up the receiver, punched a button, got a dial tone, then hesitated. He'd promised to call Susan after the meeting with Clake, and she'd be anxious now because he hadn't. But what the hell was he going to say to her?

He replaced the receiver in the cradle, slung his jacket over the back of his chair and sat down. 'I don't want to be disturbed for an hour, Stella,' he called out, and closed his eyes against a headache that was becoming acute. 'I'm due to play squash at seven with Archie Warren. Could you call him and cancel?'

'Do you want anything? Coffee?'

He shook his head, heard the door shut, and sat motionless. His insides were drawn into a tight, hard, knotted ball and he felt queasy. John had always had a fear of heights, and he felt this way sometimes on a balcony or in a cable car, this dreadful, helpless fear that he was experiencing now.

He had to collect his thoughts, think his way through this, somehow find solutions to the two different problems that had kicked him into touch today. The intercom on his new telephone warbled; he ignored it. A bluebottle thudded against the window. Outside, a delivery truck rumbled along the mews.

He stared bleakly ahead of him. His life stared back. Glossy software packs framed and mounted on the walls. *How to Play Bridge ... How to Plant a Herb Garden ... How to Build a Space Rocket ... How to Wire a House ... How to Make Love Properly ... How to Eat Healthily ...*

John's business had been built on a simple idea. His company made computer programs that told people how to do anything they wanted, and provided information at the touch of a keyboard. They'd started with CD-Roms, but now it was mostly on-line multimedia through the Internet. On-line medicine had been his biggest success of the past couple of years – in particular, the Virtual Gynaecologist.

He'd pulled off a great coup in getting Harvey Addison, London's most fashionable obstetrician, to be the presenter of this service to which women could log on, ask any questions they wanted and get a seemingly live consultation – although it was, in fact, incredibly smart software that used pre-recorded filmed responses to every conceivable question, which gave the illusion that Harvey Addison was appearing live. People knew, of course, that it wasn't live, but women loved it. For just a couple of pounds they could have their own personal, and thorough, consultation with the great man – and in their own home!

DigiTrak had been hugely successful. There were framed gold CDs on the walls. Statuettes, plaques. The company had won innovation awards from computer magazines, medical magazines, television stations. Its products had a good reputation and were respected.

John had made it all happen. He had smart ideas and a knack for picking great people and getting the chemistry right. His sixty employees were mostly computer-technology graduates, working either on improving the existing programs or designing new ones. He looked after his staff, paid them well, encouraged them. And last year he had found the perfect premises, a large mews building in the middle of South Kensington, which had previously been occupied by an advertising agency. It had great open spaces, split levels, wild spiral staircases. Staff liked working here and clients liked visiting. He had proudly named it DigiTrak House.

The one constant hassle was that the business had always been short of cash. As it expanded, DigiTrak gobbled money faster than it made it so it was constantly chasing its tail. John wasn't alone: all fast-growing businesses tended to have the same problem.

But right now he was alone.

Bill Williams, who had protected him, had gone and now he had Mr Clake. And Clake didn't want to know. In another year's time, maybe less at the rate they were growing, they would be in a position to go public. An analyst John had talked to reckoned that if John could deliver the right figures, they could float the company for maybe twenty million pounds. But there was a yawning chasm between now and then.

John looked down at the workload on his desk. Letters that were unread, letters that awaited his signature, purchases to be approved, cheques to be countersigned. He touched his keyboard and his monitor sprang into life. The icon told him he had new mail. He touched the keyboard again. Seventeen new e-mails awaited him.

Susan stared at him from the photograph on his desk, a big, warm smile on her face that shouted, *I adore you!* at him. He adored her, too, and he needed her right at this moment more than ever. Susan was smart, she was level-headed, she had good ideas and she never panicked. She was a wonderful person and, he thought bitterly, she deserved better from him than failure.

He punched a number on his new telephone and eleven voice-mail messages repeated themselves to him; he jotted down on his pad the ones he would phone back when he could summon up the enthusiasm.

God knows when.

He buried his head in his hands, pinching the bridge of his nose to try to relieve the ache, and sat for some minutes, just thinking, compiling a list in his head of everyone he knew in banking, everyone he knew who had access to investment money, but he was finding it hard to think clearly. He stood up, wandered around the office looking at all the plaques and certificates, then unhooked a framed gold CD from one wall, the first Home Doctor he'd produced, and stared at it.

This is the kind of work we do, Mr Clake, he thought, angrily. The best. Our products are better than anyone else's, because we care. Every single person in this company cares. You might sneer at technology, but the women whose lives we've saved because we showed them how to examine their breasts for lumps aren't sneering at it.

He hung the frame up again then, gripped with a terrible, helpless sense of frustration, stared around the office, wondering if he would still have it in a month's time. Wondering if he would still have *anything* in a month's time.

He lifted the slats of the blinds and looked out of the window. Someone who was trying to get past the truck down below was pissed off and blasting their horn. It was going to be a fine evening. He and Susan were looking forward so much to this summer in their new home. How the hell could he possibly break it to her that they might have to put it on the market?

And they might not even have her income for much longer if the takeover of her publishing house went ahead.

Shit. Oh, shit. Oh, shit.

He thought about the house. He loved driving home to it, and almost every time he pulled up outside he had to tell himself he wasn't dreaming, this really was his house. He thought about all the change-of-address cards they'd sent out, and the friends they'd already had round to show the place off to. Everyone had loved it, told them how lucky they were. They were going to look foolish, having to move straight out. And he thought about his staff. How could he face them? How would he feel, throwing them all out of work? How were *they* going to feel?

He sat down on the sofa, beneath the overhang of a huge potted plant, and closed his eyes again. *Must be positive.* There will be a solution. You always find solutions. Remember what you've always told other people: *The best form of revenge is success.* Stuff Clake by *succeeding.*

The intercom on his new telephone warbled; he ignored it; it warbled again; he ignored it again. He got up and walked over to the one-armed bandit, an original, mechanical one he had bought years ago in an antique shop, slotted in a coin, pulled the lever: a cherry, a lemon and an orange clattered to a halt.

The bluebottle smacked the window again. It was trying to get out and it was trapped. He knew how it felt. He was trapped too. Bluebottles were also called blowflies, he remembered. Blowflies ate corpses. He thought about a CD they had made called *How to Mummify a Corpse.* It had sold hugely well; they still had it up on the Web.

The phone warbled again. The horn blasted outside. His brain was spinning but got no traction. He knew what he should have done; he should have played squash with Archie Warren and he might have felt a bit better afterwards, but he wasn't up to coping with Archie tonight. Archie was his most successful friend, but he was loud, garish, and John always found himself bullshitting about how well DigiTrak was doing just to keep up with him. And he wasn't in the mood for bullshitting tonight.

He made a decision. He'd leave early, pick up a couple of steaks from the butcher round the corner from the mews, stop to buy a couple of good bottles from that terrific little wine merchant Susan had discovered near their house, and fire up the barbecue. Then they could sit out on the brick patio, get smashed and talk their way through this.

The thought of getting smashed cheered him. He stood up, wormed into his jacket, slammed his PowerBook into his briefcase and was out of his office, telling Stella he'd see her in the morning.

But as he walked out into the corridor, his partner, Gareth Noyce, attached himself to him. Gareth needed to speak to him. Urgently. He needed to speak to Gareth too, but not now. He didn't intend telling his partner unless it became absolutely necessary, because Gareth was not good at dealing with pressure. Nor was he much good at dealing with people. If you gave him a computer, any computer, didn't matter how bad shape it was in, didn't matter how pissed off it was with life or how stressed out, within a few minutes it loved Gareth, treated him as if he was its favourite uncle, and gave Gareth anything he wanted. But Gareth did not have the same charm with people.

Gareth was tall, beanpole thin and, although only just thirty-one, his hair had been grey for as long as John had known him. He had a complexion like someone in intensive care, and dressed in clothes that looked like he'd partied in them all night.

'Look,' he said to John, 'we have to talk.'

Reluctantly, John went into Gareth's tip of an office and sat down. As his partner, John knew he had an obligation to tell Gareth what had happened with Clake and the lawyer, but Gareth had only a childlike grasp of money and it would have meant nothing to him, other than to panic him. Gareth lived on a different planet from John, one that had its own subset of reality. This was one of the reasons the partnership had worked so well. John handled the finance and marketing, Gareth the technical side. There was no crossover.

Gareth started talking so fast that John had difficulty catching more than the basic drift. It concerned a game they had in development. A glitch had surfaced. It was important to Gareth, but there was nothing John could do about it, and besides, this problem was nothing, *nothing*, compared to the ones John was carrying inside his head.

'It's a configuration parameter problem, right?' Gareth said. 'But it's not just configuration, right? We're getting software conflicts – I mean, for Christ's sake, Microsoft –' Gareth launched into a screed of technical jargon that lost John in seconds, but carried on, as he usually did, oblivious to the fact that John had no idea what he was saying.

John tuned him out. He let him carry on talking, watched him smoke two cigarettes in succession, the smell driving him nuts. He was tempted to cadge one, but managed to restrain himself. He'd quit three years ago, making a promise to Susan, and was staying quit. Finally, at some point, when he wasn't even sure whether Gareth had finished or was just pausing for breath, John stood up. 'I have to go. We'll talk about it in the morning.'

'You realise this could delay the launch?' Gareth said, darkly.

'Yup, but we can't go with it until it's right.'

'I suppose there is a way round it,' Gareth remarked, as John reached the door.

John waited for him to continue.

'Yup,' Gareth said, perking up. 'Yup, I know what to do! Don't worry, leave it to me.'

John left it to him. He took the lift down to the lobby, wishing he could find a solution to Mr Clake as easily as Gareth had found a solution to his software problem.

Chapter Six

'This is the master bedroom. We have one phone in here.' Susan pointed to it. She even felt proud guiding this stranger around the house – it was still a novelty to her and she was like a kid with a new toy. In particular, she liked showing off this round room in the turret, with its views in all directions.

Kündz followed the line of her finger and saw the telephone beside the bed. He noted the panic button just above the skirting board, but mostly he was taking in the scents of this room. He was separating out the smells this woman had left in this room from those of her husband.

Rich, musky smells from her vaginal juices lingered in the air. They were soured by the metallic tang of her husband's semen, still quite fresh. Maybe they had made love this morning, but if not, certainly some time during the night.

'Two lines to this phone,' she was saying.

Two lines, he heard. The third was for the fax in her study. The fourth was for the burglar alarm. There were four panic buttons. Kündz had seen these, by the front and back doors, by the bed and in the kitchen, right beside the wall-mounted cordless phone; he remembered their positions exactly. The ISDN was for Mr Carter's e-mail.

His thoughts veered to the loft. He had seen the hatch in the landing and the thought of it excited him – not as much as the smell from Susan's vagina or the mental picture he carried of the red pubic hair inside those jeans, but it excited him a lot. His heart was full of gratitude to Mr Sarotzini for the gift of being here. Mr Sarotzini always seemed to understand the things that excited him

They stopped on the landing. He pointed up to the hatch. 'The access by that way is the only one?'

'I think so.'

'Is there a ladder that you have?'

'Out back.' Susan watched this giant of a man with his odd way of

29

speaking and wondered if he enjoyed his work. She wasn't sure why but he just didn't seem to be in the right job, it didn't fit him. Maybe he couldn't get a job doing what he really wanted to do, she thought, and he was doing this because it was better than nothing. Because he was desperate, like a lot of other people.

Susan climbed the ladder first. Kündz stood beneath her. It tormented him to watch her: he was drenched in her smells as he stood there, his face brushed by her legs as she climbed past him. She lifted her feet to another rung and Kündz caught a glimpse of the bare flesh of an ankle exposed beneath her jeans. He'd never been aroused by an ankle before: this was a new experience.

He'd never made love to a woman with red pubic hair before. He thought about her husband's sperm and wondered if it would be slippery inside her.

Above him she pushed open the hatch, and switched on a light.

Kündz looped his metering equipment over his shoulder, then gripping his blue metal tool box in his hand, he began to climb.

The traffic was moving slowly south of the river. John sat in his black BMW coupé, with the sun-roof open, Brubeck on the CD turned down low.

He wasn't enjoying the warm summer air eddying in around him nor the music, which he was playing to try to relax. With a sudden rise of impatience he blipped the accelerator, watched the rev counter spin round to the red line, then did it again, childishly. The man in the car in front glanced at him in his mirror: there was nothing he could do, they were at an intersection and there were four cars ahead of him.

John was angry with himself now for blowing out tonight's squash game with Archie Warren. It might indeed have relaxed him, but more importantly, Archie, who was making a fortune as a commodity broker in the City, had terrific connections. He was one of those people who knew *everyone*. John had joked about Archie's contacts in the past: he had once told Susan that if she ever wanted to meet the Pope, she should start by talking to Archie.

He looked at the clock on the dash. It was six twenty. He dialled Archie's mobile on his car phone, but the answering machine kicked in after one ring. He tried Archie's office number – if John dashed, he could still just about make the Hurlingham in time. But all he got was Archie's voice-mail. He hung up, disappointed, without bothering to leave a message.

There was a fleck of dust on his sunglasses; he took them off and blew it away. Across the road people stood on the pavement in front of a pub, glasses in hands. They were winding down for the day, and there was a carefree air about them that John found himself envying.

A handful of men were clustered around a brand new Porsche convertible, parked ostentatiously with two wheels on the kerb, and he thought gloomily that it would be a long time before he could buy a new car. The ageing BMW had 90,000 miles on the clock, but replacing it was out of the question now.

The traffic moved on and John dropped down two gears, trod hard on the accelerator and overtook the car in front, ignoring the flashing lights and angry hooting as he cut into a gap that did not exist. He did the same with the next car, and the next.

He did not slow down until, pulling up outside the house, he realised he had forgotten to pick up any wine.

He saw the Telecom van. Susan was in her element, supervising the workmen, watching all her decorating schemes take shape. She had a great talent for decorating. She also had a great talent for spending and, right now, they seemed to be haemorrhaging money – money they no longer had.

For some moments he sat, looking at the house, his heart riding up and down like a ship at anchor, in a swell. How was he going to tell her she had to stop everything? How was he going to tell her they ought to postpone the housewarming party? She had the guest list all worked out and the invitations were being printed. They'd decided to include the close neighbours, although they weren't too sure about the ones next door, the Merrimans, they were pretty old. The husband, a retired major who looked gaga, sat out in the garden in a sun-hat on fine days, just staring ahead, and once in a while he shouted at the trees. Every so often his wife hobbled out on a zimmer frame, and when the old boy saw her, he would bark a command at her and she would stagger back indoors.

John had teased Susan that he thought they'd really make the party swing, and Susan told him not to be cruel, that they might be like that themselves one day.

Her words had touched a nerve. At thirty-four, old age seemed a long way off – although, he thought uncomfortably, not so far as it had once seemed. Nothing stayed the same, and he'd never felt that so acutely as now. In the space of a few seconds your whole life could change.

One thing that had not changed was Susan. She was still the same strong, beautiful girl she had been when he had first met her. She had accepted so much in marrying him – uprooting, leaving her family behind and coming to a country where she knew no one but him. And the way she had settled down, won the hearts of all his friends, found herself a great job and run their home, had impressed him even more. Everyone who met her liked her – she was lively, warm-hearted and there wasn't a trace of malice in her.

The only thing that concerned him was the way she had accepted his determination never to have children – something John had made clear to her right from the early days of their dating, before he had proposed to her. He could see a look in her eyes sometimes when she saw friends' children, or even when they were out somewhere and they passed a mother nursing a baby. He was certain that those moments made it hard for her. Not that she ever brought it up.

There had been occasions when he had overheard her at parties responding to a question about when she and John were going to start a family, and invariably she replied cheerily that they had made a decision not to have children. The disarming, end-of-conversation way she put it, as if this had been her idea instead of one to which she had agreed with mixed feelings, always made him feel proud of her.

Susan deserved better than Mr Clake.

His eyes were watering. No one was going to take this place away from him and Susan. No balding, four-eyed creep of a bank manager, with a lopsided mouth and a Bible on his desk, was going to wreck the life they'd created for themselves.

He turned the car round and drove to the wine merchant.

A long time ago someone had done a loft-insulation job here. The spongy yellow material was packed into every crevice, and Kündz was pleased about this as he picked his way carefully along the joists. He rounded a corner, stepped over the desiccated skeleton of a mouse crushed in a trap that someone must have set then forgotten about; small patches of fur were still attached to the carcass, but any smell of decomposition had long gone.

There were other smells up here, of a dead bird somewhere close and the dankness of a cistern full of water, and rotting timber where the flashing, probably on the join between the chimney and the roof, had lifted. But there was only one smell up here that mattered to Kündz, and with every step he took, he breathed it in deeply. It was the smell of Susan Carter, and it was making it hard for him to concentrate.

It was only the ever-present thought of Mr Sarotzini that helped him to stay focused. The thought of what Mr Sarotzini might do to him if he failed. He wondered, sometimes, if Mr Sarotzini became really angry with him, how long the pain he inflicted would last. No pain that Mr Sarotzini had given him so far had ever lasted longer than a few days. But he had seen other people suffer pain inflicted by Mr Sarotzini. Pain that had lasted days, weeks, months after they had screamed to be allowed to die.

People had often spoken of hell on earth – it was an expression with which Kündz had become familiar from books and films, and he knew it was just a metaphor. Even among the survivors of the Holocaust, there were few people who had experienced a hell of the kind suffered by those who had angered Mr Sarotzini.

Susan Carter was right behind him. She followed him into the total darkness around the corner, and she was excreting no smells of fear. She trusted him and that was good.

John sat in his car outside the wine merchant, digging at the cellophane around the packet of Silk Cut with his thumbnail. He removed the wrapping, opened the flip-top lid, tore away the gold foil and pulled out a cigarette. The dry, cedary smell reminded him fleetingly of his childhood. Furtive cigarettes hidden under his socks in a drawer at school and smoked in a loft or in a derelict bomb shelter beyond the bounds of the school grounds.

He lit it with the car's lighter and inhaled deeply. There was an unpleasant rush of blood to his head and he felt slightly giddy. With the second drag, he felt even more giddy and broke out in a cold sweat.

In disgust he opened the door, tossed the cigarette into the gutter, then guiltily stared at the opened packet on the seat beside him. He got out, dumped it, the cellophane and the gold foil into a litter bin, then pushed a stick of Doublemint gum into his mouth. He leant back in his seat, feeling terrible. He couldn't go home yet – he needed a drink before he faced Susan. There was a pub in the next street along. He started the car and headed there.

Anticipation. Kündz had learned that anticipation could often be greater than the pleasure that followed. The Twenty-first Truth stated that pleasure was merely the release from anticipation. But he didn't think this would be the case here, not with this woman. With Susan Carter he was certain that the pleasure would be even greater than the anticipation.

'Do you need me any more?' she asked, suddenly.

He said nothing. He liked her being in this darkness with him, it gave

33

him a feeling of intimacy between them. Then she called out again, 'Hallo? Do you still need me?'

He liked the change of pitch in her voice, this tease of silence was fun, he was enjoying himself. He waited a little longer before calling back, 'No, everything I have need of is up here, thank you.'

Kündz followed her back round the corner, directing the torch beam to guide her, then stood still, watching as she climbed through the hatch, savouring her smells, which lingered on, greedily lapping them up.

Then he moved back down the loft, and turned his attention to the first part of the work that had brought him here. He set down his tool box, knelt, and from the top tray removed a small metal box, two inches long and an inch wide. He also took out a copy of the plans of the house he had obtained from the Planning Department. A spider's web rocked just above his face.

Moving carefully around the loft spaces, he located the optimum position, then screwed the box to the side of a joist where it would be safe, concealed by the insulation and not in danger of being trodden on. It would pick up the signals from the microphone transmitters he was about to place inside each telephone in the house, and relay them to a low-orbit satellite.

From anywhere in the world, Kündz would be able to hear every word spoken in this house, whether it was a phone call or a conversation taking place in any room. He had connected the system to the house's mains electricity supply, but had added a back-up in the event of any power cut. If necessary he would have to return in three years' time to replace the nickel-cadmium battery inside this small metal box. He had noted the date.

Checking his work, he applied the meter he had brought with him to the box, and was satisfied with the reading. Next he made a test transmission, and was pleased to see that the signal was strong.

Now he had completed the first part of what he had come to do in this loft. The next part would take longer, at least two days, he estimated. But it would give him such pleasure to work up here immersed in Susan Carter's smells, with her presence all around him. He thought about the wisdom of the Eighteenth Truth: *Anything that can be dreamed can be true.*

Every night since Mr Sarotzini had shown him her photograph, Kündz had dreamed of Susan Carter. He wondered at Mr Sarotzini sometimes. Mr Sartozini always knew exactly what he would like. In return, of course, there was always a price he had to pay. But he did not mind. For Susan Carter there could be no price too high.

He closed the hatch and climbed down the ladder. One quick job to complete now and then he would be off. He knew that on his first visit he must not outstay his welcome. He had the rest of his life to enjoy her.

Chapter Seven

When she heard the front door open Susan was in the kitchen. She went out anxiously into the hall. One look at the ghastly white of John's face told it all.

'Darling,' she said, alarmed, swinging his briefcase out of his hand and setting it on the floor. She put her arms around him and kissed him. There was no response: it was like embracing a statue. She could smell cigarette smoke and alcohol on his breath – he hadn't smoked for three years.

'Hon,' she said even more alarmed, 'what happened? Tell me?' She held his face tightly to hers and felt him give, just a little. 'Want a drink? A whisky?'

As she worked his tie loose, she sensed a nod. 'I'll fix you a drink,' she said, aware of her own voice shaking now, not sure how to handle this, not sure what to say to him. He was like a stranger.

In the kitchen, she poured him a large measure of Macallan, twisted out four ice cubes, and added a splash of filtered tap water. She was about to pour herself a glass of rosé wine, then decided she needed something stronger and poured another slug of whisky.

'Telecom – were they here?' John said distractedly, looking at a duplicate work-sheet on the table.

'An engineer – he just left. He was putting in a ringing converter, I think he said – does that sound right?' She looked at John.

He shrugged. On another day he would have mentioned the phone engineer's visit to his office – Susan was nuts about coincidences – but he let it go.

Although she had been desperate to hear about the bank, perversely now Susan found herself wanting to delay getting round to it, and she sensed that John did too. 'He's coming back tomorrow to install your ISDN line,' she said, 'and he's going to put in new wiring for the rest of the system.'

'Good,' John said absently. 'I didn't think we had a very good connection. Crackly. Did you get him to check the phones?'

'Uh-huh. He seemed pretty thorough.'

The conversation dried.

John swirled his drink and an ice cube cracked loudly. He turned and faced away from her, towards the window. 'It didn't go too well at the bank. The new manager –' He grimaced, took a half-hearted sip of his drink, then propped his elbows on the pine worktop, cradling the tumbler in his hands. 'He's a prat, he's just a total prat. I – I can't believe –'

Susan slipped her arms round him and gently turned his face towards her, watching him in alarm. His voice was unsteady – he was fighting back tears. She had never seen him cry before. 'Darling, poor darling,' she said, taking the glass out of his shaking hand, then holding him more tightly. 'Hon, it doesn't matter, nothing matters except you and me.'

John pulled out his handkerchief, dabbed his eyes and sniffed. He said nothing.

'So what did this new manager say?' she asked.

'He's given me a month to pay off the entire overdraft.' He sniffed again, then was silent. Very quietly, he said, 'If I don't, they're pulling the plug.'

Three miles from the Carters' house, Kündz turned the Telecom van off the road, drove several hundred yards along the cutting beside the disused railway siding and pulled up beside the plain blue Ford he had rented for this switch.

He did not enjoy driving this van, neither was he looking forward to getting back into the Ford. Mr Sarotzini had bought him a beautiful black Mercedes sports SL600, with black leather seats and a Blaupunkt CD ten-way autochanger with twenty-band graphic and separate amp with bass bin, for his thirtieth birthday last October. The car was in the underground garage beneath his apartment in Geneva, and he missed it. He felt cool driving that car; he did not feel cool driving a rented Ford. But if that was one of the sacrifices Mr Sarotzini had forced him to make to have Susan Carter, he could accept it.

He pulled a thick wad of fifty-pound bank-notes from his pocket and gave it to the Telecom engineer, who was lying out of sight in the rear of the van, peering at him like a cornered rabbit. 'The interim payment,' Kündz said. 'The last amount you are getting when we have finished.'

The engineer, a diminutive man close to retirement age, took the money, looking scared as hell. 'I just hope you did it properly,' he said.

Kündz assured him that he had, not that it mattered to the man. In a few days' time the engineer would throw himself out of a tower-block window. Anything odd that was ever found about the telephone system in the Carters' house would be down to him, working while the balance of his mind was disturbed.

Back in the Ford, Kündz switched on his satellite receiver, which was built into the shell of a mobile phone, and set the voice-activated digital recorder. Then he lifted the receiver to his ear, punched in a channel-seek command and listened. It required one small tuning adjustment and then, with perfect clarity, he heard Susan Carter's voice.

Instantly it aroused him. Her smell had soaked into his clothes and was all around him in the car. He was going to be reluctant to take off this uniform, which the engineer had 'borrowed' for him. Maybe he would keep it.

Susan Carter said, 'How? How can they do this? John? How can they do this?'

'They can do what they want,' John said. 'It's crazy, I know, but it's their money and they can do what they want with it.'

Susan had been expecting the bank to be tough on him, but not this ruthless. 'They can't treat people like this,' she said.

John drank some more whisky and was regretting having thrown away the cigarettes. 'They do it all the time, these days.'

Susan ran some water into her whisky and sipped it. She was trying to think of something positive to say. There would be a solution to this, there were solutions to everything, it was just a matter of keeping a clear head and not panicking. And of staying confident. If you looked confident, people had confidence in you. Failure in your eyes scared people away. 'Let's take our drinks out in the garden and relax, and talk this through. We could go to the Thai restaurant if you like,' she said.

'I – left the steaks in the car.'

'Steaks?'

John nodded. 'And the wine. I – thought – I – I'd do a barbecue.'

Susan smiled at him gently. 'Sure. Is that what you'd like? I could put some jacket potatoes in the oven.'

He shrugged. 'Better start saving money, no more eating out.' He pulled open a cupboard door, peered in. Then he removed a jar bearing a Fortnum and Mason label and examined it. 'What's this?'

'Pesto.'

'Uh.'

'It was in the hamper Archie sent us as a moving-in present.'

John continued to stare at it, as if, printed somewhere on the label, he might find the solution to his problems. 'We shouldn't have gone for this house, that's the bottom line,' he said.

Susan took another sip of her whisky and stared out at the garden. It looked so intensely beautiful in the soft evening sunlight, and she thought about how it would feel to move back into a tiny house, like the one they had left, or an apartment. But if they had to, they would, and they'd make the best of it, and hopefully, in a few years' time, they'd have enough saved to buy somewhere nicer.

But would they ever find anywhere like this again?

'Have you spoken to Bill Williams?' she asked. 'He'd be horrified if he knew what was happening.'

'Bill's history. He's out of it. He's on the golf course.'

'I know, but he was your friend. We had him round for dinner, we took him to the theatre, to Glyndebourne, to Ascot. I had to put up with his two-brain-cell wife. Surely Bill could do something. He *owes* you.'

John replaced the jar in the cupboard and picked up his glass again. 'I don't think Bill can do anything – I was the reason he got stuffed. One of them, anyhow. That's how I read it from Clake.' He drained his whisky and began to pour himself some more.

Susan made no comment about it: maybe it was the best thing tonight for him – at least he usually became docile when he was drunk, and not aggressive, like her father. Maybe they should both drink themselves into oblivion tonight. 'What's this Mr Clake got against you? You're a good customer. I don't understand why the bank's being so hard suddenly.'

'Officially? Clake says the bank is over-exposed in the technology sector. They've had their fingers burned by a few high-tech companies going down on them – a couple of which were Bill Williams's babies. Our balance sheet isn't great, and they don't believe our projections. They don't think we're going to be able to meet our borrowing repayments and they're cutting their losses.'

'And unofficially?'

'Clake's a born-again Bible-basher. Technophobe. Reckons technology is the work of Satan – you know the kind of guy.' John always trod carefully around the subject of religion with Susan because she was a believer. In the early days of their marriage she had gone to church quite frequently. He had joined her a few times, reluctantly, while they were engaged, to pacify the vicar before their wedding, but had steadfastly refused to go since. And she went only rarely now.

Susan had a mental image of Clake as an immaculately coiffed, cadaverous man, with grey hair and a grey suit. Although she had never met him she was suddenly frightened of him, of his power, of the hold he had over them. She remembered now, with chilling clarity, the evening when Bill Williams had come apologetically to their house in Fulham with a briefcase full of forms. He'd told her that she would not have to be a guarantor for long, he'd see to that personally, just a few months until DigiTrak's figures improved.

Their figures did start to improve, but then they'd bought this house and John had told her the bank needed her to stay as guarantor just a while longer so that Bill's superiors at the bank had the comfort factor of the security of the house.

Susan knew enough about the law to be aware that if she hadn't co-signed the papers, the bank would not have been able to touch the house.

Bill Williams was out on the golf course, with a stack of severance money, a handsome pension and not a care in the world. She found herself hating him with a vengeance for landing them in this.

And now Kündz, who was driving the Ford and listening in on the satellite cellphone, knew they had a problem. And he thought to himself that this was good. Mr Sarotzini was going to be so pleased with him.

Years ago, Mr Sarotzini had taught him how to fish for salmon, on a great estate in Scotland. Mr Sarotzini had placed in his hands a huge, whippy, hand-made rod, with a beautifully engineered reel, and stood patiently with Kündz for hours, on a river bank, teaching him how to lay the line far out across the water.

Finally, when Mr Sarotzini had been satisfied, he had attached the fly that Kündz had tied under his guidance, to the end of the line, and allowed Kündz to make his first real cast.

Kündz had never forgotten that moment. The line snaking out over the foaming black water of the Dee, the fly touching the surface and then, seconds later, the explosion of water around it, the flash of silver, and that incredible jigging sensation through the rod.

That thrill, that same deep thrill he had experienced then, was the same thrill he was experiencing now.

He could scarcely believe his luck.

'What's the total amount you have to find?' Susan asked. 'Your overdraft is around five hundred thousand, isn't it?'

John cradled the crystal tumbler in his hands. 'Bill increased it a few months back to seven fifty. And we have a quarter of a million term loan,

40

which is due – Bill would have extended it. Plus the mortgage on this place.'

Susan swallowed nervously. Christ, it was even worse than she'd thought. A loud crack startled her.

The tumbler had splintered in John's hand.

Susan recoiled in shock as ice, whisky and sparkling shards of glass fell to the floor. Blood streamed from John's palm where a sliver had embedded itself. He pulled it out, then stood still, like a child who has not fully understood what he has done.

Susan checked that there was no more glass in the wound, then pressed a wet towel against it, steered John away from the mess and into a chair. 'Hon, try to relax. You just sit down and I'll do everything.'

'I don't want to be poor again,' he said. 'No way. I'm not going back down that alley.'

'We're not going to be poor,' she replied quickly, fetching some rags and a dustpan and brush. 'We're going to find a way out of this. I'll go and speak to your Mr Clake.'

John managed a faint smile. He could imagine Susan bursting into his office, and letting rip with her fireball temper.

'Maybe you should try going higher – above Mr Clake's head. Do the directors of the bank know about this? Are they happy about losing one of their best customers?'

'If they fired Bill for loaning me too much, they probably are,' John said.

Susan knelt and began to clear up the mess. 'You've had a big shock today and you're too tense to think straight right now. Why don't you go change, and we'll sit outside, light up the barbecue and try to relax a little? OK?'

Twenty minutes later, comfortably dressed in old jeans and a sweatshirt, John had flames licking up evenly through the charcoal in the barbecue. He sat down on the bench and drank some of his fresh whisky. Susan brought out a bowl of salad and a clutch of cutlery dropped them on the table, then joined him.

On the other side of the fence, they heard the voice of the old man next door. 'Go away, woman!' he shouted.

Then a dog barked excitedly in the park. There was a deep rumble like thunder. John looked up and saw a jumbo jet on its landing approach to Heathrow, it seemed scarily close and low.

 In spite of the warmth of the air he shivered. If you were poor you didn't get to fly off in aeroplanes. If you were poor you were trapped, you lived your whole life like a fly crawling around inside an empty jam-jar, scavenging traces that hadn't been licked away, and beyond caring whether you got out or not.

His mother had been trapped by his father, and then by giving birth to him. She'd struggled all through his childhood, trying to find ways to supplement the dole money in between taking him to school and fetching him, and she'd found some pretty unsavoury ways. When you were poor the world could despise you, could dump on you, and you had nothing to hit back with. His mother had had nothing with which to hit back at the social services people when they'd tried to take him away. She had had nothing with which to hit back at his father.

And now he had nothing with which to hit back at Clake. It felt as though Clake was standing at the top of the long, greasy pole John had spent his life climbing, and just when he had almost reached the top, had given him a hard shove sending him hurtling back down towards the cesspool at the bottom.

'Honey,' Susan said, softly, 'DigiTrak itself is doing well, right? I mean in terms of orders and reputation.'

John hesitated. 'Sure.'

'There must be other banks that would love to have your business?'

John said nothing. The sound of the jet was fading. The sky was turning deep cobalt; the colour was so intense it seemed unreal. It reminded him of a painted backdrop in a theatre.

'If it wasn't for the lawsuit, yes,' he said.

'With the composer? Zak Danziger? I thought that was sorted out, that he was dropping it.'

'So did I,' John replied. 'Tony Bamford thought so too. We'd agreed a royalty payment, based on sales.'

Tony Bamford was John's lawyer. DigiTrak had used a piece of music for the Home Doctor series from a young composer they'd hired, whom Gareth had discovered, part of which turned out to be a possible copyright infringement of an old work of one of Britain's highest paid composers, Zak Danziger.

DigiTrak's composer had denied vigorously that he'd ripped off Danziger's work, but when the two pieces were played side by side, the similarities were evident. The onus of defending the accusation fell on DigiTrak, and they had little chance of recovering any of the costs from their youngster.

'What's happened now?' she asked, alarmed.

'Someone sent Danziger to a hot-shot brief. He's been advised that he could probably get three to five million out of us. We have an errors and omissions insurance limit of one million, and the court costs alone could easily run to half of that. Not too many people are going to want to jump into bed with a five-million-pound lawsuit.'

John stood up and gloomily rearranged some of the barbecue coals. Even the smell, which he normally loved, failed to lift his despondency. He prodded the steaks, which were lying in his own special hot 'n' spicy marinade, and scooped a few spoonfuls of it over them.

'So,' Susan said. 'You have a month. At least we have time.'

Inside the house a phone rang. John started, then checked himself. Susan made a move. 'I'll get it, hon.'

Then the ferocity of John's reply halted her in her tracks. 'No!' he said. 'Dammit, *leave* the fucking thing. Let the machine get it.'

She left it, and on the fifth ring it stopped.

'You haven't any more news about your job?' he asked.

'No.'

Susan worked as a non-fiction commissioning editor at Magellan Lowry, a good, solid company, and one of the few independents left in publishing. 'Not since Peter Traube came in to give me his reassurances that if the Media International Communications Group take over does go ahead, there won't be any redundancies in Editorial.'

'Traube's the head honcho, right?

She nodded. 'Managing director.'

'And he's a man of his word?'

Susan thought before she replied, and then said, 'No, I don't think he is.'

John drank some more whisky, and watched the trees at the end of the garden, and in the park beyond, turning dark, like silhouettes against the sky. His mind was scrabbling around for straws to clutch. The bank would seize the equity in the house, but with Susan's salary, and cashing in his pension fund and the few stocks and shares he had, they could, perhaps, just about manage the mortgage for a while. Except there was another problem that neither of them had yet spoken about. Susan's kid sister, Casey.

'OK,' Susan said. 'You owe this money, but what about your assets? Your order book's healthy, you have all the computer and office equipment, the lease on the offices, that must have some value –'

John cut her short. 'We paid over the odds to get those offices, and the second-hand value of all our kit is peanuts. Our cars are mostly leased.' He thought for some moments. 'We'd be talking about a fire sale,' he said, bitterly. 'It's not an option.'

'Hon,' Susan said, 'don't forget the little bit of money I have stashed away in the States. It's close on ten thousand dollars and you can have that if it'll help. And I could sell my jewellery – not that I have much.' She reached out, took his bandaged hand and kissed his fingers lightly.

John shook his head. Casey was in a coma in a home in California. She'd been there for nine years and might go on living, in her persistent vegetative state, for many more years yet. 'That money is for Casey. You need to keep that back for when the insurance runs out,' he replied.

'Archie Warren,' Susan said. 'Why don't you talk to him?'

'I will.'

'It's Tuesday – shouldn't you have been playing squash with him tonight?'

'I cancelled, wasn't feeling too great.'

'I'm sure Archie will be able to help.'

Susan moved across and sat on his lap, and looked straight into his eyes. They were a deep nut brown, hard as nuts sometimes, but there was a warmth and kindness that never left them. 'We'll survive,' she said. 'We can find a solution to this problem. And if we can't, we still have each other. If we have to sell the house, we'll sell it. We're still young – well, young*ish* – we can move back to a smaller place again, even a little apartment if we have to, start over again. It's no big deal.'

'No big deal,' John echoed. He could see Clake's face and his lopsided smirk and the Bible on his desk. And he wished he could agree with Susan, but he couldn't. It was a *very* big deal, it was huge.

It was everything.

Chapter Eight

'So?' Archie Warren said. 'What do you think?'

They were driving down the Fulham Road in Archie's Aston Martin Virage Volante. The car was brand new: he had taken delivery of it that morning, and there were only seventeen miles on the clock. The roof was down and John was cocooned in the cockpit in cream Connolly hide with red piping. The car smelt like a saddlery. A reverberating boom from the exhaust accompanied the Dr Hook song erupting from the speakers, 'I'm rich and I'm having a ball.'

Archie Warren was having a ball.

And John, who was normally a bit of a show-off himself, was not up to all this today. He felt self-conscious in this gleaming haemoglobin-coloured monster that was deafening the passers-by, as well as more than a tiny bit jealous.

In answer to Archie's question, he thought that, driving along like this, Archie looked like Mr Toad. But he didn't tell him that.

And the more he looked at him, the stronger the resemblance to Mr Toad became. Archie had fair, thinning hair that was more like bum-fluff, and he'd probably be completely bald on top in a few years' time. He was wearing a loud silk tie, chalk-striped suit and tiny oval sunglasses that were cool to the point of being sinister.

Archie was thirty-four and had the figure of a Vietnamese pot-bellied pig. Yet he usually beat John at squash, and at tennis, and could swim much faster than John and get out of the pool less out of breath. And, what made John really mad, was that Archie could do all this in spite of smoking twenty, maybe thirty, cigarettes a day.

John had always been something of a loner, driven by his ambition, and had drifted apart from his few childhood friends. From school he'd gone to technical college to study architecture, and after only a couple of months working on the Computer Aided Design systems, he had realised the potential market for serious and informative software for home computers.

Building DigiTrak had been his life ever since, and the friends he now had – not by design, but because that was the way it had happened – were all, with the exception of Archie, connected in some way to his business. Susan's friends were drawn from her publishing world.

He probably liked Archie the most because he was different and because Archie always amused him. Another part of the attraction was that Archie was well bred, with a public-school background, and had the careless air of aristocracy about him to which John secretly aspired.

They had met on a ski lift in Switzerland seven or so years ago, both highly ambitious men with an enjoyment of the good life. Although Archie came from the hunting, shooting, fishing set, he had made his money, not inherited it. He had a brace of Purdey shotguns he had bought at auction for over fifty thousand pounds – an amount that had staggered John when Archie had told him. He had an impressive country estate, a villa in France, a small aeroplane, and the rest.

Archie earned an obscene salary, trading Japanese convertible bonds and warrants in the City. In a bad year he cleared a million before tax, and in a good year a whole heap more. He spent as much as he could, some on girlfriends – he was still single – but most on toys and food.

The restaurant to which he took John for lunch seemed happy to oblige Archie's whim for emptying his wallet. Its speciality, *assiette de fruits de mer*, arrived at the table embedded in crushed ice and stacked on four tiers, accompanied by a full set of surgical instruments. Tackling it, with no appetite, John felt like an archaeologist encountering a cryonically frozen tableau of some past civilisation's excess.

Archie split open a crab claw and the juice squirted onto John's cheek, but Archie didn't notice: he was busy chewing the remnants of a sea snail and washing it down with a glass of Chablis to make room in his mouth for the crab meat. John dabbed his cheek discreetly with his napkin.

'Those whelks are yours,' Archie said, pointing. 'And that crayfish.'

'Thanks.' John removed the legs from a prawn. He'd had a million questions he was going to put to Archie today, but so far Archie had been more interested in talking about his new car and this new restaurant he'd heard about than suggesting whom John might approach for funding. And John's hint, earlier, that Archie might like to invest in DigiTrak had fallen on deaf ears. That had been his own fault for being impatient. He needed to pick a better moment, perhaps now.

They were on to the second bottle, with most of the first one inside

Archie. 'I can think of plenty of places,' Archie said, suddenly. 'No problem. But you're going to have to get rid of that lawsuit before we go to 'em.'

'How do you mean?'

Archie snuck in a quick prawn before the crab meat. Its tail poked through his lips as he talked, slowly working its way in and disappearing. 'Settle it.'

'I don't have the money to settle, and besides –'

'John, no one's going to touch you with a barge pole with a lawsuit like that hanging over you. That's your problem, that's your real buggeration factor.'

John picked up a narrow stainless-steel implement with a hook on the end. He tapped the prickly spines of a raw sea urchin, but left it on the stack. Half the creatures in front of him should have been left on the ocean floor, he thought. They looked more like relics from the gene pool than anything that would pass a selection committee for the human food chain.

The eyes of a spider crab were eerily fixed on him. 'We have a good defence,' John said.

Archie pulled the head off another prawn and dropped it on his side plate, then dunked the remains in the mayonnaise. 'How about biting the bullet, letting DigiTrak go under and starting again with new finance?'

'DigiTrak isn't a limited company, it's a partnership. If it goes under, I go under. We lose the house, the lot.'

'Shit.'

'And there's another problem.'

Archie had the grace to stop eating.

'Susan's kid sister, Casey, I told you about her, right?'

Archie's forehead narrowed. 'The one in the home?'

'Yes. She costs two thousand dollars a month, and the insurance runs out in September.'

Archie whistled. 'That's a lot of boodle. You're going to pay for her?'

'Susan and me, between us. Susan's going to contribute.'

'What about her family in LA?'

John smiled at him and shook his head. 'They haven't a bean. They can look after themselves but nothing else.'

A waiter filled Archie's glass and put a token splash into John's, which was still full. John asked for another mineral water. Archie nodded at the stack of crustaceans in front of them. 'Come on, you're lagging.'

John selected a half lobster; lobster was normally one of his favourites, but as he ate the first mouthful of this, he was so deep in thought that he barely noticed it. 'If I do go under, Susan's going to take it really hard – quite apart from losing everything herself.'

Archie nodded. 'I'll make some calls this afternoon.' He lifted a large crab onto his plate.

Swallowing an enormous amount of pride, John said, 'I – I was wondering, Arch, if you might be interested in coming into DigiTrak yourself? It's a great business, and – we're looking at the very real possibility of going public in the next couple of years.'

Archie shook his head. 'I'll take a look, but I don't think so. Nothing personal, but I'm a trader not an investor. I've sunk money into half a dozen businesses in the past few years – a door-to-door wine outfit, a car-tyre dealership, a mobile-phone operation. Truth is, I've saddled myself with a fucking great mortgage on that pile I've bought in the country and I'm losing a bundle on my investments. I don't have the kind of money you need lying around in readies.' Then he smiled at John kindly. 'But if you get into real shit, let me know. I'll lend you something to tide you over.'

'Thanks, I appreciate it,' John replied, 'but I don't want to do that.'

Archie, who had never done anything he didn't want to do in his entire life, smashed open the crab's belly and said, 'We all have to do things we don't want to do, sometimes.'

Chapter Nine

'OK, this is how I understand it,' Susan said. 'You freeze water and it turns into ice cubes. You warm those ice cubes and they turn back into water. The state of those molecules is reversed, but that change is still taking place in linear time.'

She twiddled with the tag hanging from the new telephone that had been installed early this morning, before she had arrived in the office. There had been some fault with her previous phone, apparently, not that she'd been aware of it.

Fergus Donleavy gave away about as much in his expression as he might if he'd picked up a bum hand of cards in a poker game. He was sitting, in Susan's cramped, hopelessly cluttered office that looked out through grimy glass on to a Covent Garden rooftop, his tall frame folded like an Anglepoise lamp into the solitary armchair in front of her desk.

He was dressed in an old tweed jacket, lumberjack shirt, drainpipe jeans and black boots. His greying, wavy hair was carelessly long. His face was thin and lean, handsome in a Marlboro Country way, which was exactly what he looked like, Susan always thought – an ageing cowboy.

Over the past five years working as his editor she'd grown very fond of him: he had become almost a father figure to her. Fergus had been the first person she'd rung to tell when they'd made the decision to buy the house, and he'd approved of the area – although a couple of decades ago, he had warned her, it had been a lot less salubrious.

'You boil an egg,' he said, in his quiet voice that was close to a murmur, 'and there's nothing you can do that is going to turn it back into a raw egg. A sperm fertilises an egg, there is no way you can reverse that. That's linear, but that's chemistry not physics.'

Fergus talked laconically, the voice of a man who had been around life's block a few times, although he wasn't jaded: life was still vibrant for him. 'Susan, the point I'm trying to get over to the readers is to make them imagine time as being that water. It can be liquid, fluid, but it can also be solid, like the ice, three-dimensional. It's just a question of how we perceive it at any given moment. Time is both linear and static. It's like Schrödinger's cat, the wave and the particle –'

Susan stopped him in his tracks. 'Fergus, if I'm confused by your argument, and I have a physics background, how's the average reader who has no science background going to feel?'

She had spent the past two weeks grappling with his manuscript. Although worrying desperately about John's problems with DigiTrak, for which there was still no solution on the horizon, she had tried her hardest to concentrate on her work and not be distracted, and all her instincts were telling her that the manuscript in its current form did not work. At the end of the day, this would reflect badly on her.

She sipped coffee from the yellow mug John had given her a couple of years back for her birthday. On it was printed, in bold black lettering, YOU DON'T *WANT* TO KNOW WHAT I THINK.

'Fergus, when Einstein published his theory of relativity, there were something like only five people in the whole world who could understand it.'

Dr Fergus Donleavy, professor of physics at University College, London, grinned. 'I heard it was six, actually.'

'Well, we want to outsell *A Brief History of Time* with this one, and we're only going to do that if people can get their heads around at least *some* of it. I'm not knocking your thesis, it's the way you've put it across.'

Fergus looked at her thoughtfully. 'Is it chapter seventeen you're worried about?'

Susan genuinely believed this book could be an international best-seller. Fergus Donleavy had the credentials and the book had the content. That was how it had looked from his six-page synopsis. Now she had on her desk eleven hundred pages that were almost impenetrable. He was going to have to drop everything else he was doing for the next six months and rewrite it. She was trying to be tactful, and had hoped that by gentle manoeuvring she would bring him round to see this, but so far it wasn't happening.

She felt a deep responsibility for this book: she had planted the seed for it in Fergus's head, sold the outline to her firm and commissioned it. It was a great concept: Fergus was going to argue that physics proved the existence of God – or a Higher Intelligence, at any rate. He was going to *prove* that some being, smarter than humans, had created the universe.

In the book, Fergus demolished the Big Bang theory. He trashed Darwinism as a means of explaining human existence. He demonstrated how it was possible to travel faster than the speed of light. And he had hard evidence to show that earth was not man's natural habitat – that the first humans had been brought here from elsewhere in space.

Her mind veered briefly back to John. He was having another meeting today, another bank, a contact of Archie Warren, and then he was seeing Archie. John had thoughts of trying to put together a consortium of backers, including people who had a vested interest in DigiTrak, like the gynaecologist Harvey Addison who hosted their best-selling series, but so far the response had been lukewarm.

It was the lawsuit that was the bitch. John had now been served with a writ from Zak Danziger, and it was looking bad. Although John was trying to keep up a brave face, she knew that he was running out of options. And, to make matters worse, people here at Magellan Lowry were getting increasingly nervous about the impending takeover.

Tomorrow Archie had invited her and John to Ascot and she was looking forward to that break from their worries. Archie did Ascot in style every year, taking a box, and always brought along a string of influential people. Maybe John would meet someone willing to take a punt. But it seemed more likely that he'd lose a few hundred pounds on the horses.

At least Archie's company would be cheerful. She liked him: he made her laugh.

And tonight held possibilities too. They were going to a seriously smart black-tie do at the Guildhall. She wasn't sure why they'd been invited, and neither was John. The invitation had arrived only a week ago, as if they were an afterthought. There seemed to be some link with a book she had once edited on Oriental antiquities, but beyond that she was unclear.

The invitation had impressive names on it – Mr and Mrs Walter Thomas Carmichael. She knew that Walter Thomas Carmichael was one of the richest men in America, a philanthropist and a patron of the arts. Initially, John hadn't been that keen to accept, but Susan had persuaded him, telling him that wealthy people would be there and that he might find someone who could help him.

Susan took Fergus Donleavy out to lunch, which was the gentlest way she could think of to break the news that he was going to have to rewrite his book. In the airy restaurant above Covent Garden they ate seared tuna, drank Sancerre and talked about everything except the book. Fergus told her that his daughter by his one and only marriage, which had ended years back, was starting psychology at Duke University, North Carolina, in the autumn. 'Now that you've moved into this big house, are you going to start a family?' he asked.

'No.' She could see that Fergus was afraid he'd touched a raw nerve, and quickly bailed him out: 'We made a decision not to have one. Didn't I ever tell you?'

Fergus cut a slice of tuna and pushed it around to scoop up the juices, but did not eat it. Instead he made a noise somewhere deep in his throat that could have been either approval or disapproval. When he responded, his face was stern, but his voice remained gentle. 'That was then.' He raised his eyebrows. 'You told me that it was John who didn't want children because he'd had a terrible childhood. I was under the impression you went along with that, but hoped to change his mind.'

'No,' she said awkwardly, because he *had* touched a nerve inside her. 'The – the move isn't going to change anything.'

'It's good that you have such a strong marriage.'

Susan had to strain to hear his quiet voice against the babble of conversation. 'Sure,' she said, almost equally quietly. Fergus knew a lot of people. She was wondering whether to tell him about John's problems. But she decided that, in spite of their friendship, it would be unprofessional. The purpose of this lunch was Fergus's book, and she needed to keep the focus on that.

'A lot of people who get married have children because they've run out of things to say to each other,' Fergus said.

She smiled. 'Maybe.'

'So it's good that you and your husband still haven't run out of things to say to each other. If you haven't run out after seven years, you probably won't.'

'Did you and your wife run out of things to say to each other?' she asked.

Fergus put the piece of fish in his mouth and chewed it slowly. He looked sad, an old wound opening up again. 'There were a lot of things.' He fell silent.

Susan drank some wine, letting the subject drop.

'Something I've never asked you,' Fergus said. 'How do you cope with the biological urges to be a mother? Or don't you have them?'

Susan glanced around the room, checking out who was sitting near them. This was a personal conversation and she didn't want anyone from work hearing her. The publicity director and three men she did not recognise were seated at a nearby table, engrossed in a heavy discussion. 'Sure I have them, but I don't let them dictate the course of my life.'

Fergus drank some more wine, set down his glass, made that noise again deep in his throat, and murmured, '"Stars rule man, but a *wise* man rules the stars."'

'That's smart. Who said it?'

'Francis Barrett, in *The Magus*.'

'I didn't know you were knowledgeable about magic.'

He inclined his head. 'How well do you know me?'

'I don't know you,' she said. 'Not really. We've been friends a long time, but I don't *know* you.'

He have a distant smile. 'How well do you know anyone?'

'How do you mean?'

'How well do you know your husband? Do you really know him? Do you know yourself? Do you *really* know yourself?'

Susan raised her hands. 'I – think I do but I – I guess I can't be sure.'

'None of us knows what we are capable of, until we have to do it.' Fergus picked up the stub of lime on the side of his plate and squeezed the last drops of juice onto the remains of his tuna.

'I thought you were a scientist,' she said. 'Magic is the realm of the paranormal. How do you reconcile that?'

'Arthur C. Clarke once said that *magic is any sufficiently advanced technology*. I think he's right. The paranormal is the name we give to things science hasn't yet found an explanation for.'

'You really believe that?'

'Yes,' he said.

'You think eventually we'll find explanations for everything?'

'Yes. But I don't know when.'

'Or what they will be?'

He shrugged. 'C. I. Lewis said *there is no a priori reason for thinking that, when we discover the truth, it will prove interesting.*'

Susan smiled. 'I hope he's wrong.'

Fergus looked at her strangely. 'I think it's quite possible he's wrong.'

She picked up her glass. 'So, if none of us knows what we're capable of, you think few of us ever fulfil our destiny because we are not aware of it?'

There was a long silence. Then he said, 'You will. You will fulfil yours.'

He looked so serious that it made her want to laugh, but she held back hard because he looked *so* serious. And then she felt uncomfortable. He was no longer looking *at* her, he was looking *through* her, into some compartment deep inside her. And he seemed deeply disturbed by what he saw. Almost as if he were afraid.

She felt a sudden wintry chill blow through her. 'What is it? What are you looking at?' she asked.

But the expression was gone. He replaced it with a smile and changed the subject.

Chapter Ten

John hadn't seen the child on the bicycle.

He was doing fifty and accelerating hard, in a thirty m.p.h. limit. The rat-run. This was the traffic-dodging route he took home from the office. Because it was through residential streets, he normally took care, but tonight he was going much too fast.

With that amount of alcohol inside him, he shouldn't have been driving at all. He'd gone for what should have been a quick sandwich lunch with Archie. It had turned into an oyster-downing session, accompanied by champagne mixed with Guinness, over which Archie had delivered the depressing news that he was having no dice finding investors for the consortium.

So far the only firm commitment John had had was from Harvey Addison, who had agreed to invest twenty-five thousand pounds, subject to them raising the rest of the money.

The lawsuit. Zak Danziger, that was the problem. Archie had told him yet again at lunch today that John had to settle that damned suit. And John had tried really hard to do that in the last fortnight. They'd even had a meeting at Danziger's lawyer's office, at which John had had to restrain himself from lashing out at the arrogant little composer. Danziger had strutted in an hour late, his wiry hair gelled back into what looked like a fantail, his ratty face covered in designer stubble, his denim suit ornamented with diamanté studs, and proceeded to call John, in rapid succession, a shit, a thief and a capitalist turd.

John told Archie that his own counsel's opinion was that Danziger's case might look strong on the surface but had holes in it. He had advised John there was a fair chance that Danziger would eventually realise this and that they should be able to settle out of court, before legal costs rocketed, for a few hundred thousand pounds – well within the insurance limits. The problem was, as Archie had pointed out in response, what would happen if Danziger refused to settle?

Then when John had got back to the office, Gareth had cornered him. His partner was in a bad state, shaking with nerves and on the edge of one of his famous tantrums, telling John he was seriously worried about him.

That was rich coming from Gareth, whose erratic behaviour caused John constant anxiety, particularly if Gareth was ever left to deal on his own with a major client. But today John had listened to him, aware that Gareth was right. Apparently all the sales team had been complaining that John's mind seemed totally off the ball. He hadn't been returning phone calls, or responding to e-mails or snail mail, nothing.

And it was true, he thought guiltily. All he had done for the past two weeks was write proposals to banks and fund-raisers, make phone call after phone call to everyone he had ever met who might either be a likely prospect or know one, and turn up to meeting after meeting at which he was mostly told the same thing: 'Great company, great products, sort out the lawsuit, come back and talk to us again.'

He still hadn't told Gareth the truth, knowing that not only would Gareth freak out but he would immediately tell everyone he knew because he was hopeless at keeping anything secret. In many aspects of business, Gareth had a mental and emotional age of seven. All geniuses have their flaws and this was Gareth's.

John was frightened that as soon as word got out his staff would start looking around for other jobs. His competitors would be hovering like vultures. He had a moral duty to tell them all soon so that they would not find themselves out of work with just a few hours' notice, but he couldn't bring himself to do it, not while there was still hope. And there *was* hope, there had to be. As he drove, fuelled by the two pints – or maybe three – of real ale he had just downed with Gareth, John felt a renewed charge of optimism.

Harvey Addison had pledged twenty-five thousand and they weren't making enough use of his name. Surely he could use Harvey's commit-ment to encourage others? The gynaecologist was famous: he had his own daytime television show on BBC 1, with huge ratings. He tried to think of a way to capitalise on Harvey as he drove.

A single spat of rain burst like an insect on the windscreen, startling him. The sky was dark, heavy, laden. They were going out tonight to some smart function, something to do with Susan's work, but he couldn't remember what. The beer was kicking in now, making him feel drunk, and he could not see much more than a blur beyond the end of the BMW's bonnet. He saw the square hulk of a removals truck ahead, parked along the kerb. As he raced towards it, doing over sixty now, he saw a faint glint, something red, shiny, moving out fast, straight into his path.

It was the front wheel of a bicycle.

Susan looked anxiously at her watch. It was twenty to seven and they were due in the City, half an hour's drive away, at seven thirty. John had promised to be home in good time so that they didn't have to rush, but he still wasn't back.

She balled her hands and banged her knuckles impatiently together. *Come on, hon.* She wanted them to get there early because it was at the pre-dinner drinks, when they could circulate, that they would have the best chance of finding people whom they might interest in DigiTrak, and they had already agreed a strategy on how they would work the room when they got there.

Susan, who was much less shy than John, was good at getting on with it at parties and introducing herself to people. She would work the pack until she found a financier, then signal to John, who would come over and be introduced by her. She would move on, hunting out another prospect.

She was already changed, wearing the black silk dress that she felt she had worn too many times and which was starting to feel tired, even if it didn't *look* tired – although, with luck, there wouldn't be anyone at the dinner tonight who had seen it before. She wasn't even sure there'd be anyone at the dinner they would even *know*.

Determined to dress to kill, she'd changed earrings, necklaces, brooches and shoes half a dozen times before she was satisfied that she looked classy rather than showy.

Come on, John, darling. Come on!

She tried phoning his mobile, but it was not switched on and debated whether to try the office. But he would have left by now, surely?

She sat down on a sofa in the living room, in front of the marble fireplace, and admired the colour scheme and the paintwork. She was really pleased with the soft, warm effect of Not Quite White and it looked stunningly elegant with the contrasting black woodwork. As soon as they'd hung up their pictures and paintings, which they planned to do this weekend, and got the grey and white striped curtains, which should be arriving next week, the room would really come alive.

At least, she thought ruefully, the place would be looking wonderful if they did have to put it back on the market. But she wasn't going to dwell on that now. John needed her to be positive, and she needed to be positive herself. If you believed in something enough you could make it happen. If she and John showed people that they *believed* DigiTrak had a future, that must help.

She picked up the latest copies of *Publishing News* and the *Bookseller*, which never reached her desk until several days after they had arrived at Magellan Lowry, and scanned the Company News and the Who's Moved Where columns, checking for new rumours about the impending takeover or whether anyone she knew had been promoted into a position where they might be able to offer her a new job if the crunch came.

Then she remembered that the garbage men collected early on Thursday mornings, and busied herself emptying the waste-bins into a large black bin-liner, which she carried out through the side door in the kitchen.

As she opened the door, she was surprised by the wind that had got up and felt a few spots of rain. Fergus Donleavy's words at lunch today echoed again inside her head. They had been disturbing her all afternoon.

'You will. You will fulfil yours.'

Destiny.

And although he appeared to have seen it, Fergus had refused to tell her what her destiny was. He would not say another word on the subject other than to assure her that it was nothing, nothing at all, and that she should forget it.

But she couldn't forget it. She had a sense that Fergus had a deeper interest in the paranormal than he had let on. Lunch had left her with a deep chill, a sense of foreboding that was haunting her now even more deeply.

As she lifted the dustbin lid, a small piece of paper blew out into her face, then fell to the ground. As she picked it up, she saw it was a lottery ticket, with all seven rows filled in, and as she was about to put it back into the bin, she noticed more in there. Dozens of them.

'Christ.'

She scooped out a handful: a piece of eggshell fell away from one. All carried last Saturday's date. Doing a quick, rough count she reckoned there were about forty. At seven pounds each, John must have spent over two hundred and fifty pounds on the lottery and had said nothing.

She wondered, alarmed, whether he had turned to any other forms of gambling. During the first couple of years of their marriage, he had played in a regular weekly poker school but had stopped when he had got too busy with DigiTrak. She knew he gambled with his friends, quite ludicrously high stakes sometimes, on their regular Saturday-morning golf games.

A thought struck her: could John have been lying to her about their financial problems? Had gambling debts caused them, not business problems?

No, that was ridiculous. She knew John too well: he liked a flutter but he was not an addict.

But then something else she remembered from her lunch with Fergus began to disturb her.

How well do you know anyone? How well do you know your husband? Do you really know him? Do you know yourself?

And she realised that Fergus was right. She didn't know John, didn't *really* know him, and he probably didn't *really* know her either. They just knew little bits about each other, like pieces of a jigsaw that slowly gave you more and more of the picture the longer you were together. She wondered if all couples were like that, strangers who never realised they were strangers.

The kitchen door slammed, and she looked around guiltily as if she was prying, which in a way, she felt, she was, dumped the black garbage bag on top of the tickets, and put the dustbin lid firmly back on.

Going inside, she puzzled again about why Fergus Donleavy had looked so strange, so frightened. She wondered if he was just playing some game with her head, but she didn't think so. Fergus was not the kind of man to mess with people's heads.

Was he psychic? She couldn't get his expression out of her mind. She could picture it vividly, the way he had been looking at her, seeing something.

Her destiny?

Whatever he'd said in denial, he had seen something there.

And it was bad.

John could see the child's face. A girl, short blonde hair cut in a fringe, and she hadn't seen him. *She still had not seen him.*

His foot was rammed to the floor and the car was juddering and grating violently as the anti-lock brakes gripped and released. He tried to find the horn, missed, his hand jamming uselessly against the boss of the steering wheel.

And she kept on coming, kept pedalling out from behind that removals truck, filling the whole road in front of him.

Filling his whole windscreen.

John didn't have time to think, he was just reacting, his ears numb, ringing with the yowl of his tyres on the tarmac. He caught a glimpse of a skip on the other side of the road stacked with broken plasterboard.

The girl had seen him now. Her mouth was open, she was staring at him, she braked, stopped dead, dropped her feet onto the tarmac. *The dumb girl had stopped dead in front of him.*

Get out of –

He jerked the wheel over, and the car swerved wildly. The skip disappeared, then he saw it again, close, too close, it felt for an instant as if he was motionless and the skip was hurtling across ice towards him.

He felt the impact even before he heard it, even before he'd had time to swing the wheel again. The car bounced off, like a dodgem, rocked, then a tremendous metallic boom exploded in his ears.

Then silence.

John sat shaking, unsure in which direction he was facing, trying desperately to orient himself. Trying to see the girl.

Oh, Christ, where was she?

Then he saw her behind him. She had dismounted and was holding her bicycle, staring at him. There didn't seem to be any expression on her face, no shock, no relief, no surprise, nothing. Blank.

He'd missed her.

She was all right.

He had hit the skip instead.

His brain was working jerkily, fumbling with bits of information. The noise. People would have heard the noise. At any moment they would start running out of their houses. But they didn't. Nothing was happening. Just the silence, and the girl staring at him expressionlessly.

And he remembered, with sudden panic, all the alcohol in his system.

Must get out and make sure she's OK, he thought. But when he tried to open his door, it was jammed. He unclipped his seat belt, yanked the handle and threw his weight against the door. It gave.

He climbed out onto the road on unsteady legs. The girl with the red bicycle was still standing there, staring at him. He leaned against the side of the car, feeling a little sick, and looked down in horror at the dented, twisted, torn, scraped mess that was the driver's side of his BMW. The outer skin of the door had been ripped open, as if by a tin opener, and a clutch of wires and part of the window mechanism were exposed.

'Are you OK?' he shouted at the girl.

She gave a single, shocked nod.

The rear bumper was sticking out sideways like a wing flap. He tried to push it back, but it would not move. The alcohol, he thought. Got to get out of here. He pushed it again, but it still wouldn't move. Then in panic he pushed still harder and it bent back, not quite flush but good enough Someone was running towards him now.

John decided to run, too. He needed to get the hell out before the police arrived.

He cast a glance over the rusting skip, climbed back into the BMW and started the engine.

In his mirror he watched the man who had been running stop, stare at him, then reach for something inside his pocket – a notebook, or maybe a mobile phone.

John rammed the gear lever forward and accelerated away, faster than he'd intended.

Chapter Eleven

John came in through the front door looking like a ghost.

Susan smelt the alcohol before she'd reached him. He staggered clumsily into her arms, and she had to take a step back to prevent both of them falling over.

'Shorry – so late,' he said.

As she hugged him, she noticed his face was clammy with perspitation.

'Darling,' she said. 'Hon.' It hurt her to see him like this, this man of whom she was so proud, letting himself go, drunk and dishevelled. And it frightened her. This pillar of strength on which she had depended was crumbling and her life was crumbling with it.

How drunk was he, she wondered. 'Hon, are you OK to go out?'

He said nothing.

'I've put your dinner jacket and shirt out on the bed, and your patent leather shoes and some socks.'

He eased free of her, sat on the bottom step of the staircase and sank his head in his hands. He was silent for a little while. Then he said, with choking emotion in his voice, 'I nearly killed a child.'

A ripple of goose bumps rose up through her. 'What do you mean? What happened? When? How?'

'It was just now – I was driving too fast. Stupid.'

'Is the child OK?'

'Yes.'

'You didn't hit him – her –?'

'No.'

'Hon,' she said gently, 'you have to pull yourself together. We're going to be OK, we're going to come out the other side of this.'

He looked up, like a child himself, and nodded.

Susan decided that he wasn't as drunk as she had first feared. He was as much shaken as drunk. She had a sudden fear that if she allowed him to start finding excuses not to get out and meet people, it could be the start of a slippery slope. He *must* pull himself together, and she had the feeling that she was the only person who could make him. 'You were keen to go to this do tonight, you said there might be some good people there to approach –'

'I know,' he cut in. 'I just –'

'We've accepted, we should go.'

'I must have a shower.'

She looked at her watch. 'We don't have time. Slap some water on your face and get changed. Come on, this is for both of us.'

'I can't drive – over the limit – I – you want to phone for a taxi?'

'I don't mind driving,' she said. 'We have to economise. I'm sure we can save a lot just by being careful.'

'Bugger that.'

'Come on, upstairs! You're not going to let that man Clake beat us, are you?'

John looked at her, and she could see that she was getting through. The mention of the name Clake had triggered a spark of determination in his face. 'Because that's what you're doing right now. You're letting Clake get you down. You have to fight back at him. And you have to remember, hon, that even if we do lose the business, the house, everything that we own, that we're still not going to let Clake win, because we're going to go on loving each other just as much, and he'll never take that away from us, ever. OK?'

'I – I'm shorry,' John said. 'I've had a bloody awful day. No dice. None at all.'

'You can tell me about it in the car,' she replied.

Downstairs, fifteen minutes later, she picked up his car keys from where he had left them on the hall table.

'Let's go in your car,' he said, hastily, his voice still slurring a little, but not so badly. 'Easier to park.'

Susan wondered why he was reluctant to take his, but, as she walked round to the driver's side of the BMW, she saw the reason. 'What happened?'

He told her the full story on the way. She took it calmly, trying to encourage him to snooze for a few minutes, telling him he'd feel better when they got there, masking her concern. And she decided to say nothing about the lottery tickets. She wasn't going to gain anything by criticising or prying. And she had a good feeling about this dinner tonight – she had picked up positive vibes from the invite.

Maybe they had been invited as an afterthought, or even by mistake, but she was determined to milk the opportunity for all she could. What did they have to lose?

Susan drove recklessly fast, and they made it to the Guildhall only twenty minutes late, which John told her was almost respectable.

Inside the building, they presented their tickets to a liveried master of ceremonies, who announced them to a roomful of glittering people who were not listening. Their hosts, Mr and Mrs Walter Thomas Carmichael, were presumably somewhere in the vast, elegant hall, with its glittering chandeliers and fine statues and coats of arms and carvings.

For some moments, overwhelmed by the grandeur of the setting, Susan's confidence deserted her. Almost everyone appeared older than her and John, and she felt as though she had arrived at a club where everyone, except them, knew each other well.

John was tired. The alcohol and the shock were wearing off, leaving him with a dull headache and a thirst. A waitress came up to them with a tray containing glasses of champagne or mineral water. John knew he needed to sober up and that he should drink water but he took a glass of champagne. Before the waitress had moved too far away, he had drained it and taken a second.

'John ...' Susan said.

He feel more confident, and a little punchy now. 'Poor show when the hosts can't be bothered to meet their guests. I still don't understand why we're here.'

Susan was scanning the room. She had thought an author might be here whose book on the discovery of rare Oriental antiquities she had edited for Magellan Lowry six years back. She turned to John. 'We probably haven't got long to dinner. Shall we circulate, give it a whirl?'

He swigged most of his drink. 'Sure, let's go for it.'

As they made their way into the crowd, John detoured to a tray laden with canapés, and stuffed three scallops wrapped in bacon into his mouth in rapid succession. When he looked round, Susan had disappeared. He swallowed the last of his champagne and, as he did so, caught the eye of a tall, distinguished-looking man, who seemed to be on his own.

The man smiled at him.

'Beautiful room,' John said.

The man replied, in a cultured voice that carried only the faintest hint of broken English, 'Yes, a very *pleasant* room.'

They were in perhaps the most beautiful banqueting hall in Britain – the

Queen Mother liked to eat here – but John detected an air of put-down in the man's tone, as if this room was too small for him, as if he normally dined somewhere infinitely grander.

John struggled, unusually, to come up with anything more to say. He looked at the man's face, trying to put an age on him, but found it hard; late fifties perhaps, but possibly older. It was a handsome, distinctly aristocratic face, just a fraction gaunt, with dark, youthful hair streaked elegantly around the temples with silver, and brushed immaculately back.

The man's eyes were grey and sharp, alive with observation and a twinkle of humour, and his countenance suggested a *bon viveur* who took care of himself and an air of rather old fashioned courtly elegance. He wore a dinner jacket trimmed with velvet, which John instantly coveted, and his bow tie put John's small black clip-on one to shame.

'Are you a friend of the Carmichaels?' John ventured, helping himself to more champagne from a tray.

'We go back a long way,' the man said, in a polite but rather distant manner, his eyes overtly roaming the room as if he was in search of more interesting company.

'Ah.' John resisted the urge to swig from his glass and took just a small sip. He knew that he needed to find out what this man did but his companion's attention was elsewhere.

With his nerves still jumpy from the accident, John found it hard to think of a polite way of moving on. He glanced around, trying to spot Susan.

'And yourself?' the man said, still distant. 'You are a good friend of Walter and Charlotte?'

'I – ah – no. My wife's in publishing – she has an author – Oriental antiquities. That's how we – the invite –' John dried.

The man inclined his head and, with a polite smile, said, 'Very charming to meet you. If you'll excuse me, I must circulate a little before dinner.'

As the man moved away into the crowd John cursed himself. Where the hell was Susan?

He scanned the sea of faces but there was no sign of her. He tried to enter the thick of the crowd, but his path was blocked by an impenetrable wall of people locked in conversation. He stood by one group for a couple of minutes, trying to catch the eye of any of the three men engaged in an animated discussion about stock-market prices, but failed.

Turning away, he noticed an area to the side where people were reading something. As he walked over, he saw that it was the seating plan. After some jostling he got close enough to locate his own and Susan's places. They had been put on separate tables, which pleased him because it gave them more opportunities to meet people.

He was on Table Four. On one side of him was Lady Trouton and on the other Mr E. Sarotzini. Neither name meant anything to him. He was about to set off again in search of Susan when he heard three loud knocks and a booming voice announced that dinner was served.

According to the plan, Table Four was towards the far end. Lady Trouton was already at her place: she looked very old, wore tinted glasses and did not respond when John said hello. Not a good start, he thought, looking at the empty place on his right and hoping that this character, whoever he was, might be a more promising companion.

As he reached forward to take a look at a menu, the portly man opposite him nodded without breaking off from his earnest conversation with the steel-haired woman next to him. John picked up the menu and glanced at it. There were some fine wines, and the food was elaborately described, six courses ending in a savoury, Angels on Horseback. No speeches were listed, and the sole clue on the menu as to the purpose of this dinner were the gold printed words, A DINNER HOSTED BY MR AND MRS WALTER THOMAS CARMICHAEL.

As he put the menu back on the table, John was aware of a man taking the place next to him. He turned to acknowledge his dinner companion, and immediately tried to mask his disappointment with a smile.

'So, we meet again,' Mr Sarotzini said, peering at John's place name. 'Mr Carter. How very pleasant.'

Grace was said.

John held Lady Trouton's chair for her, but she didn't thank him, and when he tried again to introduce himself, she peered at him suspiciously. 'You are a friend of Walter and Charlotte?' she enquired in a tone of haughty disdain.

'No,' he said. 'Are you?'

A plate arrived, smoked salmon artistically arranged around a mousse. Simultaneously, a gloved hand poured white wine into one of John's glasses. Then a basket of rolls appeared, which Lady Trouton waved away dismissively, before turning back to John. 'Tell me,' she said, 'your views on unemployment.'

John, taken aback, unwrapped a pat of butter while he considered the question. 'It's going to increase,' he said. 'Technology is –'

She raised a hand to halt him. 'I'm sorry, dear, I find it difficult to talk and eat.'

John ate a mouthful of salmon, then drank some white wine, Bâtard Montrachet 1982, he remembered from the menu. He glanced at Mr Sarotzini, who had not yet touched his food.

Without looking at him, his neighbour asked: 'You are here alone or with your wife?'

John peered around, found the table Susan was sitting at and pointed her out to the man.

'A fine-looking young woman,' Mr Sarotzini said.

'Thank you.'

'How long have you been married?'

'Seven years.'

A silence fell between them again. They ate for a few moments, then John said, 'And you? You're married?'

Mr Sarotzini nodded slowly. 'Yes.'

'Is your wife here?'

John saw sadness in his expression as he replied, 'I regret, no.'

John sensed that the man did not want to talk about his wife. Perhaps they were separated, or she was ill. He felt sorry for him. 'Do you have children?'

Mr Sarotzini broke off a piece of his roll and buttered it carefully. His hands, with their long, elegant fingers, were a little unsteady and seemed to belong to an older man than his face suggested. 'No. No children.' His grey eyes clouded. 'You are blessed with them?'

'No. I'm not sure if they're a blessing or a curse!'

There was no reaction from Mr Sarotzini. Awkwardly, John picked up his wine glass, but when he brought it to his lips he discovered it was empty. He hadn't realised he had been drinking so quickly.

He glanced at Lady Trouton, who was engrossed with cutting her salmon into tiny squares. 'It's the coloureds who are to blame,' she announced suddenly.

John wondered for a moment who she was speaking to, and then realised she was speaking to him.

'I beg your pardon?'

'We should never have let them in, to drive the buses, back in the Fifties. They've taken over, haven't they? And look at the promises Mountbatten made to India. Now you can't buy a newspaper from a white man.'

John looked at her again, and wondered if they were both on the same planet. Disturbingly, he knew they were.

Mr Sarotzini was now engaged in conversation with the man on his right. John ate his salmon in silence, while Lady Trouton continued, with studied concentration, to cut hers up into squares, eating only the occasional morsel.

'A blessing,' Mr Sarotzini said, startling him. 'Children are most definitely a blessing.'

Soup arrived in a silver tureen. Mr Sarotzini waited until John had been served, then tested the soup and seemed to find it wanting. He munched a croûton. 'Yes, children. We must all remember, Mr Carter, that we have not inherited the earth from our ancestors, we have borrowed it from our children.'

John was warming towards him a little. 'Do you mind if I ask you – my wife and I, we're not sure what the purpose of this dinner is?'

'The Carmichaels are just marvellous hosts,' Mr Sarotzini answered. 'They always put on a little gathering for their friends when they are in London. They are here, of course, at the moment, because it is Ascot week. But you know,' he said, 'they're not people who require much of an excuse to throw a dinner party.'

'No,' John concurred, trying to give the impression that he was no stranger to the Carmichaels' stratosphere.

'Are you a racing man?' Mr Sarotzini asked.

'Yes. I prefer the flat season.'

'Of course. Steeplechasing is –' he waved a hand dismissively '– how should I put it? – rather inelegant. Were you at Ascot today?'

'No, I'm going tomorrow.' John was thankful for Archie's invitation.

Rack of lamb was served. The conversation moved on to travel: Mr Sarotzini had homes in Switzerland, America, England. He knew California well, and seemed familiar with the Venice Beach area of Los Angeles where Susan had grown up. 'Where did you meet your lovely wife?' Mr Sarotzini asked him.

'On the UCLA campus in Westwood,' John said. 'I was giving a talk at a conference on on-line publishing and Susan was working as an assistant to one of the delegates from Time Warner.'

'Synchronicity,' Mr Sarotzini said, giving him a quizzical stare. 'Perhaps you were brought together. It was meant to be.'

'My wife is a fan of Jung. She believes in synchronicity.'

'Are you familiar with the old Chinese proverb, "I hear and I forget, I see and I remember, I do and I understand?"'

'No,' John said, 'but I like it.'

'Your wife,' Mr Sarotzini said. 'I imagine she would like it also?'

'Yes, I expect she would.' John was a little surprised by the question. He cut a slice of lamb, chewed it, then washed it down with a mouthful of Mouton Rothschild '66. His glass was instantly refilled.

It did not seem to matter how much John drank tonight, it just made him feel increasingly alert and alive. Now he was thoroughly enjoying his conversation with Mr Sarotzini, they were getting on famously, and neither had yet asked what the other did. John was starting to feel that, if he played his cards right, Mr Sarotzini might be the man to help him, and deliberately kept away from the topic of business, not wanting to seem pushy.

'Your wife,' Sarotzini said, suddenly, 'does she find it hard, sometimes, not having children? Does she find people, at dinners such as this, making tactless remarks that wound her?'

'Yes. But she's very good about it.'

'And there is no biological reason preventing her from conceiving?'

'We've never checked.' John cast a glance at Lady Trouton. She was cutting her lamb into tiny squares, totally preoccupied.

'Forgive me for being so personal,' Mr Sarotzini said. 'It is a fault of mine.'

'No problem.' John smiled. 'Did you and your wife make a conscious decision not to have children?'

The question brought back the air of sadness to Mr Sarotzini's face and John wished he hadn't asked it.

'Yes,' Mr Sarotzini replied. 'Yes, a conscious decision,' he echoed, and his face seemed to age ten years.

With the arrival of *tarte tatin* Mr Sarotzini finally enquired about the nature of John's business. At first John gave him only sketchy details, but then, when he saw the man's interest, he opened up a little more. And then more still. By the time port was being poured and the cheese board presented, John was entertaining Mr Sarotzini with a detailed account of his meeting with Clake.

And Mr Sarotzini was surprisingly sympathetic, telling John of his deep scorn for high-street banks. 'You know,' he told John wryly, 'such a bank will only lend you money if you can prove to them that you really and truly do not need it.'

John smiled, and said, finally, 'So what do you do?'

Mr Sarotzini smiled back. 'I'm a banker,' he said.

John had to make a supreme effort not to let his elation show in his face or his voice. 'Oh, really?' he said. 'What – what kind of banking are you involved in?'

Mr Sarotzini handed him a business card. On it was printed: *E. Sarotzini. Director. Vörn Bank.*

Beneath was a PO box number in Zürich.

John studied the card. Something was missing.

'No phone number?' he asked.

'We like to choose to whom we speak, Mr Carter. We are most selective. We have interests in a number of companies in the technology and biotechnology sectors. Perhaps we should have a further conversation?'

John pulled out a card of his own. 'Yes,' he said. 'Thank you, I'd like to very much.'

Chapter Twelve

It was quiet in the Carters' house. Kündz, wearing his headphones, did a routine flick through the channel selector. He could hear the hum of the fridge in Susan's kitchen, but in all the other rooms there was silence.

But even listening to this silence gave him pleasure, because this was *Susan Carter's silence.*

The Carters were out tonight at dinner with Mr and Mrs Walter Thomas Carmichael, and he wondered how they were getting on. Mr Sarotzini was at this dinner also, and Kündz was not quite sure about the agenda there. Sometimes Mr Sarotzini only told him so much, leaving him a little in the dark, almost as if he was teasing him; that was one of the things that seemed to give Mr Sarotzini pleasure, playing games with him. But Kündz didn't mind. He knew from experience that Mr Sarotzini did nothing without a reason, which always eventually became clear.

He continued listening to Susan Carter's silence, picturing in his mind the exact position of every item in that round bedroom in the turret perfumed with her smells.

It was quiet also in Kündz's attic flat in Pembroke Road in Earl's Court. The walls, floors and ceiling were lined with soundproofing material he had installed. The room beneath the eaves, in which he was now sitting, his monitoring room, had no windows: it was completely secure, and as quiet as the grave.

It was also as solitary as the grave. Kündz felt lonely in London. He missed his apartment in Geneva, the only home of his own he'd ever had, and he felt insecure being so far away from Mr Sarotzini. Although he was never really far away from Mr Sarotzini. Physical distance made no difference because, wherever he was, Mr Sarotzini was always with him, connected to his thoughts, reading his mind, sometimes letting him get on with it, other times instructing him. It was as if Mr Sarotzini could step in and out of his head, from wherever he was in the world, and manipulate him.

And Kündz did not mind this. Mr Sarotzini had always given him guidance, and he was never wrong. Kündz understood implicitly that it was his life's duty to serve Mr Sarotzini.

He had been groomed for this role since the earliest days of his conscious memory, in the *château* above Lake Geneva to which Mr Sarotzini had brought him all those years back and which he had left only rarely throughout his childhood, mostly to accompany Mr Sarotzini on his travels. Mr Sarotzini had instilled in Kündz from an early age that he had been put into this world for a higher purpose than ordinary mortals, and Kündz had accepted this without question.

And now, here in London, Kündz was afraid that on this important mission he might fail Mr Sarotzini. It wasn't the pain that Mr Sarotzini might inflict that worried him. It was the fear of being rejected by him that was really terrifying.

But, so far in London, everything was proceeding well, Mr Sarotzini had been pleased with the first results, more pleased than Kündz had dared to hope. He sensed Mr Sarotzini's presence in the room with him: Mr Sarotzini, at the dinner table, was thinking about him. Kündz picked up the warm thoughts, and felt a little less lonely; he was grateful to Mr Sarotzini for this small kindness he was showing him.

Kündz tried to send back a signal of gratitude. Mr Sarotzini had taught him that it was possible to transmit thoughts, and even, if you concentrated hard enough, to influence other people's minds.

He wondered if the signal had reached Mr Sarotzini. He wondered if Mr Sarotzini was close to Susan Carter and if he could smell her. Then he picked up his book, Homer's *Iliad* in Greek – Mr Sarotzini had taught him that one should always read a book in its original language, never in translation – and began to read.

This was something else he missed in London: his books. The vast library in Mr Sarotzini's house had been his starting point where, under Mr Sarotzini's tutelage, he had read every volume on its shelves. His own apartment was overflowing with books, which he had regretted having to leave behind. He valued them far more than he valued the company of people, for they presented interpretations of the world, past, present and future, from which he was able to form his own understandings.

Sometimes he interpreted his understandings with the intricate drawings he made with his airbrush. He was a fine artist; Mr Sarotzini had often praised his work, and that made him proud.

He missed the gym, too, where he did his daily workout, and the special muesli with blueberries in the *konditorei* on Rue de la Confédération where he had his breakfast, and the cool breezes off the lake, and his black Mercedes SL600 – but he understood that that was too conspicuous, and in London he needed to blend into his surroundings.

And he missed his wardrobe. He had racks of hand-made suits, in fine wools, silks and linens, shelves stacked with hand-made shirts and hand-made shoes laid out in long lines. Mr Sarotzini had taught him about the value of quality, and detail. Everything that Kündz wore was the best, and the luggage in which he carried them was the best also, beautiful leather with hand-stitching finish, all of the cases matching.

When he had been alone in Susan Carter's bedroom and had been through the drawers and wardrobes, he had noted that John Carter's suits and shirts were brand names, Boss, Armani, Conran, off-the-peg. It hurt him to think that Susan Carter could be penetrated by a man who bought ready-to-wear clothes. She deserved so much better. The words of the Twenty-third Truth came into his mind: 'Mediocrity recognises nothing higher than itself. Talent instantly recognises genius.'

Many eminent and famous people came as guests to Mr Sarotzini's château from all over the world: heads of state, cabinet ministers, senators, royalty, movie celebrities, scientists, industrialists. Mr Sarotzini had taught Kündz to imagine each of these people sitting on the lavatory, excreting then wiping their backsides. He wanted to make Kündz realise that title, rank, noble birth or any level of fame only made a human being different from his fellow man in some ways, not all.

Susan Carter was different.

She was truly different.

Kündz found himself thinking of Claudie and wondered if Mr Sarotzini had put this thought into his mind to distract him from Susan Carter. It was hard, sometimes, to differentiate between thoughts that were his own, and those that Mr Sarotzini planted in his head.

Claudie. He imagined himself in his apartment with her, doing something dirty with her; she liked to do things that were dirty. Before he had been inside Susan Carter's house, and had stood in Susan Carter's presence and breathed in her smells, he had missed Claudie. But no longer.

On the small desk beside him was an envelope containing a ticket for a performance of *Don Giovanni* at Glyndebourne on Sunday. It was a reward from Mr Sarotzini for his good work. He wished he could take Susan Carter with him and make love to her afterwards, with the roiling energy of the music bursting through their bodies.

But that would not be possible.

'Susan,' he whispered quietly.

Susan stared at him from every wall. Photographs he had taken from the tiny camera concealed behind the badge of his British Telecom uniform those three glorious days when he has been in her house.

They were grainy, which irritated him. She was inanimate and that irritated him too. He wanted to see Susan Carter move, he wanted to see her undress, he wanted to see her doing dirty things with her husband.

He wanted, although he did not need, an excuse to hate her husband even more than he already did.

He switched to a different channel and listened in to his apartment in Geneva. From the living room he could hear voices, the television. He adjusted a filter and the sound of the television faded. Then he listened for other voices, for any sound that Claudie might have a man in the apartment with her.

He checked out the bedroom and that was fine. Then he tapped a command on his computer keyboard. The screen came to life. On it appeared a colour image of Claudie, his favourite photograph of her: she was sitting naked on a chair, facing the camera, her legs spread open. He imagined that it was not Claudie, but Susan Carter.

He picked up the phone and punched a number. Claudie answered. He imagined he was hearing Susan Carter's voice.

He asked, 'What are you doing?'

'Watching television.'

'What are you wearing?'

Teasing. 'Nothing much.'

'What do you smell of?'

'You,' she said.

'I want to see you,' he said.

'And I want to see you, too.'

He keyed in another command and logged onto the Internet. A new image appeared: an empty chair facing the camera. In a moment, Claudie, naked, moved into the frame and sat in the chair. The technology was not yet perfect. He was watching her now, in real time, but each movement was jerky as if in slow motion, as the images travelled down the cables from Geneva to London.

He stared at the live image of Claudie, naked, her long brown hair resting on her shoulders. She was looking directly at him and knew he was watching her. But she did not know that in his mind he was no longer seeing her but Susan Carter.

'Touch yourself,' Kündz said.

He watched her touching herself. The jerky images added to the sensuality. He watched her pressing her fingers up inside herself. He watched the expression on her face change. As she worked her fingers, a certain dreaminess softened her face, and he wondered if this was how it would be with Susan Carter also.

Then her lips were moving, she was speaking. Yes, speak to me, oh, my Susan, speak to me.

'Now let me see *you*,' she said.

Chapter Thirteen

John felt queasy, tired, and he had a blinding headache. Port always did this to him, and at the dinner last night he had poured it down his throat recklessly.

On the advice of his accountant, he had been to see an insolvency practitioner, and was talking on the phone to him now. The news he gave John about what he would be able to salvage from the business if the bank pulled the plug wasn't good. If John had seen the writing on the wall a year back, he could have formed a separate company and started transferring business into it. But he hadn't made any such preparations.

He replaced the receiver, deeply gloomy. His secretary brought him in a second cup of coffee and gave him a strange look, making him wonder whether she'd overheard him. Stella wasn't stupid, she knew something was going on, but in her usual discreet way she hadn't asked.

She'd been with him right from the start, when he had been operating from a tiny office above a pet shop in Marylebone, and Gareth had been moonlighting from his day job in computer graphics at a firm of architects. Stella was a bright, sassy girl, pretty and elegant, with short brown hair, and a tiresome boyfriend she supported, a permanently resting actor with an ego the size of the Atlantic. She'd get another job quickly – anyone in their right mind would snap her up – but losing her was going to be a terrible blow.

He would have to tell Gareth soon, and all their employees. So far the only person in the company who knew anything was the financial controller, a quiet, efficient, conscientious woman called Janet Pennington. She had prepared the figures for John's pitch documents to other banks and institutions, and he knew he could rely on her to say nothing.

He had just thirteen days left until Clake's deadline. And last night there had been a slim ray of hope, the Swiss banker with the odd name.

'How's your headache?' Stella asked.

'Bad.' Headaches had become an almost daily feature of his life but this was the mother of them all.

'I'll give you two more paracetamol before you go.'

It was a quarter to ten. In an hour's time he would have to leave the office, get home, change into his morning suit and drive with Susan to join Archie's party at Ascot.

He was glad to be out of the office today – there was no way he'd be able to concentrate on much in his state – and Susan was right: someone there might be willing to take a gamble on DigiTrak. And that banker last night had given him a couple of tips. John had checked the horses in the morning paper and they were both outsiders. He decided he would bang them hard.

His head took a turn for the worse, and he pressed his knuckles into his temples, trying to ease the pain. Looking lamely up at Stella, he said, 'Be an angel and get me a Coke, full strength.'

'Sure.' She smiled sympathetically, knowing from experience that when he asked for a Coke, he must be in bad shape: it was the hangover cure he used as a last resort.

John fished in his wallet, and found the banker's card. E. Sarotzini. He started to compose a letter in his head, then picked up his dictating machine. As he did so, his telephone warbled. It was Stella: she had a Mr Sarotzini on the line, did John want to speak to him?

Mr Sarotzini sounded polite, but much more formal than he had last night, as if he had moved from party into business mode. 'It was very pleasant to make your acquaintance,' he said.

John remembered the man's use of the word *pleasant* in his rather condescending appraisal of the banqueting hall, and wondered, his heart sinking a little, if in the banker's eyes the same mediocrity applied to himself.

'Likewise,' John said.

'I may perhaps see you at Ascot today?' It was clear from the way Mr Sarotzini spoke that this remark was merely a courtesy and not a serious invitation to rendezvous.

'I'll keep a look-out for you. I've remembered the tips you gave me.'

'Don't put your house on them,' Mr Sarotzini said. 'But they are worth a little flutter.'

Something about the way Mr Sarotzini spoke convinced John that he should bet on these two horses even more heavily than he had already intended.

There was a brief silence, and then Mr Sarotzini said, 'I have to return to

Switzerland at the weekend. I wondered if by any chance you might be free to join me for lunch tomorrow, Mr Carter?'

John looked at his diary. Friday, 18 June. Lunch with his accountant was marked in. 'Yes,' he said. 'I have something I could move, I can manage that.'

'I will come to your office at midday.'

'Sure, fine.'

'It would be most helpful if you could have prepared for me the last three years' audited accounts, your forward projections, your cash flow – and a five-year plan?'

John tried not to give away his excitement in his voice.

Chapter Fourteen

The Venerable Doctor Euan Freer, Professor of Systematic Theology of the University of London, and Archdeacon Emeritus of Oxford, was the most intelligent and influential clergyman Fergus Donleavy knew.

Fergus sat, ignoring the broken spring beneath him, in an ancient leather armchair in the sitting room of Freer's residence at the university. It was a masculine room, with battered furniture, threadbare rugs, sagging bookshelves and a small open grate; the sash window was raised and the sweet air of freshly mown grass filled the room from the communal gardens below.

He took a bite of a digestive biscuit, and drank some coffee, savouring the cool air in here after the blazing heat of the June sun outside. He and Freer were old friends and they had been trying to work out how many years it was since they had last seen or spoken to each other.

Fergus bided his time while they caught up on each other's news. He told Freer that the church had kept him looking young (although he did not tell him that he had become rather plump and that his hair had turned alarmingly grey) and Freer, in his black cassock, laughed and told Fergus he wished he looked as fit as him.

If Freer had not elected this vocation, and the vow of celibacy that went with his Brotherhood, he could have been a devastating womaniser. He was good-looking, in a swarthy Latin way that caused many people, including Fergus, to comment on his resemblance to Robert de Niro.

Freer asked Fergus about his books, and what he was currently working on. Fergus became a little subdued. 'It's Steven Hawking, *Brief History of Time* territory,' he explained. 'But it goes a lot further.'

'When's it coming out?'

Fergus shrugged. He had some rewriting to do, he told Freer, and that was a bitch.

Freer told him about a book he had published a couple of years back on the history of exorcism in Britain, and the editor who had made him rewrite whole chunks of it. They both agreed that editors were a bitch.

Fergus dunked a segment of digestive into his coffee, shook off the drips and ate it. 'This bloody woman, Susan Carter,' he said. 'I like her, she's bright, but sometimes she drives me nuts. She doesn't think the general public are as smart as I do – she tries to get me to explain things in baby talk.'

Freer smiled. 'But you have faith in her judgement?'

'Yes, I suppose – yes, of course I do.' Fergus shrugged again. 'I'm just pissed off, but that's my problem.' He pulled out his cigarettes and offered one to the priest.

Freer shook his head. 'I gave up – just smoke my pipe occasionally. There's an ashtray beside you.' He settled back in his chair while Fergus lit his cigarette, and watched him with an expectant smile. He knew that this visit was not purely social. 'So?' he said.

Fergus drew deeply on the cigarette, tilted his head and blew the smoke directly up at the ceiling. 'Nietzsche said that sometimes when you stare into the abyss, the abyss stares back at you.'

Freer nodded, his gentle, alert eyes fixed on Fergus.

'Have you ever had a bad feeling, Euan, about something?'

'Like a presentiment? A premonition?'

'No, it's more than that. I don't know how to explain it. I suppose, I mean, OK, we both agree that the birth of Jesus it *did* happen in some way – although we come at it from different directions, right?'

Euan Freer looked at him questioningly, the thread eluding him.

'The Three Wise Men,' Fergus said. 'The Magi. They saw the bright light in the sky, right? The star? They knew the messiah had been born. Right?'

Freer nodded, unsure where this was going.

Fergus cut the air in front of him with his hand, smoke trailing from his cigarette like cotton thread. 'I happen to believe the "star" was a space craft bringing Jesus from another, smarter civilisation. You happen to believe that the Virgin Birth brought him. But that doesn't matter. This is what is important: how do you think those three wise men *felt* when they saw that star?'

'They felt that something quite extraordinary was happening.'

'And that whatever it was they sensed was a force of *good*?'

Freer smiled. 'I wasn't there. But yes, probably, that's one of the things they sensed.'

'And now it's the end of the millennium and a lot of people have a sense that something bad will happen. There's been a raft of predictions about this, going back a long way.'

The cleric poured more coffee. 'How far do you want to go back? Nostradamus? The Bible?'

'Further than that, maybe.' Fergus stood up and walked around the room, then leant against the window-sill and peered down into the garden. A man with a ponytail was weeding a bed. 'You must believe that I'm being serious, Euan.'

'I always take you seriously, Fergus. I even defended the paper you published in *Nature*.'

Fergus turned, startled. 'You read that? It was about six years ago.'

'Of course. People's auras. You still believe that we have auras?'

'It's not a question of believing, it's proven scientific fact.'

'And you can read people's futures in these auras?'

'No, I can't do that. It's nothing visual, nothing physical – it's just a sense I get.'

'And how often have you had that sense?'

'Half a dozen times in my life. The first was before my mother died – that was clear, I kept seeing the car accident in my dreams, and I saw the aura of death around her, and it happened exactly as I saw it.'

'And now you've had it again?'

Fergus sat down, crushed out his cigarette and told him exactly what he had sensed, and what he felt it meant. Freer listened in silence, without interrupting. When he had finished, Fergus could not tell from his friend's expression whether the priest believed him or not.

'Tell me, Fergus,' Freer asked, 'these feelings you get – how many have been accurate?'

'All of them.'

For what seemed a long time Freer reflected on this. Then he asked, 'Do you want to tell this woman?'

'I don't have an image. I don't have anything to tell her.'

'Shall we pray for her?'

Fergus had rejected prayer years ago. And yet now, here with Canon Euan Freer, it seemed the right thing to do.

They knelt and said the Lord's Prayer aloud together. Then Freer said, 'Lord, protect this woman.'

And Fergus mouthed silently into his cupped hands: 'Susan, whatever it is you are about to do, don't do it. *Please don't do it.*'

Chapter Fifteen

The three-pointed star on the radiator of Mr Sarotzini's elderly black Mercedes Pullman floated with the eerie grace of a gun-sight tracking a target, as the chauffeur robotically helmed the limousine through the London traffic.

John, tense and anxious, watched the view through the smoked glass of the windscreen. Thirty years ago, this was the kind of vehicle the dictator of an emerging Third World nation might have bought to demonstrate his status. Now, mellowed by age, it had an imposing, rather noble presence.

The star hovered on a taxi, then on a cyclist in a smog mask, then on a traffic light. A smartly dressed woman crossed the road, a scarf flapping from her shoulders. It was a dry morning but heavily overcast, the darkened glass making it seem even more so, and it had turned cold. With the air-conditioning set uncomfortably low, it felt wintry in the car.

Mr Sarotzini seemed a different man altogether from the person John had sat with at dinner. He had the same distinguished appearance and natural air of superiority, and he was again immaculately dressed – today in a finely tailored grey worsted suit, yellow Hermès tie, and a complementing yellow handkerchief protruding with flourish from his breast pocket. It was his expression that had changed.

At dinner he had exuded all the charm of a *bon viveur*, a relaxed man with barely a care in the world. Today he was hard, remote, chillingly serious. The warmth that John recalled, and the sparkling humour, was gone, and John's attempts to break the ice had so far failed. He tried again now.

'Those two tips you gave me,' he said. 'I really am impressed.'

Mr Sarotzini stared out of his side window, as he had for most of the journey, his long, elegant fingers calmly entwined in his lap. Even his voice seemed different today. At dinner his accent had carried a charismatic trace of Italian but that had been replaced with an equally cultured but harsher, guttural Germanic undertow. 'Horse racing is the sport of kings and fools, Mr Carter. If someone gives you a tip and it wins, you should put it down to coincidence or corruption, no more or less.'

John looked at him, unsure from his tone which of the two applied in this case. Both of Mr Sarotzini's tips at Ascot yesterday had won, the first at 20 to 1, the second at 15 to 1. John had bet two hundred pounds on each, plus a further fifty pounds on a forecast, and had come away with a twelve-thousand-pound profit.

Yet instead of being thrilled, as Susan had been – she was treating it as a great omen – he was kicking himself for not having backed the horses harder. If he had been bolder (and if he'd had the money available, which he didn't), he could have solved all his financial problems on just those two tips. Except, of course, he couldn't have taken a risk big enough for that.

'On your balance sheet, you show a capital loss of £48,751 carried forward two years. Can you explain this to me?' Mr Sarotzini asked.

'Yes, of course, it's …' John had to rack his brains. 'It's the way we treated the depreciation on some computer graphic equipment we bought from a bankrupt firm. We acquired shares in the company at the same time to give us a loss we could carry forward.'

'And in last year's accounts there was a note from the auditor about a payment of £35,687 into an account at the Crédit Suisse bank in Zürich. I did not understand what that was in respect of.'

This was a little embarrassing for John, although he felt that, as a Swiss banker himself, Mr Sarotzini would understand. 'That was part of our arrangement with the gynaecologist Harvey Addison. He's very important to us – he hosts our most successful online show. But the deal is that we have to lose – hide – part of his salary overseas.'

John was increasingly surprised at the extent of the detail Mr Sarotzini had remembered. The banker had no notes and he had spent less than half an hour in John's office, scanning the figures that had been prepared for him, yet everything now seemed to be stored in his head.

'This composer,' Mr Sarotzini said. 'Zak Danziger. Do you think a quick settlement is possible?'

John considered his reply carefully, and decided it was wisest to be truthful. 'No, I don't think so. At least, he might settle but not cheaply.'

He had been concentrating so hard on the questions that he had not noticed the car pull up. They got out and entered a club in Mayfair that had about it an air of discretion. The Georgian building, off Curzon Street, had a certain grandeur, but the exterior was in need of a fresh coat of paint. There was no doorman, and no name, simply an entry bell and the number 3 on the door.

Inside, it became evident, from the reverential manner in which he was treated, that Mr Sarotzini was well known here, and he warmly greeted each member of staff by name. They passed a porter's desk and entered a large, panelled hall hung with portraits and a row of green baize notice boards.

The staff were elderly, but all were unctuously polite to John, treating him, as he imagined they treated all visitors, as if he were the most important guest ever to have entered these portals. Yet from the silence that fell as he followed Mr Sarotzini through a doorway and across another hall, he had the impression that he was being studied and assessed by them all.

The dining room was decorated in Baroque grandeur, with gilded columns and crystal chandeliers, yet it was not so large that it lacked intimacy. Like everything else about this club, the room seemed a little tired. The stuccoed ceiling was stained an uneven ochre from years of rising nicotine, the green velvet curtains had faded badly, and the nap had worn thin on the carpet. Even the handful of other diners, all elderly men dressed in dark suits, looked a little faded.

John was glad that he had dressed conservatively, in a navy suit, white shirt and a striped golf-club tie that might have passed for an old-school tie.

He was given a menu, but Mr Sarotzini was not. 'I always have the same,' the banker said, sitting with a ramrod straight back. 'But please help yourself, enjoy. The food here is really quite pleasant.'

John ordered smoked salmon and Dover sole. The salmon arrived almost immediately, along with a plate of quails' eggs for Mr Sarotzini. Mineral water and white Graves were poured. John raised his wine glass.

'Cheers, your health.'

Mr Sarotzini smiled politely but did not respond, and John put down his glass. He said, awkwardly, 'This is very nice, this club. Beautiful building.'

Mr Sarotzini opened his hands expansively. 'I find it convenient.'

'What's it called?'

'The name is private, known only to members. This is one of the rules.' Mr Sarotzini smiled again, but his expression seemed to John to have turned a little frosty.

'How does one become a member?'

Mr Sarotzini carefully poured a small mound of salt at the edge of his plate. 'You have an enquiring mind, Mr Carter. Please, time is short today, permit me to ask the questions. I must make a report about your business this afternoon if we are to have a chance of helping you by your deadline.'

'Of course.'

John squeezed lemon onto his salmon, and his eye caught an oil painting on the wall depicting a group of cherubs picnicking beneath a viaduct. There was something carefree about it, in contrast to the atmosphere in this room, and John fleetingly found himself envying those anonymous characters their simple pleasure.

Mr Sarotzini cracked a quail's egg on his plate, shelled it, then dipped it into the salt. 'Tell me, what are your religious convictions, Mr Carter?'

John, an atheist, took a moment to think before answering, wondering if he was stepping into a minefield. Was this another Clake? Was Mr Sarotzini a deeply religious man? 'I – I have an open mind,' he said finally.

'How open?'

Mr Sarotzini's eyes were fixed on his now: it was as if the banker could see into his mind, and that the truth was the only option.

'I suppose I tend to look towards science for explanations, rather than religion, mysticism or the paranormal.'

'And your wife?'

'She's a believer – a committed Christian.'

'How committed?'

'She goes to church. She used to go every week, but now only occasionally.'

'And does this difference in your beliefs affect your marriage, Mr Carter?'

'No, it's not an issue. I guess we agreed to differ a long time back, and we hardly ever talk about it.'

'Of course. Forgive me for being so personal.'

They ate in silence. John waited for Mr Sarotzini to continue, but with deep concentration the banker began to shell another egg. John wondered if he had disappointed him, and whether he should say something to retrieve the situation. But then Mr Sarotzini said, 'Forgive me again for being so personal, but has religion ever entered your reasoning for not having children?'

John sensed that Mr Sarotzini was deliberately trying to avoid the subject of business, but he was anxious to get back to it. There were some big deals in the pipeline that he wanted the banker to know about, and he needed time to explain these in detail as they would significantly affect DigiTrak's profits over the next couple of years and make the figures look much better.

'No, that's not an issue. Susan's pretty relaxed about religion. We're godparents to a small boy, and I'm happy about that. It's no big thing in our lives.'

'But your decision not to have children, Mr Carter, that is a big thing?'

John tried to side-step the question, but Mr Sarotzini would not let him, and John found himself getting into the full story of why he and Susan had decided not to have children. He was nearing the end of his Dover sole before he had finished.

Mr Sarotzini, eating his boiled fish with slow deliberation, commented, 'So it is your family upbringing that is responsible?'

'Yes.'

'You had no stability. Your father drank, he drove a taxicab, he cut hair, he bought a corner store and lost his savings. He became a salesman, then he dropped out and became a shepherd on a remote Scottish island. Finally he returned home, bitter and angry, and blamed your birth for destroying his freedom and his marriage.'

John felt a lump in his throat. It still hurt. Over the years he had tried to bury it, to confront it, and once he had even tried therapy, but nothing had worked.

'And then he threw himself beneath an underground railway train?'

John had been at school then in North London, fourteen years old; it had made the local newspaper. Kids whispered and pointed; groups fell silent as he passed them in the playground. If your father threw himself under a train, you were tainted with it. Whatever sickness in the head your father carried, you carried too.

Stay away from John Carter he might take you under a train with him.

The banker disinterred a bone from his fish. 'And your mother?' he said.

John did not want to tell Mr Sartozini about his mother. He thought about the presents she used to buy him, and the terrible rows she always had with his father over how much they cost. He remembered the model of Apollo 11, when he'd been hooked on the moon landing. The Action Man. The model aeroplanes, the encyclopaedias, the Lego sets.

It was around her gifts that his childhood had revolved. They became his brother and sister, his best friend, his window on the world. He huddled in his room, reading, learning, making models, living his life vicariously through Action Man's hair-raising adventures, and closed his ears to the moans of his mother with the men who visited her when his father was out or away, and to her screams when she opened his bedroom door some days and blamed him for ruining her life. If he had never been born their marriage would have been wonderful.

And always he escaped into his fantasy world. Into board games, Dungeons and Dragons and, finally, into computers.

He told Mr Sarotzini a modified, more palatable version of this.

Coffee arrived. They had discussed no business over lunch and Mr Sarotzini was now looking at his slender, old-fashioned Cartier watch. John reached beneath the table for his briefcase. 'I have copies of the accounts and projections for you,' he said.

The banker pulled a tiny gold dispenser from his pocket and tapped two sweeteners into his *demi-tasse*. 'How thoughtful of you, but that will not be necessary.'

John looked at the man, alarmed by his tone. The hope that had buoyed him earlier had been dashed on rocks. Was it something he had said during lunch? This sudden change in Mr Sarotzini was not making any sense. He could not understand why the man should have gone to the trouble he had and then ask him only about his private life and his background.

As the banker dabbed his mouth carefully with his napkin, then rose from the table, John wondered whether the man had all his lights on. Yet he had remembered incredible details about the accounts and he had not in any way seemed a fool.

As the Mercedes headed back towards John's office, Mr Sarotzini sat in distant silence. When John tried to steer the conversation back towards the chances of the Vörn Bank coming on board, Mr Sarotzini replied, finally, that the more he had thought about it, the more Zak Danziger presented a deeper problem than he had at first realised.

By the time they parted company, John was deeply despondent. Mr Sarotzini hadn't taken any paperwork, he couldn't be interested.

The calendar on the computer in John's office told him that he had eleven days left. It was Saturday tomorrow, golf with the lads if he felt up to it. On Monday morning he would have eight days left. Gloomily he picked up the receiver and phoned Archie Warren.

Archie had run out of suggestions.

Chapter Sixteen

The cellar was the only part of the house Susan didn't care for.

The heavy door had sagged on its hinges and she had to give a back-breaking heave to move it. As it scraped open, she was greeted by dank-smelling darkness. She switched on the light and went down the steps, ducking her head. She particularly didn't like the claustrophobically low ceiling, or the little spiders that hung around everywhere in their webs.

She walked past a cluster of old Chianti bottles, lengths of drainpipe, empty packing cases and a stack of rusty strips of metal, reached the chest freezer and opened the lid. It came free with a loud cracking of ice from the frozen rubber seal and a blast of cold air. As she peered at the contents, she cursed her stupidity in not having labelled anything when she had stocked up. She lifted out something that might have been a leg of lamb, searching beneath it for the frozen tiger prawns she was sure were in here. She pulled out more packets. Even this simple task was an effort today: she was too distracted by her worries to concentrate on anything normal. They had guests coming tonight, and she usually loved entertaining, but today it was an ordeal.

Last night John had arrived home more miserable than ever. He'd had high hopes of the Swiss banker he'd met at the dinner at the Guildhall, and so had she after the success of the man's racing tips. But now it seemed that, like everything else, it had come to nothing.

She jumped as the boiler, at the far end of the cellar, rattled and thumped into life. Then she continued to dig, her hands numbingly cold. Alex and Liz Harrison were coming tonight. Alex, who had been John's best man, was marketing director of a large software company and John was going to pick his brains to see if he could think of any company that might buy DigiTrak. Liz was Susan's closest friend in England, next to Kate Fox, her colleague in the office.

Harvey Addison and his wife, Caroline, were coming too. Susan didn't much care for the gynaecologist, whom she thought rather precious and arrogant, but John wanted to keep him sweet. If DigiTrak went to the wall, he planned to offer him a partnership in a new venture.

Susan found Caroline pleasant but dull and self-obsessed. Attractive, in a Barbie-doll way, her conversation was limited to the walk-in wardrobes she was having built, the diet she was on, and updates on her children, on whom she lavished the same Stepford admiration she held for her husband. In the five years that Susan had known her, she could not remember Caroline Addison ever having asked her a question about herself.

It was Saturday morning and John was on the golf course. He needed to relax, and she was glad that at least he was out in the fresh air for a few hours. Then he was going on to the office, to meet a liquidator, someone Archie Warren had suggested, a bit of a rough diamond, according to Archie. The liquidator was going to advise him on how to salvage what he could between now and when the bank pulled the plug. Nothing *illegal*, John told her last night, but his tone had told her something different.

His desperation was scaring her. Until this crisis she had always been able to trust his judgement, but now she was worried that he might do something that could land him in trouble. Or worse. She was beginning to fear that he might try to kill himself.

Until now John and she had always discussed everything openly, but now they could hardly communicate with each other. He had drunk heavily again last night and had snapped at her when she had tried to talk about other avenues they could try. Then he had fallen asleep in front of the television.

A bad childhood either destroyed you, warped you, or made you strong. John's had made him strong; his father's failure had made him determined to succeed, to prove that failure was not in his genes. He had never been a quitter, but now he seemed close to becoming one. From what he had said last night, she thought he was beginning, alarmingly, to see the end as a release.

And she could see that, in some ways, it would be a release. He could start again, although it would take time for him to get back to where he was now, or anything close to it, and yes, it would be a wrench, but if they had to leave this house, she could accept it. The serious problem was Casey.

If only her own job were secure.

When John had asked her to marry him and move to London, only Casey had made her hesitant about leaving LA.

Tinseltown held mostly images of tragedy for her. Her father, a bit-part actor who hadn't had a role in thirty years, earned a living gassing up the yachts and powerboats of the rich, the famous and the just plain successful at Marina del Rey. At the age of fifty, he had taken up painting, and still dreamed of being discovered, if not as an actor, maybe now as a water-colourist. But Susan knew, sadly, that he wouldn't be. He had talent but he didn't have *drive*.

Her mother, whose biggest movie break had been a part riding an elevator with Clint Eastwood in *Dirty Harry*, which had been cut in the televised version, now worked in a ticket booth at Universal Studios and had stopped dreaming a long while back.

Casey, who was fun, wacky and stunningly beautiful, had dropped a contaminated Ecstasy tab at a party when she'd just turned fifteen. She had lain ever since in a persistent vegetative state in a clinic. Susan's mother would not allow life support to be switched off, and Susan and her father, although with some misgivings, had always supported her decision.

Susan blamed herself for Casey's condition. In spite of her parents and friends telling her repeatedly that it hadn't been her fault, she couldn't help the guilt she carried. Her parents had gone away for the weekend and Casey had been invited to a party. Susan had been reluctant to let her go but Casey had begged, promising to be home early, and Susan had relented.

If only ... Susan had thought a thousand times.

For the first five years, Susan had visited Casey for an hour every day. She had sat by her bed, talking and playing her favourite rock music. Slowly it had drifted to an hour every few days, then once a week.

Since she had moved to England, Susan saw her only twice a year. She had compensated for this with the knowledge that the money she and John made in England would enable her to keep Casey in the luxurious clinic in Orange County rather than have to put her into state care. Now the realisation that she might not be able to help Casey was hurting deeply.

Right at the bottom of the last compartment she found the tiger prawns. As she packed everything back in, she thought about children, suddenly. Alex and Liz Harrison had four, two boys and two girls, all three years apart. Liz was a perfect mother, attentive, intelligent, attractive, funny, and Susan, who had always preferred flawed people to perfect ones, was filled with a deep, irrational loathing for her friend.

And with the loathing came the yearning.

She knew it well: it was an ancient enemy that returned to her every few months, and she had her ways of dealing with it, of talking herself through it – until the next time.

All the old arguments came out now. She told herself there were too many people in the world, that kids killed the romance in a marriage, destroyed their parents' freedom, cost a fortune to feed and educate, and anyhow, she and John might not even be able to have them if they did want them. She had stockpiled an arsenal of defences but none worked.

The truth was that she loved John and John did not want children. She loved her job, too, and that gave her no time to have children even if she wanted them. And besides, she was only twenty-eight, she had plenty of time, John might change. Somehow, in time, she would *make* him change. Or maybe *she* would change, and go off the idea for good.

And anyhow, in their current situation, children were more unthinkable than ever. So why was she thinking about it? Strongly.

Her thoughts were interrupted by the front doorbell, right above her head. Who was it? Harry the painter? He was due to bring a builder mate to do some odd jobs, like fixing the cellar door. No, he was away on holiday, it was next Saturday he was coming.

She hurried up into the hall. The bell rang again just before she reached the door. Then, as she opened it, she remembered.

The tall, rather simple-looking man in the Telecom uniform stood there, holding a toolbox in one hand and a large sealed pack in the other. On the street, parked behind her little Renault, was the Telecom van.

'It is convenient?' he said.

'Yes, yes, of course.'

'I was worried you had forgotten, perhaps.'

'Er – no – I –' She saw him looking at the bag of frozen prawns in her hand. 'I'm sorry, I was in the cellar. No, I hadn't forgotten. A new circuit board? Mother board? Something like that, you said.'

'Exactly like that.' Kündz smiled. It felt good, so good, just being close to her, smelling her again. No sperm this time, and he was glad about that; she did not smell as if she had made love to her husband since he was last here, and he wished desperately that he could reward her now, here on the doorstep before they even went inside.

Susan, my darling, you have been a good girl.

Chapter Seventeen

Dr Doomandgloom needs cheering up. One of the three boxes on the screen will cheer him up. Click either of the other two boxes and he will stamp his feet, burst into tears and pull the lever that will release the trapdoor on which you are standing. The trapdoor will drop you into a stinking sewer, where you will have to negotiate a maze of tunnels infested with giant mutant rats and man-eating crocodiles to get out.

One of the boxes tells Dr Doomandgloom that in your morning break you ate a chocolate bar; the second tells him you ate crisps; the third that you ate an apple. Clicking on the box that tells him you ate an apple really makes his day. His eyes light up, his ears wiggle, he bursts into song and performs a hand-stand followed by a back-flip.

'What do you think?' Gareth asked. Then, before John could reply, he added, 'It's coming along, right?'

'I think we have a problem,' John said, and undaunted by his partner's look of sullen hostility, continued, 'I think kids will be more enticed to the sewer than seeing Dr Doomandgloom look happy. This has been bothering me for a while.'

'We can change it, but it'll delay the launch and we're already behind schedule,' Gareth said, then added petulantly, 'None of the teachers who read the script felt that way.'

John was standing over a workstation in the development room. Twenty-five of his staff were concentrating all around him, and normally John would have stopped by each of them in turn for a brief word. But today he was trying to avoid eye contact. Neither did he want to get into an argument with Gareth.

Cliff Worrols, ponytailed with granny glasses, dressed in the unofficial DigiTrak uniform of T-shirt and jeans, looked anxiously up at him, seeking approval of his work on the Doomandgloom graphics. John nodded at him. The program, aimed at getting kids to understand about nutrition, was fraught with minefields, but he was too distracted to apply his mind to it. It was Wednesday, there were just six days left, and he had decided to break the news to Gareth today, at lunch-time.

He was also going to have to tell him about his meeting with the liquidator, and about the liquidator's salvage plan. It needed a few phoney invoices, a bit of backdating here and there, which meant screwing the creditors, just a little. John was concerned that Gareth might have a problem with this, because he was scrupulously honest to the point of naïveté.

He had decided that the way to sell him the idea was by pointing out that, if they could salvage some cash, they had a chance of starting up again and paying back those creditors – something John genuinely intended to do.

He stared again at the graphics on the computer screen, and at Gareth and Cliff's anxious faces.

Worrols's phone warbled. He answered it, and turned to John. 'Stella. Call for you.'

John took the receiver and Stella told him she had Mr Sarotzini on the line. John felt as if he was standing on a rolling floor. 'I'll take it in my office,' he said. 'See you at one, Gareth. Good work, Cliff!' He hurried out.

In the sanctuary of his own room, he picked up the receiver, with a strong image in his mind of the banker as Dr Doomandgloom.

'Mr Carter? You are well, I hope?' Mr Sarotzini sounded better-humoured than he had been on Friday, much more the warm, caring man John had sat next to at the Carmichaels' dinner at the Guildhall than the dry, cold one with whom he had had lunch. But he was a bag of nerves. 'Yes, thank you. Thank you for lunch last Friday. I enjoyed going to your club very much.' He'd dropped the banker a thank-you letter to the PO box address on his card, and wondered if he had received it.

Mr Sarotzini did not mention it. 'I'm so glad you enjoyed it. It was a pleasure to meet you again and to get to know you a little better. One can be so private there. So many places it is difficult to be private, do you not find?'

'Yes,' John said politely, despite his impatience for Mr Sarotzini to come to the point. From the tone of the man's voice, there might be hope.

'And your quest for funding, Mr Carter, how's that progressing?'

'We've had some interest,' John lied, trying to stop shaking, aware that he sounded breathless. 'But nothing firmed up yet.'

'Ah.'

There was a long silence. John waited for Mr Sarotzini, but the silence continued. 'Is – is there any further information you'd like?' he asked, trying to think of an enticement he could offer.

'No, I think at this stage not. I have talked to my associates, and before I took matters further I wanted to establish that your requirements remain unchanged.'

'Yes, they're unchanged.' John's brain was racing. *Before I took matters further.* That sounded positive. What else could he tell Mr Sarotzini? What had he forgotten last week, or had anything changed since then? 'Well, actually, we've had some good business developments, since we spoke, which might interest you.'

'Ah? Tell me.'

'I can't remember if I mentioned – with Microsoft. It looks like we could have a terrific distribution deal – the junior version of our Home Doctor series. They came back to us on Monday. It could become part of a package with their online version of Encarta.'

Mr Sarotzini did not sound as if he had connected with this. 'Good,' he said. 'Yes, that sounds very good, most encouraging.' He was silent again. 'So, your requirements are exactly as we discussed?'

'Yes, they are.'

'No developments with your lawsuit?'

'I'm afraid not.'

'Allow me to come back to you, Mr Carter, in a few days.'

It seemed an odd formality that he still did not use John's first name: it contradicted Mr Sarotzini's good-natured tone, John thought. 'The deadline I have with my bank is next Tuesday.'

'Yes, of course, I am aware,' the banker replied, chidingly. 'How could I forget a date of such gravity? But thank you all the same for reminding me. I am indebted to you for the opportunity to help you. We will speak again before Tuesday.'

The phone went dead.

John stared at the receiver in surprise, then replaced it. He sat quietly, analysing the call. It was definitely a plus that Mr Sarotzini had phoned him – he had not expected to hear from him again after the banker had expressed his concerns about Zak Danziger.

Feeling a sudden burst of optimism, he phoned Susan to tell her that there was still hope. She was in a meeting so could not talk freely, but he could hear the relief in her voice. When he hung up, he decided not to say anything to Gareth after all, until he had heard from Mr Sarotzini again.

If he heard from him again.

But he had a feeling he would. He reckoned Mr Sarotzini might at least come up with some kind of proposal rather than give him a flat turn-down.

That evening, he suggested to Susan that they went to the Thai restaurant round the corner.

The owner greeted them like long-lost friends, gave them a powerful free cocktail each, and plied them with new experimental dishes all evening, as well as massive brandies on the house afterwards.

It was close to midnight before they finally rolled out, drunk and giggly and so stuffed they were groaning. Unkindly John waddled up and down the pavement outside their house mimicking the restaurateur: 'Hawoo, plizz, you tlie now, gleen plawns in coconut!'

Susan, hysterical with laughter, hushed him, and dragged him inside. They tripped out of their clothes, scattering them over the bedroom floor, and made love for the first time in almost a fortnight.

And Kündz, who had installed a video camera above their bedroom on Saturday afternoon silently watched them, on the monitor in his attic room, aroused and angered by the sight of them making love.

It was erotic to see them give oral sex to each other simultaneously, and then to watch John Carter climb on top of Susan and enter her. But it hurt that John Carter was making love to *his* woman, and it made Kündz ache to see the expressions on Susan's face, to see her chewing her husband's ear, to hear the sounds of her breathing, her cries of pleasure.

It hurt him to see how much *she was enjoying this*.

She rolled John onto his back and sat astride him. Then the expression on the man's face became almost too much for Kündz. But he continued to watch, as Carter threw back his head and shouted out, his mouth bursting with yells of pleasure that bordered on laughter, until he reached his climax.

Finally, his heart heavy, Kündz switched off the monitor. He hoped that, one day soon, Mr Sarotzini would allow him to punish John Carter for this.

But at least tonight Kündz had something that made him happy. On the table beside him, among the remnants of his Kentucky Fried Chicken dinner and empty Coke cans, lay the white envelope with a Swiss postmark, which contained his gift.

Mr Sarotzini did things like this sometimes. Just when Kündz was feeling really depressed, Mr Sarotzini would do something for him. It was further confirmation that a part of Mr Sarotzini resided inside his head, always knowing his mood, sensing if he was down.

Fondling the envelope, Kündz began to hum, softly, to himself.

Chapter Eighteen

Don Giovanni was sinking through the stage floor and down into hell. Flames erupted all around him, and Kündz smiled.

Hell.

He remembered the words of the writer, T. S. Eliot, whose work Mr Sarotzini had encouraged him to study. *'Hell is oneself.'*

And Don Giovanni kept singing, lamenting, as he went down into hell. Alone. The huge voice of the tenor filled the auditorium. This was great music, and Kündz could not have been happier. He was sitting at Glyndebourne, in his box which could have accommodated half a dozen people but tonight was for his sole pleasure.

Susan Carter would have enjoyed being here with him. He smiled, wallowing in the music that cascaded down on him. Yes, she would have enjoyed it. The air was balmy, and rich with the scents of all the women in their finery. None of their scents was as good as the smells of Susan Carter, but tonight Kündz didn't mind. He had Mozart to make him happy, he could wait. It would be soon now. And then Susan Carter was going to make him happy for the rest of his life.

That had been a promise made by the man who always kept his word.

Beauty is truth, truth beauty, that is all ye know on earth and all ye need to know. Keats, Kündz remembered. He had been introduced to Keats by Mr Sarotzini.

He had been introduced by Mr Sarotzini to so much beauty. To this joy of great music, to the riches of fine painting, to the sensuality of great food. And to so much wisdom. He recalled a film he had once watched in Mr Sarotzini's private screening room. In it, the actors Joseph Cotton and Orson Welles met in a gondola high in the air above an amusement park, the Prata in Vienna. And that was the point at which Mr Sarotzini had stopped the film, instructed him to listen carefully, then restarted it.

And Orson Welles, who was playing the role of a man called Harry Lime, turned to Joseph Cotton, angry but restrained, and said: '"In Italy for thirty years under the Borgias they had warfare, terror, murder, bloodshed – but they produced Michelangelo, Leonardo da Vinci and the Renaissance. In Switzerland they had brotherly love, five hundred years of democracy and peace, and what did they produce? The *cuckoo clock*."'

Then Mr Sarotzini had stopped the film again, turned to Kündz and asked him if he understood. Kündz, who had never dared to lie to Mr Sarotzini, told him that no, he did not understand. Mr Sarotzini replied that one day he would.

And now Kündz looked down into the stalls, which were erupting into applause, as the curtain fell. People were rising from their seats and he rose with them, clapped with them and joined in the call, the cry for the *encore*. And he imagined that he was in that gondola, high above the Prata, he imagined he was Joseph Cotton and that Harry Lime was speaking to him.

Below, and around him, the audience chanted, 'More! More! More!'

He chanted as well, and then he wept for joy. Tears torrented down his cheeks. He wept at the sheer beauty, and because of all the emotions the music had stirred within him, and because of the magnificence of the secret he kept in his heart. He wished he could share it with all these people who had been swept away, like him, by the music. He wished he could rush down onto that stage, and hush them all, and call out: *It is near, it is so near!*

But Mr Sarotzini would never have forgiven him.

So instead he contented himself with looking down at them, watching them clapping, watching the rapture on their faces. Few noticed him, alone in his box, none was aware of the true nature of the elation he was feeling.

None knew of the white envelope in his pocket, the one in which the ticket for this box had been sent to him. None knew that to receive a white envelope from Mr Sarotzini was an honour for which there was no equal on earth.

Minutes later Kündz moved through the jostling crowds pressing themselves into the exits. Those who noticed him saw a man in a dinner jacket, a tall guy, built like a American-football quarterback, a foreigner, perhaps. They did not hear the special way the music of Mozart still played on inside his head. They did not know he had a white envelope in his pocket. They could not hear his thoughts, they could not know the things that Kündz knew, that secret he carried.

They should have been grateful for their innocence.

That was what Kündz thought as he stood outside, waiting for Mr Sarotzini's black Mercedes limousine to collect him.

Chapter Nineteen

The wind flailed John's hair, and the spray flecked his sunglasses. The prow of Archie's powerboat skimmed across the glassy blue water of the Solent, heading towards the battlements of the Royal Yacht Squadron and the entrance to Cowes harbour. There was a flat, steady drone from the twin inboard engines, and an occasional smacking thump as they crossed another boat's wake.

Archie was now Mr Toad of the waterways. In his tiny oval sunglasses and rope-patterned short-sleeved shirt, he sat at the helm, high up in the open cockpit, surrounded by the monitors and dials of enough high-tech navigational aids to have enabled a fleet of spacecraft to circumnavigate the universe.

Behind them, on the sumptuous, white-cushioned sun-deck, Susan and a striking brunette Spanish model named Pila, Archie's current girlfriend, lay spread out, sunbathing topless.

Archie dug his fingers into his gin and tonic, pulled out a small piece of ice and lobbed it at Pila. It was a bullseye, landing right in her belly-button. She sat up with a start. 'You bassard!' She lobbed it hard back, with wild aim, and John had to duck as it went past him and struck the windscreen. He could not tell whether Susan, eyes masked behind her sunglasses, was awake or asleep. He smiled as Pila waved him an apology, then turned and continued looking out across the water at the vast canvas of the hot June afternoon.

There were boats as far as the eye could see, mostly sail-boats, some on their own, some grouped in races, all motionless, their sails hanging listlessly, waiting for even the smallest puff of breeze to fill them.

He watched a fort slip past, breathed in the salt, seaweed, ozone tang of the sea and could not get the thought out of his mind: it was Monday tomorrow. And there had been no further phone call from Mr Sarotzini.

'So,' Archie said, suddenly, 'you reckon your Swiss connection, this Sarotzini man, is blowing you out?'

'I'm sure I would have heard back by the end of the week,' John said.

'I did a search on his bank for you,' Archie said.

'You did?' John was surprised.

'Uh huh. The Vörn, right? V-ö-r-n?' Archie spelled it.

'Yes. Thanks, what did you find?'

'Goose eggs.'

'Goose eggs?'

'Zilch. But that doesn't necessarily mean much. Vörn could be its trading name – it might be registered as something different.'

The boat thumped hard through the heavy wake from a ferry and spray fogged John's sunglasses. He removed them and wiped them, with only moderate success, on his salty T-shirt.

'Half my clients are banks that only exist on paper,' Archie continued. 'You try to trace them back, you end up with nominee directors in Liechtenstein who are working for nominee directors in Panama, who are working for the subsidiary of a shell that's registered in the Cayman Islands. Classic Mafia money-laundering technique.'

John frowned. 'Think this could be Mafia?'

'Do you?' Archie threw the question back at him, and shook out a cigarette. He lost his concentration as he reached into a cubby-hole for his lighter and the boat veered off-course, then rolled sharply as he over-corrected. Some of John's gin and tonic slopped out of the glass.

'I hadn't thought about it.'

'This Sarotzini character. Sounds sort of Italian. Is he Italian?'

'No, I assumed he was Swiss, I suppose, I don't know. His accent is more German than Italian.'

'I can't find anything on him, either. Nobody's heard of him.'

'Is that unusual?'

'There are players who keep a low profile. Might not be his real name – you didn't ask him?'

'Oh, sure,' John said, with a grin, taking a long pull on his drink. 'First thing I said to him, Arch – "Can I borrow a million quid and, by the way, is that your real name?"'

Archie grunted, his concentration distracted by a flashing orange blip on one of his navigation screens. 'Don't know what the fuck that means,' he said, twiddling a couple of knobs. He called up a help menu and began to study it. 'Keep an eye out ahead.'

'I am.' John scanned the water: at the speed they were going, sail-boats came up fast.

Still studying the menu, and fiddling with more dials and buttons now,

Archie said, 'It's a long shot, but I've got an Arab client who's looking for technology companies to buy. I've given you a hard sell.'

'Thanks. Did he bite?'

Archie hesitated. 'No, I wouldn't say that, but he didn't turn you down flat. He's in the frame. How're you getting on with Big Jim?'

That was the liquidator Archie had recommended. John had signed and carefully filed away a wodge of phoney, backdated documents Big Jim had helped him prepare, and he was nervous: it was the first time he had ever done something fraudulent, although the liquidator had assured him that this went on all time, that it was almost standard practice for any company going down the tubes.

Archie's Arab didn't sound much of a prospect and John suspected that his friend had only mentioned it to try to keep up his morale. He was dreading tomorrow and all that the coming week was going to bring. *Dreading* it. He was going to have to tell Gareth and the rest of his staff, although he was going to have one final last-ditch attempt at reaching a deal with Zak Danziger. He had asked his lawyer to set up a meeting for tomorrow, to try to persuade Danziger that if DigiTrak did go to the wall there would be nothing at all for him.

He wasn't looking forward to that meeting either. Next to the subhuman Clake, Danziger was probably the most unpleasant person John had ever met.

'Got it!' Archie said suddenly. 'The orange blip. It's an aeroplane going overhead!'

'Well, that's useful to know,' John said.

Archie gave him a sideways glance, unsure whether he was being serious or taking the mickey.

John was normally at his desk before eight o'clock, but on this Monday he'd dragged his feet while getting ready. Susan, her voice heavy with emotion, had wished him lots of luck and, unusually for her, had set off for work before him.

Because he had left late, he got caught up in heavier traffic, and it was nine fifteen before he reached the office. Stella greeted him with the news that Mr Clake had phoned and needed to speak to him urgently.

'Fuck him,' John snapped, startling her. He slammed the door behind him, hung up his jacket, then sat at his desk and switched on his computer. A stack of post awaited him and another of e-mail, none of which he had any enthusiasm to tackle. His back and the tops of his shoulders were raw – sunburned yesterday on Archie's boat.

Why had Clake rung? To remind him of what he already knew, that he had just two days left to his deadline? To gloat? Calming down a little, he buzzed Stella and asked her to get the bank manager for him.

Moments later, Clake was on the line. He did not sound like the same Mr Clake John had met almost a month ago.

'Mr Carter,' he said. 'This is a *very* encouraging development!'

John wondered if the man had misheard his secretary and thought he was talking to someone else. The only encouraging development he could think of was either that Clake was terminally ill or that he was leaving the bank. What the hell was he talking about? 'Which development exactly do you mean?' he asked, cautiously.

'The one and a half million pounds from the Vörn Bank.' It was Clake's turn to sound a little strange.

John heard the words but took several moments to comprehend them. 'The *Vörn* Bank?' he echoed, finally, his pulse starting to race.

Some of the good humour evaporated from Clake's voice. 'You do know about this, I presume, Mr Carter?'

'Yes – I – I –' John started to bluff. 'I've been in negotiation with them, but –' He wasn't sure how to go on, and was almost too excited to think clearly. 'I wasn't expecting the funds quite yet.'

'I have explicit instructions from a Mr Sarotzini. The sum of one point five million pounds has been transferred from the Vörn Bank in Geneva in Switzerland and lodged in a temporary account they have opened with us, pending transfer to DigiTrak when documentation has been completed. The Vörn Bank has indicated to us that they anticipate the transfer should occur by the end of this week. In view of the circumstances, Mr Carter, should it be necessary, I am prepared to allow you a few days' grace on my bank's original deadline.'

John could not believe that this was happening. He wanted to throw his arms around Mr Sarotzini and hug him. Tears were welling in his eyes, and his voice was choked. He swallowed, trying to compose himself, not wanting Clake to know that this was a complete surprise.

'Thank you,' he said, pausing again to control his voice. 'I appreciate the extension.'

'No bank likes to see a valued customer go out of business,' Mr Clake said. 'I can assure you, Mr Carter, that no one is more delighted by this news than myself.'

'I'm sure,' John replied, swallowing the man's hypocrisy. Right now he was filled with almost as much gratitude towards him as he was towards Mr Sarotzini.

Just after he put down the receiver on Mr Clake, the phone buzzed. It was Stella. She had Mr Sarotzini on the line.

'I've just had a call from my bank,' John said to him. 'Thank you – I'm just incredibly grateful.'

Mr Sarotzini replied, in a tone that was coldly formal, 'We have deposited these funds, Mr Carter, to demonstrate our good faith. You have yet to agree our terms.'

John barely heard him. He was thinking about Susan's face when he told her the news, about how he was no longer going to have to say anything to Gareth or his staff, about the house that they were going to be able to keep, after all. He didn't care about terms, he was going to have to accept them. 'Of course,' he replied.

'Are you and your wife free to join me at my club for dinner tonight, perhaps?'

'My wife?' John said, a little surprised.

'Yes, I should like to meet her.'

It struck John as an odd request, but he and Susan had no plans, he was certain, and even if they did they'd have to cancel them. 'Sure, yes – I – I'm sure she would be delighted.'

'Good,' Mr Sarotzini said. His voice was still cold, but John hardly noticed. 'My driver will collect you both from your home at seven thirty this evening.'

John was so elated, and his brain was in such a whirl, that all he wanted to do right now was call Susan and tell her the news. It did not occur to him that he had never given Mr Sarotzini his home address. 'Seven thirty,' he said. 'Perfect.'

Chapter Twenty

It was quiet in Mr Sarotzini's club, and John wondered whether the establishment was more of a lunchtime venue than an evening one. Although, of course, it was a Monday night. Only a few tables were occupied, and many were not even laid. One elderly steward was occupying himself by aligning the cutlery on a nearby table.

'The Napa Valley,' Mr Sarotzini said. 'Yes. The French have much reason to be grateful to the Americans. When phylloxera destroyed so many of the great vines of Bordeaux in the 1880s, they were replanted with rootstock from the East Coast. You have been to any of the wine regions, Mrs Carter? You know the Napa Valley?'

They were in an alcove, which could not have been more private. John stared at Mr Sarotzini across a small cut-glass vase of yellow carnations. The banker was eating quails' eggs. Susan, who had a plate of Parma ham and melon, told him that she had been there.

She looked stunning tonight, and John felt more proud of her than ever before. She was wearing a new suit, which she had rushed out and bought after he had phoned her the good news; the jacket was stone-coloured with black abstract markings, and the matching skirt was plain and elegant. Under the jacket she had on a simple white open-necked blouse, and a silver pendant on a velvet band round her throat. She always dressed well, but he had never seen her look classier.

Mr Sarotzini reeled off a list of towns, villages, vineyards, and Susan responded enthusiastically. She talked about soil, escarpments, canyons and valleys, about specific density, alkaline soil, late harvesting, and John remembered now that a couple of years ago she had edited a book on Californian wines, a technical, scientific guide to the industry.

Mr Sarotzini raised his wine glass and said, '"Forsake not an old friend, for the new is not comparable to him. A new friend is as new wine; when it is old, thou shalt drink it with pleasure."' He stared pointedly at her.

'Ecclesiasticus,' she responded.

105

Mr Sarotzini smiled. 'Remarkable.' He turned to John. 'You have a remarkable wife, Mr Carter. You are aware of this?'

Susan laughed freely. 'He needs reminding sometimes!'

John grinned. He peeled a quail's egg, dipped it into some salt and ate it. He'd never tried one before, and had decided that if Mr Sarotzini ate these for lunch every day, they must be special. But it was disappointing. It tasted, in his view, as bland as any ordinary hard-boiled egg.

Susan was enjoying herself: she had taken an instant liking to Mr Sarotzini. She loved his elegant appearance, his old-world courtly charm, his cultured voice, the humorous twinkle in his eyes, although she was finding it hard to put an age on him. At one moment his features looked delicate to the point of frailty, particularly in the way he ate, taking tiny mouthfuls of his shrimps and bread and butter, chewing slowly like an elderly man nervous of choking. But at the next there was an assured, confident flow in the way he moved, in the way his manicured hands gestured animatedly as he conversed, and in the power that his erect, lean body radiated. It was then that she could see a deep strength within him, the grace and power of a lion.

This was a man she would have loved to have had as an uncle, or a grandfather. He had so much knowledge, exuded such passion for life: she felt she could talk to him for ever.

The conversation moved from wine to opera. John disliked opera. He knew Susan loved it but, even so, her savvy surprised him as she talked, well able to keep up with Mr Sarotzini whose encyclopaedic knowledge of wine was nothing compared to his authority on opera. John found himself a bystander, left out of the conversation, but he didn't mind. This was brilliant, he thought. Susan and Mr Sarotzini were hitting it off famously, she was impressing the man, she was winning this battle for the money single-handed.

John peeled the last of his eggs while they compared Rimsky-Korsakov operas, each enthusing about their own favourite, and then, over lamb cutlets, they moved on to ballet. John knew even less about ballet and loathed it even more than opera.

He could see in Susan's eyes that she was captivated. She had gone beyond a mere show of good manners, of common courtesy to her husband's potential business associate. She had really connected with the man. Mr Sarotzini was making plans (with John's permission, of course, he said, with a smile): he would like to take Susan for lunch one day soon, and afterwards show her his favourite gallery, a room where there were paintings from the Renaissance of which few knew. And, perhaps, one evening a concert? And Glyndebourne before the end of the season. John must come to Glyndebourne as well, they would see something accessible, Mozart, perhaps, *Don Giovanni* – would John care to see *Don Giovanni*?

John was aware, suddenly, that both Susan and Mr Sarotzini were looking at him, awaiting the answer to a question he had not heard. 'I'm sorry,' he said, 'I was miles away.'

'Mr Sarotzini is inviting us to Glyndebourne,' Susan said, '*Don Giovanni*? I think you'd enjoy it, it's not heavy.'

John thought that he'd rather spend an evening in hospital, having his gall bladder removed without an anaesthetic, than have to sit through an opera, but he didn't say this. Instead he replied politely, 'I'd be delighted.'

After dinner they went through into the club's large drawing room, which they had to themselves, and settled into wing-back leather chairs. Coffee arrived, and Mr Sarotzini insisted John had a brandy. He ordered one for himself as well. John hesitated as a box of Montecristo cigars was offered, then selected one, acknowledging Susan's glance which had said, 'Go ahead, you're allowed this!' The banker selected one too.

The conversation had moved to the English romantic poets. Mr Sarotzini favoured Shelley, and quoted 'Ozymandias, King of Kings', in its entirety and, from John's memory, word perfect.

With literature, John was on better terrain: he could get a toehold into the conversation here. But he was beginning to feel agitated. Not one word of business had been spoken the entire evening, and he wanted to steer the conversation around to this now, while Mr Sarotzini was in such good humour. All his instincts were telling him that this would be a smart time to negotiate.

As if he sensed this, Mr Sarotzini shifted his position in his chair. For some moments, he worked on his cigar, puffing out several thick clouds of smoke; then, careful not to disturb the half inch of ash, he rested it in the ashtray. He picked up his brandy balloon, and cradled it in both hands, his fingers outstretched around the contours of the glass as he seemingly studied the contents. 'I'm glad,' he said, 'that we are able to feel so comfortable together.'

He gave each of them in turn a piercing stare that made John feel uneasy. 'It is so pleasant to have so many interests in common.' The banker smiled, an easy, warm smile. 'There is something else we have in common also.'

John watched Mr Sarotzini expectantly, sucking on his cigar, trying to draw it back into life. It was the first he had smoked in several years and he was enjoying the taste but it was making his mouth hot and parched.

'You see, Mr and Mrs Carter, you are childless. My wife and I are also childless, but there is a difference. You are childless by choice, my wife and I by unfortunate circumstance.' He paused to sip a little brandy, and there was sadness in his voice when he spoke again. 'My wife is unable to conceive or bear a child, the result of a cancer operation some years ago.'

John glanced at Susan and saw her looking at the banker with apparent sympathy. Susan was again trying to work out his age. He must be in his late fifties, she thought, at the very least, and could be quite a bit older than that. Perhaps his wife was much younger.

Circling the rim of his glass with his index finger, as if he were stroking a cat, Mr Sarotzini said, 'This is my proposition. I am prepared to give you, Mr Carter, the one million pounds you require to pay off your bank, together with the five hundred thousand necessary to pay off the mortgage on your house, by way of the Vörn Bank acquiring a fifty-one per cent equity stake in your business.'

Mr Sarotzini paused to pick up his cigar and John's brain raced. On the surface, this seemed fair, far more so than he had been expecting. A bank taking an equity stake in a business would customarily want around thirty to thirty-five per cent but, under the circumstances, and considering that no bank would normally allow any such investment money to be used for private purposes, the deal seemed, the more he thought about it, incredibly generous.

Then Mr Sarotzini continued. 'In exchange for this, I would like you to be the surrogate parents for the child my wife and I cannot have.' He drew hard on his cigar and blew a long plume of smoke up at the stuccoed ceiling.

John looked at him, unsure that he had heard correctly. He caught Susan's eye and saw the same uncertainty. 'Surrogate parents? How exactly do you mean?'

Mr Sarotzini stared John straight in the eye. 'Mrs Carter would be artificially inseminated – in a clinic, of course – with semen provided by myself. She would act, until the birth of the baby, as its natural mother. Then you would hand over this child to my wife and me.'

John turned to Susan. She had gone white and looked rigid with disbelief. *What the hell's going on here?* Susan was signalling. And John signalled back that he had no answer. Something deep inside him had gone cold, as if he had been given a lifeline, which had been cruelly snatched away before he could reach it. He could not believe what the man had said.

Susan asked unsteadily, 'Why? I mean, why me – us?' She was in turmoil, trying to read the expressions on her husband's and Mr Sarotzini's faces.

As if anticipating this, Mr Sarotzini said, calmly, 'Mrs Carter, let me assure you that your husband was wholly unaware of this proposition. Please believe that there has been no conspiracy between us over this.'

Trying to think clearly through her shock, Susan wanted to say something that would keep the deal alive for John. There must be hundreds of women who would be prepared to have a surrogate child for money. If that was what the banker wanted, she could find someone, there were organisations in America she had read about. 'This isn't something I'd want to do, but I'd be very happy to help you find someone,' she said, sounding calmer than she felt.

Mr Sarotzini smiled. 'Mrs Carter, to choose a parent for one's child when one's criteria are high is not an easy matter. Good looks are required, a sound medical history, high intelligence. You have all these qualities.'

She rounded on him, unable to hold back the flash of anger at his casual arrogance. 'Oh, yes? How do you know I have these qualities? How do you know I don't have a wonky circuit in my brain, or some inherited disease?'

The banker allowed her the outburst with no hint of rancour. 'Because – forgive me the intrusion – I have done the necessary checking on you.' He gave a placatory smile and raised his hands. Then his voice became profound and sincere. 'Mrs Carter, I appreciate that what I am asking of you carries an enormity of implications and emotions. I am not expecting an answer from you tonight, and I would not like one tonight. This is something you must think over very carefully, and that you must discuss privately between yourselves, that you must be absolutely certain about before giving an answer.'

Susan turned to John again and said, accusingly, 'What have you told him about me? What have you said?'

'Nothing, darling.' He shook his head and said weakly, 'Nothing. I didn't know anything about this.'

There was a long silence. Unable to face Mr Sarotzini's stare, Susan looked anywhere but at him. She studied the paintings, the faded curtains, the furniture, the badly worn carpet. Frightened, and feeling desperately insecure, she slipped her hand down the side of her chair, searching for John's, wanting to feel it, to hold it, but it wasn't there.

In the back of the Mercedes as they travelled home, she held John's hand, and then suddenly she pulled away from him, leaned against the window, feeling the cold glass on her cheek, and the sensation of the darkness and the lights gliding silently by, beyond.

There was just the driver and themselves. Mr Sarotzini had remained at his club, and maybe he was staying there, she wasn't sure, she didn't register his plans, she was just relieved to have got away from him. She had a strong urge to tell John to stop this car, she wanted to get out, determined not to be in Mr Sarotzini's pocket one second longer. But she checked herself. Her heart was pounding. She was angry with John, he had set this up, he *must* have known about it. John and Mr Sarotzini had been planning this.

Why the hell hadn't he told her? Had he really thought she was just going to sit there and say, 'Yes, of course, darling, anything to help the business?'

Suddenly she hated him.

Since they left the club John had barely spoken. He put an arm round her now and tried to pull her towards him, but she did not budge. 'Hon, I'm sorry, I had no idea. No clue. You have to believe me.'

His voice sounded so small, so miserable, so helpless. Maybe he was telling the truth, after all. She took his hand again and held it, squeezed it, squeezed her rock, and her rock squeezed back.

She thought about how they had set out so happily this evening, and about the hopelessness of the mess they were in. The takeover of Magellan Lowry and the job she might no longer have in a month's time. DigiTrak. The house. Casey.

One and a half million pounds.

Nine months was not that long. And, who knows, she might not get pregnant anyway. If she tried, perhaps Mr Sarotzini would let them keep the money. And it wasn't that big a deal to have a baby. What the hell? She could have the baby, it would be taken and they'd have their life back.

And then she started to think how having this baby would affect their love for each other. Her carrying another man's child. Could it ever be the same between them again? She turned to John and looked at his face. She loved this man so much. He was her world. Was anything worth risking this love for?

110

And John, sitting in his silence, was turning the same thoughts over in his mind. He was trying to gauge how he'd feel seeing Susan with another man's sperm inside her, another man's child growing inside her, and the notion upset him. He was angry with Mr Sarotzini, angry about the way in which he had been manipulated and had been made to look a fool in front of his wife.

'It's out of the question,' he said.

Chapter Twenty-one

'Einstein said, "I want to know how God created this world. I am not interested in this or that phenomenon. I want to know His thoughts, the rest are details."'

That was fine, Susan did not have a problem with it. She read on 'Einstein said, "People like us, who believe in physics, know that the distinction between past, present and future is only a stubbornly persistent illusion."'

She rubbed her tired eyes. Her whole body felt weary today after a restless night of lying awake, tossing and turning, churning Mr Sarotzini's proposal over and over in her head.

One moment she decided that as John had never wanted a family, this might be her only chance to experience childbirth; at the next the thought of being impregnated by someone else, however clinically, filled her with horror. And the knowledge that she would have to live with that not just for the nine months of the pregnancy but for the rest of her life made her decide each time that no, she could not possibly do it.

In the corridor outside her tiny office an animated conversation was taking place about a copy-edit deadline on a book that was being rushed into print. Susan sat surrounded by piles of manuscripts. She chugged down some coffee, then noticed the flashing icon on her computer, and checked her e-mail; it wasn't important, just a memo about a two-week shift in a publication date.

It was pelting outside. Hard summer rain lashed the rooftop that was her view; high above it, a crane was swinging a steel girder across the slate-grey sky. She liked this attic office. Magellan Lowry had moved into this building over seventy years ago, and most of the offices, like her own, appeared not to have been redecorated since. But it didn't matter, it added to the character of the place, to the pleasure of coming here. Cracks in the walls, gaps where chunks of plaster had come away and ugly damp stains were all pasted over with jacket designs, cartoons and photocopies of brilliant reviews. And how many other people in London, she wondered, had a working gas fire in their office?

She turned her attention back to Fergus Donleavy's manuscript, but almost immediately her phone rang. It was her secretary, Hermione, a seriously bright Sloane whom she shared with Kate Fox, telling her that Mark Rivas was on the phone. It was the second time he'd rung this morning, and he had said it was urgent.

She took the call. 'Hi, Mark,' she said. 'Sorry I didn't get back to you, got stuck in an editorial meeting that went on longer than I expected.'

Mark Rivas was an agent she particularly liked. He had the knack of finding good new science writers with original ideas, and he had a finger on the pulse of what was wanted.

'How's things?' he asked. 'What the latest on ...?'

He didn't need to finish the sentence. Everyone had their own personal shorthand for the takeover of Magellan Lowry, and this was his.

'Not much change in the last week. Rumours about job losses still flying. Denials in the trade press.'

'I saw.'

'So?' she said.

'Susan, I have a hot new writer, name of Julian DeWytts, *Dr* Julian DeWytts. He's stunningly good-looking, very charismatic, and is hosting his own seven-part series on genetics for BBC 2 this autumn, called *The Gene Lottery*. He's written an accessible book on inherited diseases, and I thought of you immediately.'

'Me and how many others?' she asked, good-humouredly.

'Four,' he said, which, Susan knew, probably meant eight.

'Is there a floor?'

'It's going out to everyone simultaneously.'

'And what kind of money are you looking for?'

'A lot,' he said.

Susan was a little dubious. 'There's already been a ton of stuff on genes and inherited diseases,' she said. 'Steve Jones has covered the territory pretty thoroughly, in his books and on television. And Dawkins.'

'Julian's in a different league. Take a look at the manuscript – you won't be disappointed.'

She told him she would, and promised that if she was interested she would get back to him with an offer within ten days, mentally shifting further back into the future the other five manuscripts she had to read.

Then she started to concentrate again on the first six chapters of Fergus Donleavy's rewrite. He was anxious to hear if she felt he was now on the right track. She struck her pencil through the second Einstein quotation, putting a note in the margin, which said:

'Not necessary, you already made this point on page 28.' Then she added, because her tiredness was making her feel punchy today, 'I'm not even sure this entire chapter's necessary. What does it contribute?'

Kate came in, holding a book. She was a couple of years older than Susan, married to an economics researcher, and had two children. Tall and well-built, Kate had a booming, jolly personality, and a handsome face beneath a bob of straight brown hair. Susan liked her because she was one of that rare breed of people who are totally unfazed by anything life throws at them.

Kate was the first person in whom she had confided when she and John had decided to buy the house – and they had snuck down to see it in an extended lunch hour. Kate thought the place was wild, and loved it.

'This the one you meant?' Kate asked.

Susan looked at the cover. It was a photograph of a pregnant woman's abdomen, except, as if by X-ray, the foetus was visible inside, snugly curled up. The book was titled *Pregnancy – The Myths and the Reality*, by Dr Maria Anscombe.

Susan turned it over, glanced at the back of the jacket, then looked up at Kate. 'It's the one you edited, right?'

'It's brilliant. She's a terrific communicator. I found it really helpful myself – it's the best guide to pregnancy.' Kate gave Susan a quizzical look, then smiled. 'Hey! Is there something you're not telling me here?'

Susan shook her head, but could not prevent herself blushing. 'It's for a friend.'

She waited until Kate had left her office, then pushed Fergus Donleavy's manuscript to one side, opened the book and started to read.

'So?' Archie said, as he padded, naked, across the cork matting into the men's shower room, sweat was running off him. John was looking at Archie's flesh. Great flaps hung from his belly; he was beginning to develop a figure that would make a Sumo wrestler proud, and yet he had just thrashed John on the squash court. Trounced him.

Archie turned on the shower, adjusted the temperature, tilted his face up into the spray. 'Tell me your friend Sarotzini's terms.'

John's lungs were aching – he had really tried in this game today. But his mind hadn't been on it. 'They're crazy,' he said. 'I mean, the guy's not in the real world.'

Archie soaped his hair. 'You seem pretty pissed off with him.'

'I *am* pissed off with him. He made me look a fool.'

'So what does he want to do? Sleep with Susan?'

John had been on the verge of telling Archie, but he held back. What if –
and he knew it was a crazy notion – but *what* if they decided to accept
Sarotzini's terms? Susan wouldn't want any of their friends knowing, and
neither would he. And, in any case, someone else had come into the
shower room.

'No, not that kind of a scene. It's – it's guarantees,' John said.
'Percentages. *Control.*'

Archie turned off the shower and began to towel his hair. 'Better to have
ten per cent of something than a hundred per cent of nothing, isn't it?'

John did not reply. As he sat on the locker-room bench, tying his shoe
laces, Archie sat down beside him and patted his thigh gently. 'Listen, it
might not seem that great a deal, after you've had this long run owning
the business yourself and doing what you please. But this is the real world,
John, and few people get to hang on to their businesses. Sarotzini is
offering you a deal. Would it enable the business to survive?'

John nodded.

'Would it enable you to keep your house?'

John hesitated. 'Yes.'

'Would you be able to draw out the same income you're currently
getting?'

'I don't know, I presume so.'

'Do you get to keep shares?'

'Yes.'

'Then what the fuck are you worried about? Go for it! Bite the man's
hand off!'

They dressed, went up to the bar, and ordered their usual beers. John
drank his straight down and requested another. Archie, puffing on a
cigarette, reminded him that Mr Sarotzini was the only game in town.

John knew this. He'd lain awake thinking about it all last night, and
he'd been thinking about it all day today. Susan had told him this
morning that she could do it. Sure, she *could* do it. He wouldn't be
affected, physically, but –

And that was where his thoughts hit the buffers each time.

After her initial anger had subsided, Susan seemed to have taken the
proposition better than he had, and he admired her for that. But he didn't
know how she felt now about motherhood. They hadn't talked about it
for a long time, and on the rare occasions he'd thought the subject might

rear its head, he had quickly steered the conversation away. Did she still feel the same way as he did?

He suspected not. When they had got engaged, he'd tried to encourage her to be sterilised, but she'd resisted. He had made no big deal about that, and she took the pill instead. But he had seen the way she had been looking at babies recently. The way she had held Liz and Alex's new baby at their barbecue last week. The way she doted on Kate Fox's two small children. Maybe Sarotzini's proposition had touched a nerve inside her. That this would give her the chance to experience pregnancy and, perhaps, to be a fulfilled woman.

Did *he* still feel the same way?

Uncomfortable, suddenly, he tore that thought straight out of his mind, balled it up, threw it in the bin. Are you going *crazy*, John Carter?

But the money was sitting there. One and a half million pounds under Mr Clake's lock and key.

All they had to do was say yes.

But Archie didn't know the truth.

Chapter Twenty-two

John stayed downstairs long after Susan had taken her manuscript up to bed. He went out into the garden and sat there for a while, Archie's advice resounding in his head. The skies had cleared and the air was fresh and cool. Then he went into the kitchen and poured himself a whisky on the rocks. Gloomily he looked at a pile of interior-decorating magazines, that, only a month ago, they had been leafing through, tearing out pages of anything that interested them.

At last he went upstairs, dragging his weary legs up each step. Susan was sitting up in bed in a baggy white T-shirt, reading the manuscript. He could tell that she was finding it hard to concentrate.

As he came in she smiled, her face pale with tiredness and stress. Some loose strands of hair, which she hadn't bothered to flick away, hung down over her forehead. She looked so vulnerable, and he felt an almost overwhelming tenderness towards her. She was so lovely. He adored her. There hadn't been a day, an hour, a moment since they'd met when he had faltered in his love for her. Susan was everything to him.

He still had the card in his briefcase that she'd given him soon after they were married. There was a soppy-looking bear on the front, and inside was printed: I LOVE YOU MORE THAN I DID YESTERDAY, BUT NOT AS MUCH AS I WILL TOMORROW.

And he felt the same way. After seven years, he still found himself loving her more every day.

Mr Sarotzini's presence hung in the air so strongly, it could have been written on the walls in Dayglo lettering. All evening, between long silences in which Susan had read and John had channel-surfed the television, they had talked about Mr Sarotzini's offer. Shortly before going up to bed, Susan told him that she would do it. John had not replied.

Now he sat on the end of the bed. He was still holding the tumbler and shook the ice cubes around before he drained the last of the whisky. 'There's no way,' he said. 'I'm telling him no. I could get the backing to start again, and you can get some freelance work if you lose your job. And if we lose the house, we lose it. What the hell? We were happy before in our little house. Right?'

'And Casey?' she said.

The way she said the name startled him. It was a rebuke. It was a reminder that, to Susan, Casey mattered more than anything else – including him.

He remembered all the times he had sat with Susan at Casey's bedside in the clinic. That stunning apparition, lying there, ventilator tube cannulated into her windpipe, drip line in her wrist. Her eyes were mostly closed, and even when they were open she couldn't see the fine view of the canyon right outside her window, and she was never going to see it. He knew in his heart, but dared not say it, that it would make no difference to Casey whether she was in a state home or a luxury clinic. Casey had no idea where she was; she was *never* going to know where she was.

In the morning, Susan sat at the breakfast table, *The Times* unopened in front of her, toying with a grapefruit. She looked up at John, who was spooning yoghurt onto his cinnamon crunch cereal.

'You'll tell him,' she said. 'Hon?'

He pushed a slice of wholemeal bread into the toaster.

'Please?' she said. 'If it's not for us, it's for Casey, OK?'

But it was not OK. John had made up his mind too. He was not going to put either of them through this humiliation. Mr Sarotzini must have a heart, he was thinking. Perhaps he could buy time by dangling the bait that he and Susan might agree at some point in the future if he would help DigiTrak now.

He rummaged around inside *The Times* and pulled out the Interface section, which he propped against a tub of Flora. They just needed time. If the Microsoft deal came good they would be out of the woods – a couple of months, tops, that was all they needed.

Avoiding Susan's eye, he scanned the pages of computer and Internet technology, forcing each mouthful down to give himself some energy, aware that he was feeling a little weak from having eaten barely anything lately.

He needed to be alert today. In his judgement, he would get just one shot at bringing Mr Sarotzini round. It was not going to be easy.

He gulped down his apple juice, his vitamin pills, his tea, then kissed Susan goodbye.

'You're going to say yes?' she pleaded.

'I'll sort something out,' he said grimly, and left.

At five past ten Mr Sarotzini telephoned John and asked if they had come to a decision.

In spite of his preparation, John found himself breaking out in a nervous sweat, and shaking. 'I'd like to meet,' he said. 'I have a proposal to put to you.'

His reply was greeted by a long silence. When Mr Sarotzini spoke again, his tone was icy. 'My car will collect you from your office at a quarter to one, Mr Carter. We will lunch at my club, which I trust will be convenient.'

John wondered if he ever ate anywhere different. He had planned to suggest that they met somewhere else, in a restaurant of *his* choosing, but before he could respond, the banker had disconnected.

The Mercedes collected John, and he rode alone, but for the silent chauffeur. Although at the club he was now on increasingly familiar territory, the place made him feel uncomfortable, to the point of intimidation, and some of his remaining confidence left him.

He was greeted politely by the staff and wheeled straight through to the dining room, as if his arrival had been rehearsed.

More people were eating there than he previously remembered, and there were strong aromas of food in the room, of roast meat and, more pungently, of garlic. Above the general murmur of conversation he heard the sharp pop of a cork.

Mr Sarotzini was already at his table, sipping a glass of mineral water and checking through a wodge of documents. He rose to his full height to greet John, and John noticed for the first time an almost reptilian feel in his handshake: it was cold, moist and bony.

In surprising contrast, Mr Sarotzini's voice was warm and sincere, as was his expression 'Mr Carter, a pleasure to see you again. It was enchanting to meet your wife, such a remarkable young lady, truly remarkable.'

'Thank you,' John said. 'I think so too.' A steward held his chair for him to sit down, unfolded a starched napkin and placed it on his lap.

'Would Sir care for a drink?' he asked.

'Mineral water, please,' John said. 'Perrier or Badoît.'

'You are a very lucky man, Mr Carter,' Mr Sarotzini said, sitting down. 'A most fortunate man.'

Now, seated across the table from him, John remembered the banker's awesome presence. He wondered about Mr Sarotzini's wife and tried to form a mental image of her, but could not. Was she a tall, steel-haired aristocrat? A small, dumpy little *hausfrau*? A beautiful young gold-digger?

He made himself concentrate on his reason for being here. Mr Sarotzini looked relaxed: life would go on for him whether DigiTrak survived or not; he would find someone else to provide a surrogate baby, no problem. He did not look the type of person to be unduly concerned by anything. He would go to Ascot, to polo, to the opera, to private art galleries, to great dinner parties and banquets regardless of whether John and Susan were a part of his life or not.

A menu was presented, but John gave it hardly a glance. He wasn't hungry, and eating wasn't the point of this meeting. He ordered the same as he'd had before, smoked salmon and then sole, no wine, he said in response to Mr Sarotzini's offer, although he could have happily drunk a bottle straight down. He needed to keep a clear head.

When the waiter had moved away, Mr Sarotzini leant across the table towards him, and asked, quietly, 'You would not mind if I were to take your wife to the opera, Mr Carter? I have the impression that you yourself are not particular about opera.'

'No,' John said, momentarily thrown by the question. He had been expecting Mr Sarotzini to get straight down to business. He took this as an encouraging sign. 'No, I'm not,' he said. 'Please do, she'd love it. I'm afraid it's rather wasted on me.'

'The next time I come to England, I shall arrange for tickets.' Mr Sarotzini seemed almost childishly pleased. Maybe he was lonely, John wondered. As rich as Croesus but lonely. He clung to this dreary club because he was known here. He bought friendships, and he thought, even, that he could buy a family.

Let's keep the illusion going.

Then, very calmly, Mr Sarotzini said, 'I have prepared the documents.'

John watched as he spread them out into neat piles, wondering if the banker had misunderstood him earlier.

'There is a clinic here in London, Mr Carter, close to Harley Street. It is owned by the Vörn Bank and offers the finest medical care in this country. There is nowhere more discreet, more private. This is where the insemination will take place.'

The smoked salmon and quails' eggs arrived. John said nothing as Mr Sarotzini continued, 'You are no doubt aware that it is not against the law in England to have a surrogate child, but it is illegal for money to change hands in such an arrangement, other than for expenses.'

John, squeezing lemon onto his salmon, nodded. He'd had a brief word earlier with his lawyer about surrogate law, wanting to understand at least the basics.

'This documentation acknowledges myself to be the legal father, which will circumnavigate the law.' Mr Sarotzini raised his eyebrows and received acknowledgement. 'Now, who knows what emotions can take place during a pregnancy?'

John said nothing, watching Mr Sarotzini's face, listening carefully, waiting for his chance.

'You will understand that I need to protect my investment, Mr Carter. So, your house, and all but the ten per cent of the shares in DigiTrak owned by your partner, Mr Gareth Noyce, will be transferred into my ownership until the infant is in my possession. At this point the house will be transferred back to your ownership, together with thirty-nine per cent of the shares in DigiTrak. I trust this will be acceptable.'

John cut a piece of salmon, playing for time while he thought out his reply. He put down his knife and fork and played with his napkin. 'Look, there's a problem we need to discuss. Susan is finding this difficult. I think I can persuade her, but I'm going to need time. We can't rush into this.'

Mr Sarotzini shook his head, looking relaxed. 'I don't have that impression, Mr Carter. I don't think your wife finds this difficult at all. I think you are misreading her. On the contrary, I think it is you who finds it difficult, perhaps.'

John was taken aback by the certainty in his voice. Taken aback because the man was right.

The banker gestured to John's plate. 'Please, Mr Carter, eat.'

John ate his salmon, like a child scolded by a parent, while he tried to find a way back into the negotiations.

'This lawsuit that you have with your composer still worries me, Mr Carter.'

'My barrister feels it's unlikely that Danziger will go the distance. He feels we have enough evidence to show a judge that we didn't deliberately set out to steal someone else's work.'

'But at what cost?'

John was surprised that the banker was bringing all this up again. He relayed everything his barrister had told him, pointing out that copyright was a grey area of the law, nothing was certain, and maybe if they had a bank like the Vörn behind them, Danziger would back off or, at worst, accept a small out-of-court settlement.

They reached coffee without any further mention of the surrogacy, and

John was feeling a little more hopeful. He had been able to turn the conversation into a serious discussion about the future potential of DigiTrak, and to demonstrate to Mr Sarotzini the company's viability. The man was a banker, after all. He might be desperate for a child, but surely he wouldn't want to let a good business opportunity slip past? Of all the pitches John had made during the past four weeks, none had been so receptively received as the one he was making now. He was certain that he had swung Mr Sarotzini into believing in the merits of DigiTrak in its own right. Bolstered by this, he made his play. 'This is my proposition, Mr Sarotzini. If you will put up the funding for DigiTrak, just on an interim basis, I will give you my undertaking to do my best to persuade Susan. I'm sure I can, given time.'

Mr Sarotzini raised his tiny coffee cup, holding the handle between his forefinger and thumb in a dainty manner. This was not matched by his expression, which had turned to steel. His voice had turned hard also, and impersonal. 'You do not appear to have registered what I said to you earlier, Mr Carter. It is not your wife who has objections to my proposal, it is *you*. Let me make it clear to you that my terms are not negotiable. You will understand, if you ever do business with me, that I am fair to the point of generosity but I am firm. I have offered you a solution to your problems. You have to take it or leave it.'

John's heart sank. He stared back into the grey eyes, and felt clumsy because Mr Sarotzini had seen through him. Clumsy and cheap. Even his suit, which was from Paul Smith and had cost a fortune, felt cheap in Mr Sarotzini's presence.

He took a breath, hating this man now with all his heart. 'I appreciate your offer, but it's not acceptable. My wife and I aren't for sale.'

Without any visible reaction, Mr Sarotzini slowly scooped up the pages of the documents and tidied them. There was a matter-of-factness about the way he did this, as if he really did not care one way or another, and John watched him helplessly, aware that he had badly misjudged the banker.

'Mr Carter, please realise that I do understand the complexities of emotions in this situation. It was a thought, an idea I had to help you out of your dilemma. We will talk no more of it. I will transfer the funds back to Switzerland and that will be the end of the matter.' He paused to wave away a waiter, who was trying to refill his cup. Mr Sarotzini smiled. 'I have enjoyed our brief friendship, Mr Carter, and perhaps our paths will cross again one day. Who knows?'

From beside his chair Mr Sarotzini produced a slim black briefcase. He opened it, put in the documents, and closed each of the catches with a sharp click. Then he downed the remnants of his coffee, nodded at the head waiter and got up from the table.

As John rose also, the finality hit him. Mr Sarotzini was moving towards the door at a speed that startled him, as if John already belonged in his past. Hurriedly following him out past the porter's desk, he thought about the expression on Susan's face this morning. It had been that of someone looking forward to a challenge.

Maybe he was being too hasty. Perhaps this was the perfect solution: Susan could experience motherhood without them having to bring up a child. They would be out of their financial mess. And she wouldn't have to worry about Casey – neither of them would.

He followed Mr Sarotzini into the street with a mounting sense of panic. Without even turning to acknowledge him, the banker was getting into the back of his Mercedes. John realised he had no fax or phone number, no e-mail address for this man. His last chance to save his business, his home and, perhaps, even, his marriage was about to glide away into the London traffic.

As the chauffeur closed the door, John ran forward. 'Mr Sarotzini! Wait, please. We'll do it!'

For a moment, as the chauffeur climbed in behind the wheel, John thought the car was going to pull away. Then the rear window began to slide down. Mr Sarotzini peered through it, staring into John's eyes with an intensity that scared him.

'Let us be absolutely clear on this, Mr Carter. I will give you one and a half million pounds. Your wife will bear the child my wife and I are unable to have. The day the baby is born you will hand it over to us. You will never see it again. We have a deal?'

'We have a deal,' John replied.

Chapter Twenty-three

'Nietzsche said, "That which does not kill me makes me stronger."'

On channel 4 on the monitor in Kündz's attic, John Carter, leaning against the kitchen table, said to Susan, 'What time do you have to be there?'

Kündz, in his armchair, read several more paragraphs of the book on the German philosopher, Nietzsche, that Mr Sarotzini had recommended to him, then looked at the television screen again.

This was the shape of his life now. He watched, he read, he sketched, he reported. Sometimes, at his discretion, he hired extra people to maintain surveillance on Susan Carter when she travelled. Nothing could be missed, no place that she visited, no people she met, no conversation she had.

'Ten,' Susan Carter said.

'And you really don't want me to be there, you're sure, hon?' John Carter asked.

Susan was wearing jeans, a white T-shirt and yachting shoes. Kündz liked her in this casual outfit. She was making supper, roasted peppers with anchovies, then grilled lamb chops, followed by raspberries and *fromage frais*. John Carter did not appreciate the effort his wife made each evening, cooking for him, and this angered Kündz. Susan's job was just as demanding as her husband's, yet she was the one who always had to work at home too. He hoped Mr Sarotzini would allow him to teach John Carter a lesson for this.

And now, while she worked, John Carter was doing nothing except drinking whisky. He was still drinking too much, Kündz thought. This was weakness: he didn't need to drink this much, not now he had got what he wanted.

Kündz was concerned about the amount John Carter drank because sometimes it made him snap at Susan, and Kündz could see the pain in her face when he did this, and the pain hurt him. *Burned* him. This made him hate John Carter even more than he already hated him.

John Carter switched on the television in the kitchen, but he didn't watch it. Instead he flicked through the pages of a magazine.

'I'm sure,' Susan said. 'I'm *really* sure, OK?' She'd left off cooking the meal and was watering a row of plants in pots along the window-sill. They might have been herbs, Kündz couldn't tell. Although he was becoming an expert on poetry, philosophy, painting, opera, he knew nothing about plants. One day Mr Sarotzini would teach him about plants, but not yet.

And there was only so much that could be taught, Mr Sarotzini said. That which is truly important had to be *learned*.

Mr Sarotzini had explained this to him, telling him always to carry inside his head the words: 'I hear and I forget, I see and I remember, I do and I understand.'

Kündz read these words now. Then he looked at the date on his watch. It was the twenty-first. And tomorrow was the twenty-second: 22 July. Yes. For three weeks he had watched John and Susan Carter, had listened to them day and night, and all the time they kept on talking about it, debating it, discussing their visits to the clinic.

They had been to the clinic eleven times now. On five occasions John Carter had gone with Susan, on the rest she had gone on her own for the injections to improve her chances of conception. Kündz had listened to them discussing the doctors they had met there, and they were impressed with the clinic, there was no doubt about that.

Mr Sarotzini had been very pleased to hear that.

July 22. The centre of her ovulation cycle. Tomorrow.

And that was more than good.

Susan walked out of the kitchen towards the living room and Kündz switched to channel 3, picked her up, watched her carry the glass vase she was using as a watering can over to a plant, a potted palm perhaps, he wasn't sure. Susan knew about plants: maybe *she* would teach him about them.

He carried on watching her, in no hurry to return to Nietzsche, although he was enjoying the book. But he was enjoying Susan Carter in her jeans, white T-shirt and yachting shoes even more.

John Carter came out into the living room now, put an arm around her and kissed her cheek. 'It's not too late, darling. We don't have to go through with this, OK?'

'Everything's signed.'

'It doesn't matter.'

Susan wished – and neither John nor Kündz could read this – that John would take his hands off her. She wished he would stop kissing her, stop giving her the option to quit, every five minutes.

She had made up her mind, she had come to terms with all the voices inside her head that screamed at her not to do this, and now all she wanted was her own space. She wanted to make a box and hammer a label on the outside of it that said, NINE-MONTH BOX, and she wanted to climb inside it, close it, bolt the hatch, have this baby, and let Mr Sarotzini take it away. Then she could climb out and get her life back.

But it wasn't going to be like that, however much she wanted it to be. And it was this that made her angry, this fear that she was not going to be in control, that Mr Sarotzini was already in control and, from tomorrow, doctors would be in control too, and then the baby, if she conceived, would be in control, too. And what was going to happen to her emotions – and to her marriage?

Layered beneath those fears lay her curiosity. She had convinced herself that she was doing this for Casey. But she knew, also, that she was doing it for herself. A few days ago in a magazine she had read that it was important for health reasons for a woman to become pregnant at least once. She had shown the article to John, taking consolation in it.

She was dying for a drink, although she'd been told strictly no alcohol tonight.

Kündz watched in dismay as she poured herself a glass of rosé wine. This gave him a problem he would rather not have had, because he should report it. But if he did, what would happen? Would they delay?

And the timing, he reflected. If he reported this one glass she was now drinking, so much would have to be changed that it hardly bore thinking about. And Mr Sarotzini might be angry with him, might blame him for not stopping her from drinking.

Just one glass, Susan Carter, that's all.

He remembered something Mr Sarotzini had taught him, the story of the strong man who said, 'Give me a firm place to stand and I will move the world.'

'We can all be that man,' Mr Sarotzini had told him. 'We can all push the lever that moves the world, it is inside us, we just have to learn how to recognise it, how to use it, that is all we have to do.'

Susan moved to the dining room and Kündz turned the channel selector to 6. There wasn't much in this room, just a trestle and some rolls of wallpaper. Kündz wasn't sure why she had come in here.

She walked to the window and stared out at the garden. Now he understood: she had come in here to be alone.

And Kündz, watching her so closely, almost breathless with adulation, knew. He *knew*. He was certain that Susan was the lever that would move his world. But there was a lack of clarity that bothered him. There were events going on, wheels turning. He thought again of Mr Sarotzini's words, 'I hear and I forget, I see and I remember, I do and I understand.'

July 22.

Tomorrow.

The excitement was rising inside him, it had an operatic quality, yes, like Don Giovanni, the music of the excitement was erupting inside his head, and he had to struggle to contain himself.

Now the Carters' phone was ringing. Susan had heard it and hurried through into the living room shouting to her husband that she would get it. She picked up the receiver.

Kündz punched a button on the control panel and immediately heard the caller. He knew this voice: Susan spoke to this man regularly – she was editing his new book.

'Susan?' The writer sounded anxious, Kündz thought. 'I'm sorry to bother you, I need to see you urgently. Are you free tomorrow, for lunch or a drink?'

Susan sounded friendly, she liked the man, but she was evasive. 'Oh, Fergus, I'm sorry, it's not possible. I'm out of town for a couple of days.'

'How about breakfast before you go?'

She laughed. 'No *way*! I'm leaving at the crack of dawn.'

And Kündz was impressed. She sounded so natural – she was a great liar, this lady was terrific.

'Susan, it's important, I really do need to see you.'

She promised to call him over the weekend, when she was back. The writer again tried to persuade her to meet before she went, but without luck. He also tried to get a phone number out of her, but she didn't have one to give him. She'd call him, she promised, the moment she was back.

Good girl.

Kündz's adrenaline was racing. He needed to speak to someone, to share his excitement. Even if he was not allowed to say anything about Susan Carter, he could still share his *sense* of excitement.

He picked up the phone and dialled Claudie at his apartment in Geneva. But there was no answer. He telephoned her own apartment, got the answering machine and hung up. She was out and he didn't like that. He had not spoken to her for ten days, but he did not like the fact that she was out. Claudie was his woman, Mr Sarotzini had given her to him. Susan

127

Carter was going to become his woman, but until then Claudie was his woman, and his woman was out.

He replaced the receiver and began to read Nietzsche again. Mr Sarotzini's words came back once more. 'I hear and I forget, I see and I remember, I do and I understand.'

He looked up from the book and watched Susan turning over the lamb chops, all the time thinking to himself, *Tomorrow.*

Tomorrow I will understand.

Chapter Twenty-four

The WestOne Clinic was a modern, four-storey building that blended reasonably unobtrusively with the Victorian red-brick façades of Wimpole Street. Inside, it did its best not to look or feel like a hospital. The entrance was plushly carpeted, there were tapestries on the walls, vases bursting with fresh flowers, bowls of pot-pourri, and huge sofas. It could have been the foyer of a small, immensely luxurious hotel, except for the smell.

The cocktail of disinfectant, fresh laundry and institutional food was ever present. Not even the huge bunch of flowers from John, and the even bigger bouquet from Mr Sarotzini, could mask it in Susan's room, which was as plush and spacious as a hotel suite, and had a fine view of the street as well as a glimpse of Regent's Park. Dusk was falling, and in a few minutes they were going to take her into the theatre. She was feeling nervous, and very alone.

John had phoned a couple of hours ago to wish her luck, and again offered to come over. But she couldn't have him here. She did not want him around while she was having this – this thing – done to her. She felt as though she was being unfaithful to him, and it was easier to be alone, not to have to see his face.

The door opened and a nurse came in, followed by a doctor; neither wore a badge. She had been introduced to them already but she couldn't remember their names – maybe, she thought, because she didn't want to. There was something unreal about being here, and that was how she wanted it to stay. It was just a bad dream. In nine months' time she would wake up from it. In the meantime no one, other than herself, John and Mr Sarotzini, would know the truth. Her friends and colleagues would see her pregnant, sure, but they wouldn't know the truth. And in nine months' time they would be telling her how sorry they were, that it was awful for her and John to have had a stillborn child. And she'd act out the charade, and John would too, and then it would be over.

The nurse had a hypodermic in her hand. Susan hated injections, and it normally took all her courage to have one in the doctor's surgery. She'd lost count of the number she'd had today and over the past few weeks.

'Pre-med,' the nurse said.

'Pre-med,' Susan echoed. 'Right.' It didn't matter, they could do what they wanted. Her body didn't belong to her for the next nine months.

She felt the prick, and a lot of fluid went in. A build-up of pressure began to hurt her arm as the nurse kept pressing the plunger. There was a numb sensation in Susan's hand, as if someone had whacked the nerve in her funny bone.

The nurse jigged out of Susan's line of vision and she saw the doctor's face clearly now. He was good-looking, in a movie-actor-playing-an-American-senator way, with a Mediterranean tan, dark hair with jet black streaks, like highlights in reverse, and a perfect smile. So perfect. Maybe he was an actor? She thought he looked familiar. Had she seen him in *ER*? Was he that doctor – what was his name? – Dr Doug Ross?

She wasn't sure if the nurse had finished or not. Dr Ross from *ER* kept looking at her with that perfect smile. There were several questions she wanted to ask him about the show.

She wondered whether she had her arm back yet. Not that it mattered, she was feeling nicely floaty. Like a boat, or maybe a lilo. And it was good that Dr Ross from *ER* was here. Could she bring Casey over and have Dr Ross from *ER* look after her?

She was about to ask him this, but he had gone. The nurse had gone, too, and now the room didn't look familiar any more. The walls were moving, they were changing colour as they slid past her and now she was fifteen years back, at Epcot, Disney World, in Florida, on a ride, travelling though a cave and they were going to stop at an exhibit in a moment.

She tried to turn her head, but it didn't move, and she was aware, although it didn't bother her, that she couldn't move it. Someone would be along in a minute to fix it, probably nice Dr Ross from *ER*.

The motion of the ride changed, making her feel giddy. They were going up, or maybe they were going down. Her mind was rising up and her body was sinking downwards, and then the motion reversed and it was her mind that was sinking down while her body rose.

Her eyes closed against the giddiness. They shut out one world but opened another inside her head. There were people all around her, gathered inside her head.

She could see her mother and father, and Casey now, coming into focus. Casey was standing up, she was fine, they had fixed her. John was standing in here too but there was no light on his face and she was having difficulty identifying which one out of all these people he was. And Mr Sarotzini was here too – she could see him clearly and he was smiling at her, a great warm smile that told her she was doing just great and everything was going to be fine.

And there was another man she had seen before, but she couldn't put a name to him and she couldn't place where it was she had seen him. It was recently, she knew that much. She had definitely seen this man recently. He was a big man, built like a quarterback.

And then her brain connected. Yes, it was him, the man from British Telecom who had come to fix the ring tones in the phones.

And this was a strange part of her head she was in, lights criss-crossing, sharp long slivers of cold white light, like knife blades. Lasers. Hundreds of lasers, their beams making strange patterns on the inside walls of her skull. And figures were moving in and out of the darkness between the beams. Her parents had gone now, Casey too – and where was Dr Ross? Mr Sarotzini was still here and the man from Telecom, and there were others in here now, strangers inside her head, they were all looking down at her, but with the lasers behind them, it was impossible to see their faces. All she could see were the silhouettes of their bodies.

Now the lasers were burning away the walls of her skull and she could see the room beyond them. She could smell burning, a pungent, aromatic smell that was both sweet and bitter. The room was large and packed with people, all back-lit by the lasers. She could see glints of shiny metal. The people all seemed to be wearing dark polo-necks, but she still couldn't see their faces, just blackness on blackness.

She could recognise Mr Sarotzini – even though she couldn't see his face she could sense his presence. And in front of him this man from Telecom, a faceless silhouette carrying the strength of all these people behind him.

Where was Dr Ross from *ER*? Well, if he didn't want to be here, that was his loss. Suddenly she felt very important. All these people had come inside her head to see her. And the man from Telecom was standing in front of them, laser beams playing on his body now. He was huge, far bigger than she remembered, and he had this tremendous physique. But he wasn't wearing his uniform and, unlike everyone else here, he was naked, and he was holding this serpent, and it was uncoiling outwards, reaching towards her, rising like a striking cobra towards her from this dark bush of hair that covered his groin.

The serpent shone, it gleamed, and this man from Telecom, with his face in darkness, didn't need to move towards her. The serpent was doing that, it was still growing, and he was standing between her legs now, and this serpent was reaching out with a hunger, and she wanted it. She wanted it desperately.

She cried out for it.

She prayed for it to come closer to her.

And it did come closer. It was so close that now she couldn't see its head, but she was starting to feel it, and it felt, oh, it felt quite incredible, probing around, so gentle, softly nosing its way, finding an entrance into her.

She guided it with her hands, helped it, but it was OK, it was fine on its own. It nuzzled so gently, just for a moment it tickled, but it was too big, there was no way, it was not going to be able to enter.

She cried out in fear.

Then a laser lit the man's face a ghostly white. But his eyes were full of comfort. He held her with his dark brown eyes. And she felt the serpent starting to work its way in, burrowing, and this now, this was a great sensation, it was like it was opening her up, pushing, it was so big it was impossible, but still it kept on, levering its way in, further, further, inch by inch it was coming inside her, filling her entire body, and one moment it hurt like hell and she heard herself emptying her lungs with pain. Then the pain turned to pleasure. This serpent was gliding, surfing its way up inside her, it was pushing these huge great waves out in front of it, they were swimming up through her, one following another. . .

She was shimmering now, she was like heat waves rising from rippling desert dunes. She was air, her body had dissolved into gaseous vapour, she was just particles of energy, she was waves and beams. And now she felt her body again, she wanted to keep feeling it, this thing inside her, to keep feeling it for ever, never to let it go, never, ever, ever, ever.

Oh, please.

And it was still pushing up, filling her more and more. She had no idea where the head was now, it was somewhere up around her stomach and these waves, she wanted to cry out, wanted to let him know it could come further, there was room, it might not feel like there was room but there was, oh, yes, there was room, and she could make more room, and she was swimming, her whole body was liquid, it was dissolving, and then it was rippling, her body had become the ocean, there was a swell running through her and that swell was increasing, and she saw this ghostly white face, this man from Telecom, his face was right up close now, she couldn't see anything but his face and she couldn't feel anything else in the world, just this serpent, just the swell of the ocean, she was just exploding, she was on fire but this fire was good, she felt this electricity, it was shooting down her legs, up through her arms, great spikes of electricity were shooting up into her brain, deep down into her stomach.

And now she was still, and there was a fuse that was lit, this deep warm glow burning inside her, and she felt so safe, so wanted, and this feeling, this depth inside her, she wanted to hold it, wanted to curl up in a corner with it and live it and never let it go, but she couldn't hold it, she could not hold the ocean together any more, it was disintegrating apart inside her, it was erupting and she was surfing, out in bright sunlight, she was surfing, the waves were inside her, beneath her, and she was screaming, her whole body was exploding joy, the ocean was erupting through every cell in her body, blowing her apart as she screamed, *'Please, yes, oh, yes, oh, yes, oh, yes, oh, yes.'*

There was a long silence.

Motion, it felt like sleeping in a train. Then Susan realised her bed was moving, it was being dragged along, she was travelling down a corridor.

She heard a harsh, intrusive sound.

Metal shutters?

A clatter.

Then darkness.

Chapter Twenty-five

Something was bothering Kündz. It had been on his mind since Tuesday night, but now it was coming at him with an urgency that was clouding all his other thoughts.

Mr Sarotzini had taught him to open himself up to his intuition, to free it from its shackles, to nurture it, to learn to trust it. So he opened himself up to it now, and Tuesday night returned to him in precise detail. The phone was ringing in the Carters' house and Susan had answered it. Kündz knew it was this conversation she had had that was bothering him.

He keyed a search command. The tape wound back, stopped.

He played the section of the tape over, listening carefully.

'Susan?' The writer sounded anxious, Kündz thought. 'I'm sorry to bother you, I need to see you urgently. Are you free tomorrow, for lunch or a drink?'

It was the tone of this man's voice that was bothering him. And what was this urgency? Although Susan was making him rewrite huge chunks of his book, the deadline was movable – what mattered was getting the book right.

Kündz's intuition, fuelled by the tone of this man's voice, was screaming at him.

He played the tape again. Then again. *Urgently*. This word. It had got him by the balls.

For the second night running Fergus Donleavy had woken from the same nightmare.

It was a simple dream and he could recall it with clarity. He saw a baby, a tiny new-born infant, alone in a terrible darkness. It was crying, and it was this cry that was the real nightmare: there was such utter terror in it. Then in the dream he saw Susan Carter: she was fumbling around in the pitch blackness with a torch, and she was crying, she couldn't find the baby, and she was begging Fergus to help.

And he told her, no, leave the baby, don't try to find it, let it die. *For God's sake, let it die.*

Then he woke.

He looked at his wristwatch beside the bed. There was a dull ache midway between his eyes. Jesus, what the hell had he drunk last night? He chucked his feet out of the bed and his body followed, wobbled a little but stayed upright, one benefit of four hundred thousand years of evolution as a biped, he thought, but not very clearly, then opened the curtains.

The Thames was outside, which still surprised him every morning, although it had always been outside, all the ten years he'd lived in this docklands flat.

A rusty lighter slid past, heavily laden and low in the water. The barge towing it could have been on rails fixed to the river bed, it was so unshaken by the spring ebb chop. He watched the froth, the spume, the shit-brown water then, craning his neck to the right, could just see Tower Bridge. Grey against a grey sky. It might be drizzling: it wasn't much of a day.

He hauled on his dressing gown, found his slippers, padded through to his den, which, like the living room and dining room and everywhere else in this flat, apart from the lavatory seat, was covered with pages of the damned manuscript that this bloody woman was making him rewrite. Oh, Christ, he was bored with this book, wished he'd never started it, but he needed the money for the mortgage on this flat, which was not worth even half the fortune he'd paid, and which his university salary didn't cover. There was no way he could afford to dump it and repay Magellan Lowry their advance.

And, don't forget this, Fergus, this book is important, it's needed: this book *really could change people's thinking.*

Bollocks. It was just a good sales pitch, Fergus, that was all, and you know that.

And he did know that, but only the modest part of him was buying that right now. There was an immodest part, a massive, mountain-sized ego part of him that didn't buy that at all. This part was thinking Dr Steven W. Hawking has not got it right, and the only truly great scientific mind in the world holds tenure inside the cranium of Dr J. Fergus Donleavy.

He ground coffee beans and tried again to interpret the dream. He had an entire shelf of books on dreams: he knew all the possibilities and none worked for this dream. Nothing resonated. He knew the reason, and the reason frightened him. This dream was not about symbolism.

This dream was a premonition.

This was the presentiment, the feeling he'd been having of something bad happening to Susan for these past few weeks, the feeling that had been worsening every day.

It was even stronger this morning than it had been two days ago, and it had been strong enough then to have made him call her.

What would he have told her? She didn't want children, so how could he warn her that he had seen something really bad to do with her having a child?

She would dismiss it, reminding him that she and her husband were not going to have children.

Goddamn you, Susan Carter, stop messing with my head. He thought of her face across the table at lunch, the sleek red hair, those beautiful, intelligent eyes, the way she looked at him with humour, curiosity – and something else.

Did some part of her want to go beyond a pure editor-author relationship?

Then an even wilder thought occurred. Was she making him do all this rewriting because she was trying to reject her attraction to him?

Come on, Fergus, you trashed more brain cells last night than you realised.

He poured the coffee into the machine, filled it with water and switched it on. The morning post and the *Independent* were on the floor. He scooped them up, glanced at the headlines, glanced at the envelopes, nothing of interest, and sat down again.

Susan hadn't phoned him. Tuesday night, he had rung her. It was now Thursday morning. She had said she would call and she hadn't. And she'd sounded mysterious when he had spoken to her. Going away, she said, but she didn't say where. Surely when people are going away they say to Manchester or Paris, or wherever the hell they are going. So why hadn't she?

Christ. Did Susan have a lover? He'd never met her husband, so he couldn't gauge the man or the relationship. Women took lovers because their marriages were unhappy. Had all those meaningful looks she had given him been a hint? A cry for help? And he'd been too blind to see?

He felt a twinge of anguish. He had been deeply attracted to Susan from the moment they had first met. He liked everything about her. It wasn't just her looks, it was the way she moved her hands, the way she smelt, her voice, her mind, her clothes, her confidence, and the way she *cared* for her work, for people, for everything. If she had a lover, and this was a big speculation, but *if* she did, and therefore her marriage was rocky, now was the time to make a move himself.

136

He shook his head. He had to switch his mind from this. He had to concentrate on the manuscript. But he kept coming back to the dream, to Susan's red hair, her legs, her smile, those brilliant blue eyes, her freshness, her vitality.

The thought that right now she might be in bed in a hotel room with her lover was tormenting him.

But the dream tormented him just as much. It stayed with him through his shower, through his one slice of cremated toast, through the first half-hour of his work.

He wanted desperately to talk to Susan. And he needed to tell her his dream, to see whether any part of it resonated. And the parts were: darkness; a baby crying; Susan trying to find this baby with a torch. And then himself, telling her to leave it, to let it die.

He was about to pick up the phone to dial her office and see if by any chance her secretary, who had been so adamant yesterday that Susan could not be contacted, had a number for her today.

But before he could pick up the phone, it rang. Maybe it was Susan, he thought hopefully.

But it wasn't. It was a man from British Telecom, polite and most apologetic. A line fault of some sort. The computer showed them it was coming from the equipment Fergus had installed in his flat. Would it be possible for an engineer to call? Would there, perhaps, be someone at home this morning?

Chapter Twenty-six

A sliver of light appeared in the darkness. A flat, steady monochrome, growing a little wider now but no brighter. Susan, drowsy and disoriented, watched it, trying to figure it out.

It was a window, she realised. Trails of rain were sliding down it, and the sky beyond was the colour of a television screen that was switched off. Her bedroom window. But it was in the wrong place. John must have moved it. Or moved the bed?

She closed her eyes again, but she felt a deepening disquiet. Something wasn't right. She opened them. Pale grey walls. Hotel, she thought. We're away somewhere. She tried to turn her head to see John. It took an enormous effort to roll it a few degrees, just far enough to be able to see that no one was beside her.

A coil of fear spiralled through her.

This isn't a hotel, I'm in a clinic.

Something had happened that wasn't right. Something, last night, the operation –

She tried to move, but her body was leaden, weighted down like a diver's. It took all her energy just to turn her head again, to see if her watch was on the bedside table, or if there was a clock in the room, but after a few moments, she gave up. Her eyes returned to the wall with the window. They shifted, stopped at a painting on another wall, a copy of a Lowry, a wintry northern industrial landscape filled with matchstick people. And that was a coincidence, she thought, incongruously. She worked for Magellan Lowry and there was a painting on the wall by Lowry.

A smoke-detector sensor and the nozzles of a sprinkler system poked down from the ceiling. Somewhere a phone was ringing. Her mouth was parched and her throat was raw. She tried to think back; fragments of a dream, or a hallucination, indistinct, a bad dream, the fear was growing.

And at the edge of her peripheral vision the door was opening. A nurse came in, efficient-looking, rather hard face, dark-haired, late thirties. She stood a short distance from Susan, her mouth opened and her pale lips moved up and down, and one word at a time, with gaps in between, her voice reached Susan. A smell of food had come into the room, breakfast food, toast, eggs, which increased Susan's nausea.

'Ah. Good. She's. Awake.'

The words told Susan that someone else was in the room too, but she couldn't see who. Then a man moved right in front of her, blocking her view of the window. She had seen him before: dark hair with jet-black highlights, a Mediterranean tan, yes, Dr Ross from *ER*.

He looked at her without speaking, holding her with his friendly brown eyes, and then he said, 'How. Are. You. Feeling?'

Susan felt a little queasy and she also had a raging thirst, but she didn't want to tell him because she was too tired. She didn't want to have to make the effort to drink. She wanted to go back to sleep. 'OK,' she said.

'You're going to be feeling a bit woozy for a while from the anaesthetic. Any tummy pains?'

She was able to shake her head. But a memory was starting to clarify, rising steadily from some great depth towards the surface, like a bloated corpse.

She shuddered.

Alarm registered in the face of Dr Mediterranean Tan from *ER*.

She could recall, suddenly, the violently erotic sensation inside her of the serpent, the phallus, the *thing*, of the man from Telecom. Christ, she could see it, could feel it so vividly, it was all rushing back now, and she was aware that her face was flushing, and she was aware, too, that it must have been a dream, something Freudian, that was all, *it must have been.*

With no warning, a fierce pain ripped through her abdomen; it felt as if a knife had been plunged in and twisted. She cried out, gasping, as the pain struck again.

'It's from the incision. We'll just take a look at the stitches,' the doctor said. The nurse lifted away the sheet, untied the front of her gown, then removed the dressing. Looking down at her abdomen, Susan could see the stitches and the livid flesh.

Dr Ross began explaining to her exactly what they had done in the operation, but she only half listened because she already knew. Mr Van Rhoe, the obstetrician, had already explained it to her in great detail.

Mr Van Rhoe was the man Mr Sarotzini had insisted would take care of her, and Susan had had to admit to feeling a little flattered. Miles Van Rhoe was in a different league from even Harvey Addison. For over thirty years he had delivered babies for the rich and famous, for the aristocracy and the nobility; she had read in newspapers and magazines that many members of the Royal Family would consider no one else.

And Dr Abraham Zelig, the director of this clinic, had also explained everything that would happen to her in the greatest possible detail. Dr Zelig, Mr Sarotzini had told her, was one of the world's foremost authorities, perhaps *the* foremost authority, on *in vitro* fertilisation.

Dr Ross was patiently explaining now to her that they had made an incision, removed the eggs from her ovary, selected the healthiest-looking one, mixed it with semen provided by Mr Sarotzini, and then returned it to the womb.

As she listened, the pain gone now, and looked back into those kind eyes, she had a sudden urge to blurt out to him that he was wrong, it hadn't been Mr Sarotzini's semen, it had been the man from Telecom's semen. But she held back. Of course she'd had the operation – Christ, she had the sutures and the pain to prove it. The stuff in her dream, that crazy erotic dream, that was all just hallucination. Anaesthetics did freaky things to the brain, everyone knew that.

The effort of being awake for just these few minutes was exhausting her. She started to think about Mr Sarotzini's semen and felt a sudden wave of repulsion. It was inside her, mixed with one of her eggs, fertilising it at this very moment. Was she pregnant?

She felt hot, then very cold. Dr Ross was there, and then he was not there. Then he was there again. She suddenly remembered that Dr Ross in *ER* was a paediatrician.

Of course, she needed a paediatrician now, or would soon.

The nurse was looking at her strangely. Dr Ross went out of focus then came back in again. Susan felt dizzy and desperately thirsty. She asked now if she could have a drink of water.

Shortly after six o'clock that evening, Mr Sarotzini's chauffeur pulled up the Mercedes outside Susan's house, and she was relieved to see that John wasn't home yet. She dreaded facing him. She hadn't even had the courage to return the call he'd left for her this morning at the clinic.

Mr Sarotzini had been in to see her at lunch-time, and that encounter had been awkward. He had brought her an enormous basket of fruit, which was in the trunk of the Mercedes now, but in spite of all their common interests, she had been too tired – or confused – to be able to converse with him. She had been relieved when he left.

The sky was dark and it was still raining. The automaton chauffeur only broke his rigid silence to offer to carry her overnight bag inside for her. She declined, then immediately regretted it. The basket of fruit, and her small bag were heavier than she'd realised, and pulled on the stitches in her abdomen.

Dr Mediterranean Tan Ross had been reluctant to let her go home, wanting her to spend a further night in the clinic, but it was vital she was in the office tomorrow. The directors of Magellan Lowry were now keen for the firm to acquire the Dr Julian DeWytts book, and tomorrow was the deadline for upping their bid in the auction.

As she unlocked the front door and stepped into the hallway, she felt a sense of relief that she had made the right decision. She could see straight through to the French windows in the living room, and the garden beyond. Even in the gloomy rain, it was looking gorgeous. It was a beautiful welcoming sensation, this whole house felt just so good. How could they ever have let it go?

She walked slowly around; she'd only been away one night, but it felt like a month. Everything was unchanged, although she noticed that some of the plants needed watering. Harry the painter had finished the dining room and was starting on the first of the spare bedrooms upstairs, the one that John had chosen for his den, and she was eager to see how that was shaping.

She stood by the marble fireplace in the living room, first looking out at the garden, then at the walls of the room, thinking for the hundredth time how pleased she was with the colour scheme she had chosen. Some white colours were bland, or too pink, or too stark and cold. But this colour was both fresh and airy and, even on this dark day, warm at the same time.

Soon need to start looking at colours for the baby's room, she pondered, wondering which of the three spare ones upstairs would be best for a nursery. And then with a start, she remembered: *What the hell am I thinking about?*

Susan didn't know how she had been expecting John to react when he came home, but it was none of the ways that she'd imagined. He said nothing at all.

Susan was in the kitchen; in spite of her tiredness she was trying to make a nice meal for them out of pasta and a piece of monkfish she had in the freezer. She heard the front door open and shut, and the sound of John's briefcase thunking down on the bare oak boards of the hallway, and waited for him to come into the kitchen. He must know she was here

– onions, chopped garlic and tomatoes were frying on the stove, and the radio was on.

But he didn't come in.

John had never been a creature of habit. He was unpredictable, enigmatic, spontaneous, but in seven years of marriage he had one invariable routine: the moment he arrived home, he came into the kitchen and poured himself two fingers of Macallan whisky, with three cubes of ice and a splash of water, except on Tuesdays, after squash, when he had a Budweiser instead.

Susan waited, turned down the radio and, to her surprise, heard the sound of the television. She went through into the living room. John was sitting on the sofa, still with his jacket on, channel-surfing.

'Hi,' she said meekly.

He continued to stare at the television, punching the remote every couple of seconds, before locking his attention on truck-racing on the Sky Sports channel.

For the first time ever Susan did not know what to say to her husband. Was he angry because she hadn't returned his call earlier? She suspected it was more complicated than that.

She turned away, and walked back to the kitchen, a tear rolling down her cheek. She dabbed it with a strip of kitchen towel, and the next one, stirred the mixture in the frying pan, then leant on the edge of the sink and stared out of the window.

The kettle barbecue, the wooden picnic table and benches were all glossy from the rain. A thrush, the one that was often there, was twitching around in the grass, which needed cutting. It dipped its head and began to pull a worm out of the ground. It was having a struggle, a tug-of-war, as if something out of sight beneath the earth was holding the other end of the worm and pulling just as hard. Finally the thrush won and the worm dangled briefly, shrank in short jerks, and disappeared into its beak. The food chain, Susan thought.

Rain pricked the puddles on the patio. *We think we're so smart because we're human, because we're at the top of the food chain.* A robin hopped around on the lawn, another regular visitor. Susan watched it, catching little splashes of the orange colouring on its chest as it hopped around. It was a pretty bird, she thought, but it was probably savage. Robins were tough and mean; if you were a small bird you didn't want to mess with a robin.

Everything was deceptive. Nothing was what it seemed. She blotted up another tear, taking a deep breath, thinking suddenly: *Oh, Christ, what have I done?*

And then, a short while later, she was laying the table and John was still watching truck-racing, and she was thinking, hoping, that this thing she'd done, this *in vitro* fertilisation, maybe it wouldn't work.

Suddenly she hoped, desperately, that it wouldn't.

The next morning, all she wanted to do was to stay in bed. She forced herself up, though, because she *had* to go to the meeting at work today.

She showered and went downstairs. John was about to dash out of the front door. 'Made you some coffee, hon,' he said. 'On the table.'

She kissed him. 'Thanks.'

'How are you feeling?' he asked.

'Tired.'

'Do you really have to go to the office today?'

'I'll come home early.'

She kissed him goodbye, went into the kitchen, sat down and picked up the newspaper. As she was reading the main front-page story, she picked up her mug and sipped the coffee.

It had a slightly different flavour from usual. Not unpleasant, but it left a faintly metallic aftertaste. She wondered if John had opened a different packet.

In the board meeting at Magellan Lowry, coffee had just been brought. Susan was reporting that there was a bid on the table, she didn't know who it was from, it could be HarperCollins, she suspected, but she knew Transworld were interested, so were Random House and maybe Little, Brown as well. She'd heard from a friend at Simon and Schuster that they'd dropped out and, from what little she'd managed to glean from DeWytts' agent, she reckoned that so had Viking Penguin. But this latest bid was £175,000 for UK and Commonwealth rights, and that was big money.

She didn't think the book was that special, she told the board. It wasn't accessible, in her view, it was too technical and wouldn't grab the broad, popular readership it was intended for. 'I don't think this book is going to be big at all,' Susan said. 'I think we should pass.'

She reached out for the cup that had been passed to her, and took a sip. It was perfectly drinkable, but seemed to have the same metallic aftertaste as the coffee John had left her. She wondered if she was imagining it.

Chapter Twenty-seven

John brought up the papers and breakfast on a tray. This was Susan's weekly Sunday-morning treat. Only once in seven years – when he'd had a truly terrible hangover – had he forgotten it.

She was feeling fine today, and she was relieved that their relationship was getting back to some semblance of normality. John looked sexy in his towelling dressing gown, and she felt aroused and had to restrain herself from slipping her hands inside the robe. Instead, freeing herself with only a tinge of reluctance from the last snug remnants of sleep, she hauled herself up in bed.

The curtains were open and brilliant morning sunshine belted in through the huge east window of the turret. She loved this room – it felt like waking in a castle and they'd decorated it as much like a castle as they could. The floor had been kept as bare wood boards, which they'd had sanded and polished and then thrown with rugs; there was a copper chandelier, with rather suspect modern wiring, which she'd bought in the Bermondsey market, and a minimal amount of furniture, all antique.

When they could afford it, they were going to buy a four-poster bed or, even better, have one made to measure, but that was going to have to wait a while, although John had said it wouldn't be long. Already, in the short time since they'd accepted Mr Sarotzini's deal, DigiTrak was booming. Susan told John it was because he was confident, now that he didn't have his financial worries, and that confidence was infectious.

And he was feeling confident, so much so that he hadn't even bothered with the lottery or the horses recently.

He kissed her. 'Morning, sleepyhead.'

'Morning. Thanks, that looks great,' she said, taking hold of the tray. The past few days since she had come home from the clinic had been horrendous. They had barely talked, and last night John had exploded because she wouldn't make love to him. Miles Van Rhoe had told her strictly that she and John must not make love for a fortnight after the

144

fertilisation attempt, not even with a condom. She wasn't to risk any kind of sexual contact with him.

She met his eyes fleetingly now, and thought she detected in them a glimmer of understanding. Maybe today, she thought, would be the start of the thaw. They were going to have to deal with this problem. They couldn't go on not talking, letting it fester and, besides, this hadn't been only her decision. John couldn't keep on walking around the house looking at her as if she was a leper or a whore. Surely their love for each other was strong enough to get them through this.

'How did you sleep?' she asked.

'OK.' His voice was tepid, suddenly, imbued with the unsaid 'I'd have slept better after a bonk.' 'You?'

'I woke a few times.'

There was a strange smell in the room that seemed to have accompanied John's entrance, a faint stench of burnt rubber. Maybe the old couple next door were having a bonfire. The woman was a pyromaniac; she had a bonfire almost every week, chucked all kinds of rubbish on it while the old boy sat in front of it. Susan had seen him from the west window, which looked right across their neighbours' garden, sitting in his chair, in his Panama hat, watching the bonfire as if it was a great movie, and shouting out when it needed stoking.

John poured her coffee, set it down beside her, then climbed back into bed and turned straight to the Innovations section of the *Sunday Times*. Susan picked up the main section, glanced at the headlines, then took a sip of her coffee.

She spat it straight out.

John looked at her in alarm. 'What's the matter?'

The taste in her mouth was something else. She didn't want to tell him, didn't want to risk upsetting him just when he was in a good mood, but this coffee was seriously nasty. It tasted like rusty metal. And the stench of burning rubber – she knew now where it was coming from. It was the coffee.

'Susan? Darling? What is it? What's the matter?'

It must be her imagination she thought, and tasted it again. This time it was even worse and the smell was making her feel distinctly queasy. Either he was going to have to take the coffee out of the room, or she was going to have to leave the room herself.

'Hon,' she said, 'is this a different brand? The coffee?'

'It's the same we always have, the medium roast, the one you like. Why?'

145

She wondered, wildly, if something from Harry the painter had got into the percolator, some paint stripper or something. Surely not. 'It tastes – different.'

John sipped his coffee, then hers, frowning. 'It's fine.' Then he put down his cup and raised a hand. 'Uh-oh. I've read about this. You know why it tastes strange? You're *pregnant.*'

She sat in silence. She'd been suspecting it since Friday. But that had been so soon – too soon, surely.

Oh, God, please let it be something else.

'It's too soon,' she told him. But she had to get away from this stench. 'I need some air. Why don't we have breakfast out in the garden?'

John shrugged. 'Sure, why not?'

Susan took *Pregnancy – The Myths and the Reality* and sat in a chair outside, sipped some orange juice and nibbled a dry biscuit, which was all she fancied.

The first chapter of the book dealt with the time immediately following conception. Susan read that morning sickness occasionally came on within twenty-four hours. Revulsion to foods, drinks, smells might occur almost as quickly.

Then she put down the book and peered inside her nightdress at the ugly red weal in her abdomen, and the stitches, which were already beginning to dissolve. Miles Van Rhoe had promised there would be no scar.

She thought back to the weird dream she had had when she was under the anaesthetic, and in spite of the warm sunlight, she shivered.

It had been just a dream. Or a hallucination. She thought about the strange man from Telecom, trying to work out why he had been in the dream. She knew that everything in dreams was significant and that any people you saw were there for a reason. Maybe the man from Telecom represented work being done on the house. Maybe she had dreamed about him because part of the point of her having the operation was to save the house, and he represented progress with it. But why him and not Harry the painter too? Or any of the other tradesmen who had come and gone over the past two months.

There had been a time when she and John had discussed their dreams, and she toyed with mentioning this one, then dismissed the idea: it was too personal and she did not want to raise the subject of sex.

Abandoning her dream, she returned to the *Sunday Times*. When she'd finished the main section, she picked up the *Mail on Sunday* and began to read it. When she came to an article on page seven, she stopped, read it carefully, then read it again.

Hon?' she said.

John was buried in a supplement. 'Uh?'

'This composer you've been having the problems with – it was Zak Danziger, right?'

John did not look up. 'Snivelling little turd.'

She handed him the paper, tapping the top of the page with her finger. 'Look, here.'

John looked, reluctantly, irritated at being disturbed in the middle of an article he was reading about a new BMW sports coupé; it was a model he fancied buying, and he was wondering if Mr Sarotzini would have any objections if he splashed out. Although, of course, he could lease it, and then the figures wouldn't look bad.

And then he saw the small photograph, the name Zak Danziger, followed by the word *dead*.

Gripping the paper tightly he read straight through the article. It was short and did not go into detail. It simply said that British composer and former rock singer Zak Danziger had been found dead of an apparent drugs overdose in his suite at the Plaza hotel in New York yesterday morning. Danziger had written the lyrics for three hit musicals that had played in over twenty languages around the world and the scores for over thirty films. He had been married three times and was estranged from his current wife. He left a son and two daughters by previous marriages.

'Bloody hell!' he said.

'What does this mean?' Susan asked quietly.

'It means the lawsuit is brown bread – dead.' John smiled. 'I should feel sorry for the poor bastard, but I don't, not after the way he behaved. It's very good news for us. Mr Sarotzini's going to be delighted.' He read through the piece again, and said, 'God, why couldn't it have happened a month ago? We'd have been out of the woods, wouldn't have had to go through any of –'

He stopped in mid-sentence, having seen the troubled expression on Susan's face. 'I'm sorry,' he said. 'I shouldn't be feeling like this – I know I shouldn't be happy at news of a tragedy, but I am, with this bastard I really am.'

'It's quite a *coincidence*, isn't it?' she said, quietly.

'Uh?'

'His dying – so soon.' She shook her head. 'It's nothing, I'm being silly.'

John gave her a sideways look, then read the report again. He

147

remembered the old dictums about not speaking ill of the dead, but he still couldn't prevent the smile spreading across his face each time he looked at Danziger's photograph and remembered the composer that afternoon in his lawyer's office, with his studded denims, lavatory brush hair and arrogant scowl.

Susan looked at the sky: there wasn't a cloud in it, and she wondered what was draining all the heat out of the sun today.

Chapter Twenty-eight

Coffee was causing Susan real problems. Even the faintest scent of it right now made her stomach feel like she was on a bad funfair ride, and Fergus Donleavy was due any minute – he ran on caffeine. She sometimes thought Fergus had Colombian dark blend double roast rather than blood in his veins.

It was Tuesday. Last Wednesday night she had been in the clinic. In one week's time her period was due, and she was thinking, maybe this coffee thing was just coincidence. Except it wasn't just coffee, it was the smell of alcohol now too, and cigarettes, and the only thing she wanted to eat was dry biscuits.

It could be flu, she tried to convince herself.

Sure, Susan Carter, it could be flu. And that would be a real coincidence to catch a flu that gave you the same symptoms as pregnancy, just a few days after you'd been in a clinic having artificial insemination.

Artificial?

That question had taken up residence in the first compartment she reached each time she took a walk around the inside of her head. The man from Telecom was always in there, smiling at her, stepping out of the darkness towards her, and however much she tried to shut him out, she couldn't. Only this man knew for sure whether it had been a hallucination.

In one week's time, she would know if she was pregnant or not. She had to ride this week out and pray hard for her period to come.

Tony Weir experienced a similar reaction to John when he heard of Zak Danziger's death. The solicitor's voice down the phone was filled with good humour, even though he'd just lost out on Lord-only-knows-how-much loot from defending DigiTrak against the composer.

Tony Weir was the only person who knew the truth about John's arrangement with Mr Sarotzini: he'd gone through the Vörn Bank's

149

documentation with John before he had signed. A quiet, hard-working man, Weir had a wise head and lived modestly, although he was a partner in a major London law firm, pulling in upwards of £350,000 in a bad year. He had been John's solicitor from the early days of DigiTrak.

'I'm getting the impression,' John said, 'that Susan thinks there's some agenda behind this guy's death connected to our deal with the Vörn. She's in a strange mood – a bit paranoid about things.'

Tony chuckled, then said, 'This cutting you faxed from the *Mail on Sunday* – the New York Police Department don't sound suspicious about the death. Danziger had split up with his third wife, just lost a custody battle, was heavily into drugs – sounds to me like all the ingredients for depression. These composers, they're a pretty flaky lot.'

'Sure. And I don't give a fuck. This guy nearly ruined my business and my entire life.'

'How are your partners working out?'

It was a good question. John had not seen or heard from Mr Sarotzini since he'd handed him the signed documents three weeks ago. It was a little surprising, after all the promises the banker had made to Susan about taking her to the opera, concerts, art galleries, but it was early days, and he had plenty of time to come good on those. And, besides, that wasn't important. What mattered was that the money had been transferred to the company's account.

'Fine, terrific,' he replied. 'So far, so good.'

There was a silence.

Tony Weir was not comfortable about the deal. He had warned John that it put him and Susan into Sarotzini's pocket, and he had even suggested that Susan should consider counselling before accepting. But he'd had to agree with John that DigiTrak weren't exactly knee-deep in other options. Now, lowering his voice to almost a whisper, he asked, 'So? Has Susan? You know?'

'Last Wednesday.' John's good humour evaporated and he had a dry, unpleasant taste in his throat.

'And you're OK about it?'

John had to think. He would have liked to have confided in Tony Weir that he felt as if Susan had been violated, and that he had too – that it was as though she was having an affair right in front of his eyes and he was powerless to do anything about it.

He wanted to tell Tony Weir that every time he looked at her, even at the photograph on his desk, all he could think of was Mr Sarotzini's sperm inside her. And he wanted to tell him that she seemed to be locking him out of her life. Sure, she smiled at him and talked to him, kissed him hello and goodbye, good morning and good-night, but shutters had come down.

But John didn't tell Tony Weir this. Instead, he said,·'Yup, I'm OK about it.'

Kündz was listening to this conversation while he did his housework. Except that this wasn't just housework, this was ritual, the closest Kündz came to prayer.

This was purification.

He was purifying his flat, with the same thoroughness and the same pleasure with which he had purified himself. He was clean, every part of him, every crevice, every orifice. Now he was finishing washing the walls of the flat, and then he was going to spray them with disinfectant. It would be as clean as an operating theatre.

This whole world needed purifying.

Mr Sarotzini understood that.

All the time Kündz was purifying his flat, he was listening: channel 9, the telephone in John Carter's office, and channel 14, the telephone in Susan Carter's office. He listened to both at the same time, that was no problem. He had also been listening to channel 17, Fergus Donleavy's study overlooking the Thames, but the writer had gone out now. He was on his way to meet Susan, to take her to lunch at a restaurant called Mon Plaisir. Kündz did not like this. He did not want this man to be close to his Susan. He felt a confusion of emotions, anger most of all, and some sharp, indefinable pain, like a tourniquet tightening somewhere deep inside his heart.

Kündz had already booked a table at this restaurant, for one, in the name of Dr Paul Morris. He had learned from Mr Sarotzini's teachings that a professional title always carried weight. So *Dr* Paul Morris dined out a lot, always alone. His real name was Rikky Berendt and he was sitting at this table now, apparently reading a paperback novel. Within its pages were contained a directional microphone and photographs of Susan Carter and Fergus Donleavy. He was destined for a fruitless wait. Susan and Fergus weren't going to turn up.

Kündz had a hard time controlling his temper when he heard Susan say to Donleavy, who had just arrived in her office, 'Fergus, would you mind if instead of going to a restaurant we went for a walk?'

Kündz heard Donleavy clear his throat and then say, 'No, of course not. Where would you like to go?'

'Anywhere. I don't mind – a park? Along the Embankment?'

Kündz, moving fast, dialled a mobile-phone number and two early diners at Mon Plaisir glanced in momentary irritation at a rather well-dressed man who put down the book he was reading and answered his cell-phone.

'How far are you from Susan Carter's office?' Kündz asked.

'Five minutes.'

'Get there in two.'

They were like a couple of tourists, except they weren't carrying cameras, and they strolled easily in the fine lunch-time sunlight, down St Martin's Lane, across Trafalgar Square, stopping to look at the pigeons and the lions. Susan had never realised how big these lions were, she didn't think she'd ever walked across Trafalgar Square before, never been this close to them.

She was wearing black jeans with a white T-shirt, and a linen jacket, and it was comfortable in this heat. Fergus wore what he always wore: an old tweed jacket, open shirt, rusty cords, lace-up brogues. Seemingly impervious to the temperature, he seldom wore an overcoat in winter and equally seldom took off his jacket in summer.

They did not start talking about anything in particular until they'd reached the Embankment. Fergus was enjoying his new role as a tourist guide, and Susan was realising, with some embarrassment, how few of London's sights she'd learned anything about in seven years. On their way past, Fergus explained that Nelson's Column had had to be built higher than the Duke of York's statue in the Mall, and a short while later, stopping in front of Cleopatra's Needle, he explained how the Egyptians erected their obelisks.

And Kündz heard Susan say to him, with a tease in her voice, 'How come you know so much about all these *phallic* monuments?'

Then he had to listen to Donleavy telling Susan that Egyptian priests took it in turns, had a rota, to masturbate in the inner sanctums of their temples.

Seething with anger, Kündz wanted to take Donleavy by the throat and tell him to stop talking dirty to Susan Carter.

And then, almost as if Donleavy had heard Kündz's thoughts, he changed the subject, asking, 'Where did you go last week?'

'A clinic,' Susan said baldly. 'A minor op. A woman's complaint. Not something I want to talk about.'

That did the trick. It stopped Donleavy asking any more difficult questions. Susan leant on the Embankment wall and looked out across the water. 'You must love living by the Thames,' she said. 'I think I would.'

Fergus grunted, or maybe he cleared his throat – neither Susan nor Kündz were sure. He studied a well-dressed man sitting on the Embankment wall – he might have been a lawyer, or perhaps a doctor, reading a paperback. Simple pleasures, Fergus thought, his gaze staying on the man. Such a simple pleasure to sit on a wall and read a book, but how often do any of us do it?

Finally, Susan couldn't wait any longer, and asked Donleavy directly, 'What was it you wanted to talk to me about so urgently last week?'

Fergus made that same noise again, deep in his throat, then sat down, looking a little awkward. He retied one of his shoe laces. When he had finished, he said, 'I'm a little bit psychic, hrmmn?'

Susan nodded. He'd told her about his premonitions, his telepathic experiences, the auras he could sometimes see around people, and she'd read most of what he'd written in this area.

'Well, this is going to sound strange, and I don't want to alarm you.' He fell silent.

Susan waited patiently for him to continue. He rummaged in his pockets, pulled a cigarette from a battered flip-top pack, then lit it with a Zippo. As the smoke drifted past her, she smelt the now familiar burnt rubber stench.

She watched him draw on the cigarette again, gazed at the shaggy mane of grey hair that hung down over his ears and touched his shoulders, his lean, hard-but-warm face, and thought, as she often had, how much he reminded her of a cowboy, the Man With No Name, the loner of the prairies.

She had such faith in this man's abilities, and his presence always excited her. He carried so much knowledge, so many wild ideas, in his head. She loved John deeply, but she had thought, and more than once, that had she met Fergus under different circumstances, something could have happened between them.

'I've been getting a recurring dream.' He drew on his cigarette again, without looking at her. 'I know you and John have made a decision not to have children, but in this dream I see you pregnant.'

She prompted, 'And?'

He swung his head to look at her, and his eyes narrowed against the glare of the sun on the water behind her. A light breeze lifted a few strands of his hair and batted them around. 'I shouldn't be saying anything, worrying you, it's nuts.'

Susan tilted her head and looked at him sideways, not giving away anything in her expression. 'But you felt strongly enough about it to ring me at home.'

He smoked some more of his cigarette. 'Well, this is none of my business, and anyhow, you're not planning to have children, are you?'

She hesitated and saw that he'd picked up on this hesitation. 'No.'

He raised his hands. 'So, good. It's OK.'

'And if we changed our minds – decided to have children – is there a problem? What have you seen?'

He thought hard, gazing into her face, smelling her perfume, watching strands of that sleek red hair lifting and dropping in the breeze. Last week it had seemed desperately urgent. But out here, in the sunlight, she was looking so anxious and vulnerable, and she'd just assured him she was not about to have a child, and he didn't want to make her worry, he didn't want to mess with her head. He just wanted to put his arms round her and see how she responded.

A moment sometimes presents itself between people. A tiny window opens: within seconds it could shut again. He sensed now that the window was open.

He really had thought last week that she was going to have a baby, and he was picking up vibrations from her now that it was in her mind, but it didn't seem that anything was imminent. It wasn't in her mind with John. But with someone else? Her new lover? 'Nothing,' he said, finally. 'It would only have been important if you were pregnant.'

She nodded, avoiding his eyes.

Then he made his move. He swung his arms around her shoulders, but she flinched, backing away, and he ended up holding her rather clumsily. 'I love you, Susan,' he said.

She looked back at him, startled, her face flushed. 'Fergus, I –' She was shaking her head, and he was still holding her shoulders firmly, but awkwardly, his face close to hers, blocking most of the light.

Then he released his grip, stepped back half a pace. 'Look, I – I'm sorry, but I can't help it, I really do love you.' He smiled sheepishly. 'I – I'm not sure about your situation – with your marriage?'

Susan wondered what she had done to make him feel like this, and tried to find a way to defuse the situation without hurting his feelings. 'Fergus, I'm sorry, you've rather taken me by surprise.' She smiled. 'I mean, I'm flattered, and I like you a lot. But I have a good marriage and I love my husband.'

Fergus was blushing profusely now. 'I'm sorry.'

She smiled again, not knowing whether to look at him or down at the pavement. 'I like our friendship, Fergus, I really value it.'

He smoked the cigarette down to the stub then crushed it on the pavement. 'I'm around, OK? You can telephone me any time, day or night, I don't mind. Just promise me that if anything starts troubling you, you'll call me. Will you do that?'

Susan promised.

And Kündz, struggling to contain his fury, decided that Mr Sarotzini should hear this conversation.

Chapter Twenty-nine

The picture on the monitor was fuzzy black and white, or more like grey and white, and it took a while before Susan saw what Miles Van Rhoe was pointing at with his finger. Then when she did see it, she wasn't sure she was looking at the right thing.

'That?' she asked. 'The sort of oval?'

'The inter-uterine sac,' the obstetrician told her, sounding as excited as a kid on Christmas morning. It was difficult for him to point, because he was holding the probe with his right hand, and trying to keep it steady.

Susan was lying with her feet hooked up in stirrups, and a cold, gelatinously coated vaginal scanner inside her, and she was craning her neck to see the monitor.

She was still not sure that she was looking at the right thing. 'That – the dark bit that looks like a bladder? That's my baby?'

'Yes. Congratulations, Susan, you are five weeks pregnant. You are going to be a mother!'

Susan continued staring at the sac, fascinated. Then her eyes moved to the obstetrician's nurse, a tall, rather stern woman in her fifties, with grey hair pulled back harshly and clamped either side. The nurse was smiling, but it was a cold, formal smile, as if she knew something that Susan did not and was holding it back.

Unnerved by this, Susan looked at the obstetrician and said, 'It's all right? The baby? He – she – it's all right? It's healthy, I mean?'

'Yes, Susan, everything looks absolutely fine. But please remember it is very early, and we're only seeing the sac at this stage.' Van Rhoe gently removed the probe and handed it to the nurse. Then he peeled off his rubber gloves and went over to the sink. The nurse handed Susan a tissue. She put on her knickers and linen skirt, then followed him back into his minuscule office.

The size of the room surprised Susan: this man regularly delivered babies for the British Royal Family, the rich and famous, and yet these consulting rooms, two floors above Harley Street, were not much larger than a pair of broom cupboards.

She rather liked this modesty: it seemed to make Miles Van Rhoe more accessible, somehow more human, and it reinforced the strength of his reputation for her. He must be pretty terrific for some of his clientele to put up with this poky little place, she reckoned.

And there was a down-to-earth quality about Van Rhoe that she liked. She didn't know his age, but put him at around sixty. He had a large frame, but he wasn't tall, and a dreadful hairstyle, short and spiky as if he cut it himself. His suits were all fine quality but they looked old-fashioned and tired, as though he'd bought them when he'd first qualified and worn them ever since. He had self-assurance though, buckets of it, huge, finely manicured hands, beautiful blue eyes and a silky voice to die for. She felt comfortable with him: he exuded the endearing air of a favourite teddy bear.

Holding a fountain pen, an old Parker, he said, 'So, metallic taste from tea and coffee and stench of burning rubber. Cigarette smoke is unpleasant and the smell of alcohol makes you nauseous. Loss of appetite, apart from a craving for dry biscuits.' He jotted all this down on an index card. 'Anything else?'

'Bath Olivers,' she replied. 'They're the biscuits I crave most.'

He smiled as he wrote this down, then peered at her over the top of his half-rims. 'Pity it's not something a little less pricy.'

She grinned. A question sat in her mind, which it was getting harder and harder to ask. She had known that she was pregnant before she had come here – she had done a test that she bought from a chemist, although she hadn't told John.

She had made the decision that she was going to induce a miscarriage, and had told John last night that if she was pregnant, she wanted to terminate it. Perhaps they could go and see Bill Rolands, their doctor, who was a personal friend. John had responded indifferently and it was impossible to gauge what he felt. All Susan knew was that this baby would destroy her marriage, and she could not go through with it.

But now she felt different. There was such warmth coming from this man that sitting here in front of him, as he wrote his notes, she felt as if she had just been congratulated by a teacher on a brilliant essay, which made her want to go on pleasing him. And seeing this living thing inside her had excited her. She was feeling so proud.

It was a powerful feeling.

She hadn't expected to feel anything like this.

And couldn't ask him the question now. She had been going to ask him how many weeks she had to go in which a miscarriage could happen, but now she couldn't. The image of the sac was too strong. *Her baby was growing in it.*

Van Rhoe rummaged in a drawer and pulled out a fresh hypodermic in its wrapping. 'I'm just going to give you a little injection,' he said. 'Some vitamins that will help the development of the foetus.'

She rolled up the sleeve of her blouse, all fear of needles gone. This was for the baby. As he dabbed her upper arm with a swab, he said, 'Before you leave, I'd like you to see my secretary. We need to make a regular weekly appointment, at a time convenient for you.'

'Weekly?'

'Until we're out of the danger period.'

'How long is that?'

'The next couple of months.' He dropped the syringe into a receptacle, and Susan rolled down her sleeve; she had hardly noticed the jab.

'Do you mind if I ask you a personal question, Susan? How is your husband taking this?'

She took a moment. 'OK, I guess.' Then she blushed a little. 'I – we haven't made love, since –'

'Is that you or him?'

'I – I'm not sure. Both?'

He smiled. 'It's not an easy situation.'

'No, it's not.'

'But you're strong. You'll get through it.'

She smiled back. 'Yes.'

Van Rhoe wrote something else on the index card, then looked up again. 'How do you think he'll take this news?'

'I don't know,' Susan said.

And she didn't.

Chapter Thirty

'We got the contract!' Gareth told John. 'I mean, this is unreal, right? We've bid on ten jobs in the past month, and we've got nine of them. And we could have got the tenth if we'd wanted but we effectively turned it down. What's going on?'

John sat in the pub, sipping his beer and smoking the cigarette he'd bummed from Gareth. He'd bummed so many from his partner in the past few weeks that he kept buying new packs for him. But that was better than buying a pack for himself. As long as he was just *bumming*, it didn't feel as if he had started smoking again.

He wondered if Susan had noticed the smell of smoke on him; she must have done, he thought. In fact, thinking about it, the other evening she had told him that she didn't mind the smell of coffee any more, that it had stopped smelling like burning rubber, although it still tasted metallic; and she had said that she didn't mind the smell of cigarettes any more, either.

Had that been a barbed hint? If it had, why hadn't she just said something? That was the problem, they weren't communicating: they were like two strangers living under one roof. He knew that it was as much his fault as Susan's. Probably more. And he knew the reason.

'How do you mean, what's going on, Gareth?'

Gareth, in a red cotton jacket and baggy green shirt, gave him a weirding-out look. 'You have to admit this is spooky, right?'

John drew on his cigarette in silence. It was spooky.

'I mean, these new backers of ours, they must be impressed, right?'

Six o'clock, the pub was filling up. Someone was playing a slot machine, and kept reaching a level that set off a twangy musical tune that John found irritating. And Gareth was irritating too. And the fact that he'd been weak and had started smoking again.

But the real issue was Susan, his marriage, their life. What life? They didn't have a life any more. She was eight weeks pregnant. Just a couple more weeks and she would be out of danger of miscarrying, and the way he was feeling right now, he wanted to go home and throw the bitch downstairs and make that miscarriage happen.

He crushed out his cigarette. Gareth was talking and he wasn't listening. DigiTrak was going so incredibly that he didn't need Mr Sarotzini's money any more. Christ, if Clake had just let them hang on for another month they wouldn't have needed Sarotzini and the Vörn Bank in the first place. There were two things he wanted to happen. He wanted Susan to miscarry and he wanted to get Mr Sarotzini out of his face.

Except Mr Sarotzini wasn't around and he hadn't responded to either of the reports John had sent to the Vörn Bank. John had asked Tony Weir to find a loophole in the agreement they had made. Weir had responded that there was no problem in finding a loophole – it was illegal under British law to have a surrogate child for money. The problem would be with Mr Sarotzini, who held legal ownership of DigiTrak and the house until the baby was handed over. The deeds, shares, everything were assigned to him.

Before Susan's pregnancy had been confirmed they had talked about inducing a miscarriage. It had been Susan who had made the suggestion. But she had changed. She'd become sanctimonious about the baby and absurdly protective. Every time he tried to bring up the subject of miscarriage, she changed the conversation abruptly, or walked away.

He finished his second pint, and ordered a third. While Gareth talked enthusiastically about a new RAID server he wanted to order, and compression algorithms, John drank his beer, getting more and more angry with Susan. He finished it, told Gareth he'd see him in the morning and headed for the door.

He was going home. He was going to grab that bitch wife of his by the throat.

He was going to make her miscarry.

'"He who begins by loving Christianity better than Truth will proceed by loving his own sect or church better than Christianity, and end by loving himself better than all,"' Mr Sarotzini said to Kündz.

And Kündz, sitting in Mr Sarotzini's great office in Geneva, replied, 'Samuel Taylor Coleridge.'

And this pleased Mr Sarotzini. And then he read the list that Kündz had prepared for him. 'Archie Warren? Fergus Donleavy? Tony Weir? Just these three? Why is John Carter's name not on this danger list also?'

Kündz had to think. 'Because,' he started, and then he stopped. 'Because

160

that decision has been made,' he said, and he knew, immediately, that this was the wrong answer.

And this answer did not please Mr Sarotzini, Kündz could see that in his expression, and suddenly he was afraid. He could smell his own fear rising from his body. He could smell the leather in this room, the polish that had been applied to the wood, the chemical that had cleaned the carpet, but he could not smell Mr Sarotzini.

And this was a strange thing that had Kündz found about Mr Sarotzini: he never, ever had any smell and Kündz found this hard. He was certain it was a game Mr Sarotzini played with him, deliberately blocking his ability to smell him by putting something disabling into his mind.

Kündz had never come across a person before who had no smell. Without smell, Kündz could not read Mr Sarotzini. He was the only person Kündz had ever met whom he could not read.

Mr Sarotzini could read every cell in Kündz's body, and he could hear them. They were all speaking to him now. They were deeply afraid.

'Stefan, who made this decision?'

Kündz sensed the temperature in his body changing: for an instant it rose, then it plunged, dropping away so fast that all his hairs stiffened, turning hard as needles.

'I believed we had no other option,' Kündz said.

Mr Sarotzini, behind his desk, in his fine suit, barely moved. 'John Carter, is he special to you, Stefan?' Now he leaned forward a little. 'Tell me, Stefan, would it cause you pain to hurt Mr Carter?'

Kündz was careful. He wasn't sure of the answer Mr Sarotzini was expecting, he was trying to remember what Mr Sarotzini had taught him. It was one of the Truths, the Third, or was it the Fourth? He couldn't remember, not exactly, and he did not want the pain Mr Sarotzini would inflict if he got it wrong.

'The Fourth Truth, Stefan? "The only true pain is to hurt the thing you love"?'

Kündz answered, 'No, it would not cause me pain to hurt John Carter.' And secretly he was thinking that he would love to hurt John Carter, more than anything in the world, but he was careful to smother this thought. Mr Sarotzini could take thoughts straight from his head and read them.

And Mr Sarotzini was standing up now, walking across his office to a cabinet. Kündz knew what was inside the cabinet and he did not want this.

Mr Sarotzini swung open the teak door to reveal a large television screen. He touched a button and the screen came alive. Kündz braced

161

himself, using all the training Mr Sarotzini had given him to control his emotions, but this was still difficult.

The picture on the screen was of Claudie. She was sitting, naked, in a big wicker chair in Kündz's apartment in Zürich, and she was doing what Kündz had always loved her to do, which was to press her hand up between her legs while he was intoxicating himself on the smells of her body.

Claudie was smiling that big, sexy, provocative come-and-take-me smile. She was playful and she was pretty – but in a different way from Susan Carter. Susan had fresh, healthy, all-American outdoor looks, but Claudie was an indoor girl. Her glossy black hair was razor cut in Goth style, and her flesh was as white as death. But it was soft flesh to touch: she was slim enough to be vulnerable, but carried just a hint of voluptuousness.

Being pregnant would make Susan Carter voluptuous, he thought suddenly.

Claudie was moving that hand so slowly, gentle strokes with those long fingers, and sometimes she brought them out from inside her and sucked them, and caressed her body with them. But there was no soundtrack playing with this recording.

The sound that was coming into this room now, through the speakers on either side of the television, was live and, Kündz knew, it was coming from within this building.

The sound was Claudie screaming.

And the sound of her screaming was almost beyond imagination. The agony, the fear, the terror, the despair, the pleading it carried.

And Kündz was aware that Mr Sarotzini was watching him and he must pass this test. And this was hard, because he knew exactly what they were doing to Claudie and the thought of it churned even him up.

Claudie screamed again, and this was even worse, and then she cried out, 'No, please, oh, God, *noooooooooooooo.*'

Her voice turned to a shriek so fearful that Kündz wanted to put his fingers into his ears and turn away. But he couldn't.

He daren't.

Then Mr Sarotzini turned off the television and the speakers, and closed the cabinet door. He returned to his desk and asked Kündz, 'Do you love Susan Carter enough to feel pain if you hurt her?'

For the first time in her life, Susan felt she was doing something for herself, and not for someone else. She was doing it because she *wanted* to do it, and it was elating.

Standing on top of the step-ladder in the freshly painted front spare bedroom that overlooked the street, with two picture nails gripped in her lips and a hammer in her hand, she felt deeply happy and content. Maybe it was the hormone change in her body, or just the excitement she had felt this afternoon when Miles Van Rhoe had put the ultrasound scanner on her abdomen and let her listen to her baby's heartbeat.

If John would just calm down about this whole thing, everything would be perfect. It wasn't a big deal having this baby, it really wasn't, and she was doing it for them both, for their marriage, for everything. And even though this wasn't their child, it was a human being, it had as much right to her love and care as if it were their child. She owed it that much and she was determined to give it that much. And it was an adventure. And, most important of all, in a little more than seven months it would be over. It was just a matter of getting John to see it that way.

And she would. She had experienced his stubbornness before: it was like a defence mechanism for him, a toughness he had developed to shield him from the horrors of his wretched childhood. Confrontation never worked so she just had to be patient, take it a day at a time, be nice to him, swallow the insults, slowly win him round.

She hammered one nail into the wall, fixing the picture hook on the pencilled cross she had marked, and at that moment the door crashed open behind her. As she turned round in shock, the remaining nail she had been holding in her mouth pinged onto the bare floorboards.

John was standing in the doorway. His expression frightened her. She could smell the waft of alcohol and cigarette smoke and he seemed to be having difficulty in holding himself steady and focusing. He must have driven home in this state, she thought with horror. This wasn't the John Carter she married, this wasn't her rock, she didn't know this man.

'Hi, hon,' she said, nervously, because almost anything she said these days seemed to make him fly off the handle.

He just kept staring at her, and the way he was looking at her unnerved her. There seemed – and she hoped she was imagining it – to be pure hatred in his face.

John was staring at a bitch stranger in his house. He was thinking that if he pushed this ladder over, right now, she'd fall to the ground, which might make her miscarry. It would be easy, he thought. She was balanced precariously on the top step, hammer in her hand, picture hook hanging

163

lopsided from only one nail on the wall. He could walk over there, blunder into the ladder, she wouldn't realise it had been deliberate.

But what if she broke her arm instead? Or her neck?

And then as she turned her head, instead of a stranger, John saw his wife standing at the top of that step-ladder, he saw Susan, and she looked so radiantly happy. She was in this home that she loved, and she was doing what she liked to do, decorating, making this place into the dream they both had.

He took a deep breath, swallowed down the hatred that had been growing inside him these past weeks, remembered.

It's only for seven months, for Chrissake.

And then it will be over.

Nine months, it was nothing, it was already eight weeks now, just seven months to go, they could handle this, they could keep the lid on this cauldron of emotions, fuck Sarotzini, fuck everybody.

'How was your day?' he asked.

'I went to Miles Van Rhoe – another scan.' Uncertain about his mood, she decided not to tell him that she had listened to the baby's heartbeat. 'I came home afterwards to work on Fergus's manuscript. Thought I'd get a few pictures up in here – thought I'd put up that one of the Suffolk harbour – the one you've never been crazy about. It would look OK in here, don't you think?'

'Sure. Do I get a kiss?'

Sensing his lightening mood, she blew him a teasing one. 'Pass me that nail I just dropped, then I'll give you a great big one!'

John knelt, found the nail and she hammered it in. Then he passed her up the picture, a rather uninspired sunset behind a fishing port, which they'd bought some years back in a car-boot sale.

'Fancy a movie? There's several things on I want to see.'

'If you like.' She didn't sound enthusiastic.

'No?'

'It's just that it's such a gorgeous evening and there won't be many more this year when it's warm enough to sit out. Why don't we have a barbecue? We haven't for weeks.'

John thought about it and she was right. It was the third week of September; the summer had slipped past. 'Weather's been shitty,' he said. 'That's why we haven't.'

But they both knew it had been a glorious few weeks, just the last couple of days it had rained, that was all. It was something else that had been shitty.

Susan hung the picture, straightened it, and John steadied the ladder as she came down, then put his arms around her and held her. She nestled into him, pressed her face to his shoulder, their cheeks touching. John smelled her hair, the sweet coconut scent of her shampoo which he liked.

'I love you,' he said.

The alcohol and the smoke gave him a manly smell. When they had first gone out, he always smelled of smoke and she'd liked that because it reminded her of her father, who had smoked throughout her childhood. 'And I love you,' she replied. 'More than anything in the world.'

Instead of having a barbecue, they went to bed and made love. A few hours later, John woke up and heard the flick of a sheet of paper as Susan read her way through further pages of Fergus Donleavy's rewrite, and he had a close-up view of her left breast. He realised that her breasts had become bigger recently, and that was a turn-on.

He gently traced the contour with his finger, stopping to give the nipple a circular stroke, and Susan wriggled, giving a tiny murmur of pleasure.

'Hungry?' she asked.

'Uh-huh. What do you fancy?'

'I don't mind, something light. Scrambled eggs?'

'Sure. I'll make it.' John kissed her and got out of bed.

'God, you've got a hard-on *again*!' she said.

He grinned. 'Yup, well that's a problem I've always had with you.' Then he pulled a towel around his waist and padded downstairs to the kitchen.

Tonight at any rate, he thought, they had their life back.

Chapter Thirty-one

Ten weeks. And now it had been pointed out to her, there was no mistaking it. Even on this fuzzy grey and white screen Susan could see it clearly. She could see the arms, the legs, she could even, when Van Rhoe indicated, make out a foot.

This is incredible, she thought, this baby, alive, inside me.

A leg moved, then the other, and she wanted to keep on watching, but Van Rhoe removed the probe and she was left with a whiteout on the screen.

The obstetrician looked down at her and smiled. 'I can confirm viability, Susan. Everything looks normal, the baby is healthy, and the results of the mucal thickness scan are fine, we have no worry about Down's syndrome. And your worst danger period for miscarriage is now past.'

'Were you worried before about Down's Syndrome?' she asked, suspicious of his concern.

He reassured her silkily. 'No, but it was too soon to carry out the examination then. This Down's syndrome test is routine, Susan, and you're well below the risk age.'

She knew a little about Down's syndrome: older parents had a higher risk of producing a baby with it, and she wondered if that meant just the mother or included the father. Suddenly she shuddered, and Van Rhoe looked at her, concerned.

'Are you all right, Susan?'

She nodded. It had been a sudden feeling of revulsion that it was Mr Sarotzini's baby and not John's that she had been looking at; that a part of Mr Sarotzini was growing inside her. It was a feeling that kept returning. Everything would be fine for a few days, and then this sudden horror came back that she was carrying another man's child.

But it's not just Mr Sarotzini's baby, this is my baby also, she reminded herself, reassured herself.

And now she was at the point-of-no-return. Her body had not rejected the baby and now it was only her mind that could. Abortion was still an option, but not one she was even remotely considering. The image of the screen replayed in her mind. Those legs, the way they moved. That was – just so – *incredible*.

'Could I listen to the heartbeat again?' she asked.

'Of course, Susan.' He placed the scanner on her abdomen, moving it around until it picked up the sound, and Susan lay still for some moments, entranced by the steady boof-boof-boof.

Then Miles Van Rhoe gently lifted her legs from the stirrups and handed her a paper towel. As she stood up she felt a power that she had never felt before. Even the frosty nurse was smiling.

'Is it a boy or girl?' she asked, and immediately noticed the briefest glance between Van Rhoe and his nurse – or had she imagined it? Did they know something?

'Sixteen weeks is the earliest we can tell,' the obstetrician said. 'Are you sure you would like to know the sex in advance, Susan? Most mothers don't want to.'

'I'm not sure,' she said, fretting about the glance between them that she had seen. What did it mean?

'Let's deal with the question of sex when we come to it,' he said. 'What I say to my patients is, all that matters is the health of the baby. And if you want your baby to be really healthy you must love it with all your heart while it's still in the womb. Do you love your baby with all your heart?'

'Yes.'

He smiled warmly. 'Good, then it's going to be a healthy baby.'

Susan looked up at the nurse, who was beaming at her. So was Van Rhoe, and the warmth was infectious. She was starting to forget the exchange of glances that she'd seen – convincing herself she'd imagined it – and was getting caught up in the excitement. She felt so happy that she wanted to kiss Miles Van Rhoe, and nearly did.

She followed him skittishly and sat down in front of his desk.

She was thinking so much about those legs moving on the scan that she found it hard to concentrate on what Van Rhoe was saying, and he had to repeat himself. He was giving her advice about exercise, not lifting things, rest, diet. They had been through most of this stuff before, but she could see why he was so well thought of: he was so thorough, he was treating her as if this was his own baby.

And he was setting off a chain of thoughts in her mind. Ante-natal classes. People at the office like Kate Fox – especially Kate – were going to think it strange if she didn't make preparations for the baby after it was born. She would have to keep up some sort of pretence. People who were having babies bought clothes, got the room ready.

Miles Van Rhoe had asked a question and she'd missed it. She gave him a blank look and said, 'Sorry, I was somewhere else.'

'Your husband?' he asked again. She knew this question: he asked it every week without fail. 'How is he taking all this now?'

'Fine,' she said. 'Better. Much better now.' She smiled. 'I think he's getting used to the idea.'

The obstetrician folded his massive hands. 'This can't be easy for him. I sympathise.'

'It's not easy for either of us.'

He held her with his huge eyes and she wasn't sure how to read his expression. She thought she saw the tiniest hint of mockery, and realised he'd picked up on the elation she was feeling.

His expression told her that he thought she was secretly enjoying this, and she wanted to tell him that he was wrong, that this was a waking nightmare, and if she had the chance over again she would have said no.

But she didn't tell him this. Because, deep inside, she was aching with happiness.

Kündz could hardly believe his eyes, but he had no choice. It was there, it had happened. Susan's face had a green hue, the night vision lens did that. He was looking at her tight buttocks now – they hadn't fattened out, none of her had, she didn't look pregnant at all.

The bedclothes were off, she was spread-eagled across John and she had taken him in her mouth. He was clawing at the sheets.

This was tough to watch.

Now she was moving around, so agile, like a horizontal ballerina, she was sliding across his body and she swung her legs over him, and now she was sitting astride him. Kündz could see her back arched as she guided him inside her, heard her let out a tiny cry, but it wasn't pain, it was just a murmur, she was smiling.

And this was hurting Kündz so much.

And he saw John Carter's face, green too, with a remote expression. He was somewhere else: his penis was inside Susan – but his mind?

Where is your mind, John Carter?

Kündz fought the anger that was swelling so big inside him it was hard to contain it. *You are doing this to my woman, but your mind is somewhere else – on another woman? Who is she, John Carter?*

One day you will tell me.

One day you will scream out her name for me.

Kündz could not watch this much longer. Susan's ginger green hair tossing and shaking, those breasts, flashes of milky whiteness breaking out of the green, and the nipples, brilliant deep crimson nipples, he wanted to touch those breasts so badly. And he tried to imagine that what Susan and John were doing was not real, just a movie on television, that was all.

Kündz now remembered the Sixth Truth that Mr Sarotzini had taught him, and it was this: 'Reality is what you believe it to be.'

This helped him, but not totally. For the Truths could not help you totally until you understood them totally, and he knew, Mr Sarotzini had told him this, that his understanding was a long way from complete.

And now, was Susan having an orgasm or was she faking it?

He stopped the tape and the rage that was like a crazed animal trying to tear its way out of him subsided. He switched to channel 9, the bedroom, in real time, seeing what was there now, at this moment, and that made him feel better.

He watched John reading an Internet magazine. Susan was reading a manuscript. She wouldn't let John make love to her tonight, she told him she was tired, and that she had to finish this manuscript by tomorrow. Kündz was proud of her: this made him so happy he could almost forgive her for the one slip she had made two weeks ago.

But not John Carter. He could not forgive John Carter. John must be purified.

And Mr Sarotzini had promised him this.

John turned a page of his magazine, then another. Then he gazed up at the ceiling.

Kündz looked straight into his eyes.

And John, lying in bed in his dressing gown, had this strange feeling that he was being watched. He wasn't sure why, but it was making him uncomfortable.

He glanced at Susan, but she was concentrating on her manuscript. He slipped out of bed, walked over to the window, peered through the curtains. He could see the street lights on the far side of the park, the shadowy outlines of bushes and trees, his own reflection in the glass pane.

He turned, looked up at the ceiling, then around at the walls.

'What's the matter, hon?' Susan said.

'I thought I heard something,' It was better, John thought than telling her he was being watched by something invisible.

He stood still and they both listened. 'Must've imagined it,' he said.

169

Then Susan said, 'Oh, I meant to tell you, I heard something up in the loft earlier. I think we have mice, or,' she wrinkled her face, 'rats.'

John shrugged. 'Could be a bird.'

'Maybe we should put some mousetraps up.'

'I'll do it at the weekend,' John said. 'Actually, I've been meaning to have a good root around up there – haven't really checked out the loft. Never know, there might be some old masters hidden away up there.'

Susan grinned. 'Sure – and the Holy Grail at the bottom of a tea chest.'

Kündz switched off, leaving the Carters' house on the default Voice Activated record setting, and picked up the novel by Marcel Proust he was half-way through. John Carter could root around in his loft to his heart's content. He double checked that the tape machine was on the right setting, then settled down.

It was not until the next morning, when the computer scanned the tape for anything that might have happened after he had stopped listening, that Kündz heard Susan Carter's terrible scream.

Chapter Thirty-two

In the darkness the solitary candle guttered, tossing a ribbon of light across the old man's face.

The curtains were drawn against the night outside, but it made no difference to the old man, with his sightless eyes, who lay motionless in his bed. For him, darkness was a constant and had been so for over a decade now. It was not important, he had seen enough.

The light that did matter still burned brightly inside his head, behind the cruel, lined carapace of his face. It was fuelled by the knowledge he had retained, and to which he had unfettered access. There were perhaps five thousand books lining the walls of this room, and this man could recite, at will, any line from any page, from any book, and from thousands more books beyond these.

And he knew, from the change of smell, from the change of the rhythm of the air in here, that someone had entered the room, and he had identified this person before he had even closed the door behind him. He greeted his visitor good evening, quietly, in a language that less than a thousand people in the world could speak.

And Mr Sarotzini responded in this same language as he approached the bed, returning the greeting. He inclined his head out of respect to the man, even though he could not see. And he remained standing. Not even Mr Sarotzini was permitted to sit in this room.

We are all afraid of something. This was the Ninth Truth, and Mr Sarotzini knew it. He had just one fear. And that was this man lying before him in this room that smelt of old leather and decaying paper.

'You have news?' the man asked.

'Ten weeks. The danger of miscarriage is nearly behind us. Everything is well.' There was more that he could have told him, but he did not.

'And do we know the sex?'

'No, it is too soon.'

The man smiled, as if enjoying a cruel, private joke. 'It will be a girl. For

171

two thousand years they have been waiting for a boy and we are giving them a girl.'

'You are certain it is a girl?' Mr Sarotzini asked.

'I *know*.'

'Of course,' Mr Sarotzini demurred, smarting from the reply that was delivered like a slap. He watched the ribbon of light, trailing backwards and forwards across the old man's face. This candle provided enough light for visitors to see him, and its scant beam was gentle on his frail skin. The old man had once been striking-looking, with the proud, aristocratic features of Eastern Europe, but now, blotched by liver spots and ravaged by skin tumours, only his silhouette was still proud. And even though he was deeply afraid of this man, the tenderness Mr Sarotzini felt towards him remained undimmed, and if anything, grew stronger with every passing year.

'When will you come again?'

'Soon, when I have more news.'

'And you are confident?'

'Yes, I am confident. I am very confident.'

It was the answer the old man wished to hear.

Miles Van Rhoe sounded upset. 'Why didn't you phone me about this immediately it happened?'

Kate Fox barged into Susan's office and stood in front of her desk, holding what looked like a copy-edited typescript bound with rubber bands. She was mouthing a question, and Susan didn't have a clue what she was saying. All she could think was that she did not want Kate in this room while she was having this conversation.

'Can you hold?' she asked Van Rhoe, then covering the mouthpiece, told Kate she'd come and see her in a moment. When her colleague had left the office and closed the door, Susan lifted her hand from the mouthpiece and apologised to the obstetrician. 'I didn't phone because it was eleven o'clock at night. And because it was just this one sudden sharp pain and then it stopped. I figured maybe it was some muscle twinging, some after-effect from that probe when you were examining me yesterday.'

'You mustn't try to diagnose yourself, Susan, and *please*, the time of day is not important. You have all my phone numbers. I *want* you to phone me at eleven o'clock at night, or at three in the morning, or five. The only thing that can make me upset is you *not* phoning me at eleven at night, or three in the morning. We're a team, you and I, we are working together on this, and we're going the distance together. You must never do this again. I want you to promise me that.'

Susan mumbled an apology.

'I want to hear it, Susan. I want you to say loud and clear to me now, "Mr Van Rhoe, any time I have any pain, or any abnormality, or even just any concern, however tiny, however trivial, I will call you, at eleven o'clock at night, or three o'clock in the morning, or five o'clock in the morning". Come on, say it!'

Susan said it, then giggled when she had finished. Her other line was flashing but she ignored it.

'OK?' Van Rhoe said. 'We understand each other a little better now?'

'Sure.'

'And you've had no more pain since?'

'No.'

'No bleeding?'

'None.'

'And absolutely no more pain? Discomfort?'

'No.'

'Nothing at all? Not the slightest twinge?'

'Nothing.'

Well, almost nothing, she was lying now, because she did not have time to visit Van Rhoe now. There was still a little pain, but nothing like that sharp twinge last night that had made her scream out.

And she wasn't worried – Van Rhoe had done the scan yesterday morning and said everything was fine. If there had been anything wrong, he would have told her, surely?

'Our next appointment is Wednesday,' Van Rhoe said. 'And today is Friday. I don't like the sound of this, Susan. I think you'd better come over and I'll take a quick look.'

She was regretting having rung him. 'I have to go into a meeting.'

'Susan, this baby is more important than any meeting.'

The rebuke made her feel guilty. 'I know.'

'I insist you come. Please get in a taxi and come straight over. I'll see you right away and you'll be back in your office within half an hour.'

Susan hung up, gulped a mouthful of mineral water and told Kate she'd be back in half an hour. But she wouldn't. She knew that, with the traffic, it would be an hour at least, probably more.

And then, as she reached the door, her secretary buzzed to tell her that John was on the line.

'Take a message,' she said.

'He just wants to know how you are.'

'I'm fine,' she snapped. 'Tell him I've never been more fine in my goddamn life.'

John had heard that chocolate was the thing for mice, not cheese. He knelt in the loft, pushed a tiny piece onto the spike, set the spring of the crude trap, and laid it on the orange insulation, alongside a joist. There was a steady drip … drip … drip … from the feeder pipe in the water tank just beside him.

He moved away from the mousetrap, picking out the joists and low beams with the flashlight as he headed into the darkness beyond the range of the bulb above the hatch, methodically exploring each of the roof spaces, looking for a Rembrandt the previous owners might have left behind. But he had no luck: they hadn't left *anything*.

A sound close by startled him and he stiffened. Then he heard it again: it was nothing, just a bird in the eaves. He eased past a chimney breast and frowned as he noticed a crack of daylight ahead.

As he investigated it, he saw that the roofing felt in this space looked much newer than that in the rest of the loft, and he wondered why – maybe the previous owners had had a problem with this part of the roof? If they had, they hadn't fixed it well, because there seemed to be a tile missing.

He finished his inspection then climbed down the ladder, closing the hatch behind him.

It was a fine Saturday afternoon, and Susan was out in the garden. She doubted that Miles Van Rhoe would have approved of what she was doing, which was raking up the leaves that had begun to fall on the lawn. She was also raking up two McDonalds cartons, a half-eaten burger, a couple of plastic cups and a McDonalds carrier bag that some asshole had thrown over the fence from the park during the night.

The beech hedge had started showing a few gold leaves, and the trees in the park were beginning to turn. She was looking forward to the fall: it was going to be beautiful here in the house, watching the changing colours of the trees and bushes. That was one thing she loved about England, the intensity of the seasons that she had never experienced in LA.

She knelt down to scoop up the small pile of leaves and litter and, with no warning, the pain happened again. It felt as though a wire was being ripped straight through her insides and she cried out, dropping to her knees, pressing her hands to her abdomen, closing her eyes.

I'm going to lose the baby.

'Susan? Darling?' John was at her side. He was staring at her in alarm. She looked up at him, her eyes unnaturally wide, her pupils dilated, her complexion waxy. He put his hand on her forehead, which felt clammy.

She held her breath, waiting for the pain to strike again. She had to be ready for it.

'Susan?'

She heard him but did not respond.

'Darling?'

'I'm OK.' She held her breath again.

After some moments John eased her to her feet and steered her into a garden chair.

'I'm OK,' she said again.

He was looking at her with deep concern. 'What's causing this?'

'A nerve. Or something,' she said, in a near gasp. 'Or a pulled muscle. Cramps. Wind. Maybe I'm a little constipated, I don't know.'

'Did Van Rhoe say you might get more pain?'

'He. He said. Might.'

'Cramp?'

She nodded. Van Rhoe had assured her that nothing was wrong, that it was probably cramp, and he'd given her some capsules to take against it. Some vitamin supplement – he seemed to be big into those. She looked at John's anxious face, then up at the trees. She was starting to feel better now: the pain had gone as fast as it had come.

John's mention of Van Rhoe's name had reminded Susan that when she had rung the obstetrician yesterday morning he had not seemed as surprised about the pain as she'd thought he might. It was almost as if he had been expecting it. But then, of course, he would have been, she realised. He must get hundreds of calls every day from patients with all the usual complaints.

'Still got the pain?' John asked, tenderly.

'No, it's gone.'

'We'd better ring him.'

She shook her head. 'No, hon, it's OK.' She smiled, shakily. 'How did you get on in the loft? Did you set the traps?'

'You sure you're OK?'

'I'm OK. Maybe I shouldn't have raked the leaves. He told me not to do any heavy work.'

'Yup, well, from now on you're obeying your doctor's orders.'

She nodded. Then they were both distracted by the old boy next door;

recently he had been getting worse and they could hear him shouting urgently to his wife that he'd just peed in his pants.

Susan grinned. 'At least I'm not as bad as him.'

'Yet.'

'Thanks a lot.'

John kissed her. Then he asked, 'Darling, that survey we had done – any idea where it is?'

'In the file you have on the house – it's in one of those piles on the floor in your den. Why?'

John walked a few paces backwards, trying to spot the section with the missing tile. 'It had a report on the roof.'

'Problem?'

He shook his head. 'Got a tile off, that's all.'

'Harry, the painter, I think he knows someone, a handyman. Want me to call him?'

'I think you should have a rest.' His eyes shifted back to the roof. John was not an expert on roofs but something was bothering him about that loft. Something was not right.

But he had no idea what.

Chapter Thirty-three

Archie Warren sat at his desk in the dealing room of Loeb-Goldsmid-Saxon, twenty storeys up in the City of London. It wasn't much of a desk. It was about the size of a fold-down table on the back of an airline seat, and had leg room to match. All it contained was a computer screen, keyboard, two telephones, an ashtray, a packet of cigarettes, a gold Dunhill lighter and a paper cup of coffee.

Like all the other sixty traders in this room, Archie had a phone jammed to each ear, while his fingers hammered the keyboard. He dealt in Japanese convertible bonds and warrants, buying and selling them for his clients, which were companies, banks, pension funds, and a handful of seriously rich individuals.

It was six fifteen a.m. Archie had been at his desk for an hour and ten minutes and had smoked two cigarettes. Smoking was banned but Archie didn't give a shit, and neither did Oliver Walton next to him, or half the other people in this room who slugged out their working week on the stalks of their nerves. On a quiet day Archie turned over one hundred million dollars worth of business.

There were six traders in Archie's section; the company had two thousand employees world-wide, but Archie and his colleagues had produced 40 per cent of the company's entire profit for the past three years. No one was telling Archie he couldn't smoke here.

Names of clients chased each other down his screen, Morgan Grenfell, Scottish Widows, Newton's, Nomura, Sumitomo Trust, Julius Baer, State Street, Soros. A voice bellowed down the squawk box from Tokyo: 'Yamaichi are a buyer of ten million dollars of Sumitomo bank convertibles at $99^1/_2$ or better.'

As the Tokyo market closed, Archie lit his third cigarette and did a quick audit of his positions in preparation for the day ahead in London. He did a flick through the overnight trades coming in from Japan, and as he did so, noticed a trade for five million dollars in a little traded issue, and this immediately drew his attention. The name of the client looked familiar and he wasn't sure why. The Vörn Bank. He saw that the dealer had been Oliver Walton.

Vörn Bank. Why did that name ring a bell? Archie yawned. Maybe if he hadn't drunk so much port last night he'd have a few more brain cells to swing together today. He turned to his colleague. 'Hey, Ollie, the Vörn Bank. Who are they?'

'Switzerland,' Walton said. 'Private bank. Private *private.*'

Archie knew what that meant. 'Serious players?'

'Big time.'

Archie leant back in his chair and sucked at his cigarette, thinking hard. Then he connected.

John was sitting in his new BMW. He'd decided to buy it – the business was going so well it could easily afford it, and he did not imagine Mr Sarotzini would be concerned by this one extravagance.

In almost five months he'd received just a brief fortnightly phone call from the banker. Mr Sarotzini wanted a bulletin on Susan and barely commented on John's regular reports on DigiTrak, other than to say it all looked satisfactory.

There had been no mention of his promises to take Susan out, and he had not once called her. Perhaps, John wondered, he thought she might find it awkward. He sensed that Susan was disappointed not to have heard anything.

And maybe Mr Sarotzini was right, because he and Susan seemed to be coping by not talking about it. They were five months into it now, only four or so to go, and they were handling it, they were keeping the lid on the emotional cauldron, and he was proud of Susan's stoicism.

It was going to work out fine. They had the business and the house and this new car. He'd offered to buy Susan a new car too, but she was quite happy with her battered Peugeot. He'd bought himself the convertible he'd been hankering after, dark metallic blue with cream-leather interior, air con and all the toys – he was playing with some of the toys now as he sat in the early-morning jam on the Albert Bridge. Seven fifteen was early for a hold-up here: roadworks were causing the problem.

There was so much business coming in at DigiTrak that for the past couple of months he'd been having to go in this early just to cope with the workload. Gareth was close to a nervous breakdown.

John hit the selector on the CD and sent Phil Collins's voice soaring around the car. He'd recently seen a programme on television that said if you played rock music it got your brain going, so he'd taken to playing it on his way into the office each morning. After a few moments he tuned his brain into the prospect of Christmas, which was only three weeks away. Where to spend it? What to get Susan? The usual problems. Except worse than usual.

He'd like to have gone skiing, as they had in previous years. Archie had suggested he and Susan join him and Pila, in Switzerland, but skiing wasn't an option with Susan's condition. And, anyway, she didn't want to travel. Miles Van Rhoe wanted her close to hand. And maybe that was sensible. John was worried about her; she was still getting those terrible pains. Originally Van Rhoe had insisted they were cramp, but a couple of weeks back he'd diagnosed an ovarian cyst. He said it was nothing to worry about, but he hadn't seen Susan have an attack of pain.

Susan insisted that Van Rhoe was the best obstetrician in Britain but John had doubts about the man. It seemed strange to him that one day the pains were from cramp, the next, a cyst. Had Van Rhoe failed to spot the cyst before?

But it wasn't just the pains, it was . . . His thoughts were interrupted by his mobile phone.

'We squashing tomorrow?' Archie asked.

'Yup – booked the court.'

'Just found out something interesting. This bank of yours, the one that's backing you, it's called the *Vörn* Bank?'

'Yup.'

'I just discovered they're clients of our firm. How's that for a coincidence?'

John thought about this. 'How come you didn't find that out before?'

'They've only been clients for a couple of months.'

'What do you know about them?'

'What do you *want* to know about them?'

'I don't know, it's not so important now. I originally wanted to check them out before we climbed into bed with them.'

'And now you've been shagged by them without a condom so it's a bit late, I guess.'

'Maybe you could use a better metaphor.'

'Uh?' Archie knew nothing about that part of the deal.

Suddenly the line was breaking up and it was hard to hear him. 'Nothing, it's OK.'

'Hey.' Then John didn't catch the next word. All he caught through the crumbling line was, '... movement. Gotta ...' Then 'Eight. 'Bye.'

The traffic moved and John dialled Susan. She wouldn't have left yet, she didn't usually leave for the office until shortly before nine.

'Hi,' she answered, sounding surprised and pleased to hear him.

'Listen,' John said. 'I just had an idea about Christmas. I know the Harrisons have invited us, but I don't want to have to spend it with their brats. How about just the two of us going to a hotel in England? A nice country-house hotel, somewhere close to London.'

Susan was silent, then she said, 'Hon, I had this thought. Why don't we have a real family Christmas at home? Mom and Dad don't have any plans – why don't we bring them over as a treat, a present?'

John's heart sank. And then it rotated sharply when Susan added: 'I thought, you know, with the baby, Mom could help out.'

'Uh?'

'She might get a real bang out of the idea that she's – she's going to be a grandmother. Could be kind of useful to have her stay for a month or two after the baby's born.'

John didn't notice that the traffic lights at the end of the bridge had changed to red, and jammed on his brakes far too late. The BMW howled to a stop almost half-way into the junction. Horns blared and lights flashed at him but he hardly noticed. All he could think about was what Susan had just said. 'Susan, *what* do you mean?'

'Well, you know, women often have their mothers come stay, look after the baby, because they've done it before, they know what –'

John raised his voice. 'Susan, we're not keeping the baby! Day one, the day it's born, Mr Sarotzini takes it. For God's sake, don't start getting your mother involved, this is just going to make it worse for you – us.'

There was a silence. John waited a moment, cars still hooting at him, drivers gesticulating angrily as they wove their vehicles around him. Then he checked that the line hadn't disconnected. 'Susan?' he said. 'Hallo?'

He heard a sniff. Then another sniff. She was crying.

Chapter Thirty-four

Susan took a bus and then the tube to work. There were no parking spaces at Magellan Lowry and, in any case, she didn't mind the journey, which took close to an hour each way, as it gave her time to read.

But this morning, sitting upstairs on the double-decker bus, she gloomily watched the rain sliding down the windows, unable to concentrate on the manuscript she was trying to finish, which was yet another new theory on how the Egyptian pyramids had been built. It would interest Fergus Donleavy, she thought, because the author claimed to have definitive proof that the pyramids had been built on the instructions of aliens.

Her emotions were in turmoil and she was feeling very tired. Housework was exhausting her, and she'd stuck an ad for a daily help in the local newsagents' window. So far she'd had no response.

God, it was only Monday, a whole week's work to get through, and all she wanted was to go home, curl up and sleep. She'd woken with a dull ache in her abdomen, which was new, and she was afraid that it was going to turn into one of the ghastly sharp pains again. She was putting on weight now, which she was not happy about – although John liked her enlarged breasts – and the bump was just starting to show. And she was going through a phase of craving dark, bitter chocolate. She took a bar out of her handbag now, broke off a square and slipped it into her mouth, sucking it, resisting the temptation to bite, to make it last longer.

They were having a big supper party at home on Saturday and she wished she could cancel it – although it had been her idea in the first place. She was determined for life to go on as normal and not be a wimp to her pregnancy – surely all women went though this pain and tiredness? – and, besides, they hadn't yet had a house-warming party.

She pulled her battered Filofax out of her handbag and looked through the checklist. John had bought her a Psion electronic organiser for her birthday last year; she had almost got the hang of it but still preferred the

181

familiarity of her old leather-bound friend. They'd invited fifty people, a dozen of whom couldn't come, which left them to cater for either thirty-six or thirty-eight plus themselves – they were still waiting to hear from Harvey Addison and his wife. Susan had told John she thought it rude of the obstetrician to leave it so late, and John had promised to call him this morning.

She went through her checklist. The waitresses were confirmed: the owner of the Thai restaurant was organising them and the food – lemon grass chicken and Thai vegetable curry. The drink, red and white wine plus Australian fizz, was being delivered on Friday morning from Bottoms Up, on sale or return, and they were lending the glasses.

They'd debated about whether to have a disco and dancing. Susan was for it but John was against: half the people coming were to do with his business and he had said he wanted it to be a networking evening. To compensate she had bought several hundred poppers, streamers, blowers, silly hats, as well as boxes of crackers.

The tough thing was going to be everyone at the party congratulating her on being pregnant and asking when the baby was due.

She flicked a few pages of her Filofax and glanced down the Christmas card list. She'd already mailed off the ones to the US, with a specially large one for Casey, as the last postal dates had come and gone, and she should complete the English ones this week. Turning to her Christmas presents page, she made a mental note that she should do the tradesmen's tips next week.

Then she looked at the list of presents for John. Three books that he wanted. A wild waistcoat to go under his tuxedo. A Victorian bronze horse statuette she'd bought in the antique shop near the Thai restaurant, and a golf gizmo she'd ordered from the Innovations catalogue, which hadn't yet arrived – a kit for making a lost ball give off a bleep. John would be upset if there wasn't at least one gizmo in his stocking.

She would send a huge bouquet of flowers to Casey, and as for her parents – well, that would depend on whether or not they came over. If they didn't she'd buy them a treat, maybe a weekend at Caesar's at Vegas.

And then, as if reminding her that there was someone else who should not be left off the Christmas-present list, she felt a light stroking inside her. This had only started happening a few days ago and it was an incredible sensation.

She put her arms protectively around her abdomen. 'Hi, Bump,' she whispered. She had started calling the baby Bump because she did not want to think about a real name. John had told her that if they gave it a name – Alice or Tom or Nicholas or whatever – they might start getting too attached. 'This is your first Christmas, Bump. How do you feel about it? Have you written out your list for Santa yet?'

Mr Sarotzini had not been in touch with her since that morning he had come into her room at the clinic after the operation. She had told John that she didn't mind, that it made things easier, but deep down she did. She was hurt because it made everything seem even more clinical and businesslike than it need be.

What was going to happen to Bump?

What kind of life was Bump going to have with Mr Sarotzini? What kind of parent would an elderly man make? And what about Mrs Sarotzini? She'd had cancer, which was why she couldn't have children, according to Mr Sarotzini. Was she sick now? Or a glamorous international jet-setting clothes-horse, who didn't have time to have babies, found it easier for other people to have them for her? Like those women who insisted on having Caesareans so their vaginas didn't get stretched? Sure Mr Sarotzini could afford anything – but was that going to be enough? Was Bump going to be stuck in a nursery in some remote Swiss mansion, to be wheeled out and shown to his parents once a day – a trophy child?

As if echoing her concerns, Bump stroked her again.

The bus was slowing for a stop. It seemed fuller than usual today – people going into town for their Christmas shopping, she guessed. A heavily pregnant woman began walking down from the front of the bus. Susan caught her eye, giving her a *me-too* smile, with which the woman failed to connect.

Suddenly, before she realised it, Susan's eyes were watering with the terrible homesickness she'd felt earlier when John had rung.

However much her mother and father had failed in their acting careers, they had still been good parents to herself and Casey – in as much as any child could judge these things. They had always been there for her when she'd needed them, home had always been a welcoming place, and they'd never grown bitter over either the failure of their careers, or the tragedy of Casey. Susan knew they would love to become grandparents, and she remembered how disappointed they had been when she had told them, soon after getting married, that she and John did not intend to have a family.

Now she was pregnant and she wanted to share something of this with them. She wanted to see the delight it would bring to their faces, wanted to experience the sensation of being with them and sharing this, this – this what?

Joy?

Or, as John had said, would it be cruel to do this to them? To raise their hopes and then have to tell them the baby was gone, dead, stillborn? Was John right that it was best to keep it quiet, as far as they were concerned?

She couldn't do that. What if they found out from someone that she was pregnant? Or had been pregnant and hadn't told them? That would be much worse, surely.

Why, she wondered, had she made that remark to John about her mother staying on in England to look after the baby? It had just come out so naturally, as if she really believed that was going to happen.

She shook her head. I really am in a bad state, she thought.

Shortly before eleven that morning, Susan was typing a rejection letter to a promising writer from the slush pile. The book, on case studies of people driven by their genes to commit crime, had had good readers' reports and she had liked the young writer's style. But the board had felt the book, clearly a modified PhD thesis, too scientific for a broad readership.

She was trying to find a way to let the writer down gently by encouraging him to find a way to rewrite the book more commercially, when her phone intercom rang. It was her secretary, telling her she had a Mr Sarotzini on the line.

Susan's brain went into tilt. Weird, she thought, that he had been on her mind only an hour or so earlier this morning. 'I'll be with him in a moment,' she said, and released the button, feeling, suddenly, like a bag of jelly.

Absurdly, she ran her fingers through her hair, tidying it, tossed some away from her forehead, then looked behind her to make sure her door was shut. Then she pressed the button again. 'Put him through, Hermione.'

A moment later she heard his unmistakable voice, pleasant, courteous, a little more formal than before, a little stiffer.

'Good morning, Susan,' he said. 'I thought I should enquire how you were. And, of course, the baby.'

'We're both fine, thank you,' Susan said, almost blurting the words, feeling breathless. 'How are you?'

'Oh, yes, I am well, thank you.'

There was a silence in which Susan flailed around for something to say. There were a million questions she had been wanting to ask him when they next spoke, but all of them eluded her. Finally she came up with: 'And your wife, how is she?'

Mr Sarotzini seemed to hesitate, then replied, 'Yes, thank you, she is well also.' There was another silence. He said, 'You must forgive me for not having been in touch sooner. I am aware of promises I made to you about concerts and the opera and art galleries, but I have been detained by business activities. I wondered, perhaps, if tomorrow or Wednesday you were free for lunch, and to come and see a remarkable collection of Impressionist paintings. I recall from our discussions that you care for the Impressionist school very much.'

Tomorrow was her secretary's birthday and she and Kate Fox had promised to take her out to lunch. 'Wednesday would be good,' she said.

'Perfect, it would suit me better also. I will collect you at twelve forty-five.'

Chapter Thirty-five

During the regular Wednesday morning editorial meeting Susan was tense and finding it hard to concentrate. She had arrived late in the office, having changed her mind several times about what she was going to wear for her lunch with Mr Sarotzini, and her hair, with which she normally had no problems, had not come out well after she had shampooed it.

To make matters worse, John had been in a strange mood last night, almost as if he was jealous that he had not been invited today. He had pranced around the bedroom, mimicking Mr Sarotzini, making crude jokes about the man's virility and, even though she had not been in the mood, had virtually forced her to make love, as if to establish his superiority – or his territory.

When reception buzzed her to tell her that Mr Sarotzini was waiting, she put on her navy coat and went downstairs as nervously as if she were going for a job interview. She normally felt confident in her most formal suit, a black two-piece, with a high-collared white blouse, the neck pinned with a silver brooch, but now she felt stiff and awkward.

Mr Sarotzini stood in the reception area, in a long camel coat with a velvet collar, looking out of place among the racks of new titles. The only other occupant was a ponytailed illustrator, who was awaiting his lunch date. The banker greeted Susan with a polite smile and a stiff, almost absurdly formal handshake.

'How very good to see you, Susan,' he said, and indicated the door. 'My car is outside.'

It was strange to see him again, this tall, debonair man with his fine clothes and his worldly air, and to know that his child – their child – was inside her. She kept trying to look at his face, to try to learn more about it, to lock it into her memory. Her thoughts kept oscillating: one moment this man was the father of her child, the next he was a stranger and she could not connect the baby growing inside her with him.

As they sat in the back of the Mercedes making small-talk about the weather, Britain's problems with the EC and the worsening state of London's traffic, Susan was trying to imagine how the baby might look – which of her features, and which of Mr Sarotzini's, Bump would inherit. Mr Sarotzini had an assertive nose – it wasn't overly large but it would look better on a boy than a girl, she thought. But those grey eyes were gorgeous, anyone would be happy to have them.

She continued to study him over lunch, still trying to put an age on him and finding it impossible. He smiled and he looked fifty. He turned his head to the right and he looked seventy. He angled his head down to concentrate on a quail's egg and he looked eighty. He turned his head to the left and he was sixty, tops. She searched for the usual telltales of age, but he had no turkey-neck, few liver spots on his hands and just the tiniest one on his face. When he smiled, his eyes were bright and creased with crows' feet but otherwise not excessively lined. There was energy in his movement, in the animated way in which he spoke, once they had moved on to the topics of art and music, and yet all the time it was there, this aura of old age he wore like a shadow that he could not quite shake off.

In spite of her earlier nervousness, Susan began to relax a little, finding him as good company and as charming as when she had previously dined here with him and John. He regaled her with anecdotes, privileged insider tittle-tattle about great singers, including Pavarotti and Maria Callas, about great conductors like von Karajan and Previn and Simon Rattle, about the great composers. There seemed to be nothing of the world of classical music that he did not know, and few of the world's greatest names in this field that he had not met.

Susan listened with interest, but absorbed only part of what he told her, because all the time she was going over the questions she wanted to ask him. She had no appetite, and hardly touched the soup she had ordered; neither did she eat more than a couple of mouthfuls of her liver and bacon.

Somehow their conversation had moved to paintings. Mr Sarotzini told Susan stories of great art treasures plundered by the Nazis, and sold illegally to private collectors around the world, and he regaled her with case histories of fakes: some of the most famous people in the world had been duped into paying millions for faked old masters or Impressionists, and concealed the fact to this day.

It was only when coffee was served that Susan, anxious now about time, managed to bring up the subject of the baby's future. Would his wife look after the baby or a nanny? It was the first of many questions she wanted to ask, and the banker answered it with a glib but evasive, 'This is under discussion.'

She got the same response to her questions about where the baby would live, where it would go to school, whether it would be christened or brought up in any religion at all. Everything was, in Mr Sarotzini's words, 'Under discussion.'

It rapidly became clear to Susan that the period beyond the birth of the child was shuttered off, and although she tried not to show it, his attitude angered and disturbed her. It seemed strange that Mr Sarotzini and his wife should so badly want a child, yet be so undecided about the kind of life they proposed for it. Besides, this wasn't just his baby, it was *theirs*. She was the mother, however much Mr Sarotzini might have paid, so she had a right to be interested, to be informed, to be *consulted* even, on their baby's future.

Mr Sarotzini rose. 'Time is short, is it not, Susan? You have a meeting?'

'Yes, three–thirty.'

'You must not worry about the baby. It will have the very best care in the world.'

'Babies need more than care,' she said, as they walked out of the club's entrance. 'They need love.'

'Of course,' Mr Sarotzini said, as the chauffeur opened the rear door of the Mercedes. 'Love. Yes, this baby will have so much love, I can assure you of that, Susan.'

Something chilled her about the way he said this. And as she sank back into the leather upholstery of the car and the door closed with a thud against the bright December sunshine, it felt as if they had entered a smoked-glass vault. She looked at his face, which had hardened, and felt even more chilled.

Yes, this baby will have so much love, I can assure you of that, Susan.

Yes, he probably could assure her – he had enough money to fix it, to fix anything. And she thought back to that Sunday in September when she'd read about Zak Danziger's death and had wondered then whether there might have been any connection. She had dismissed the thought, but looking at that steely hard face now, it had returned, and it was disturbing her. He seemed to switch so effortlessly from being utterly charming to being icily hard. How ruthless was Mr Sarotzini?

'So now, Susan, we are going to visit a dear friend of mine, Esmond Rostoff. You have heard of him, perhaps?'

She kicked the name around for a few moments but it rang no bells. 'No, I don't think so.'

'He was a great polo player, legendary. He has played with them all, and at one time Esmond owned the world's finest team. Maybe you have not followed polo?'

'No.'

'Today he owns a huge string of race-horses, but he keeps a low profile.' He smiled. 'But we are not going to look at horses. Esmond is a collector of Impressionist paintings. He is an intensely private man and only permits his close friends to see his collection. It was necessary for me to convince him that you are very special to me.'

Susan wondered what he had told the man. 'Thank you,' she said, dubiously, her curiosity to see the paintings lost in the anxiety raging in her head.

The Mercedes pulled up outside an imposing white Georgian house just off Belgrave Square. As they walked up the steps to the front door, Mr Sarotzini informed Susan that Esmond Rostoff was a descendant of the last Russian tsar, and that he owned one of the finest – perhaps the finest – collections of early Impressionist paintings in the world, finer than any public gallery. He hinted that some of these had been removed secretly from the Hermitage in St Petersburg in the final days before the revolution and smuggled out of Russia.

When Susan asked him whether the rest of the collection had been built legitimately, or from purchases of Nazi loot, he laughed the question aside. 'Esmond Rostoff is a very proper man, Susan. He is an aristocrat of fine breeding. Such a man has no need to resort to illicit – or distasteful – methods.'

However, Mr Sarotzini's expression and the feeling she got on arrival at the house, told her otherwise. The front door was opened by a security guard who looked like a Middle Eastern thug; they were received in a red-carpeted hall, by a butler, who led them through double doors into a large, ornately decorated drawing room.

Susan had never seen a room decorated like this outside a National Trust property. Magnificent old masters hung from the walls: hunting scenes, portraits, still lifes of game and fruit. The floor was arranged with exquisite antique furniture – armchairs, reading chairs, two settles in front of the fireplace, a *chaise longue*, a love seat, all upholstered in fine muted grey colourings that toned with the carpet and the swagged drapes. There were beautiful cabinets and display cases, and no rope cordoning anything off, Susan thought. This room was lived in!

Then Esmond Rostoff came in, and someone who looked less like a Russian nobleman Susan could not imagine. He was several inches shorter than herself, sharp-faced, with a chalky complexion, crinkly blond hair, carefully combed and greased down over the bald patches on his scalp, and an immaculate goatee beard. He wore a blue cardigan, emblazoned with a gilt nautical logo, a monogrammed open-necked shirt and silk cravat, navy slacks and black suede Gucci loafers. His wrists, fingers and neck were dripping with jewellery, and he reeked of a sickly sweet cologne.

'Daaarrrhhhling!' He greeted Mr Sarotzini in the most affected accent Susan had ever heard, giving him a bear hug, kissing him cheek-to-cheek on both sides and repeating at least half a dozen times. 'It is just *soooo* good to see you!' Then he turned to Susan, 'I'm just so thrilled to meet you, my deeearrrr,' and gave her a limp, clammy handshake. 'I am told you are a greaaat expert on the early Impressionists?' He stared into her eyes with his own beady little ones, as if communicating a secret shared between her and himself. This sudden intimacy revolted her even more than his handshake.

He was grotesque.

She was having the same problem figuring the man's age as she had with Mr Sarotzini. Her first impression was that he was about sixty, but he was wearing make-up, she could see, and could have been much older. 'No, I'm not an expert, I just love that period, that's all.'

'May I offer you a glass of Krug?'

Susan was mindful of the time – it was already a quarter to three. 'No, thank you very much. I'd love just a quick look at your paintings, then I must be away.'

He found her eyes again, and once more transmitted that shared secret, whatever it was. Was he implying that he knew about the baby? She had no idea. Then, suddenly, he leaned forward and touched the silver brooch she had clipped to her neck. 'How charming, how simmmmpppply charming. Is this a family heirloom?'

'No, it was a birthday present from my husband.'

It was a simple brooch, plain, curved, beaten silver with a scrolled surround, but he continued to hold it as if he coveted it more than anything on earth. With his face so close to hers, she noticed that both his ears were pierced with tiny diamond studs. He repulsed her even more.

As he released the brooch, Susan remarked, to be polite, 'This is a beautiful room.'

He inclined his head, which almost made him look as though he was bowing. 'You are just toooo kind. It is all in need of revitalising, like ourselves.' He winked at Mr Sarotzini, who returned a modest smile.

Rostoff led them into a lift, and the smell of his cologne was so strong it made her feel queasy as the slow, antiquated car took its time, descending what seemed to her to be more than just one floor. Was this man typical of Mr Sarotzini's friends, she wondered. From the easy familiarity between them they were clearly old chums. This presumably was the world in which her child was going to be brought up. A society of rich, ageing and, perhaps, lonely people.

Something about Esmond Rostoff seemed to mirror a sadness that she had felt in Mr Sarotzini when she had met him previously. But it wasn't just a sadness, or sense of loneliness about these men, there was something else, a closeness, a bond that she was picking up. It was a feeling, although she could not in any way put her finger on why, of a hidden agenda.

They emerged from the lift into a subterranean gallery that left her, momentarily, in awe. It was vast, seemingly far larger than the house would have allowed and, in contrast to the upstairs, the interior design here, all in black and cream marble, was stunningly modern.

'This is the Van Gogh room,' Esmond Rostoff told her, leading her forward.

She could barely believe her eyes. There were about thirty paintings, of varying sizes, plus drawings, rough sketches and unfinished canvases, and she had never before seen any of the works.

Were these fakes? They couldn't be, no way. 'How?' she said, her voice coming out in squeak. 'How did you build up this collection?'

Rostoff smiled then, strutting ahead, led her through into the Monet room. 'I like beautiful things, Susan. They are the trophies that make up for all the bad times one has to endure in life.' He gave her a long, knowing look. 'For me, these are my babies.'

Blushing deeply, Susan followed him. The Monet room was even more spectacular. And, suddenly, she felt frightened being here. All these paintings were fresh to her eyes. She had studied history of art at school and she knew it was impossible, quite impossible, to see so many paintings by these great artists and recognise none, unless they had been kept out of public sight for a very long time. Most private collectors were proud of their works and loaned them to galleries. If they didn't there was a good chance that the works had at some time been either stolen or looted. So some had been smuggled from the Hermitage in 1917, but the rest?

Rostoff wasn't looking at these pictures, he was looking at Susan. He was enjoying her reaction. This was how he got his kicks from this collection, she realised. He probably didn't care what the paintings were, he got his bang out of the secrecy, out of the fact that he owned them and no one knew. He was like a child who had hoarded tuck under his bed.

She looked nervously at Mr Sarotzini. Why had he brought her here? To show off the kind of high-powered friends he had? Or because he thought she would genuinely be interested to see the paintings. The *trophies*.

And she wondered, with a chill, if that was all her baby meant to him. If, like these paintings, Bump was nothing more than a trophy, proof that if you had enough money, you could buy anything you wanted. Even life itself.

And as if reading her thoughts again, Bump stroked her, anxiously.

Don't you worry, Bump, she thought. *You're not going to be anyone's trophy. I promise you.*

Chapter Thirty-six

At five o'clock on Saturday afternoon, just when Susan was beginning to panic that their friendly Thai restaurateur had let her down, Lom Kotok arrived, in a vast, rented van filled with an army of waiters and waitresses. Susan had only requested two, but she lost count of the number of people who climbed out of the vehicle and started carrying covered dishes of food into the house.

Kotok summoned her to the back of the van, raised a conspiratorial finger and lifted a huge cloth. Beneath was an ice sculpture of a leaping salmon. 'Present,' he said. 'Look nice on the table.'

She kissed him and he looked startled. 'Thank you, you're very kind to us and we appreciate it.'

'You nice people,' he said. 'No enough nice people in the world.'

The bartender was a strikingly handsome young Thai, all smiles and dim as a plank. After the third attempt at using John's ScrewPull corkscrew he broke it, embedding the point in his thumb, and had to be driven off to hospital by Kotok. John opened the rest of the wine himself, using the hopelessly inadequate corkscrew on his Swiss Army penknife, then wandered around sucking his hand which by the time he had finished, was sore and blistered. To Susan's annoyance, he picked away at all the edible bits of garnish on the food.

The guests had been asked for eight o'clock. By seven thirty, the furniture had been pushed back against the walls, Mozart was playing on the CD, the ice salmon looked magnificent as the centrepiece on the food table, surrounded by platters of curried seafood starters, and the crew of waiters and waitresses had been briefed, including the substitute bartender.

Bowls of nuts hotter than raw chillies, another gift from Kotok, had been placed by the smiling staff on every available surface, where they lurked like land mines. Susan did not want to offend Kotok, who was not yet back from the hospital, by telling him that they were seriously, dangerously inedible.

At twenty to eight, when Susan was just getting out of the shower, she heard the doorbell ring. Moments later John called up that Harvey and Caroline Addison had arrived.

Volubly cursing their rudeness at being twenty minutes early, Susan tripped across the bedroom, trying frantically to get ready. Dark rings and bags under her eyes needed covering up, and she had to put some foundation and blusher on her pallid skin.

Then, to her horror, she discovered that her favourite black cocktail dress, which she had laid out in readiness on the bed, was too small. Holding her breath, she determinedly squirmed into it and somehow pulled up the zip.

But it was no good: it was tighter than a wet-suit and she pulled down the zip, admitting defeat. Determined to stay with black, she opted for her velvet trouser suit. But that was no good either – she couldn't even close the hooks. *Christ, how much weight have I put on?*

In the end she dug out an old A-line dress, which hung rather lifelessly but at least it was black and it wasn't killing her. She put over the top a gold-sequined jacket, added some large gold earrings, a jungle print Cornelia James scarf, and was satisfied.

By the time she got downstairs, the television writer Mark St Omer and his boyfriend, Keith, a lissom youth with a lock of dyed red hair that looked like it had been pinned to the side of his face, had also arrived, and were chatting up the bartender, who was now back from hospital proudly wearing a blue thumbstall.

She went over to Harvey Addison and his wife, who were standing in a corner of the living room on their own, while John, in a white mandarin-collared shirt and charcoal suit, was now opening bottles of fizz in the kitchen for the bartender, who was unable to put any pressure on his thumb.

'Susan, you look delightful.' The obstetrician, his usual, cool, dandified self, tonight in a Prince of Wales check suit, pink tie and flouncing silk handkerchief, kissed her. Then Susan touched cheeks with his wife, Caroline, and admired her hand-embroidered black and silver waistcoat. 'I'm so glad you like it,' Caroline demurred. She barely opened her mouth when she spoke, as if the act of enunciation was too much of a chore. The effect was to make her sound bored with everything. 'Cost me a fortune.'

'Where did you get it?

'A little shop in Beauchamp Place. I won't tell you how much it cost,' she added, in case Susan had missed her first comment.

'No, don't,' Susan said, spoiling Caroline's moment.

Caroline turned towards her husband with a sickly, cooing smile that made Susan cringe. 'You're so good to me, aren't you, darling? You never mind what I spend on clothes.'

The obstetrician, preoccupied with his reflection in the mirror above the fireplace, barely noticed what his wife had said. Susan saw him adjust the wave of his coiffed blond hair over each of his ears, then discreetly pucker his lips at himself. 'What was that, darling?' he enquired absently.

'I was saying what a wonderfully generous husband you are.'

'Ah.' He gave himself another furtive glance in the mirror, then turned to Susan. 'So sorry we arrived early. We have to go on to another bash.' Then he added, in a massive name-drop, 'At Kensington Palace.'

'Glad you could spare us the time,' Susan said, more acidly than she had intended. Although she did not care for Harvey Addison, she knew how important he was to John's business. All the same the man and his wife were both irritating her.

'Princess Margaret,' Caroline said. 'She throws a little pre-Christmas bash – we go every year.'

'Good, well, just slip away when you have to.' Susan heard the bell ring, and through the doorway saw a waitress letting in Kate Fox and her husband, Martin.

But before she could break away to greet them, Harvey said, through a mouthful of sparkling white wine, 'This really is a delightful little house.'

Susan stared at him, her anger cranked up several notches. Considering that he lived in a cramped, ordinary little terraced house like a million other Londoners, who was he to call this place *little*?

'Would you like a nut?' she asked, scooping up the nearest bowl and offering them first to Caroline, who declined, then to the obstetrician. He took a greedy handful and shovelled them into his mouth all at once. 'I'm so glad you like the house,' Susan said, smiling at him as he chewed. A look of surprise, then horror, came across his face.

'You've done so much work since we were last here, in the summer,' Caroline said. 'I do like the colour scheme – a very unusual shade of white. It's so warm.'

'It's called Not Quite White,' Susan said. She glanced at Harvey again and noticed, to her satisfaction, beads of perspiration on his brow as he chewed stoically on, then swallowed.

'Quite spicy, those,' he said, squeezing his watering eyes shut and almost draining his glass.

Kate and her husband were approaching. Susan turned to greet and introduce them. More guests were arriving now – she could see the Abrahams, and behind them a man and woman she did not recognise. He must be the man from Microsoft John had invited. And she caught sight of Archie Warren.

'Kate, hi!' Susan said. And then she stopped in her tracks as the pain struck without warning, doubling her up in agony. She couldn't move, she couldn't think straight, and closed her eyes, trying to shut it off.

I'm losing the baby, she thought, opening her eyes again and staring helplessly at Harvey Addison. *Oh, God, help me I'm losing the baby.*

The obstetrician sprang forward and knelt down. 'Susan? What's the matter? What is it?'

She moaned, then cried out, unable to help it, 'Oh ... ohhh ... ohhhh.' It was getting worse. Nothing had ever felt like this before. Nothing.

Addison's face was close to her own – she could smell the nuts and the softer vinous smell of the alcohol on his breath.

Then, just when she thought she couldn't take any more, the pain began to subside. Within seconds it had stopped.

''S OK – I – I –' She was gasping, crouched, aware that all eyes were on her.

John was at her side. 'Hon? You OK?'

She nodded, still breathless, and said, 'Yes.'

Harvey had a hand on each of her shoulders and was staring at her face with deep concern. 'Don't worry,' he said gently. 'You're OK, Susan. You're going to be fine.'

'The – the baby,' she said. 'I thought I was losing it.'

Harvey's eyes widened. 'You're pregnant?'

She nodded.

'How many weeks?'

'Almost five months,' she heard John say.

'Nineteen weeks,' she replied.

'I didn't know. You must lie down,' Harvey said.

'I'm fine, it's gone now, I'll be fine. They – they come and go. I have some pills upstairs.'

Harvey and John guided her to a sofa and she sat down, drained. Harvey stood over her, looking concerned. His kindness was making her regret her earlier rudeness. She heard voices in the background, questions, John apologising, could sense the awkward silence that he was trying to break.

'Tell me, Susan,' Harvey said quietly, squatting so that he was face to face with her, 'where exactly was this pain?'

Susan told him, then related what Miles Van Rhoe had told her, that it was a tiny cyst, nothing to worry about.

'Miles Van Rhoe is the best there is, Susan, but you shouldn't be getting pain like that, not from a small cyst, unless there's something –' He checked himself.

She looked at him anxiously. 'Something what?' She heard the doorbell ring again.

'It's all right,' he said. 'I shouldn't meddle.' Then he frowned. 'When did you last see him?'

She thought. 'On Tuesday.'

'And you've told him about these pains?'

'Yes.'

John, who had walked across, interrupted. 'Van Rhoe hasn't seen her have one of these attacks. I don't think he has any idea how bad they are.'

Susan was aware that she had to get up and stop disrupting the party. Harvey tried to restrain her. 'You must rest, lie down.'

She shook her head and hauled herself to her feet. 'I'll be fine now.' She smiled. 'Right as rain.'

Just before Susan plunged into the mêlée of her guests, Kündz in his attic, watching anxiously on channel 4, wished he could hold Susan and comfort her. He could feel all her pain, and his remoteness from her now felt worse than ever. He felt envy, too, for this glamorous party that revolved around her, envious of John, envious of them as a couple, and a pang of jealousy each time Susan kissed another guest. It was torture to watch her suffer, but it was no less torture to watch her enjoy herself.

Then he saw Harvey Addison put his arm on her shoulder and heard him say, quietly, 'Susan, we're flying off to the Caribbean tomorrow until the first week in January. I don't want to tread on Miles Van Rhoe's toes, but if you'd like a second opinion at any time when I'm back, please feel free to call me.'

Chapter Thirty-seven

It was like a finger being drawn lightly across her insides. She was being stroked. *Bump was stroking her.*

It was dark; the clock beside the bed told her it was 3.52 a.m. John, lying on his back, was snoring lightly, but she didn't mind, she liked the sound tonight. Some nights it annoyed her but tonight she found something reassuring and cosy about it.

The baby stroked her again.

She whispered, 'Hi, Bump, how you doing? Enjoy the party?'

As if in response there was another stroke, and this was a definite movement, a finger, tracing lightly, right the way across her abdomen. Bump was doing fine, really enjoyed the party. And now Bump was trying to tell her something, and she thought it was trying to tell her, *I love you, Mom.*

'I love you too,' she whispered.

It was raining outside, a light patter, and a siren screamed somewhere, way off. After the terrible start, the party had gone well and she was now unable to sleep, still on a high from it. Everyone had been so thrilled to learn of her pregnancy, and they'd all congratulated her, even the man from Microsoft and his wife, whom she'd never met before. And Kate Fox had wagged a finger at her, and said, 'I knew, I guessed, all that baloney you gave me about wanting to borrow the book on pregnancy for a friend, indeed!'

Susan could not remember ever feeling so proud, so fulfilled, in her life.

It was 11 December. Next Saturday Bump would be five months old. April 26 was looming up. Bump stroked her again, Bump knew this.

Suddenly John stirred. 'Wassertime?'

'Ten to four.'

'I've got a headache.'

'Probably the brandy. Why don't you take a couple of paracetamol?'

He grunted. 'Think it went all right?'

'Yes, I do. It went very well. Archie's Pila is pretty possessive, isn't she? The moment she saw him talking to any other woman she marched across and stood right by him. I noticed it a couple of times. I thought that man from Microsoft was nice – and his wife.'

'Tom Rockney's a good bloke, we're going to get that deal. God, your friend Kate Fox's husband – Mervyn – he's a waste of space.'

'*Martin.* He's shy.'

'He's brain dead. He's less interesting than watching paint dry. He sat in a corner the whole evening, stuffing his face and drinking, didn't say a word to anyone. I tried introducing him to people a couple of times and he stood there and gawped at them. What the hell does she see in him?'

'I've no idea.' Then, teasing, she said, 'Do you think people wonder what you and I see in each other?'

'At least we're reasonably normal.'

'You think so?' she asked.

'Glurr,' he replied. Then he made a further series of inane noises. 'Wrrogggh, glummmm, blingggg, glu glu glarp, glaarrrrrp.'

She giggled. 'What's that meant to be?'

'An intelligent conversation with Martin Fox.'

'How does an unintelligent one sound?' Then suddenly Bump moved sharply and she let out a tiny squeal.

'Wassermatter?'

'Bump's moving. Want to feel?' She took his hand and laid it on her abdomen. 'Can you feel it? Hi, Bump, want to say hallo to your d–' She clammed up, but too late.

John removed his hand. 'Perhaps he'd like to call Mr Sarotzini, then?'

Susan lay in silence, cursing herself for this stupidity. She didn't know why she'd said it, it had just came out. 'I'm sorry, hon, I didn't mean –'

He climbed out of bed and, without saying anything, padded through to the bathroom. The light came on and then she heard the rustle of paper, the sound of capsules being popped free from their wrappers. Then running water.

'I'm sorry,' she said again, when he came back to bed.

'Are you? You were bloody revelling in it tonight.'

'I was just trying to act the part,' she said quietly, trying to defuse his growing anger. 'It wasn't easy.'

'How do you think I felt? Do you think it was easy for me, watching you? Playing Mr Mighty Proud Dad-To-Be?'

'Of course I don't. It's hard for both of us.'

'Bullshit. You were loving it, you were lapping it up.'

She lay in silence. He was right, that was the problem. She hadn't thought about Mr Sarotzini all evening. She'd only thought about how good it felt being pregnant, being congratulated, feeling like a normal, fulfilled woman. How good it felt for once not having to justify, in conversation after conversation, why she and John had decided not to have children, and for once not envying all the other women who did have children.

There used to be a slang expression she'd read in books, terming women who were pregnant as being *in the club*. And that was how it felt now. That she had joined a hugely warm and welcoming club.

She thought back again to Wednesday afternoon with Mr Sarotzini and his gruesome friend with his secret art haul, Esmond Rostoff, and shuddered.

She'd tried to tell John her concerns that night when she'd got home, but he hadn't wanted to know. What happened after the baby was born was not their problem, he told her.

He was wrong. And of course he would be, because it wasn't his baby. How could he possibly understand what she felt?

John suddenly said, 'Harvey's concerned about you. He's going to be away until after the New Year, but he said if you still have these pains then, he'll have a look at you. I'm going to call his secretary on Monday and get a date booked in. If the pains have stopped, then fine, we can cancel.'

'John, Miles Van Rhoe is the best obstetrician in the country – Harvey said so himself, tonight.'

'Harvey says you shouldn't be in pain like this. He thinks Van Rhoe has missed something.'

'Don't you think it would be going behind Van Rhoe's back?'

'Then tell him, if you feel that way. Tell him you're going for a second opinion. People have second opinions all the time, there's nothing wrong with that. I'm not having you suffer like this, I want Harvey to see you.'

'OK,' she said, reluctantly.

Archie was having a quick cigarette outside the squash court before they went on. On the other side of the wall John could hear the squishing, thwacking, squeaking of the game that was ending.

'Great party,' Archie said.

'Enjoyed yourselves?'

'Yah. And great news about Susan – you've been keeping that under your hat.'

'We've been a bit worried about the pregnancy,' John replied. 'Susan didn't want anyone to know until – you know –'

'Until she was out of danger? Sensible. Going to change your life a bit, having a child. Thought you were always against the idea of breeding. What changed your mind?'

'It just sort of happened,' John mumbled.

Archie sucked at his cigarette and grinned. 'Oh, yes?' He sounded sceptical. 'Sure you didn't cave in under her onslaught? Susan's always struck me as being pretty broody.'

While John was struggling to produce a suitable reply, Archie changed the subject. 'Hey, this Vörn Bank of yours.'

'Yuh?'

The door of the squash court opened and two men came through, dripping with sweat. 'All yours,' said one.

Archie crushed his cigarette out on the ground. 'Weird City.'

'What do you mean?' John followed him onto the court.

'Chap called Kündz? Know him?'

John shook his head and slipped a sweat band onto his wrist. 'No, who's he?'

'Their man in London. Came into the office today, wanted to check us out, do the royal tour. This guy, I'm telling you, is seriously flaky.' He shook his head.

John, worried now, said, 'In what way?'

Archie unzipped his racquet. 'This Vörn Bank is privately owned, very old family business, God knows how old, centuries – Switzerland's full of them. They're quiet, discreet, low profile to the point of invisibility. The Vörn only deals in blue chip, nothing speculative.'

'I thought your bond market was speculative,' John said.

'Some and some. So you haven't come across this Kündz?'

'No, I've only ever dealt with a Mr Sarotzini.'

'The head honcho. Or one of them. Oliver Walton, my colleague who deals with them, says he doesn't know who the fuck runs them. They take this secrecy crap to the point of paranoia. You know, they're a substantial client now and we don't even have a phone number for them. Can you believe it?'

'Sounds familiar. Don't phone us, we phone you.'

Archie raised an eyebrow. 'OK, well, here's the weird bit. This Kündz character, he's six foot four, built like an American quarterback, and he looks like a goon, right? He looks like a fucking night-club bouncer, not a banker. He's wearing a shiny suit, rocks on his fingers, he shakes my hand, then spouts poetry at me.'

'Poetry?'

'In Latin.'

'You're serious?'

'It's Horace. I did A level Latin, so I recognised it. *"Si possis recte, si non, quocumque modo rem."*'

John grinned. 'What's that in English?'

'"By right means, if you can, but by any means make money."'

John unzipped his own racquet. 'Shows he has a bit of culture. What's your problem with that?'

'I don't have a problem with that. This is what I have a problem with: he's standing by my desk, looking at Oliver's screen – Oliver's giving him a demo of our system. I go and have a piss and when I come back my cigarette lighter's missing from my desk.'

John looked at him in disbelief. 'What?'

'My gold Dunhill.'

'Missing?'

'Yes.'

'It was on your desk? You're sure?'

'It's always on my desk.'

'Perhaps it fell on the floor.'

'John, I took my desk apart. I grilled the whole bloody room. Nobody else had come in. No one.'

John fought laughter – he couldn't help it, he was finding this comical and he knew he shouldn't.

Archie looked indignant. 'You think it's funny?'

John, grinning broadly, said, 'I'm sorry, I do. Here's this guy, he buys five million quid's worth of bonds and he steals your lighter.'

'Not even my client. I don't get the commission.'

'So what did you do?'

'What the hell could I do? They've got over fifty million pounds of business with us, I can hardly ask the guy to turn out his pockets.'

'Didn't you ask him if maybe he'd picked it up by mistake?'

'I did. He looked at me as if I was a dog turd and said, "I am *zorry*, I am not a man who smokes."'

Archie lobbed the ball in the air and whacked it furiously down the court. It hit the tin and died. 'Nice friends you've got.'

Chapter Thirty-eight

Swingeing cuts were due to be made by Magellan Lowry's new owners, and staff were bracing themselves for redundancy letters.

With only nine days to Christmas, there were cards up everywhere, and the art department had plastered glitzy angels and bits of tinsel all around the offices. Some wit had also produced a 3-D cut-out of a well-endowed Santa Claus having a good time with Rudolf but staff were finding it hard to be jolly. All the same, they were trying and everyone was thinking: *Maybe it won't be me.*

Meanwhile they went to all the publishing industry parties they could find and networked like crazy. A hundred jobs were being edited out and a hundred and fifty people were employed at Magellan Lowry.

Susan was about the only person who didn't have a long face: she was happy to take what she viewed as early maternity leave at Christmas and, after that, she'd have to see. She wasn't sure about anything beyond the birth of the baby. All she knew was that the feeling was growing stronger every day that after the baby was born she was not going to be handing it over to Mr Sarotzini or anyone else.

She caressed her abdomen. 'Hi, Bump,' she murmured. 'How you doing today? Looking forward to Christmas? Me, too! We're going to buy a tree this weekend. You won't be able to see it, but you can help us choose it, can't you?'

Bump responded with a tiny kick.

Her door opened and Kate Fox came in. 'Susan, you said you and John hadn't made any plans for Christmas. Well, we're having a big family do, and if you're at a loose end, you'd be very welcome to join Martin and me.'

Susan thanked her warmly, imagining what John would say. 'That's very sweet of you but we're going down to the Cotswolds that week to stay with the Harrisons, but thanks anyway.'

'Not at all. We'll have you over some time early in the New Year.'

'That would be great.'

'And how's Junior today?' Kate asked.

'Lively. Busy kicking me.'

'Now, right, that's what I've been meaning to tell you. You know, when you can feel the baby moving for the first time, it's like a finger tickling you inside?'

Susan nodded. 'Yes, I know! That's exactly what it felt like!'

'Well, I remembered what it's called. The *quickening*.'

'The quickening?'

'That's the old-fashioned term for it. From the *quick* and the *dead*.'

Susan patted her abdomen. 'The *quickening*,' she murmured. 'Did you hear that, Bump?'

Bump heard it.

'It's really good to talk to your baby,' Kate said.

'I know, Miles Van Rhoe told me that. And he said I should play music.'

'I played music to all mine.'

'I've started doing that too. Bump likes Mozart best, prefers it to rock.'

'Going to be a classy baby,' Kate said.

'You bet.'

Kate went out and Susan caressed her abdomen again. 'You hear that, Bump? You're going to be a classy baby.'

Bump kicked again.

'That's right, you got it. You're going to be the classiest baby of all time.'

Then her intercom buzzed. It was the receptionist, telling Susan her lunch date had arrived.

Susan told her she would be right down, then yawned. She felt more like going to sleep than going out to lunch. Except there was a question she very much wanted to ask her lunch date. Forcing herself to perk up, she said, 'Bump, you are privileged. You're going to have lunch with a very famous author. How do you feel about that?'

There was no reaction from Bump.

'OK, you wanna be laid back about famous people, that's OK by me, that's cool. I think you're going to be seriously cool when you grow up.'

The Very Famous Author sat opposite her, in his tweed jacket and open-necked denim shirt. There had been a stiffness bordering on a coldness in his attitude towards Susan that she had noticed ever since his attempt in the summer to kiss her on the Embankment. Susan wasn't sure how much was due to her rebuff of his advance, and how much was pique at the stringent cuts she had been continuing to make in his redrafted chapters.

However, today he seemed more relaxed, more his old self. The rewrite was shaping up, in fact it was coming along brilliantly now, she told him, this was much more the ticket.

Then, plucking up courage, Susan dropped the bombshell that he was going to have a new editor after Christmas.

'Why?' Fergus asked. Then he stared at her a little harder, and said, 'Oh, shit! I should have realised. This thing about coffee, cigarette smoke, alcohol – you're pregnant, aren't you?'

Susan nodded. She saw a wary expression appear on his face and it all came back to her, the conversation they'd had way back in the summer when he had started to tell her about a dream, and then stopped. She pushed a square of tuna ravioli around her plate, with no appetite.

'That's terrific!' Fergus said, his voice forced. 'Great news!'

'Thanks.'

'Your husband – both of you – you must be thrilled.'

She found a radiant beam somewhere in the attic of her brain, hauled it out, stuck it on like a mask. 'Yes, yes, we are.'

'When's it due?'

'April the twenty-sixth.'

'Maybe we should have a bottle of champagne?'

Susan took off the beam, and shook her head. 'No, Fergus, thanks, I don't think that's too good for the baby – and I have to work this afternoon.'

'A glass?'

She smiled. 'It's wasted on me now, tastes of metal.'

Fergus ordered a whole bottle. It was Christmas and he'd drink what she didn't want. He was in an irrepressible mood today: he was going to get the rewrite finished by Christmas, and he was determined to persuade Susan to carry on editing it – even if she was no longer at the firm, she couldn't just sit at home and talk to her swollen abdomen all day, she'd go out of her mind. 'Wouldn't you?' he asked.

'We have great conversations,' she said, 'Bump and I.'

Fergus looked at her in amazement, she'd said it with such feeling, so seriously; then he frowned. For God's sake, *she was serious.*

And he was starting to remember, a long time back, his own wife, Suki, pregnant with their child. Tammy was twenty-one now, at Duke University, North Carolina. He remembered all those feelings Suki had had. Pregnancy did this to women, made them strange. It was the hormones, but most of them came back to normal afterwards.

And he was remembering something else, even more vividly. 'Susan, earlier this year we had a conversation. You told me that you and John had made a decision never to have children. I'm interested – what's changed your mind?'

She tried to give a casual shrug and was aware that she didn't do it very well. 'Oh, you know, I guess we change, don't we?'

He gave her a probing stare. 'Do we?'

She lowered her eyes, knowing he wasn't fooled by her reply. But equally he had no way of finding out the truth. Yet something was preying on her mind that she had been wanting to ask him for some time. Now seemed the appropriate moment. 'You told me you had a dream, Fergus, back in the summer. Something about my having a child. You said that as I wasn't pregnant it didn't matter. Do you remember?'

He could still recall it vividly, every detail as fresh as if he had dreamed it last night.

A baby, a tiny new-born infant, alone in a terrible darkness, crying. He could hear that cry now, the utter terror in it. And then in the dream he had seen Susan Carter fumbling around in the darkness with a torch, crying, unable to find the baby and begging him to help her.

And his reply in the dream was to tell her no, leave the baby, don't try to find it, let it die. *For God's sake, let it die.*

But what was to be achieved by telling Susan that now, other than worrying her? 'I don't remember,' he said. 'Don't recall that at all.'

'It seemed important to you at the time.'

He looked uncomfortable. 'Not, really.'

'You saw something, didn't you?'

And then it happened. The pain, worse than ever before. It was as if a bayonet had been rammed into her stomach and twisted. She leant forward, bashing against the table in shock, her mouth open, her eyeballs feeling like they were bursting in their sockets. And then it came again, even worse. Her champagne glass fell and smashed but she didn't notice. The pain, the white-hot blade inside her, was twisting again.

Fergus was on his feet. There was a babble of voices. Susan heard the word 'doctor', then she heard the word 'ambulance'. And Fergus was saying 'pregnant', and then she heard the word 'miscarriage.'

And she was on a fairground ride, the restaurant was spinning, she was losing it. And all the time she was trying to tell them *Van Rhoe*, only call *Van Rhoe*, no one else.

And then, as suddenly as it always came on, the pain stopped.

The nausea subsided, leaving her cold, shivery, dripping with perspiration. There was still a pain inside her but it was no longer acute, just a dull throb. People were standing around her, crowding her in, Fergus, a waiter, a man who stuck his face close to hers and told her he was a doctor.

'I'm OK,' Susan said. 'Please, I'm OK, I get these, they're nothing, I have some pills.'

'You keep getting these pains?' asked the man who had said he was a doctor.

'It's all right, I have just a tiny cyst, I'm under Mr Van Rhoe. It's not a problem.'

The doctor was giving her a hard look. 'Miles Van Rhoe? He's your obstetrician?'

Susan nodded.

'Well, you're in good hands. I think you should go straight to see him today.'

'I'll call him, thank you, I'm sorry.'

'I'd better take you home,' Fergus said.

She shook her head. 'I have a meeting in the office, an author coming in, I can't cancel him.'

Fergus looked reproachful. 'Your health is more important.'

'I'm OK, I'll be fine now.' She popped two pills. Fergus handed her his glass and she swallowed them with the champagne, downing it in one gulp so that she didn't have to taste it, hoping it would help dull the pain. Then Fergus perched on the edge of his chair. 'Did you say you have a cyst?'

'It's tiny, nothing. I occasionally get a bit of pain from it, that's all.' The champagne was making her feel light-headed – it was the first alcohol she'd drunk in ages.

'That wasn't just a *bit* of pain, Susan. How long has this been going on?'

It took her a moment to answer, and then she said, 'About three months.'

Fergus told her gently, 'Susan, I know this isn't a very flattering thing to say but has anyone told you how terrible you look?'

She said nothing. He was right, she knew that she looked like a ghost. A ghost with huge dark rings beneath her eyes. Not many people had come out with it, because most of the time she'd masked it with make-up, but Fergus seemed able to see through it.

'This man, Van Rhoe, his name's familiar,' he said.

'Every time anyone famous has a baby, he delivers it. He's in the papers a lot.' Then, before she realised it, she told him, 'Mr Sarotzini was adamant that I see him and no one –'

She checked herself in mid-sentence, as she saw a strange look on Fergus's face.

A chasm of silence opened up between them. Finally, Fergus bridged it. 'Sarotzini? Did you say Mr *Sarotzini?*'

There was something about the way Fergus said the name that made her feel uncomfortable. 'Yes.'

'Is he your doctor?'

Aware that she'd trapped herself, she tried to think of a suitable reply. 'No, he's a banker. He helped my husband. He – he likes to give advice.'

Fergus pulled out his cigarettes. 'Do you mind – if I blow the smoke away from you?'

'No, go ahead, I'm better about smoke now, doesn't bother me so much.'

He lit up then spelled out the name: 'S-A-R-O-T-Z-I-N-I?'

'Yes.'

'What's his first name?'

This momentarily threw Susan. She scrolled through her mind, then said, 'Emil.'

Unless she had imagined it, his face darkened.

'Why do you ask? Do you know him?' she said.

He lit his cigarette. 'The name has connotations, that's all. And it's an unusual name.'

'What *connotations?*'

And then that knife twisted inside her again. It wasn't as acute as before and she managed to swallow the cry before it escaped her lips. But Fergus noticed. 'Susan, you're not right.'

'I'm OK, really, it was just a twinge.'

He stared at her in silence, looking dubious. Then, gently, he asked, 'What are you and your husband doing for Christmas?'

'We're having a quiet one. Going to spend the week of Christmas through the New Year down in the Cotswolds with old friends of John – he was best man at our wedding. And you?'

'I don't know, I haven't decided. There's the annual gathering of the Donleavy clan in Waterford, but I'm not much into ancestor worship. I might go to Prague, or St Petersburg, somewhere that's cold, with real snow, somewhere that looks like Christmas should look.'

'I'd like to spend Christmas somewhere like that, too,' she said wistfully, and glanced down, thinking suddenly about Bump and how Bump was going to take to the snow in a year or two's time.

'Is it going to be a boy or girl?' Fergus asked.

'I haven't – wanted to know.' Then she changed the subject. 'Fergus, you're becoming a real man of mystery, aren't you?'

'What do you mean?'

'Well, you have this dream, and now you can't remember what it was about – or you don't want to tell me. And now this name, Sarotzini, this has *connotations* and you don't want to tell me what those are.'

He tilted up his head and blew a long jet of smoke at the ceiling. It hung there, drifting away slowly over the heads of other diners until air from a heating duct caught it and it exploded, like surf. 'How old is this Emil Sarotzini?'

'I don't know – late fifties, early sixties, perhaps.'

Fergus shook his head. 'There's no connection, other than perhaps the name.'

'What is it with the name?'

He tapped ash off his cigarette, looking thoughtful. 'There was a strange character back in the twenties with that name. All kinds of rumours about him at the time. That he was into black magic, satanism – he was tied up with Aleister Crowley, part of that lot.' Fergus smiled. 'It was all a long time back in the past. He's been dead for decades. Your banker friend, presumably, is very much alive?'

'Yes.'

He turned the conversation back to his book, and Susan let the subject of Mr Sarotzini drop. There was one chapter they still did not agree on: Susan wanted it out, he wanted to keep it in.

Half an hour later they rose from the table, and a waitress helped them on with their coats. They paid no attention to the man at the table nearby who had been eating lunch on his own, his face buried in a paperback. He had already paid his bill and now he stood up. Casually, as if he had all the time in the world, he followed them out of the door.

Chapter Thirty-nine

The grass, coated with the white January frost, crunched underfoot.

The ducks saw the solitary figure approaching and, in a din of quacking, paddled urgently over to his side of the pond. He was as certain to them as any of the landmarks of their world, this man in his crêpe-soled black shoes, his dog-tooth greatcoat and black cassock, his small leather satchel slung from his shoulder, the Venerable Doctor Euan Freer.

He removed a woollen glove, dug a handful of mixed corn from inside the satchel and scattered it on the ground at the water's edge, gently chiding the ducks as they trampled each other in their greed. 'Hey, come on, calm down, there's plenty for all of you.' Then ritually, he counted them, checking that they'd all survived since yesterday. Twenty-two. Good.

It was a fine morning: the tower of the Hilton Hotel and the rest of the jagged London architecture, hazy beyond the far trees, looked surreal, like another planet. There weren't many people around yet, a few joggers, some people walking their dogs before they went to work. Freer always found innocence in the early morning, a fresh hope that lay as yet unsullied by the day ahead.

He wanted the coming new millennium to start with this same hope.

Fergus Donleavy knew he'd find him here at the Serpentine any morning after Mass. 'Happy New Year,' he called when he was still some distance behind the priest.

As Freer turned, Fergus caught those familiar de Niro looks. 'Fergus! Happy New Year to yourself. I was just this moment thinking about you. Now there's a coincidence!'

Fergus shook his proffered hand, grinning broadly. 'I can explain it to you in mathematics, if you have a couple of hours to spare.'

Freer replied, warmly, 'You can explain coincidence to me in mathematics all you like, but it won't kill the magic or the mystery. And don't tell me it has for you.'

Still grinning, Fergus raised his eyebrows. Then he hunched inside his jacket. It was a cold morning. 'So you do still come here every day. The habit of a lifetime.'

'There are worse places.'

Fergus glanced at the clear water of the pond, with its isolated patches of wafer-thin ice, the acres of sparkling frosty grass stretching away into the distance, the majestic trees. He breathed in the clear, tangy air, listening to the birdsong. Yes, there were worse places than this. 'I need to talk to you, Euan.'

Freer tossed another handful of corn. The ducks were sorting themselves out now: there *was* enough corn to go round, there always was, but they never remembered that. He responded in his soft lilt, without taking his eyes from the ducks, 'I think I know why.'

Startled, Fergus dug his hands into his jacket pockets and waited for the priest to continue.

'Last summer, when you came to see me, Fergus, you talked about a baby, as yet unborn.'

'Yes.'

'You had a presentiment about this baby, didn't you?' He threw more corn.

Fergus nodded. A traffic helicopter clattered high overhead.

'You aren't alone,' the priest said. 'I'm hearing this from other sources.'

'Good ones?' Fergus asked.

'The Vatican is concerned,' Freer replied quietly. 'Many church leaders around the world are reporting that dreams and visions are disturbing their flocks, and they are all the same dreams, the same visions.'

'The approach of the millennium brings out all the cranks,' Fergus replied.

'So, are you a crank, Fergus?' Freer turned with a sardonic smile to face him.

'Am I?'

Freer left the question hanging. 'What do you see when you look at these ducks?'

The frivolous streak in Fergus tempted him say, 'Pancakes, spring onions, chopped cucumber, hoisin sauce,' but he resisted. This wasn't a time for humour. He studied them: some were mallards, some had different markings. He wasn't sure what Freer wanted him to say. Finally he said, 'Innocence? Some kind of pecking order? Some kind of dependence on a priest who gives them their daily corn?'

'You don't just see *ducks*? Pure and simple?'

Fergus smiled. 'What do you think the ducks see when they look at us?'

'Uncertainty. I give them the corn and that gives them reassurance. They know me, I've been coming here for years, I've seen generations of them come and go, but let me try to touch one, to do one thing out of the normal, and this is what happens:'

Freer demonstrated. He knelt and tried to stroke one, and in a crackle of wings and quacks like klaxons, they were gone. Some dived into the water and paddled away, others took flight.

Fergus was still not sure what the priest wanted him to say. 'Survival?' he ventured. 'They will only trust the familiar so far, but no further?'

'Yes, the *familiar*.' Freer nodded. 'There are boundaries, demarcation lines between what is familiar to them and what is not. If I step over that line and do something out of the normal, they panic and are gone. That's how they survive, like much of the animal world, by taking flight from danger. So why don't we do the same, Fergus?'

'Because we're at the top of the food chain and we don't have these responses any more – we've evolved out of them. We tend to stand our ground, fight our corner.'

This wasn't the answer Freer was after. 'If these ducks feel a threat, they can scurry off to a different part of the pond. Or they can go to another pond. They only have a problem when they're breeding, bringing up their young. Most of the time they have their mobility and can move away from what threatens them.' He emptied the last of the corn from his satchel on to the ground. 'Make an analogy between the duck pond and our planet and you can see why we human beings are different, Fergus. We don't have another planet we can hop off to. We have to stay and confront what threatens us.'

Freer turned away from the pond and started walking slowly. Fergus kept by his side. 'I believe in the Virgin Birth, you believe Jesus was brought by astronauts, that's fine, Fergus, I've never had a problem with that because we both believe in *something*. We believe that a human was born, or an alien arrived, who was a *force of good*. Yes?'

Fergus was hesitant. 'In a manner, yes.'

The crystals of frost were sparkling all around them, and the air to Fergus seemed alive with birds singing. There was an intensity to this singing, almost an urgency: they were singing today as if there might not be a tomorrow.

Freer walked in silence and then said, 'So if you can, *in a manner*, accept the concept of a force of good, can you, in that same *manner*, accept the concept of a force of evil?'

'I came and talked to you about this last summer,' Fergus reminded him.

'I know, but you're still a scientist.'

'And this somehow demeans me?'

'I'm not saying that, no, not at all, the reverse. You are rational. Scientists come with a lot of baggage. What I'm hearing requires you to ditch that baggage. Can you? Can you cope with something that would be wholly irrational to science – at least, science as we understand it now?'

'Give me a left-luggage locker that's big enough.'

Freer had the grace to smile. 'You'll still know it's there, you'll be thinking about it, you'll be influenced by your need to make models of everything, to make experiments, to see everything repeated in a laboratory. Can you really liberate your mind from all of those constraints?'

'Religion asks *why*. Science asks *how*. I don't think there's such a big gap between science and religion, Euan. I don't think it matters how Jesus arrived or even who he really was. The thing that matters is what he did and his legacy. It's the influence he had, the charisma. He had a power that people believed – and still believe.'

'And acted upon.'

'Yes, and still do. What exactly are you hearing, Euan? Tell me.'

Freer walked on a few paces then stopped. 'There are a lot of prayers going on around the world. In the wrong places. The wrong kind of prayers.'

'What kind?

'It's nothing specific, nothing I can hang my hat on, but it's making me and a lot of other people very uncomfortable. Desecration of churches, a sudden rise in dark rituals. That kind of thing.'

'Like I said, it's the millennium. All the weirdoes are having a field day.'

Freer shook his head. 'This goes way beyond that. There's a concentration, a focus.'

'Sure, the millennium.'

'There's your baggage again. You can't leave it – you have to have a peg you can hang things on before you can feel comfortable.'

'OK, let me ask you something. It's why I'm here.'

'I guessed the coincidence of your being here had an underlying causal factor.' The priest smiled. 'Ask me.'

'The name *Sarotzini*?'

Freer frowned.

'You know it?'

'Emil Sarotzini? Of course. Who doesn't?'

'Have you heard it recently?'

'He's dead, Fergus. He died a long time ago, I don't remember when exactly, back in the forties.'

'Did he have any children?'

'No.'

'Are you certain?'

'Yes. That is one mercy.'

'Euan.' Fergus hesitated. 'Is there any possibility he could still be alive?'

Freer gave Fergus a strange look. 'No. And even if he was, he'd be –' Freer thought. 'He'd be way over a hundred, a hundred and ten, maybe more.'

Fergus fell silent. He was thinking back to his conversation at lunch with Susan Carter, when she'd said, 'Mr Sarotzini was adamant that I see him and no one –' Then the way she'd stopped, as if she'd said something she should not have.

For the past month, since that lunch, Fergus had been trying to find an Emil Sarotzini. His researcher had checked the phone directories of just about every country in the world. She'd checked the register of births, and the electoral rolls.

The last Emil Sarotzini, or indeed anyone of the name Sarotzini for which any record existed, committed suicide in Florence, Italy, in 1947, the day before he was due to be indicted by a war crimes tribunal on a raft of charges of crimes against humanity. This Emil Sarotzini had exterminated two thousand Italian Jews who had sought the help of the Vatican during the war. It was a deal he had personally brokered with Hitler, and even if it had not been actually sanctioned by the Vatican, there was controversy over whether it had tried to intervene.

'You heard the story?' Euan asked suddenly. 'About Sarotzini's cremation?'

Fergus shook his head. 'No, I don't think so.'

'He was in his coffin, in the oven, for two hours. When they took him out there wasn't a mark on the coffin or on him. Not a singed hair.'

'I'd heard something strange happened, but I hadn't heard that. So what happened?'

'The chaps in the crematorium were spooked. They wouldn't put him in again so he was buried.'

'They put a stake through his heart?' Fergus asked.

The clergyman smiled wryly. 'Maybe that's what was needed. More than a few people thought he was the devil incarnate.'

They walked on a bit. A spaniel puppy raced towards them, barked, then raced away. Fergus heard the thin whine of a dog whistle. 'He was an illusionist, Sarotzini, wasn't he?'

'He was a lot of things.'

'People are susceptible to miracles. Particularly in countries where religion is strong, right?'

'The moving statue of Ballymena? Weeping virgins? Lactating Buddhas? Images of the Madonna mysteriously appearing on walls?'

Fergus nodded. 'Maybe the gas went out. He was an illusionist, wouldn't be hard for an illusionist to pull a stunt like that, to feign death, spook a few crematorium workers, boost his mystique. Be a lot easier to turn off the gas than survive two hours at four hundred and fifty degrees Celsius. And create an urban myth in the process.'

After a few moments, Freer said, 'Why are you asking about Sarotzini? What's your interest?'

'I have a feeling, that's all.'

'A feeling?'

They walked in silence for several paces. Then Fergus said, quietly, 'Yes. I can't give you a rational explanation why, but I think Sarotzini could still be alive.'

Chapter Forty

'Susan, what's this doing here?'

Standing in the hall with his coat on, John was staring at a pram. It was brand new, still in its wrapping, sporting large Mothercare stickers.

Susan, in a chunky sweater and baggy jeans, came out of the kitchen, her hands covered in flour 'Hi, darling,' she said, going over to him, and kissing him. ''Scuse hands, I'm making pancakes.' Pancakes drowned in maple syrup were her latest craving. 'It's a present. It's beautiful, isn't it?'

'Who the hell's it from?'

'Mom. Well, I guess Mom and Dad – it just arrived this afternoon.'

'Terrific,' he said sarcastically, removing his coat. 'Very thoughtful of them. Maybe we could change it for something slightly more useful, like a piece of furniture.'

Susan looked at the pram, then back at John. She said nothing.

'I'm sure Mothercare'll take it back. Presumably that's where it came from as it's got their name on it?'

'I – I guess.'

'You can take it back tomorrow – you've got time now. Want me to put it in your car?' He saw her hurt expression. 'Susan, come on!' He cupped her face in his hands and kissed her lightly on the forehead. 'You don't want to keep the bloody thing, surely.'

She stared back at him, too choked to speak. Something about the pram, sitting in the hall, looked so natural, as if it belonged here. It made the house feel complete.

'Susan, *hello?*'

No response.

'Susan, we don't *need* a pram. As soon as the baby's born, Mr Sarotzini is taking it away, that's the deal. I'm sure he can get his own pram. I'll put it in the car for you. OK?'

'OK,' she whispered.

As John bent down to pick it up, she felt a sudden panic grip her, as if he was taking away something that belonged to *her*, that he had no right to take. 'John –' she began, but before she could say anything else the pain exploded inside her. She clutched her abdomen, let out a terrible scream and doubled up. She screamed again, then again, sank down onto her knees, curled up, screaming, screaming, screaming.

John knelt down beside her. This was ripping him apart, seeing her suffering these terrible attacks. And this one seemed worse than ever. 'Hon, darling, shall I call an ambulance?'

She looked at him in terror, but she didn't seem to be focusing. Her whole body contracted with a violent jerk and she let out a low moan. Her eyes closed and her face looked so pitiful that John was close to tears. 'Darling?' he said. 'Darling? I'm calling an ambulance.'

She reached out, got hold of his wrist with her floury hand. 'Nnnn. Nnnnnn.' She was breathing in short bursts, her face a deathly grey. 'Nnno. OK. I'm OK, I'll be OK.'

'Hon, you're not OK.'

She shuddered. John, panic-stricken, thought she was dying. In the old days women frequently died in childbirth or through complications, it must still happen. *Oh, God, please don't let it. Not Susan, please not.*

He barely realised that he was praying.

Then she gave his wrist an extra hard squeeze. 'Please don't call an ambulance. Call Mr Van Rhoe.'

She opened her eyes and John stared right into them, frightened eyes with hugely dilated pupils. 'Fuck Van Rhoe,' he said. 'OK? Fuck this creep. Months, this has been going on and he tells you it's nothing, it's just some *tiny* cyst. Well, I'm not having this any more, I don't trust this guy. He may have the greatest reputation in the universe but you shouldn't be having pain like this. I'm calling an ambulance.'

''S going – going now.'

'Are you sure?'

She nodded insistently. 'I'm OK. It goes, it always goes. Please, I don't want to go to hospital, *please*, John.'

There was something in her voice that got to him. 'Harvey Addison's back from Barbados this week and I've booked an appointment for you for tomorrow afternoon. We're going to see him. I don't want any argument from you. If he says this pain is OK, then fine, end of story, but I want this second opinion and I want it from him.'

Susan shook her head. 'No, I'm OK, it's not long now, three months, I can put up with –'

And then her stomach arched out, she threw back her head and cried out in pain to the heavens. All she saw was a blur, then the pain came again, and this time it wasn't just one knife twisting inside her, it was two knives, four knives, she didn't know any more, she was losing count, and she could see John's face and she could smell a trace of burnt rubber on his breath, and then this pain, she could feel this pain, it was coming again, like a furnace raging in her guts, melting her insides.

She screamed so loudly it felt as if something had ripped loose in her throat.

And then she was lying down, feeling terrible nausea, she wasn't sure where she was and she panicked that she was in hospital. But she wasn't, she was on the sofa in the living room and she could hear John's voice on the phone.

He was saying, 'I appreciate it, Harvey, very much. I made the appointment with your girl before Christmas – just wanted to double check. You know about it? Great. That's very kind of you, they're definitely getting worse. She won't let me call an ambulance. How was your holiday? Good. And Caroline? Good. OK, four thirty tomorrow, at your consulting rooms. I'll bring her over myself.'

Harvey Addison's consulting rooms were in a converted detached Edwardian house close to Hampstead High Street.

The obstetrician turned into the driveway, parked in the forecourt bay marked with his name, checked his hair in the mirror, and climbed out of the black Porsche Carrera that John Carter's CD and on-line series, the Home Doctor, had paid for. He pressed the button on the key fob and the car beeped and winked its lights at him, confirming that the alarm was set.

Although it was mild for January, he was still used to the warm Caribbean sunshine he had reluctantly left behind, and felt chilly. But he was in a good mood today: the jet-lag that had plagued him since arriving back from Barbados on Saturday had all but gone, and he was feeling fresh and alert.

And some seriously good news had come in the morning post. A letter from the BBC. His ratings were increasing: 3.8 million, up from 3.2 million four months ago. For a daytime television show the figures were brilliant – hell, when it had been on BBC2, *The X-Files* in prime time only pulled 6.3 million.

He strode quickly through the first few spots of an impending downpour, his cashmere coat and his coiffed blond hair flapping, and ducked in through the side entrance to avoid having to walk through the waiting room. He paused to glance at his reflection in the glass – the tan was still looking good – then went into his office suite and fixed Sarah, his receptionist and nurse, with a come-to-bed smile in those brilliant blue eyes of his. And she fixed him back with her brown eyes. An invisible wire cracked tight between them, and a smile ran down it both ways, colliding in the middle.

He was thinking, One day, you and I, one day.

And she was thinking, You have a gorgeous wife you adore, and three beautiful children you adore, and what chance do I have? And, anyway, even though you look gorgeous, you're a terrible flirt, and would I really want that situation?

And the answer, which she didn't want to hear, and kept slamming away in a filing cabinet in her brain, was *Yes, yes, I do, and maybe, who knows, one day?* But not now. His agenda was full. And the day ahead was full.

'Good morning,' she said.

'Hi, gorgeous. How's the diary?'

She turned it round for him to read. He glanced at the date, Thursday, 11 January, then scanned the entries. 'Four thirty, Susan Carter, that's John Carter's wife.'

'Yes, I know.'

'Look after her when she arrives – give her some tea or something if I'm running behind.'

'Of course.' She told him the urgent messages, and reminded him of a patient who was due to go into labour that night. She told him the BBC had rung, wanting to set up another meeting about the new series proposal they'd put to him. And then, giving him a rather odd look, she said, 'There's a man waiting to see you – a Mr Kündz?'

He frowned. 'Who's he?'

'I don't know. I thought he must be someone you knew. He seems to know you. I told him you never saw anyone without an appointment, but he's absolutely adamant that he must see you.'

'Is he a rep?'

'I don't think so.'

'So who is he? He's not the pervert who wrote to us wanting to buy all our used surgical gloves?'

Sarah shook her head with a smile. 'He said something like you'd understand the importance when you met him.'

Harvey lowered his voice and tapped his head. 'A nutter?'

She gave a your-guess-is-as-good-as-mine shrug.

He felt uneasy, suddenly. Who was Kündz? A private detective?

Someone from the Medical Complaints Board? He hung up his coat. 'You'd better get me Sally Hurworth. Did she say when the bleeding started?'

'She noticed it when she woke up this morning.'

He opened his office door.

'Are you going to see this Mr Kündz?' she asked. 'Or shall I get rid of him?'

He thought for a moment, edgy about who this man was, and remembered the many skeletons in his closet. 'I'll give him two minutes. But not yet. Let me make these calls. Anyone else waiting?'

'No, your first appointment's late.'

Five minutes later, Harvey Addison sat behind his elegant antique desk and watched the tall, powerfully built, unsmiling man come in and close the door behind him. The man was wearing a Burberry trench coat over a shiny suit, a roll-neck sweater, expensive, rather flashy black shoes, and had a leather carrying case slung over his shoulder. He didn't look like a rep or a private detective. Harvey Addison wasn't sure what he looked like – he was built like an American footballer, but he had an air of menace, not of a sportsman.

'Mr Kündz, how can I help you?'

Kündz sat down in front of the impressive desk and lowered his bag to the floor. He looked at the obstetrician silently, and then said, in his perfect English accent but with clumsy grammar, 'Mr Addison, are you a man who is familiar with the work of Thomas à Kempis who died in fourteen seventy-one?'

Harvey Addison was not and he told Kündz this, deciding that the man clearly was a nutter, but he was still wary of him. He had an intensity about him which, combined with his physique, gave him the scary, unpredictable air of a fanatic.

Kündz responded, 'Thomas à Kempis said: "It is much safer to obey than to rule."'

This was also the Eleventh Truth, but Kündz decided that Harvey Addison did not need to know this.

Addison had no idea where this man was coming from, and he was regretting having agreed to see him. And then Kündz made him feel a whole lot more uneasy: 'Mr Addison, I am of the certain knowledge that you are a busy man. If you agree to do what I ask of you, you will never see me again, you will never hear from me again, I will get out of your face. But if you are not prepared to agree, I will destroy your life. Do we understand each other?'

Addison wondered whether the man was armed, whether to buzz Sarah and get her to call the police, or dial them himself. 'No,' he said, trying to keep his cool. 'I don't think I understand you at all.'

Kündz unzipped one side of his shoulder bag and produced an envelope from which he pulled out several large photographs; he laid them in a line on the obstetrician's desk. The photographs were of the same woman and children who were smiling out from the silver frames on this desk, but just in case Harvey Addison had any problem with their identification, Kündz spelled it out for him. 'This is your wife, Julia, and this is your son, Adam. This one is your elder daughter, Jessica, and this one here, the girl on the bicycle, is your younger daughter, Lucy.'

The obstetrician stared in nervous silence at the pictures. His wife and the children all had suntans, so these must have been taken within the last few days. Briefly anger overcame his fear of the man. Threaten my family, he thought, lift one finger to harm any of my family, and you are a dead man, Mr Kündz.

Kündz picked up the photograph of Harvey Addison's son. 'Adam,' he said. 'It was his fifth birthday on Sunday, you had a Punch and Judy man come to your house at fourteen Curlew Gardens, Adam was sick afterwards and you told him he was silly to have eaten so much. He has a peanut allergy. Just one nut could kill him, that is correct?'

But before Harvey Addison had a chance to speak, Kündz continued, 'Your daughter Jessica, who is seven, kept you awake last night, because she was scared of the thunderstorm. At three fifteen she came into bed with you and your wife. You told her a story about a sheep called Boris.'

Good, Kündz thought, he could smell fear starting to rise from the man, which always made him feel comfortable. He could smell anger too, but it was nothing compared to fear.

'What the hell is all this about, Mr Kündz? Spying on me and on my family. What game do you think you're playing?'

Kündz ignored the questions. 'Mr Addison, you have a code of client confidentiality in your profession, the Hippocratic Oath. You cannot discuss a patient, but I have to ask you to break this confidentiality. She is not a patient yet, and she will not become one until you have reached this afternoon, so we'll talk about her.'

Harvey Addison was finding this man's tortuous way of speaking a little hard to navigate. 'Who is she?'

'Her name is Susan Carter. There is something that is very important for you to understand about this situation before you see her.'

Addison's voice became brittle: he was close to exploding. 'Oh, yes?'

'Susan Carter is pregnant, but John Carter is not the father. She is acting as a surrogate mother in exchange for a large amount of money, I imagine you are not aware of this.'

'I don't believe you.'

'She has an ovarian cyst which, from time to time, is twisting and this is causing the pains. If she were a normal patient, and these were normal circumstances, Mr Van Rhoe would have operated to remove this cyst.'

The surprise of this information helped Harvey Addison to contain himself. 'What do you mean by a *normal* patient? And what is this rubbish about her being a surrogate mother?'

'You will have to accept my word for it, Mr Addison, Susan Carter is a very special patient. As you know, such an operation carries a risk of the mother aborting. Mr Van Rhoe is not in a position to take that risk.'

'I can't comment about a patient, let alone one I haven't yet seen, Mr Kündz, but operations to remove ovarian cysts are carried out frequently on pregnant women with only minimal risk to the foetus.'

'I am instructed that it is not merely the risk of spontaneous aborting. There is unquantifiable damage that may be inflicted by the anaesthetics on the baby's developing brain.'

'With respect, Mr Kündz, I don't know where you are getting your information from but that is ludicrous.'

'I have not paid this visit to argue with you. These are not my instructions. I wish to remind you of the words of Tomas à Kempis. "It is much safer to obey than to rule."'

'Mr Kündz, I'm going to call the police.'

Kündz smiled. 'Mr Addison, I am not in any way of the opinion that this is your best option. You have a more important phone call to make. You need to phone Adam's school. The packed lunch your wife has given Adam. Something has happened to this lunch, a terrible error. Somehow, Mr Addison, your little son, Adam, who has this allergy to peanuts that can kill him in minutes, somehow Adam has peanut-butter sandwiches in his packed lunch.'

Harvey Addison thought about his son, with his flop of blond hair, permanent grin, and passion for bringing insects into the house. Adam, whom he had kissed goodbye not much more than an hour ago. He stared at the man sitting in front of him and wanted to hurt him. He felt a loathing for this man that was cracking the concrete edifice of his emotional dam.

Kündz watched Harvey Addison's knuckles clench and whiten. He could read the obstetrician's mind clearly: the man was deciding whether to assault him with his bare hands, but he was afraid of him. He thought about it too long, the moment for spontaneity passed, his anger was dissolving into fear for his child.

And now Kündz could really breathe in this man's fear: it was so strong, the atmosphere in this room was thick with it – not such a good perfume as the scents of Susan Carter but it had its own attraction.

Harvey Addison reached for his phone, but Kündz's hand was already there. 'Mr Addison, you have plenty of time. Adam is in class, doing a geography project, all about the Serengheti – you have visited the Serengheti?'

'Bugger the Serengheti.'

'You should know things about the Serengheti, Mr Addison. Adam may come home from school tonight and ask you questions. It is worth visiting, I can assure you. It has many insect species that would interest Adam. But you must take care with the time of year. To see the wildebeest on the move, their annual migration, that is something you should not overlook, Mr Addison. But you are right, we should not digress. For the moment, Adam: when he finishes this class, he has gym. Then he will have his shower and it is not until after his shower that he will open his lunch box. At a quarter to one. You have three and a half hours to save his life, Mr Addison, and I'm offering you such a simple deal. You save the life of Susan Carter's baby, and I will help you save your son Adam's life.'

In the silence that followed, Kündz soaked up the smell, he bathed in it, he was becoming energised by it, and always, when this happened, his thoughts turned to Mr Sarotzini. He felt such gratitude towards Mr Sarotzini, such incredible gratitude.

'And what are you expecting me to do to save the life of Susan Carter's baby?'

'Nothing, Mr Addison.' Kündz smiled. 'That's the beauty of it. It is so simple. You have to do *nothing*. You take an ultrasound scan, you tell Mr and Mrs Carter that the cyst is small, it is tiny, and these pains, they may be bad when they happen, but they are not serious, it is no worse than an insect bite. That is all you have to do, it is so simple.'

'And if I'm not happy with the scan, you expect me to shut up and live with this on my conscience?'

Kündz pulled a portable video player from his leather bag, switched it on, pushed in a tape, and turned the screen towards Addison.

When the tape stabilised, it showed a woman in her late twenties, lying on the couch in this room. A man, half undressed, was lowering his head between her legs. The date, displayed at the top of the screen said, Tuesday, 9 January.

Kündz let the tape run on, glancing every few seconds at the obstetrician, who was watching the screen stonily.

Eventually the man changed his position, preparing to mount the woman: the camera now showed a perfect side profile of Harvey Addison.

Kündz said, 'This lady is a patient of yours, her name is Charlotte Harper. Her husband is the cardiologist Kieran Harper. Also he is one of your oldest friends – you were his best man at their wedding. I am not of any opinion that your conscience affects you too much, Mr Addison.' He switched off the machine and waited. It was some moments before Harvey Addison lifted his eyes from the blank screen and looked, like a stricken animal, at Kündz.

'I have further instructions to relay to you, Mr Addison. If you do not allay Mr and Mrs Carter's fears totally this afternoon, there will be consequences for the rest of your family that I shall be unable to prevent. Your daughter Lucy, who is so pretty, will be so disfigured by acid you will not recognise her, your daughter Jessica will lose both her eyes, and your wife Caroline will be paralysed from the neck down.'

Kündz replaced the video player in the carrying case, along with the photographs, and stood up. 'I will remind you one more time to think about the words of Thomas à Kempis. I am not waiting for your answer. We will know that at half past four this afternoon.'

And then, as Kündz reached the door, he turned and added, 'Don't forget to telephone the school. Please have a nice day.'

Chapter Forty-one

John arrived home late to collect Susan for her appointment with Harvey Addison. He was in a foul mood. And it was a foul afternoon, January at its worst, four p.m. and it was almost dark, rain drumming on the fabric roof of the car, great fat sheets of it bursting out of puddles and slapping the windscreen like sea against a breakwater.

As he drove through the clogged London traffic, Susan sat beside him, the A–Z open on her knees, deciding it was best not to speak, just to let him concentrate and hopefully calm down.

Her silence irritated him, and she had the radio tuned to some classical music that irritated him even more. It was really depressing stuff, a violin that sounded like a rusty swing-door. He switched to Virgin and turned up the volume on a track of techno rock. Then he glanced at Susan. If she told him that Bump had been enjoying the music he would brain her. But she didn't say anything.

For several minutes he drove on in silence, then said, 'You took the pram back to Mothercare?'

Susan said nothing.

There was an advert on the radio now. He turned down the volume. 'You took the pram back?' he repeated, accelerating hard. 'Keep an eye open for the turning, I always miss it. Arthur Street, immediately after Vane Place.'

'Vane Place,' she said, peering down at the A–Z, then at the street names on their left. 'I'm taking it tomorrow – it's been raining like this all day.'

'Have you phoned them?'

'Who?'

'Mothercare.'

'This is it, next left, slow down, you're going to miss it. Slow down!' she said.

They did miss it.

As he held the ultrasound scanner to Susan's abdomen, Harvey Addison couldn't believe what he was looking at. This thing on the screen, which was angled away, thank God, from Susan and John Carter, was the size of a grapefruit.

It could be a dermoid cyst, a benign teratoma, which was a semi-solid mass of skin, hair, teeth, lungs, or it could be a compound malignant ovarian cancer. There was no way to tell without a biopsy, and that required an operation. And Susan Carter could not have an operation.

He could see why she was getting these attacks of pain. It had been twisting round on itself and untwisting. The pain came from the twisting motion. Although agonising, this in itself was not harmful. The danger would be if it seized up in a twisted state, because all the blood vessels supplying it would become blocked. Then it could undergo ischaemic necrosis, and turn gangrenous. He tuned the machine to make the image more fuzzy than it need be.

John came over and peered at the screen 'What can you see?' he asked.

The obstetrician knew that John wouldn't know what he was looking at. 'Nothing,' he said, more loudly than he normally spoke, for the benefit of Kündz's unseen microphone. 'It's too small to see. It must be a tiny cyst. It's quite amazing how painful they can be sometimes.'

He switched off the machine, absently telling Susan that she could put her blouse back on, deep in thought about what might happen to her.

It could be malignant, in which case if it wasn't removed it would kill her. It might turn gangrenous, and there were clear danger signs that that could be happening, in which case she would lose the baby and die of chemical peritonitis if she wasn't hospitalised. Or it might be benign. It might stay as it was, continuing to twist, giving her continual dull pain, and the occasional acute pain that hurt like hell.

Today was 11 January. The baby was due 26 April. If she could cope with the pain for another two months, then perhaps he could persuade this madman, Kündz, that they should go for a Caesarean. It would be eight months then, just a month premature; its chances of survival would be good. But two months of this pain? It was inhuman to put her through that.

He wanted desperately to find a way of asking John and Susan the truth about the baby. Was she really having a surrogate child? It seemed unbelievable, but he dared not say anything now. He would ask John quietly some time soon, when they were alone together.

He also wanted to know what Miles Van Rhoe's position was. There was no way he could have failed to diagnose exactly the same thing as himself. Did Kündz have a hold on him, too?

Harvey Addison felt a deep sense of outrage. This was criminal. All his medical training and experience was telling him that this cyst had to come out. His eyes shot up to the ceiling. He'd spent his lunch break searching for the hidden camera, for a microphone, and he had found nothing.

He was scared out of his wits.

The peanut-butter sandwich had been in Adam's lunch box. And Caroline couldn't believe it when he'd phoned and told her that Adam had a peanut-butter sandwich in his lunch box. She'd told him there was no way it could have come from their home, she kept no peanut butter or any peanut-based products in the house, she was scrupulously careful about it.

He wanted badly to speak to Van Rhoe, but he couldn't do that from here, not if he was being watched and listened to. And what if Van Rhoe was also under observation?

Sitting down at his desk again, he gave a reassuring smile to Susan and John that made him feel uncomfortably guilty. Then he told them there was nothing to worry about, it was just a tiny cyst, exactly as Miles Van Rhoe had diagnosed. It was best just to live with it, keep taking the pain-killers when it got really bad, be a brave girl.

Watching them leave, he hated himself. But it would be all right: as soon as he had the opportunity he'd tell them the truth. He would go straight home from the office, scoop up Caroline and the children and drive them all to the nearest police station and get this whole thing into the hands of the authorities.

He sped through the rest of his appointments, and then, at ten past six, grabbed his coat – his secretary had already left – and hurried outside.

The Porsche, black as the night in the rain-lashed car park, beeped at him and winked its lights when he hit the button on the key fob. Then he opened the driver's door and the dome light came on. That was when he saw the figure sitting patiently in the passenger seat.

He jumped.

'Good evening, Mr Addison,' Kündz said. 'Did you have a nice day?'

Harvey Addison stood rigid, frightened. His instincts told him to run, but that wasn't going to do him any good; this man Kündz knew where he lived. Running wasn't going to get him anywhere, talking was his best option.

He climbed into the Porsche and closed the door. Suddenly it felt very quiet in here. He was wondering, *how the hell did this man get in here?* The alarm was still set. He had been sitting in the car with the alarm set, and the sensors in the car detected even the tiniest movement.

Christ, what kind of a freak is this man?

Kündz said, 'You did well, Mr Addison, I am pleased with you, and when I report this to Mr Sarotzini he will be pleased with you also. Just one thing bothers me, and I will explain this to you as you drive – please drive now.'

The obstetrician weighed up his options. He was trying to think clearly, but fear was causing a blizzard of confused thoughts inside his head. 'W-where?'

'I will direct. Navigation is a skill Mr Sarotzini has taught me.'

'Mr Sarotzini? Who's he?'

'Turn left. This is a good car. I also have a German car, a Mercedes, I like it very much. It's the sports one, you know, but I think I have a more complicated sound system than you. Your speakers in here are very small. I can recommend some to you that will give you much better quality. I see your radio was set to classical music stations. The speakers you have here are really more suited to rock music.'

'I really need to get home, Mr Kündz. I have a patient in labour due to give birth in a few hours, and I must have some supper and then get over to her.'

'She is a fortunate lady to have such a diligent obstetrician, Mr Addison. Now – straight on over the lights – Mr Addison, in your lunch hour today you did not go out. You were looking around your room. You were trying to find a microphone? A camera? What would you have done if you had found these things?'

There was an air of quiet menace in the man's voice that riddled Harvey Addison with fear. 'I was curious how you knew so much about me, how you got the pictures.'

'Curiosity is an impure thought. This is one of the Truths, Mr Addison.'

'Pardon?'

'Turn right at these next lights, please. These actions, this looking for a camera, a microphone, I find these cause concern. Trust must be absolute, Mr Addison.'

A wild thought was going through Harvey Addison's head. He wondered if he could accelerate hard, put the car into a slide and slam the passenger side of the Porsche into a lamp-post.

'Do you understand the need for purification, Mr Addison?'

'In my work I understand the need for sterility, for cleanliness.'

'Don't let any thoughts of killing me take root in your mind, Mr Addison. If you crash this car you will arrive home to find that your wife, Julia, and your three children, Adam, Jessica and Lucy, have suffered in the manner I have already explained to you. You go straight over the next lights. From purification can come absolute trust.'

Increasingly frightened with every mile that passed, Harvey Addison could get nothing further from the man. They were driving north on the M1 now in silence. Then, several miles inside Bedfordshire, Kündz calmly instructed him to turn off the motorway.

They headed into the darkness of the countryside, passing a sign to a place called Brogborough, Addison's fear deepening as they left the lights and the comfort of other cars behind them. And then it deepened even further still, when Kündz directed him onto a dirt road which, after a few hundred yards, ended in a vast, deserted quarry. The headlights picked up a stationary car, a Ford.

'That's my car,' Kündz said. 'I appreciate the lift. Please pull up beside it and then switch off the engine, we should not cause unnecessary pollution. We must all be concerned about the environment, the ozone layer. Are you concerned about the ozone layer, Mr Addison?'

The obstetrician switched off the engine and, in a quavering voice, assured Kündz he was concerned about the ozone layer. Then he added, 'I – I thought you had a Mercedes?'

He was shaking with terror.

Kündz smiled at him. 'Yes, but she is in Switzerland, in Geneva. I think it is as well because she would have got dirty on this road. Please switch on the interior light.'

Harvey Addison did as he was told. With the wipers stopped and the rain quickly frosting the screen, he felt even more enclosed and trapped. Kündz removed a pouch from his shoulder bag and unzipped it. Inside was a piece of cardboard, the barrel of a ball-point pen, and a cellophane packet containing a fine white powder.

Unhurriedly and carefully he made a slight convex curve in the cardboard. Then he poured white powder on to it. 'This is cocaine, Mr Addison. You like cocaine very much, don't you?'

Surprised that Kündz knew about this as well, and determined to keep all his wits about him, he said, 'I don't want any right now, thank you.'

Kündz sounded genuinely hurt. 'Mr Addison, this is a reward for doing so well today. Please, enjoy, we have plenty of time, there is so much night in front of us. I have brought you this for your purification.'

The darkness, the remoteness, the silence. Christ, how the hell could he have let himself into this situation? In London he could have done something – he could have run, shouted. Surely he could have done something? How the hell could he have been so bloody stupid as to have ended up here?

He felt close to tears. His children, Caroline, what did this madman want from them all? What did he want from him, now, here?

'Please, Mr Addison, enjoy yourself. The quality is quite outstanding, I am sure you will agree.'

Harvey Addison's hands were trembling so much he could hardly grip the barrel of the pen. Hesitantly, he took a very small sniff – and then, within seconds, everything seemed much better. There was a surge inside him. He felt a power gripping him, this was great, this power, his whole stomach constricted, and a wave that started deep in his belly, rippled, spreading outwards through his whole body. It was pure, incredible pleasure, so strong it evacuated his lungs. This was sex, this was pure orgasm, but this was orgasm that went on building, spreading outwards through him, just on and on, wave after wave, each becoming stronger, more intense.

'This is incredible!' he gasped. 'My God, this is incredible!'

Kündz nodded, he was glad, he was happy. He urged Addison to take another snort.

The obstetrician shook his head.

'Please,' Kündz said. 'Do this for me. It will be even better.'

And Harvey Addison did not really want to stop now. This stuff was so good – he'd never had anything this good. He held the barrel of the pen to his left nostril, closed the right, and snorted hard. And instantly, this was just so incredible!

And for Kündz the only disappointment was the smell, the beautiful, harsh smell of this man's fear had faded. But that was a small price to pay for this man's purification. Because Harvey Addison needed this purification to achieve his absolute trust.

And to achieve this trust, Harvey Addison must experience the Fifth Truth, which stated, 'The only purification is eradication.'

This was something he would explain to the obstetrician in a moment.

Chapter Forty-two

Susan sat at her desk, staring out of the window, running through the things she needed to do. Wallpaper, she thought suddenly, and wrote it down on her pad. Pram, Mothercare, she wrote down. The cursor of her computer blinked steadily and she could hear the whir of the machine's fan. Ante-natal exercises, she added.

The rain was still tipping down – it had not stopped all night. The garden looked sad, waterlogged, the beech hedge and many of the trees stripped of their leaves, fallen twigs and branches strewn on the lawn, bits of rubbish that had blown in, or been thrown in, flapping or rolling around.

On her way back from shopping at lunch-time, she'd seen the old boy next door being taken away in an ambulance, but she didn't know why, and his wife, Mrs Walpole, didn't answer the door when she'd popped round later to see if there was anything she could do for her.

It was Friday, and she was relieved it was the weekend tomorrow and that John would be home. She was glad too that she still had Fergus Donleavy's manuscript to work on – she hadn't realised quite how much she would miss the intellectual stimulation of work, or how much she would miss the human contact of going into the office.

Although she had a few girlfriends with whom she could organise lunches and coffee mornings and teas, plus a ton of books she wanted to read, and she could break up the days with the *Today* programme and *Woman's Hour* and *The Archers* on Radio Four, concerts on Radio Three and Classic FM, plus various other radio and television treats she'd discovered – as well as housework and cooking – she had still not got used to her own company.

As if sensing her mood, Bump was restless today, shifting around, kicking, punching, having a good old rough-and-tumble. Vivaldi was playing on the CD, the *Four Seasons*. Bump still preferred Mozart but was getting to think Vivaldi was pretty OK.

'You think Vivaldi's cool, don't you, Bump?' she asked softly.

But there was no response. 'You asleep, Bump?'

Still no reaction.

'That's OK, you sleep. Wish I could sleep as much as you do. Wish I could go to sleep and wake up on April the twenty-sixth ...'

Her voice dried because she wasn't sure about that any more. A lot of thoughts were going through her mind, and some seemed to be driving her, thoughts that she couldn't help but were just there, as if someone was putting them there.

And the biggest one, which was there all the time and would never completely go away, was what kind of father Mr Sarotzini was going to make for Bump.

There was another problem: she was sleeping badly in spite of feeling tired all the time. She'd been having a lot of weird dreams recently, and last night's had stayed with her – it was still spooking her.

In the dream she was in a vast house, every room of which was painted black. She couldn't find her baby and was running, panic-stricken, from room to room, but they were all empty. Then, finally, she had found Mr Sarotzini, and he'd smiled at her and told her not to worry, the baby was fine, but she didn't trust him.

She'd tried looking up the dream in a couple of books on dream analysis, but they said different things, which made her even more confused. And anyhow she didn't need to analyse this dream to figure it out: she knew, in her heart, exactly what it meant. She had been just clutching at a straw that maybe it meant something else.

She clicked on her mouse and Netscape came up on her screen. Clicking the mouse again, she opened the search engine Yahoo, and typed in the word SURROGATE, then clicked again. A whole list of headings appeared:

> center for surrogate parents and egg donation.
>
> woman to woman fertility center.
>
> surrogate mothers' network.

She worked her way through the first ten, then the next ten, but didn't find what she was looking for. She finally exited from Netscape, called up the Usenet Newsgroups and again entered the search command SURROGATE. This time, after half an hour of going up blind alleys, she hit paydirt.

surrogate. legal.

There were forty different topics under this heading, but two immediately caught her eye and she checked out the first of these. It gave the references for the court transcripts of all cases in the British and US courts where the surrogacy had been challenged.

Then she checked out the second newsgroup topic, which turned out to be an information helpline, and felt a beat of excitement. It was exactly what she needed.

She composed an e-mail in her head, then typed it out, read it through carefully, and clicked on the command to send it. Then, in case John came home unexpectedly, she cleared it from the screen.

At that moment the phone rang. It was John. 'Harvey Addison,' he said. 'I've just had a call from Caroline.'

Sitting in his flat in Earl's Court Kündz was watching Susan typing on her keyboard, and he was appreciating the Vivaldi she was playing. This was a good thing, playing music for the baby, he approved of that. But there was too much glare coming off her computer screen and the lens of his camera couldn't pick up the detail of what she was typing. She was surfing the Net, but he didn't know why. He didn't know what she was looking at and she was not giving him any clues.

Only her face gave him clues. This expression she had. He didn't like this expression, he was not comfortable with it, he was worried by it.

'Susan,' he chided. 'I hope you're being a good girl, Susan.'

He could hear the putter of the keys: she typed fast, using all her fingers. Kündz liked it when she did that – she looked so confident, so in control of her machine and this, he remembered from Mr Sarotzini's teachings, was a very Zen thing. It was good to be in control of your machine, to know your machine, to love your machine, because all things respond to love.

You must love even the things you hate, even the people you hate, and Kündz did love the people he hated, and he remembered the words of the poet, Byron, who had said, *'Now hatred is by far the longest pleasure. Men love in haste, but they detest at leisure.'*

Kündz was in awe of this wisdom. He watched Susan; she'd had no pains today, and that was good, he did not like to hear her cry. And he hoped so much, so very much, that Susan was not going to give him a reason to hate her, because he would find that hard – maybe too hard.

He watched her face, breathed in her remembered smells, and breathed them in again, more deeply, the pangs of longing worsening. He looked at the concentration on her face, the soft pale skin of her neck, and he wanted to kiss it, to hold her, to feel the warmth of her breath against his own flesh. Why had he ever thought that it might start to get easier?

He watched her fingers on the keyboard and he wondered if she was in search of wisdom. And as he listened to the sound of her typing, his computer was listening also. But it was not the clicking that it heard, it was the electrical pulses inside Susan's computer – these pulses that were inaudible to the naked ear – and it was translating these pulses, almost as fast as she could type, back into words that appeared on Kündz's screen. And now he read:

```
hello, i need help, please, on my legal position: i am a
surrogate mother, almost six months' pregnant. my husband and
i have accepted payment for this. i would now like to know, if
i decided to challenge the legitimacy of this arrangement,
and offered to repay the money we have been given, what my
position would be. is there a lawyer you could put me in touch
with who specialises in this area?
```

And Kündz said quietly, to himself, 'Oh, Susan, my darling, *meine liebe*, my cherished one, what are you doing, my darling? What *are* you doing?'

He shook his head.

He would have to report this to Mr Sarotzini, and this made him frightened for Susan. Mr Sarotzini would be angry, and Kündz did not want this, he really didn't, he did not want Mr Sarotzini to be angry with Susan, but he must report this. What alternative did he have? And he knew that the answer was none, there was no alternative.

Susan gripped the receiver tightly to her ear. She had heard John clearly, yet she still said, 'What?'

'Harvey's dead.'

She could picture the obstetrician vividly in her mind, standing over her yesterday, tall, slim, his normally arrogant expression softened into a warm smile, holding the ultrasound to her tummy. 'I – I don't – I can't believe it. What happened?'

'I'm not sure,' he said. 'Caroline just rang me in a terrible state. He was found dead in his car.'

'But we – we saw him yesterday. He was fine. Did he have an accident?'

'No I – I –' He was silent for a moment. 'I don't think an accident. I don't know, she wasn't clear – more like a heart attack or a stroke, an aneurysm or something.'

'Shall I call her?'

'I – yes – you want to do that?'

'Yes. God, I invited her over for a coffee morning next week. I rang her yesterday.'

'I have to go to a meeting at Microsoft, then I'll come home.'

'This is awful,' she said. 'I can't believe it.'

'I can't either,' he said.

She hung up, the full shock of it hitting her now. The image again of him yesterday afternoon, holding the ultrasound scanner on her tummy. Now he was dead.

With trembling hands, feeling as if the whole world around her had destabilised, she looked up the Addisons' number in the book and dialled.

Caroline answered almost immediately, her voice weak and thin from crying. Susan spoke gently, feeling for her intensely, all thoughts of how dull, vacuous, Stepford-like the woman was now gone from her mind. 'Caroline,' she said. 'It's Susan Carter. I just heard. I'm so sorry.'

There was a long silence. Then, when she spoke again, Caroline sounded more composed. 'It doesn't seem to make any sense, Susan. Why on earth would he be in a quarry in the middle of Bedfordshire?'

'A quarry?' Susan asked.

'He had a patient in labour at St Catherine's nursing home, whom he should have been with at nine o'clock, and he never showed up. I don't understand it. We had a wonderful holiday, he was so relaxed and looking forward to this year. It – I can't make sense of …'

'What exactly happened, Caroline? He had a car accident in a quarry?'

There was another silence and then Caroline Addison said, 'Did John tell you about the peanut-butter sandwich? I mean, how did Harvey know about it? The peanut-butter sandwich in Adam's lunch box.'

Susan remembered something about the Addisons' boy having an allergy to nuts – but what did this have to do with Harvey's death? 'Peanut butter, did you say?'

'The police said he was – he was –' Then Caroline Addison began sobbing.

'Would you like me to come over?' Susan asked.

'No … mother … sister … coming. Call you later? Tomorrow? I – I'm sorry.'

Susan heard the sound of the receiver being replaced. Then she hung up herself, and wished that she was not pregnant; she could use a stiff drink.

It was starting to grow dark outside and it had only just gone four p.m. She hated these short days of winter and longed, more than ever right now, for the long summer evenings to return. Harvey Addison was dead but she still had not yet taken the news fully on board. A part of him was standing in his surgery yesterday afternoon holding the ultrasound scanner. He had seemed a little edgy, perhaps, but she'd put that down to the embarrassment of seeing a friend.

Another part of him was standing in the living room, here, just before Christmas, and he was saying, so arrogantly, 'This really is a delightful little house.' She had loathed him for that, but he had been kind to her when she'd had her attack of pain that night and he'd been kind to her again yesterday.

Quarry. Peanut butter. She toyed around in her mind with the seemingly jumbled words Caroline had spoken, but they made no sense.

She felt badly in need of comforting herself, needed to talk to someone. Five past four; it was five past eight in the morning in Los Angeles. Her parents would be up, they were early risers, and she might catch one of them before they went off to work. She just wanted to hear their voices, to be reassured that some of the foundation stones of her life were still intact.

When John arrived home Susan came out into the hall to greet him and was appalled by how shaken he looked. He was clutching a copy of the *Evening Standard*.

'Take a look,' he said, holding out the paper and tapping the front page.

'What happened?' she asked. 'I rang Caroline but she didn't really say anything.'

He shook his head. 'I need a drink.'

They went through into the kitchen. 'I'll get it for you,' she said.

'I'll get it – you read the piece.'

Susan laid the paper on the kitchen table and remained standing as she read it. The front-page splash was the discovery of an IRA explosives cache; the only other item on the page was a surprisingly large photograph of Harvey Addison beneath the headline, TV GYNAECOLO-GIST DEATH RIDDLE.

The article was disappointingly short. It said that Harvey Addison, presenter of BBC Television's popular *The Birth Miracle*, and *Private Consultation* shows, had been found dead early this morning in his Porsche car, in a chalk quarry in Bedfordshire, by workmen. There was a quantity of cocaine in the car. Police were awaiting the result of a post-mortem. He was married with three young children. His wife, predictably, was mystified and in shock.

Susan looked up at John, who was squeezing out ice cubes into his glass. 'Did you know he took cocaine?'

'No, but it's no big deal.' He stuck the glass under the filter tap and squirted a splash of water in.

'The inference is that he's overdosed,' she said.

'Did Caroline say anything?'

'I don't think she was fully *compos mentis*. She was talking about peanut butter – their son, Adam, has a nut allergy.'

'I don't see the connection.'

'Nor did I.'

John drank some whisky, sat down at the table and swivelled the paper towards him.

'Are they implying he killed himself?' she asked.

'God knows.'

'The one thing Caroline said was how relaxed Harvey'd been on holiday – and that he'd really been looking forward to this year.'

'It's a real bugger for DigiTrak,' John said. 'Quite apart from the fact that I actually liked him a lot. He was our biggest earner.' He drank some more whisky.

'I – I guess with these drugs – sometimes you don't know their true strength, if you buy them from a dealer. You don't know what you're getting,' Susan said.

'He's a medic,' John said. 'He could prescribe himself anything he wanted, I don't think he would have needed a pusher – but I'm not sure how it works with coke. And a quarry? He drove to a quarry to snort coke? Why did he do that?'

'Maybe he was having an affair, and it was where they had their trysts.'

John looked at her thoughtfully. 'Possibility. They snort some coke together, he has a heart attack, she panics and bails out?' He shook his head. 'Christ, you'd have thought he'd have a bit more style than a quarry in the middle of winter. Why not go to a hotel for that?'

'He was well known. Maybe he was afraid of being recognised,' she ventured, watching John drink some more whisky, then rattle the ice cubes around. And, like a member of an orchestra coming in on cue, a gust of wind rattled the window-pane. Then, in silent discord, Bump kicked, once.

It was as if Bump sensed something was not right.

You're reading my mind, Bump, Susan thought.

237

And Kündz listening to this conversation, was made happy by it. It almost dispelled the gloom he had been feeling about Susan Carter on her computer. *Good girl!* he thought. This is better. Oh Susan, now you are making me so much happier.

Oh, I wish I could forget your earlier foolishness. I wish that so much. I wish I could find some way of not reporting it to Mr Sarotzini. But I can't.

And he is going to instruct me to punish you.

And he stared at the photograph of Susan's sister, Casey, that he was holding in his hand, and he knew, this was perfect, this would punish Susan badly.

But Susan would be grateful for this punishment. For the Thirteenth Truth stated that 'All true gratitude is borne from punishment.'

Chapter Forty-three

The Coroner's verdict at the inquest on Harvey Addison made a few columns in some of the morning papers on Tuesday, 12 March.

Van Rhoe held the ultrasound scanner to Susan's swollen abdomen and beamed. 'The cyst is shrinking,' he said. 'It's almost completely gone, this is very good news.'

At four o'clock this morning, it sure as hell hadn't felt like it was shrinking. It had felt like her belly was filled with white-hot rocks that were trying to burn their way out through her insides. During the past few weeks she had been in almost constant pain, and coughing and sneezing were hell. She was sleeping very badly and felt shattered today. 'So why's the pain getting worse?' she asked, testily, pulling her jumper back on.

Miles Van Rhoe sat back at his desk, picked up his fountain pen and jotted some notes on a card. 'I'm afraid this stage of pregnancy is frequently painful. You're getting quite a lot of round ligament pain, which is caused by the stretching of the ligaments supporting the uterus. You're feeling a sort of aching, nagging, dragging pain?'

Susan nodded.

'And it's more severe on the right?'

'Yes.'

'Sharp stabs?'

Again she nodded.

'And these are worse when you stand up after you've been sitting for a while?'

'Yes.'

He smiled. 'All symptoms of round ligament pain. They're unpleasant but they're not doing you or the baby any harm, and they'll get better in a week or two. Any other problems?'

'A lot of backache.'

'That's normal.'

'And heartburn.'

'Yes,' he said, jotting all this down.

'And –' Susan blushed. 'I've got piles.'

'I'm afraid that's par for the course also.' He put down his pen and smiled warmly. 'I know you're not appreciating all these pains and discomforts, Susan, but I'm delighted you're having them because they are all signs that you're carrying a healthy baby.'

'Great,' she said. 'Terrific.' She gave him a wan smile and shrugged. 'He's healthy all right – boy, can he kick. I think he's gonna play football for Engl –' She checked herself, and then said, more flatly, 'For Switzerland.'

A shadow flitted across Van Rhoe's face and was gone. 'One thing I promise you, Susan, is that I won't keep you suffering any longer than is strictly necessary. The big advantage, of course, with a Caesarean is that we don't have to wait for labour, we –'

'Caesarean?' she interrupted.

'Yes,' he said. 'Of course. With your cyst ...'

She shook her head. 'No, I've been reading about natural birthing. I've got books on technique and people who've been through it, that's what I want to do.'

Van Rhoe gave her an avuncular smile. 'Susan, I'm afraid I am not an advocate of natural birthing. In my opinion, it's something primitives did before there were obstetricians and hospitals, and there are quite unacceptable risks involved. I'm going to need to operate to remove what remains of your cyst and it makes sense to do that at the same time as the Caesarean.'

He leaned forward and intertwined his long, hairy fingers. 'Susan, you have nothing to fear from a Caesarean. It's the safest way of giving birth for both mother and child.'

She shook her head again. 'I've made up my mind I want to have the baby born by natural birthing. I want to be conscious when my baby is born, I want to bond with him – or her.'

He seemed to be listening to what she said, she thought, taking it on board: there was sympathy in his expression. 'Susan, even if I agreed with the concept of natural birthing, I would have to advise you against it here. I know you're a diligent and caring person, and you're doing your very best for this baby, but you must try to avoid bonding with it otherwise you are going to find parting with it very painful.'

'I'm going to find it very painful anyway.'

'Of course you are. A mother's instincts are very powerful, more powerful perhaps than anything else on earth.' He tapped his forehead.

'Susan, you need to be finding ways, in here, of reducing your attachment, not increasing it.'

'Surely how it's born doesn't make any difference to its future', she said. 'All right, I hand the baby over to Mr and Mrs Sarotzini after it's born, but the baby needs to be born with love, not brutality. I'm suffering all this pain now. I can put up with it if at least I know it's going to be worthwhile and my baby will have a beautiful, bonding, pain-free birth.'

'If you want your baby to have a pain-free, trauma-free birth, Susan, then the only possible way to do this is via a Caesarean.'

She wondered, suddenly, whether Harvey Addison would have given her the same answer. 'Did you know Harvey Addison?' she asked, changing the subject.

He was giving her a strange look now, she thought, that made her wonder whether he knew she'd been for a second opinion. No, that was impossible!

'Our paths crossed from time to time. Why, did you know him?' He hesitated, and then said, 'Of course! Your husband made programmes with him. I saw a report on the inquest in the paper this morning. Death by misadventure. I think the coroner must have been lenient with him.'

'Why do you say that?'

'Well, I don't want to speak out of turn, but as he was a medical practitioner I would have thought he should have known what was a safe dose of cocaine and what was not.'

'Implying?' she asked.

He raised his eyebrows.

'That he committed suicide?'

'It looks very much that way to me,' he said. 'You don't agree?'

'I've seen his wife – widow – a few times.' Susan was silent. Always the peanut-butter sandwich surfaced. There seemed to be a connection but, at the same time, no connection. The police had dismissed it, saying that the sandwich must have been put there by another child – several had had peanut-butter sandwiches in their lunch boxes that day. They could make no link between a peanut-butter sandwich and an obstetrician dead from a cocaine overdose. Even Harvey's phone call to the school had been treated as a typical case of parental anxiety, rather than as anything suspicious.

'And what does his widow say?' Van Rhoe asked.

Susan was too tired to dredge up the peanut-butter story for him. Maybe Harvey'd had a brainstorm? He tried to kill his son then, in a fit of remorse, killed himself?

That did not fit together very well, yet Susan could not dismiss the connection between the peanut-butter sandwich and his death. It was another coincidence, and it made her uncomfortable.

She told Van Rhoe she looked forward to seeing him again the following week, and left.

Almost the middle of March, and there was no sign of winter ending yet. It was a bitterly cold, dry morning and, outside on the Harley Street pavement, Susan pulled her long navy coat tightly around her and fastened the belt. 'How you doing, Bump?' she said. 'You warm enough in there?'

Bump didn't respond. He must be asleep, she thought. She wasn't sure why she kept think of the baby as *he*, and she hadn't asked Van Rhoe to tell her the sex again, but for some reason she felt sure Bump was a boy.

It was just before midday; her car was safely parked in an underground lot and, although she was feeling tired she didn't want to go home yet. Instead she decided to walk down to Oxford Street and take a look in Marks and Spencer's.

By the time she'd battered her way through the crowded street to reach the store, which was further than she had realised, she was exhausted. She bought a fresh orange juice in the food department, then sat down on a chair she found near the men's department.

She broke the seal on the juice, removed the cap and drank. Miles Van Rhoe's attitude to natural birthing was angering her. It's *my* baby, she thought defiantly. It's *my* decision.

Bump kicked. This wasn't his usual penalty-shot-for-England kind of a kick: it was more tentative, more a nervous tap, as if he was trying to attract her attention. And she felt the baby's nervousness transmit to herself.

'Love you, Bump,' she whispered, and her eyes watered. 'Oh, God, how the hell am I going to let you go?'

Feeling more rested after a few minutes, she made her way to the children's department. The spring clothes were in, and she wandered slowly around looking at the baby clothes, exchanging tentative *me-too* smiles with other pregnant women there. The sight of these other women, picking up armfuls of garments and heading towards the cash desks, heightened her sense of sadness. She wished she could do the same.

Her mind racked through the dates again. March 12 today. Bump was due on 26 April. Just over six weeks. And then?

She had the phone number and the address of the lawyer in London who specialised in surrogacy law, which she'd got from the helpline on the Internet, but in spite of all her doubts about Mr Sarotzini she hadn't yet plucked up the courage to phone her.

She couldn't phone her. They had made a deal with Mr Sarotzini and she was honouring her part of it. She had to, somehow – she had to get herself through this, get herself through these crazy thoughts of keeping the baby. Only six and a bit weeks and then it would be over. Six and a bit weeks. That was all. Just six and a bit weeks.

With tears streaming down her face, she fingered a row of all-in-one suits with matching socks, in vivid colours, then a row of cotton outfits, lingering over a tiny sailor suit. She lifted it up, put it back, then lifted it up again and, unable to stop herself, marched over to the cash desk with it.

Just a present, she thought. A little going-away present for Bump.

Chapter Forty-four

'So tell me, how is she?'

'Not good. I'm afraid she's really not at all good.'

Mr Sarotzini sat at his desk in his Geneva office, his thumb stroking the receiver he held cradled to his ear. 'How do you rate her chances of survival?'

'She is deteriorating, Emil. I can't give you any guarantees that she'll survive. I'm extremely concerned about her condition. If these were ordinary circumstances –'

'Of course.'

'Or if she were a normal patient, I would have her in today, right now, not even risk a further twenty-four hours, it's that serious,' Miles Van Rhoe said.

'I understand. The date today is March the fifteenth. Six weeks remain.'

'Give or take.'

'So tell me our options?' Mr Sarotzini stroked the receiver again, his large leatherbound diary open on his desk in front of him.

'The cyst is so big there's barely room for it to keep twisting, and it will stop moving altogether shortly. If that happens when it's still twisted, the blood supply will be cut off, and within a few days it will start turning gangrenous. If we do nothing then, the baby and Susan Carter will both die.'

'And how long before you can safely remove the baby?'

'I don't want to do it for another month. I want to be absolutely sure there is no danger of the lungs not being mature enough to support the baby – there would be too many risks. At eight and a half months I would be comfortable.'

'It would be a shame to lose Susan Carter.'

'It would, I agree, but that's not our priority.'

There was a pause, then Mr Sarotzini said, 'You will bring her into the clinic the moment you sense any danger?'

'Yes, I'm monitoring the situation very carefully and Stefan Kündz has a private ambulance on permanent standby – we can't risk her being whipped off into a hospital.'

'Good. You will keep me informed?'

'Of course.'

Chapter Forty-five

She hadn't intended to take the books home. But the cheerful young salesgirl in the shop had been so insistent. That was what the books were for, she'd told Susan, you couldn't really get an idea of how any of them were going to look until you held them up to the walls in your home. Susan found herself kneeling on the floor of the smallest of the spare rooms, surrounded by pattern books of baby and children's wallpaper, and half listening to *Kaleidoscope* on Radio Four.

It was Monday, 18 March. She was more aware of the date now, in her pregnancy, than she had ever been before in her life, and almost daily she compared her condition against the calendar in her book, seeing how her swollen abdomen compared to the illustrations, making sure everything corresponded. She knew that Bump was covered in vernix, according to her book a greasy, cheesy material that stopped him becoming water-logged from his constant immersion in the amniotic fluid. The book told her also that if born premature, his chances of survival would be 95 per cent; this was a 5 per cent improvement on a fortnight ago. He – or she – was about thirty-seven centimetres long and weighed about nine hundred grammes.

She had told Bump all this.

It was going to be a long week. John was away until Wednesday night on business up in the north of England and Scotland. She didn't mind being in the house on her own, but she was going to miss him, and miss having her days broken up. She was going to the cinema tomorrow with Kate Fox, and she'd offered to take Caroline Addison out for lunch on Wednesday, but Caroline wasn't sure whether she'd feel up to it.

The doorbell rang.

Susan looked at her watch, slightly irritated. It was just after four thirty. She wasn't expecting anyone and the afternoon short story, which she always tried to catch, was broadcast at four forty-five. She'd been particularly looking forward to today's as it was by an author she knew.

On the other hand, she was pleased to have a visitor, any visitor, to relieve the loneliness, even if it was Jehovah's Witnesses with whom she could get into an argument, or a youth with a speech impediment selling dusters.

It was Fergus Donleavy.

He stood on the doorstep, the collar of his jacket turned up against the acid wind, hands in his trouser pockets, anxiety in his face.

'Susan, you got my message?'

She was both surprised and pleased to see him. 'No, what message?'

'On your machine. I rang this morning.'

She put her hand to her mouth. 'Oh, God, I've been out. A doctor's appointment, I completely forgot to check my messages. Come in. Would you like some tea?'

'I was on my way back into town – is it convenient?'

'Yes, it's nice to see you,' she said. 'Actually, this is good timing, I have some queries on the manuscript, on chapter twenty-three. I was going to ring you.'

They went through to the kitchen and she put the kettle on.

'So how are you?' he asked.

'Oh, fine, I guess.'

Susan could see from his expression that she hadn't fooled him. He paced around the kitchen, looking restless. While the kettle was coming to the boil, she got out a mug for Fergus and a glass for herself and opened a tin of shortcake. Fergus sat down at the kitchen table and munched a piece. Then, looking out of the window, he asked, 'Is that a cherry, that tree?'

'Uh-huh.'

'A flowering cherry – or do you get fruit from it?'

'We didn't get any fruit last year. I think it must be ornamental.'

He took another piece of shortcake, and held it without eating it. 'Did you ever go to the blossom festival in Washington? They have it every May.'

'Washington DC?'

'Yes.'

She shook her head. 'I never went to Washington DC. I keep feeling I ought to one day, pay homage to my nation's capital.'

He nodded, abstractedly. There seemed to be something on his mind, but he was taking his time getting around to it. He looked out of the window again. 'I didn't notice the cherry tree before.'

'It was here last week.'

He smiled, bit in half the shortcake he was holding and stared at the segment that remained as if it were an object of art, or a relic of immense importance. When he had finished chewing, he cleared his throat. 'How are the pains?'

'They're OK.'

He studied her face with concern. 'You still don't look right. You're seven months' pregnant, you should be glowing. Five to seven months is meant to be a woman's best time.'

'I know, I read the books.'

'And your obstetrician, Miles Van Rhoe, is happy about your condition?'

'He says the cyst is shrinking. Actually I had a bit of a ding-dong with him last week.' She poured water into Fergus's mug, then began prodding the teabag with a spoon to speed up the steeping. 'He's adamant that I have a Caesarean. I want to have the baby naturally. Do you take milk in tea? My brain's going, I can't remember.'

'Yes, thanks. Look, it's your baby, Susan, if you want it born naturally, that's your right. You tell him that's what you want, and if he doesn't like it, then you'll go to another obstetrician.'

She poured herself some apple juice, brought the mug and glass over to the table and sat down. 'It's not as simple as that.'

'Oh?'

Susan blushed.

'I'm sorry, I'm out of order,' he said.

'No,' she said. 'No, you're not. It's just –' Her voice tailed off. She picked up her glass and sipped the cold juice.

Fergus looked out of the window again. Susan's eyes followed his gaze. The robin was hopping around on the lawn, looking for some crumbs she had thrown out earlier that he might have missed. Then Fergus said, 'When we had lunch, before Christmas, you mentioned the name Sarotzini.'

She tried to sound off-hand but it didn't come out that way. 'Yes?'

'I don't know what the connection is, and if you want to tell me it's none of my business, that's fine, I'll shut up.'

'It's none of your business,' she said.

In the silence that followed, she was surprised at herself. Her reply had come out spontaneously and she felt a little embarrassed now. She fiddled with her cup, tilted the tin of shortcake towards Fergus. 'Have another?'

But she could read in his face that this wasn't going to go away, and part of her didn't want it to.

He was staring at her. His hands slid to his jacket pockets and pulled out his cigarettes and lighter. 'How do you find Miles Van Rhoe?'

'I like him.' She paused. 'He's very thorough, very kind. Well, I did like him up until last week. Now I'm fast going off him.' She smiled. 'He has a rather sour nurse, but I do think he's brilliant. Why?'

'Scotland Yard have a file on him.'

She looked at him in surprise. 'A *file*? What kind of file?'

He stirred his tea, although it didn't need stirring. 'Scotland Yard have an occult investigation team, as part of their porn squad. It's main purpose is to monitor satanic and black magic organisations, covens, seeing which ones are involved in child pornography, checking out rumours of sacrifice, that whole arena. It's the child abuse angle that's their main focus.'

A cold ripple shimmied through her. 'What does Miles Van Rhoe have to do with this?'

'The team raided a black mass in North London about four years ago, after a tip-off that a new-born baby was going to be sacrificed.' He set down the spoon on the table, then looked her straight in the eye. 'Miles Van Rhoe was at that mass.'

'Miles Van Rhoe?' The room felt odd, suddenly, as if she was viewing it through a distorting mirror. The walls seemed narrower, the ceiling higher. 'My *Miles Van Rhoe*?' She did not want to believe this.

'The society obstetrician.' He raised his eyebrows at her for confirmation, saw her anxious nod, then went on. 'They didn't find anything. But they reckoned that was because the coven knew they were coming, they'd been warned.'

'And *Miles* Van Rhoe was there? Are you sure?'

'One hundred per cent.'

'And how do you know this?'

He gave her a look that she immediately understood. Fergus had a lot of friends in high places. 'I had lunch with the deputy police commissioner on Friday – in a private dining room at Scotland Yard, which was rather smart.'

She smiled distractedly in acknowledgement of this. 'So what happened after this raid?'

'One of the guys from the Yard leaked the titbit about Van Rhoe to a reporter on the *Evening Standard*, called Ben Miller. His editor wouldn't go with it – probably nervous of a libel action. Miller decided to take it to *Private Eye*. Rang up the editor, arranged to meet – but he never got there. He threw himself under a tube train on his way.'

Susan swallowed, her mouth dry. 'What are you trying to say to me, Fergus?'

He held up the cigarette packet. 'OK if I ...?'

'Sure.' She got him an ashtray.

He pulled out a cigarette. 'Do you know much about the occult in Europe in this century?'

'When I started at Magellan Lowry, I was an editorial assistant on a kind of history of the occult.'

'Is there any one name that stands out in your memory?'

'Aleister Crowley?'

'Why him?'

'All the legends about him, I guess. Wasn't he called the Wickedest Man in the World?'

'That's what he styled himself, yes. Your book didn't mention the name Sarotzini?'

'No, I'm sure it didn't.'

'No books ever do. He was too smart ever to let his real name get printed – even to let his existence get known outside a privileged inner circle – and he used a raft of aliases. A lot of people reckoned that Emil Sarotzini was the Antichrist. The Devil incarnate. When Crowley styled himself the Wickedest Man in the World, Sarotzini was his role model. That's who Crowley wanted to be like. How old is this Emil Sarotzini that you know?'

'Late fifties, perhaps. It's hard to tell.'

Fergus lit his cigarette and drew on it. 'Emil Sarotzini is alleged to have died in nineteen forty-seven, although that may have been a ruse to avoid a war crimes tribunal.'

'How old was he then?' she asked.

'Sixty, perhaps older. He was pretty good at reinventing himself and hiding his past.'

She thought briefly about how difficult it was to pin an age on Mr Sarotzini, but, doing a quick calculation, this would put him at a hundred and ten. No way. 'It can't be the same man,' she said.

'No.'

She sipped enough apple juice to moisten her mouth. She felt deeply uneasy but, at the same time, there was something surreal about this conversation, as if it were some game Fergus was playing, rather than for real. 'Fergus, are – are you trying to tell me that Miles Van Rhoe is planning to use my baby as a sacrifice in some kind of ritual? Is that what you're saying?'

He stared at her with an air of desperation. 'Susan, look, I don't know

250

what I'm saying. I don't know why I'm here, putting these crazy thoughts into your head, worrying you. I shouldn't have come, it was wrong of me, I'm sorry, I don't know why I'm doing it, why I'm telling you all this.'

But he did know, he knew exactly why he was telling her this, although he still could not really believe the situation himself. There was a mistake somewhere in all this, a terrible mistake, and he was going to end up with egg all over his face, looking an utter fool for jumping to conclusions.

But what else could he have done but come here?

The inside of Susan's head was just a mass of confused data. It was like a billion busy little creatures in there all running around, all carrying jumbled-up bits of information, looking for the right places to put it and for the right sequences to put it in. She did not know why he was telling her this. But she kept thinking of Harvey Addison, couldn't get him filed away, and the name of Zak Danziger, the composer who had given DigiTrak grief last year, was floating around in all that chaos too. And a conversation she'd had at lunch with Fergus last year.

So you think few of us ever fulfil our destiny, because we are not aware of it? she had asked.

And Fergus had replied, *You will. You will fulfil yours.*

And the thought rose up inside her, like a bloated corpse rising through black water, *Mr Sarotzini and Miles Van Rhoe are going to sacrifice my baby.*

Impossible. Absurd. Ludicrous. Miles Van Rhoe was the most famous obstetrician in England. And the evil Mr Sarotzini had died in 1947, and even if he hadn't he'd be at least a hundred and ten years old now. She closed her eyes trying to visualise Mr Sarotzini, to see whether there was any remote possibility through clever surgery, diet, vitamins, whatever, that he could be that old. But there was no way, she figured. With brilliant plastic surgery you could maybe knock a decade off your looks, but not half a century.

Fergus Donleavy had been working too hard on his book. All the wiring inside his head had gotten crossed, it was shorting out. That probably explained the embarrassing pass he'd made at her. He couldn't handle the pressure of the deadline he was under. The poor guy was losing it.

And Bump rolled over contentedly inside her. Bump agreed.

But there was a dark unease riding inside her, and guilt was nagging at her. She wasn't being honest with Fergus. Not that her secret would make any difference, but she wanted suddenly to unburden it to him. She wanted to ease his mind.

And she wanted him to know, so that he could give her some confirmation, some reassurance that all was OK, that Mr Sarotzini was really a kindly, caring man, that the Miles Van Rhoe who was a satanist was a totally different Miles Van Rhoe from the one Fergus had mentioned. She wanted him to know so that all this crazy nonsense could be buried totally and utterly. Once and for all.

She wanted something to staunch the fear that had begun as a small flutter of doubt in her heart, but was now turning into a drumbeat inside her chest.

'Fergus,' she said, 'there's something I haven't told you – I haven't told anyone this, OK? Not even my parents.'

He tapped a column of ash off his cigarette and changed his position in his chair, looking at her expectantly.

'If I tell you this, it doesn't go any further, OK?'

He nodded solemnly.

'This baby – my baby.' She hesitated. 'John isn't the father.'

Fergus did not move a muscle. He didn't even blink.

'I'm having a surrogate baby for Mr Sarotzini. We agreed to do it to stop John's business going bust, and losing everything – including this house.'

She suddenly felt a huge sense of release, as if a massive spring that had been wound up inside her, day after day for months on end, had now, finally, been released. *She was telling someone her secret!* She was sharing it with someone. At last.

God, it felt good to talk.

Fergus said nothing. He watched her, smoked another cigarette, listening, nodding in agreement that Susan and John had had no choice and that anyone might have done the same in her position.

When she had finished, she was floating on a high from her sense of release. Then she looked at him with a guilty smile. 'John and I made a pact that we wouldn't tell anyone, now or ever.'

'I'm glad you've told me, Susan,' he said, feeling even more deeply troubled now than when he had arrived. 'I'm very glad.'

He needed time to collect his thoughts, unsure what to say to Susan. He was out of his depth here and needed to talk to Euan Freer, urgently.

He left, having said little more.

Chapter Forty-six

Mr Sarotzini said that all things must lose momentum and stop, this was a law of nature, this was entropy. Kündz understood this law.

Mr Sarotzini taught Kündz that Gautama Siddhartha believed that the quest for truth was like a wheel that required a fresh push every twenty-five centuries. The year 2000 marked the passing of twenty-five centuries that had begun at 500 BC. A new push was required. Mr Sarotzini told him it was coming. He told Kündz he should be proud that he was a part of it, and Kündz was proud.

And the photograph he held in his hand of Susan's sister, Casey, also made him proud. He thought of the Thirteenth Truth. *All true gratitude is borne from punishment.*

Susan was going to be grateful. But she would have to wait to feel this gratitude, there would be time for this, there would be an occasion. Now was not that time. Now he had a problem on his hands, and this problem was called Fergus Donleavy.

This was why he was sitting in the darkness in Fergus Donleavy's flat overlooking the Thames, with a heavy bag on the floor beside him. In the bag was a 12-volt car battery and a set of battery clips.

He watched the river through the open curtains; it was a fine view, much better than the one from his flat in Earl's Court, which only looked out on to the rear wall of the building behind. He could see the hull of an empty lighter riding at anchor, dark as a silhouette; there was a heavy chop tonight, a fast tide. The orange glow from the street lighting shimmered on the water like plastic wrapping.

The telephone rang. Four rings, then the answering machine kicked in. Kündz dropped his eyes to his watch; it was nine fifteen p.m. He heard Fergus Donleavy's recorded voice apologising for being out, a series of clicks and beeps, then a rich, soft-spoken voice. 'Hello, Fergus, this is Euan Freer returning your call. I'm sorry not to have got back to you sooner. Call me at home tonight, it doesn't matter what time, or else I'll be in my office tomorrow.' There was a click, then Kündz listened to the sound of the machine resetting itself.

Yes, he thought, *Euan Freer*. I know who you are.

He was enjoying himself here: he liked to be a part of other people's lives, even if it was only for short periods. He liked to share in the minutiae of their existences. He stared up at the alarm sensor, watching for the tell-tale red light to come on if it detected the slightest movement from him. But it detected no movement, and it wouldn't.

Since Kündz had entered four hours ago, disarming and resetting the alarm from the code he had obtained by listening to the touch-tone beeps each time Fergus Donleavy had set it, he had not moved. He could sit like this for hours, he didn't mind. They had taught him, as a small child in the village in Africa, to stalk animals, they had taught him how to blend in, how to be totally still. That was all they had taught him, that was all he had known before Mr Sarotzini had come for him. It was good discipline to sit still like this now. It was always harder to notice an object that was not moving than one that was.

He wondered how Susan was and hoped there had been no more pains today. This was the one bad thing, being out like this, away from his monitoring equipment, not being able to see or hear Susan, just having to try to guess what she was doing. It made him miss her even more.

Something was happening. He heard a key, the door opened and the alarm audio warning started beeping. Then it became silent. The light in the room came on but that didn't cause Kündz any problems. He wasn't dazzled by it because he had already fixed the dimmer switch so it wouldn't turn above the minimum setting.

The light was just bright enough to enable Fergus Donleavy to see both Kündz, and the handgun Kündz was holding.

Kündz did not often take this gun with him – Mr Sarotzini had warned him that one had to be careful with a gun in England. He wondered if Fergus Donleavy appreciated the special treatment he was getting.

And, from Fergus Donleavy's expression, he decided no, this man did not appreciate it. But that did not matter. Kündz was here to enjoy himself, and he had Mr Sarotzini's permission to do this. And this, this thing he was about to do, this was going to give him a great amount of pleasure. This would make Fergus Donleavy sorry he had ever put his arm around Susan, *around his woman*, and tried to kiss her. Kündz concentrated hard to control himself, to maintain the correct balance between his emotions, to ensure that he did not allow the anger he was feeling to grow so strong that it would interfere with the pleasure.

254

Fergus had been drinking tonight. Badly disturbed by what Susan Carter had told him, he'd stopped at the pub on the way home and sat on his own in a corner, downing several whiskies in succession, feeling in need of them, deep in thought, trying to fend off the inevitable conclusion to which he was being drawn.

Emil Sarotzini. Miles Van Rhoe. A surrogate baby.

It was unthinkable that Susan could be the mother. Yet someone had to be. But her? Susan? Why her?

Someone had to be.

He wanted, desperately, to believe he was wrong. And yet.

Someone had to be.

He'd rung Euan Freer four times, and each time got the answering machine. Maybe he was at home now or had returned the call and left a message. He hoped so, he hoped to hell so. He had to see him tonight.

Now he had an intruder, and he was getting confused signals from his brain. Logic was telling him that the alarm was on, so this man could not be here, he must be a figment of his imagination. But Fergus's memory was telling him that he'd seen this man before. He looked like a man who'd come to fix his telephones some time last year, and therefore the man was OK.

But the gun was telling him that the man was definitely not OK, and it was setting off a fight-or-flight response in him. Fergus knew all about fight-or-flight response: he'd written an entire book on the subject. An animal under threat gets into a state of high arousal and has two options, to run or to fight. If it does neither it gets a rapid build-up of adrenaline, which can be uncomfortable and trigger an anxiety attack.

Fergus did neither: the gun didn't look like it was going to let him get any closer or any further away. So he stood still and, in a sudden flash of anger said, 'Who the fuck are you?'

Kündz replied, 'Help yourself please, to a drink, a whisky, Mr Donleavy.'

Fergus knew his reflexes were blunted by the booze inside him. And there was something about the man's voice, an innocence, a childlike naïveté in the request that made him feel he could be dealing with a wacko here. He decided his best course was to humour him.

'Thank you, I could do with one.'

Then as he turned towards his drinks cabinet, he saw that the tumbler and the bottle of Bushmills had already been set out for him, together with a bucket of ice, a napkin carefully folded over the top, and olives in a crystal bowl.

This skewed him. He looked at the man again. The man was watching him and the gun was watching him. Was this some practical joke by – by whom? Some kind of surprise party? This had to be a set-up. Some television show – Jeremy Beadle? One of those stunts? He unscrewed the cap of the bottle and poured in a splash.

'To the top,' the man said. 'You fill it to the top.'

The slender comfort Fergus had been starting to feel slid away now as the tone of the intruder's voice hardened. He filled the glass right to the top, his hands trembling, the adrenaline roaring, his blood feeling like an express train going through a tunnel.

The whisky slopped over the top and he stopped pouring.

'Drink a little,' the man said. 'Make room for some ice. Have an olive – they're the ones you like, with anchovy inside.'

Fergus obeyed him, trawling his brain, trying to make sense of this man. He can't have been thinking straight, he can't be the man from Telecom, he must have met him somewhere else, but where? Did they eat olives somewhere? Meet in a bar?

Where?

A connection was forming, one that he did not want to make, but it was growing faster every second, every picosecond, nanosecond, attosecond.

Sweet Jesus.

But it couldn't be, it was too soon. This was too soon after he'd seen her. There was something else going on here, some other agenda. But what?

He debated whether he could use the glass as a weapon, but he knew that he had already left it too late, he hadn't fought and he hadn't run, and now he was trapped by his adrenaline and his brain was near to seizing up.

He could throw the glass.

But that wasn't going to help him. It would anger the man and the thing to do – the one thing he had to do right now – was humour this man, keep him calm, try to engage him in conversation, find out his problem. Was he a fan, pissed off about something he'd written?

'Drink more, please.'

He drank some more, and the man smiled his approval. The whisky was starting to act like a turbo boost. Half the glass was empty now, and it was getting harder to focus. What the hell? There was some kind of joke going on here that he hadn't yet latched on to.

'Drain the glass, please, all the way down.'

Fergus fixed him with a stare. He'd had enough, he couldn't drink any more, he was already seriously drunk. But the stare the man returned was so filled with warmth, with good humour, that Fergus, inexplicably, felt that he would hurt the man's feelings if he disobeyed him.

Obediently he drained the rest of the tumbler and then it slipped from his fingers, disappeared. He heard the sound of breaking glass but it seemed a long way away.

Then the man said, 'Take another glass from the cabinet, please.'

'I've, hr, had sh, sh, 'nough.' His voice slurred, he patted his pockets for his cigarettes. 'Smoke? You like one?'

'Smoking is very bad for you,' Kündz said.

Fergus grinned, feeling absurdly relaxed suddenly. 'So – so'sh drink.'

'Smoking is worse, it really is, Mr Donleavy. Please believe me, I am aware of all the medical arguments. Good health is a gift we should not squander. Please have another whisky.'

Fergus went unsteadily to the cabinet, removed another tumbler, then picked up the bottle and, barely able to guide it straight, slopped some whisky into the glass.

As he took the first sip of this second glass of whisky, someone let the brake off and the whole room started moving. He tried to take a second sip, and then the floor came hurtling up to greet him.

Some time later, Fergus didn't know how much later it was except that it was still dark, he woke. His head was pounding, his mouth was parched, and he was aware of something happening, movement, he was being shifted, or carried, or something. Then he was motionless again.

Then the pain came.

His groin exploded. Steely fingers shot up inside him, they felt like they were clawing at his brain, trying to rip it out of his skull and pull it down through his gullet. Other fingers tore at his stomach, his liver, his kidneys, fingers with brass hooks were trying to scoop out the insides of his ribcage, of his hips, of his pelvis.

The scream that erupted inside him didn't get beyond the end of his throat; something had happened to his mouth, it felt as if it had gone, been stoved in. And this made the pain worse. His body wanted to double up but it couldn't move, something was sitting on him, or holding him, he didn't know, he didn't care, he couldn't think clearly about anything except the pain.

It came again, and this time it was worse. His whole body shrank, then contracted, and as it contracted, the pain shot up through his stomach and down through his thighs. It burst into his arms, his head, then it pulled back, drawing in every muscle, every sinew in his body, constricting them, cinching them, then it released them, and this release felt as if a molten cannonball had been sent hurtling around inside his belly. He could feel the sweat bursting out of his skin, then the vomit rising. It stayed trapped in his gullet. He was trying to breathe now, but he couldn't, he was choking.

He vomited through his nostrils and pain lanced the inside of his head. Some air came in, a scrap, he coughed, his lungs clawing for more. He opened his eyes and he saw the face that his brain reminded him belonged to the man who had come to fix his telephones.

Kündz smiled. Fergus Donleavy looked so undignified strapped down on to his bed, with a balled flannel taped into his mouth as a gag, and his trousers and underpants around his ankles. Kündz had been careful, he had wound towels beneath the ligatures, there would be no marks.

Nor would there be marks from the two callipers that were clipped to Fergus Donleavy's scrotum and connected by a coiled length of wire to the car battery and the transformer.

Kündz said, 'So you are conscious again, Mr Donleavy? There are a few things I might, perhaps, my friend, have missed. You can enlighten me. Fill in the gaps. You see, sometimes there are places you have been where the signals are not good. Shall we begin with your lunch at Scotland Yard? I don't even know what you ate. Was it a good lunch? Was the bread good? Mr Sarotzini told me the quality of the bread is always a good indicator of the quality of a restaurant.'

Fergus spluttered, choking again, the name, Sarotzini, resonating in his addled thoughts. Kündz knew he needed to be careful: he wanted to make it last as long as possible, to share with Fergus Donleavy this pleasure he was feeling. He wanted, so very much wanted, this intelligent man to share a little in his wisdom and, more essentially, in the greater wisdom of Mr Sarotzini. He hoped now, tonight, among other things, he would be able to teach Fergus Donleavy to understand the Thirteenth Truth, that *All true gratitude is borne from punishment.*

He really wanted Fergus Donleavy to be grateful to him.

Because if Fergus Donleavy was grateful to him, if he was *truly* grateful, then his purification would be so much more complete.

Through his fading haze of alcohol and rising haze of pain, Fergus shivered. He could see the aura around Kündz. He shivered again, even more deeply, his soul riddled with terror. The colour of the aura around this man was different from any colour he had ever seen before.

And he knew with certainty now that his worst fear was coming true.

Chapter Forty-seven

There was a lump, an air bubble, a crease, something in the damned wallpaper, and every time Susan tried to iron it out, it just popped up further along, and she was getting fed up with this. She couldn't get the joins straight either, and she wished now that she'd got Harry the painter to do it, instead of trying to be smart and doing it herself.

Except she wanted to do it herself – and not merely for something to do. This room was special, she wanted to have her own touch in here in every sense. She had worked on it until late last night, and was hoping to have got it finished before John came home tonight. She might just do it, if it wasn't for these damned air bubbles.

The doorbell rang. Her watch said eleven twenty. It might be Harry's builder friend, who should have been here first thing this morning to take a look at the roof; there was a damp patch above one of the spare bedrooms, which John had said was caused by a couple of missing tiles, and now at least they could afford to have the work done to the roof that the original survey had recommended.

She opened the front door to see a slightly built man who looked like an ageing hippie; he had straw-coloured hair pulled back in a ponytail, a thin body, and a grin, a great big fat warm grin, that was spreading across his reedy little face. His eyes lit up with it, and before he had even opened his mouth, she was infected by his good humour and almost started laughing with him.

'Overslept,' he said, with an apologetic shrug. 'I'm really sorry.'

'Joe? You're Joe, right?'

'Yup, that's me. Mrs Carter?'

'Yes, I was getting concerned – I have an appointment.' She glanced at her watch. 'I have to be in Harley Street at half two. You want to come in?'

'It's the roof, right?'

'Uh-huh.'

'Harry said you'd had a couple of estimates and you reckoned you was being ripped off.'

'Yes.'

'I'll check the outside first – got my ladders on the van.' He jerked his thumb at a dilapidated hulk in the street that looked more like something that had been abandoned than parked.

'Would you like a cup of tea?'

'I'd murder a cup of tea.' He rubbed his forehead. 'Wow, that's a hangover, really done my head in, know what I mean?'

She smiled. 'Shall I get you some paracetamol?'

'I'm on them, thanks.' He slouched off, with a cheery roll of his head, in his donkey jacket, baggy trousers and holed plimsolls, and hefted open the rear doors of his van.

John arrived home shortly after eight o'clock. As he pulled up the BMW outside the house and reversed into a space, he did a quick calculation. It was Wednesday, 20 March. Only five weeks to go now. Five weeks and Susan would give birth to this baby, and they could hand it over and get their life back.

He wanted their life back more than anything in the world. DigiTrak was going so well, they now had the money to start doing the renovation work the house needed and to take holidays, to go off on luxury weekend breaks, to eat out in restaurants without having to worry about the cost. They had enough money to have all the freedom they used to enjoy – even more freedom now that Susan wasn't working full time – but they weren't doing any of these things.

It was as if time had frozen and they were living in limbo, and time wouldn't start moving forward again until after the baby was born and this was all over. He felt he hardly even knew Susan. Sure she always greeted him warmly when he arrived home, made great meals – if rather too many with pancakes in them – but her life, her thoughts, her consciousness were increasingly centred obsessively around the baby, not him.

Her pains scared him, but poor Harvey Addison had said they were nothing, and Miles Van Rhoe said the cyst was getting smaller and that most of the current pains she was experiencing were normal. John still wasn't happy about this. He'd talked to a couple of women at work who'd had children and, sure, they'd had some pains, but neither had had anything like this. Susan had talked to Liz Harrison and Kate Fox, and they'd had nothing like these pains either. Van Rhoe had told Susan she couldn't make comparisons, that no two pregnancies were the same, and maybe that was true. But, all the same, he was worried.

He was worried also about Susan's attachment to the baby. There was nothing specific – just little things all the time. The business over the pram that her parents had bought: he'd discovered it still in the boot of her car two weeks after he'd put it there. She claimed she'd forgotten about it, but he didn't believe that. Then, on Saturday, he had been rummaging in a dustbin, trying to find an article in a newspaper that had been thrown out, and he'd found a balled-up sheet of paper with a list of boys and girls names on it in Susan's handwriting. *Julian* had been underlined. So had *Oliver* and *Max*.

He hadn't said anything – she seemed very emotional right now so he was trying to keep calm and avoid any confrontation. But he was concerned that something was brewing in her mind, and that maybe she was inwardly starting to reject the idea that she would have to part with the baby.

He had decided he ought to have a private word with Miles Van Rhoe, and see what suggestions he had for helping Susan through the period after the birth. This was something neither of them had ever discussed, how she was going to feel after the baby had gone.

Surrogacy was in the newspapers quite often these days and he had noticed mentions of counselling. Maybe if he did a search on the Internet he might find a help group who could give him advice.

When he entered the house there was no sign of Susan. He called out, 'Darling, hi!' but there was no response. He put down his suitcase and briefcase, hung up his coat and called out again, 'Hon! Hi!'

Had she had another attack of pain? She'd sounded fine when he'd rung her a few hours earlier on the mobile – she'd just got home from her weekly appointment with Van Rhoe and had told him the obstetrician was happy with everything. Her car was outside, she must be home. Then to his relief he heard her voice up above him.

'Just finishing!'

He climbed the stairs, then called out again. 'Where are you?'

'In here!'

There was a strong smell on the landing that he thought was paste, and he could see the door of the little spare room ajar and the light on. He walked down towards it. 'Susan?'

'Come and take a look!'

He went in. And he stopped dead. And he thought, *Oh, shit.*

Scenes from nursery rhymes covered every wall. Susan, in overalls over her dungarees, was balanced on a plank between two step-ladders, smoothing a section of this wallpaper in place. 'How do you like it?' she asked, beaming at him with happiness.

'Susan, what is this?'

'Bump's room. Figured I'd better start getting it ready, in case, you know ...' She gave him a doo-lally grin. 'Sort of premature, it could happen, it's best to be prepared.'

John looked at Jack and Jill, at Little Bo-Peep, at the bright yellow background, and wondered if she had flipped.

Keeping calm, with considerable effort, he walked over to her. 'Darling,' he said gently. 'Hon, look –'

She turned away from him, carried on smoothing out the strip, trying to get the join straight. 'Like it?' she asked. Her voice was oddly detached: it sounded as if it was a stranger talking, not Susan. 'Pretty, isn't it? I got curtains to match, and I got extra material to make a covering for the cot. This room is the best because it gets the morning sun and it's cool in the afternoon, I think that's best for a –'

He raised his voice but still kept the tone gentle. 'Susan! Darling! Listen! This baby – we are not keeping this baby. As soon as it's born, Mr Sarotzini is taking it away, it isn't going to be coming home, we don't need a baby's room here.'

Now she sounded hurt. 'We have to keep up appearances, John. We agreed that. All my friends have been asking me which is gonna be the baby's room. Kate Fox told me I was mad not getting the room ready, in case it was premature.'

'Susan, you could have just painted the room a bright colour, you didn't need to get this wallpaper. If you'd just painted it we could have used it as another spare room.'

She turned towards him and the look on her face scared him. He'd never seen venom like this in her eyes before. She dunked the pasting brush in the tin and left it there. Then she came down the step-ladder, and he braced himself, because she was balling her fists and he thought for one moment she was going to strike him.

She stopped, spitting distance in front of him, and said, 'I went to Elizabeth Frazer this afternoon. The lawyer at Cowan, Walker – you've heard of them?'

He stared at her in disbelief: was she about to tell him she was divorcing him? 'They're one of the big London law firms, yes.'

'Elizabeth Frazer is the one who's been in the news recently – specialises in surrogate cases. She's the one I was recommended. Want to hear what she said?'

It felt suddenly as if the floor was made of quicksand and he was sinking into it. 'Recommended? By whom?'

'By the helpline on the Internet,' she said, in a matter-of-fact way.

John stared at a panel showing Little Miss Muffet: the spider dangling beside her looked a friendly spider, it wouldn't scare anyone. He did not want to hear Elizabeth Frazer's opinion, he really did not.

Susan said, 'She thinks we have a strong case.'

John put his hands lightly on Susan's shoulders, and drew her gently towards him. Her hair had a coarse, unwashed smell, which was unlike her: she always took great care of appearance and hygiene. Was she going to pieces? 'Hon, it doesn't matter how strong the case is because we're not fighting it. I don't want someone else's baby in my life, can't you see that?'

She moved away from him with a feral ferocity that spooked him. This really was a stranger in the room.

'It's my baby, it's not *someone else's* baby, it's mine.' She tapped her swollen abdomen. 'This – see it? This is me. It's my egg that's made this baby, OK? It's my body that this baby is growing inside. It's me that's getting all this pain. This is my body. This is *my decision.*'

John walked towards her and tried to put his arms around her again, anxious to try to tame this wild creature, to talk reason into her before things went any further, but she pushed him away so sharply that he lost his balance, tripped over an unopened tub of paste, and fell on to the bare floorboards.

Susan walked out of the room.

John climbed to his feet, shocked and mentally dazed, with a large splinter painfully embedded in his thumb. He sucked it, thinking hard. What on earth had got into Susan? Was it three nights of being on her own? Had he been stupid going away on business, leaving her with too much time on her own to think about everything?

He found her downstairs, in the kitchen, taking tomatoes out of the crisper in the fridge. He stood, working on his splinter, pinching the skin hard either side trying to force the point out and grip it with his nails or his teeth, while she ran the tomatoes under the tap. Then she put them on the wooden cutting block and started slicing them.

'Tomatoes stop you getting prostate cancer,' she said, without looking round. 'I read it in a magazine. You have to eat a lot of tomatoes. We haven't been having enough tomatoes in our diet, I'm going to change that.'

John looked uncomfortably at the sharp, serrated knife in her hands, but all the same he went up behind her, put his arms around her waist and kissed her on the neck. 'I love you, Susan.'

She yielded a little and he felt the curve of her back pressing into him in acknowledgement. She laid down the knife, but she didn't turn round.

'I don't want this thing to destroy us, Susan.'

'It's not a *thing*,' she said calmly, like a head teacher now. 'It's a baby.'

'If you want to have a baby, if this is so important to you, OK, let's have a baby, but let's have one of our own.'

'I want this one.'

'Susan, hon, I don't know what it is. I don't know what this lawyer woman's put into your head today.'

'She hasn't put anything into my head. She just told me the facts. Surrogate mothers are allowed to charge expenses but nothing beyond that. We could easily show a judge that the paying off of the overdraft and our mortgage was the consideration for the arrangement and that it was illegal. If the judge ruled for us, Mr Sarotzini would have to hand back the shares in DigiTrak and the deeds of this house. We could go before a judge in chambers the moment Bump is born, *ex parte*, and get an interim injunction and we could apply to have Bump made a ward of court.'

John found her use of legal jargon distancing. 'Susan, I understand how you feel. Turn round, look at me.'

She ignored him.

He tried to nuzzle closer, but she squirmed away. 'Susan, come on, hon, we've always been close. Don't you remember something you said to me after the first time we ever made love?'

Silence.

'You looked me in the eyes and you said, "Let's promise always to be truthful with each other, no matter what happens." Remember?'

She still said nothing.

'You're not being truthful with me now. We should have discussed this before you went shooting off to a lawyer.' He held her to him again and this time she yielded a fraction. 'You have this huge biological change going on in your body right now. All these mothering instincts are coming out, and they're bound to – it wouldn't be normal if they didn't – but they're affecting you. Maybe rather than seeing lawyers, what we should be doing is seeing a counsellor. Shall we try and find a counsellor who specialises in this area?'

Taking her continued silence as a good sign, he hugged her a little tighter and softened his voice. 'Look, hon, I know you've been through a lot, and you've been brilliant about it. It's nearly over. Forget the deal now and just think about us. How do you think I feel? You want me to look at this baby, this child, the adult it's going to grow into, every day for the rest of my life? Knowing that half of it is Mr Sarotzini?'

She still said nothing.

'And feeling the guilt that we reneged on a deal we'd made? And that we deprived Mr and Mrs Sarotzini of their child that they wanted so desperately?'

Susan said quietly, barely louder than a murmur, 'Fergus Donleavy thinks Mr Sarotzini is going to sacrifice the baby.'

John wasn't sure he'd heard her right. 'He said *what?*'

'Scotland Yard have a file on Miles Van Rhoe. He said Mr Sarotzini died in nineteen forty-seven. Mr Sarotzini wants me to have this baby so that he and Miles Van Rhoe can sacrifice it at a black mass.'

'*What?*'

'It's true.'

John released Susan. This was so absurd that he started grinning – he couldn't help it. 'When did he come out with this gem?'

'On Monday.'

He looked for the whisky bottle, saw it, and poured himself three fingers. Then he broke out some ice cubes. 'I thought Fergus was a sensible guy. What on earth did he tell you crap like this for?'

'Because he cares about us.'

John splashed a little tap water into his glass, shook the mixture around, and drank some. Then he sucked his splinter again. 'Do you believe him? What he said?'

Susan felt guilty that she'd let Fergus in on their secret. 'I –' She wasn't sure what she believed. She'd tried ringing him several times yesterday and today, but all she'd got was his answering machine. He had still not rung her back, and this surprised her because he normally returned calls promptly.

She'd been churning the same question John had asked over and over in her mind ever since Fergus had left. Whatever the truth was, she was certain that Fergus knew something about Mr Sarotzini or Miles Van Rhoe that he wasn't telling her. He was holding something back. Maybe she shouldn't have told Fergus about the surrogacy. Perhaps that had been a mistake. Perhaps he might have told her more if she'd kept that bit quiet. But why?

All she knew now was that she felt confused and incredibly tired. It was an effort to think. But each time she did think, she felt increasingly frightened. 'I don't know,' she said, finally. 'I don't know what I believe. Last year I had a very strange conversation with him, at lunch one day. He told me suddenly, out of the blue, that I would fulfil my destiny.'

'Fulfil your *destiny*?'

She nodded.

'What kind of New Age crap is that?'

'Fergus isn't into New Age.'

'I don't know what he's into,' John said. 'It sounds like he's losing his fucking marbles.'

Susan stared at the tomatoes. 'You want supper in here or in front of the television?'

'Let's have it in here and talk,' he said. 'Tell me exactly what he said about this sacrifice stuff.'

Susan told him what Fergus had told her about Emil Sarotzini, that people had called him the Antichrist, the Devil incarnate, that he had been the role model for Aleister Crowley, and that he had purportedly died in 1947 but might not have done.

'So Mr Sarotzini is a one-hundred-and-ten-year-old superman?'

She smiled. 'He can't be.'

John smiled also, relieved to see she had some sense of humour back. 'No. And if he is a hundred and ten I want to know what pills he takes, because I want some too!'

Then she told him about the Scotland Yard file on Miles Van Rhoe, and the obstetrician's presence at a coven meeting where they had been allegedly going to sacrifice a child.

John shook his head, grinning in disbelief. 'I'm sorry, I just don't buy this. I mean, OK, the fact that Van Rhoe is famous doesn't mean anything, there are plenty of people with respectable façades who get up to freaky stuff when they're off duty. But it's just absurd.'

He sucked the splinter again. 'I mean, look at it rationally. Here you have not just any ordinary guy but the most famous obstetrician in the country. He's delivered royal babies. The police raid a black-magic mass, and find him there, dancing naked around a pentagram or whatever, and it never hits the press? Come on, get real. The police love this kind of stuff. You can be absolutely certain that if it really had been your Van Rhoe, some cop who'd been on that raid would have been on the phone to every paper in London within an hour, flogging the story.'

'Fergus said a journalist from the *Evening Standard* tried to go with the story but his editor wouldn't run it. He then tried to take it to *Private Eye*, but died before he could. Don't you think that's a bit sinister? You don't want to believe this, do you, John? You're trying to blank it out. You don't care. You just want to hand this baby over and wash your hands of it. Well, it's not so easy for me.'

John sat down on the edge of a chair. 'I understand that, hon. But let's look at the facts. There is no way the Mr Sarotzini we are dealing with is a hundred and ten years old, right?'

Reluctantly, Susan nodded.

'OK, so Fergus is wrong to put crazy thoughts in your mind about him. And in the same breath he's telling you Miles Van Rhoe is a closet satanist who sacrifices babies.'

'I've known Fergus a long time,' Susan said. 'He's straight, he's honest, he's highly respected in a wide range of circles, he's not the kind of man to make wild accusations.'

'I know, I've always respected him too. If it'll set your mind at rest, why don't I call him, have a word with him? I just think he's got his wires crossed on this one. There's just a coincidence of the names here, that's what I think. And another thing, why you? There are thousands – probably millions – of unwanted babies born around the world every day. If they want babies for sacrifices there are places they could get them for a few pounds. Why pay all this money? Why should Mr Sarotzini have gone to all this trouble.'

'Exactly,' she said, challengingly. 'Why?'

'We know that. It was a combination of looks, ancestry, intelligence. Mr Sarotzini told us all the reasons.' He stood up, held her again, eased her gently round to face him. 'Maybe Fergus is under a lot of strain. Stress affects people in different ways. Sometimes the most together person can just crack up and have a breakdown. Fergus has his wires crossed. This has to be a coincidence.'

'That's one of the big differences between you and me,' Susan said. 'You can accept coincidences, they don't mean anything to you, you just think they're pure random chance. I don't. And I really don't buy this one. And I don't buy that Fergus is cracking up, either.'

She tried phoning Fergus Donleavy twice that evening. And after she had gone to bed and fallen straight into a troubled sleep, shortly after ten, John tried, but all he got was the answering machine. He left a message.

Chapter Forty-eight

Susan could hear Joe clumping around above her in the loft. She was checking the wallpaper in Bump's bedroom, smoothing it down in a few places where it had curled since yesterday, and moistening it where there were still air bumps, trying to flatten them.

Then she heard the phone ringing, and hurried out, down the landing, past the ladder up to the loft, through into the master bedroom to catch it before the answering machine did. It was a dead heat. The caller got her recorded voice together with her live voice.

'Hang on!' Susan said.

The caller waited patiently until the machine had lost interest, then Susan said again, 'Hallo? Sorry about that!'

It was Kate Fox, at the office. Her voice sounded oddly formal. 'Susan?'

'Kate, hi, good seeing you last week.'

'Yes, er – thanks for the lunch.'

'The roast peppers, with the tomatoes and anchovies, did you like them? That was the first time I'd tried that – it was a Delia Smith recipe.'

'Yes, they were good.' There was a brief silence. 'Susan, I don't know if you've already heard ...'

'Heard what?'

'About Fergus Donleavy?'

'What – what's happened?' Susan's nerves jangled as if a violin bow had been drawn across them.

'I've just had a call from a reporter wanting to speak to Fergus Donleavy's editor, to get a quote about him. It was the first I knew about it. Then two detectives came round. They've been interviewing us. I wondered if you knew any more.'

'I don't know anything. Detectives? What's he done? What's happened? Tell me?'

There was a long, awful silence, and then Kate said, 'He's dead.'

'Dead?' Susan felt as if she had been enveloped in a terrible blackness. 'Fergus is dead?'

'Yes, I'm afraid so.'

Susan's legs buckled and she sank down on the edge of the bed, the mattress making a tiny creaking sound beneath her. There was something unreal about this. Kate must have made a mistake, she *must*. 'I – I saw him on Monday. I've been trying to get hold of him for the last couple of days – I left messages – I –' She stopped talking as tears flooded her eyes. 'Just a moment,' she said, sniffing, looking around for a tissue. She found one in her dungarees pocket and dabbed her eyes with it, feeling a stark, terrible, overwhelming sense of loneliness.

Fergus dead?

There was heavy clumping up above her, then hammering, then the whine of some power tool. She was shivering: it was cold in here. There was a mistake, there must be. Fergus was too huge an intellectual, too young, too big a personality to die.

'I gave the detectives your number – I hope that's all right? One was called Shawcross, Detective Sergeant Shawcross. They wanted all of Fergus's contacts.'

'Wh – what –' Her voice was choked and she stopped again, sniffed, stared around the empty room through a mist of tears. 'What's happened, Kate? How? How did ...?'

There was another silence before Kate spoke again. 'He was found by a girlfriend last night. She'd been worried because she hadn't heard from him, and she had a key so she went round there.'

This was why he hadn't been returning her calls. Susan felt sick, desperately sick. 'And? What had happened? Was it a heart attack?'

'They haven't had the post-mortem yet but the police said it looked like booze.'

'Booze?'

'It sounds like he choked on his own vomit in a stupor. He'd been dead for some time, at least a couple of days.'

Susan stared at the floor. The power tool whined above her head again. She was thinking of Fergus, sitting here in the kitchen, so alive, so real, and her brain was churning. Sure, he enjoyed his drink – she remembered the entire bottle of champagne he had downed at lunch just before Christmas – but he'd never struck her as a hard-hitting boozer. Yet she'd never really known him outside work.

'I can't believe this, Kate. I can't believe he's – dead. Tell me it's – it's not –'

'I'm really sorry, he seemed like a nice guy.'

He was more than a nice guy, Susan thought, but she said nothing. She didn't want to talk any more, not right now, she wanted some quiet around her, some space, she wanted just the privacy of her thoughts.

He'd been dead for some time, at least a couple of days.

Monday afternoon, he'd come round to see her. Now it was Thursday morning. How soon after had he drunk himself into a stupor? And why?

'Kate, what – did they say – about funeral arrangements?'

'I didn't ask them,' Kate said. 'Has he got a family?'

Susan remembered him at lunch in December, talking about Christmas, and joking about not wanting to spend it with his family in Ireland – *ancestor worshipping,* – he'd called it. 'Yes,' she said. 'In Ireland, and his ex-wife is in the States. I'll try to find out the arrangements. I guess there are people at Magellan Lowry who might like to go.'

'Yes, I would imagine so.'

She thanked Kate for letting her know and hung up. Then she stood up, walked across to the south-facing window and looked down at the garden through a stream of tears. There had been a heavy frost last night and some of it remained on the lawn, an arc that the sun hadn't reached.

She looked at the cherry tree, and she could hear Fergus's voice as he sat in the kitchen, cradling his mug of tea, looking out of the window. *Is that a cherry, that tree?*

Choked on his own vomit.

Susan … I don't know why I'm here, putting these crazy thoughts into your head, worrying you. I shouldn't have come, it was wrong of me, I'm sorry, I don't know why I'm doing it, why I'm telling you all this.

Choked on his own vomit.

So you think few of us ever fulfil our destiny, because we are not aware of it? You will, you will fulfil yours.

Choked on his own vomit.

She could not get that line, that image, that crude, ugly image out of her mind. It didn't figure. Fergus was smart, he was not going to have choked to death on his own vomit like some poor derelict on a street corner, no, no way.

This wasn't right.

Harvey Addison, who was a doctor, who *must* have understood about drugs, died of an overdose. Was that right?

Was Zak Danziger's death right?

She heard a voice calling out, distracting her. 'Yo? Yo, 'lo, hello, Mrs Carter? 'Lo?'

It was coming from below her. Joe was standing in the hallway.

'Ah, there you are!' he said, as she came downstairs. 'Sorry, I thought you was down here. I've found something weird up in the loft, and I mean, *weird*.' He rolled his eyes and Susan wondered if he was stoned.

'Oh, yes?' She didn't want to be distracted from her thoughts about Fergus. And Joe was a chatterbox. He was a fund of knowledge on Victorian houses, no question, and some of the things he'd told her yesterday were interesting but she didn't want to talk to him now.

'You all right?' he asked, looking at her closer.

'Fine.' She nodded, and sniffed. 'I just – had a bit of a shock, that's all.' Then she noticed it was past midday and she hadn't offered him any elevenses. 'Would you like something to drink?'

'Murder a cup of tea. You sure you're all right?'

She nodded. 'Thanks. A bereavement.'

'Someone close?'

'A good friend.'

'I'm sorry – terrible thing, death, the big wipe-out. Wow.' He raised his hands. 'Got to make the most of life, you never know ...'

'No,' she said. 'You never do.'

As she put the kettle on, he changed the subject. 'How long have you lived here, in this house?'

'We moved in end of April, last year. Coming up to a year, I guess.'

He hunched up on a chair and took the shortcake he was offered, gratefully. 'I tell you, what you've got up there ... phew!' He pointed at the ceiling, then expelled air from his mouth in a low whistle.

Choked on his own vomit.

She tried to focus on the builder, but it was hard. 'It's worse than we thought, the roof?' she asked.

He nibbled the biscuit. 'No, the roof's fine, just a couple of tiles off and a bit of flashing that's lifting, fix that no probs.' He paused. 'It's what's *up* there that's blowing me away.'

She looked at him darkly, her imagination clogged by images of Fergus Donleavy choking on his vomit. 'What is up there?'

'Well, if I thought it was yours, I'd keep me mouth shut.' He finished his biscuit and Susan offered him another. 'But it isn't yours, you're not the type.'

The kettle boiled. Susan poured water into the mug and prodded the teabag with the spoon. 'The type for what?' He was beginning to irritate her. Why couldn't he just come out with it and tell her straight?

He popped half of the biscuit into his mouth and chewed. 'The occult.'

Susan knocked over the cup, then leapt back from the work surface as scalding tea poured on to the legs of her dungarees.

Joe jumped to his feet and helped her mop up the mess.

'Thank you,' she said, when they were straight again. 'What did you mean exactly, the *occult*?'

'In the loft.'

Frowning, she poured him a fresh cup. 'The loft? I don't think I'm quite on your bus.' Shakily, she added milk, then handed him the mug. 'Sugar?'

'Three, please.'

He spooned it in, and then he said, 'Did you know the people who lived here before?'

'No, they moved abroad. The husband got transferred by his company – we never met them.'

Joe nodded. 'I think you'd better come and take a look. You OK on a ladder?'

'I'll be fine.'

He held the ladder for her as she climbed. When she reached the top and had to haul herself over the sharp edge she began to think this hadn't been such a smart idea. Being careful not to put any weight on Bump, or to jar him, she hauled herself slowly and clumsily off the ladder, and crawled on her knees on to the first joist.

Then she stood up, steadying herself on a rafter, getting her balance, frightened now of falling and harming the baby. Joe clambered up after her, then switched on a powerful torch. In the beam she saw a dead mouse in a trap; it looked as if it had been there a while. She remembered that John had caught a lot of mice last year; he must have forgotten to check recently, she thought, making a mental note to remind him.

Perspiring heavily from the exertion, and apprehensive both of falling and of what she was going to see, she followed him, extra mindful of his instructions to tread only on the joists. They squeezed past the chimney breast and into the right-hand side of the dark roof space. It was here that Joe had been working, she could see the power tool; strips of roofing felt were hanging down and some had been removed completely. She noticed also that an area of the loft insulation had been lifted.

Joe pointed the beam of his torch up at a panel where the felt had been removed and Susan could see that something had been drawn or airbrushed there in black. As she neared it, she saw what it was. A pentagram.

She could not believe her eyes. It was like a slap, a taunt, a sick joke. She swallowed, her throat dry and tight, and she was trembling as if an electrical current was running through her. The ink or the paint, or whatever it was, looked bright; it had been done recently.

The beam moved to the next panel and there was another symbol she recognised: the looped-key shape of an ankh. Then another symbol, a hideous one that looked like a weather-vane with a skull on the top.

Then Joe dropped the beam down to the space between the joists where he had lifted the insulation. She saw a reversed swastika. Then in another space she saw a goat's head inside an inverted pentagram. And what surprised her, almost above everything, was that the detail in these drawings was quite incredible. These hadn't been scrawled up here by children, they had been drawn with intense care and artistry.

Her mind was flooded by Fergus Donleavy's words, all the seemingly fantastic things he had told her about the occult connections and activities of Mr Sarotzini and Miles Van Rhoe, and now this incredible, eerie stuff here, in her house.

It was as if there was a link – but there couldn't be. This really had to be a coincidence.

She shivered. *Coincidence.* She was doing it herself now, she was doing the thing she had always attacked in John and in others, she was trying to shrug off as a coincidence something that she didn't want to face. And a voice in her head was telling her that this was wrong.

The builder was looking at her. 'So what do you make of this?' he asked.

'What do *you* make of it?'

'Heavy. This is heavy. And you haven't seen the best bit.'

He knelt down, lifted away another section of the orange insulation, then shone his torch down onto a metal box, about four inches long and two inches wide, with wires running from it.

'What's that?' she asked.

'Something to do with your telephone system. I'm not sure what it does exactly – might be a ringing converter. Do you have a lot of phones in the house?'

'Yes.'

'Probably what it is.'

Susan remembered the man from Telecom who had been working up here. Christ, had he seen these symbols? What had he thought?

And then something launched itself from her memory. The man in the dream, hallucination, whatever, that night in the clinic, that strange erotic hallucination when that man from Telecom had been making love to her.

She looked down at the symbols again, then up, and she noticed more panels each time she looked. A lot of the symbols she didn't recognise. Bump stirred inside her, restless suddenly. *Are you picking up my anxiety?*

I'm having crazy thoughts. This man from Telecom. These symbols. The dream. Has to be a coincidence.

A *meaningless* coincidence.

Please let it be.

'It's not this gizmo,' the builder said, as he carefully lifted away the metal box, revealing a small indent cut neatly beneath it. It was in the shape of a miniature grave, and lined with black velvet. 'It's this. This is what's really blown me away.'

Susan peered closely. Lying in the velvet was a slender object. Although it was shrivelled and leathery-looking, there was no mistaking what it was. A human finger.

Susan's scalp constricted and a slick of fear rode down her spine. The whole roof space seemed to be shrinking around her. She turned away in revulsion from the finger, then her eyes were drawn back to it. She wanted to touch it, to know that it was real and not something from a joke shop, but she was too frightened. It was real, no question, and it looked like a woman's. Instead she glanced up and then around, stared at the meticulously painted occult symbols in each panel that had been concealed by the roofing felt.

'How far along the roof do these go?'

'Not very far,' Joe said. 'I've worked it out. They're directly above just one room. The one you're decorating with the little kiddie wallpaper.'

Chapter Forty-nine

Kündz watched Detective Sergeant Rice. The policeman was doing a thorough job, and this was only right.

Susan had been deeply shaken by what her fool builder had shown her, and Kündz was angry at the man, Joe, for distressing her. He was aware that an unborn child can sense its mother's stress, and this was so unnecessary, to upset the baby like this. But now the policeman, Detective Sergeant Rice, was standing in the living room in his uniform, and looked a picture of authority. His presence gave reassurance, his influence was calming; this was a policeman who was a credit to his force.

Time was nearly up now. Mr Sarotzini had been informed by Mr Van Rhoe that this cyst inside Susan was badly twisted and its blood supply was cut off. This meant that it was about to start turning gangrenous.

Kündz took the photograph of Casey from a drawer and studied it once more. A pretty girl: there was so much of Susan in her. It was too bad what he had to do, but it was Susan's fault.

Then he took from the same drawer a cigarette lighter, a gold Dunhill with the initials AW engraved on the lid. This was a nice lighter, beautifully made. It had such elegance that it made him wish he smoked: he could have enjoyed the pleasures of using such a lighter. He flicked open the lid and listened to the hiss of escaping gas, then closed it again. Yes, such engineering excellence. This was a lighter that was as beautifully constructed, in its own way, as his Mercedes car or his Rolex wristwatch or his Church shoes. Quality. The more he discovered about quality the more he admired it. There was beauty in quality and beauty was truth. The poet Keats had written that.

The detective said to Susan and John, 'Did you look in the loft when you bought the house?'

John replied, 'I just had a glance around. Actually, I thought there was something strange last time I went up there – something about the roofing felt – but I couldn't work out what. Now I realise it's been disturbed.'

'But you don't know when?'

'No.'

'The surveyor's report didn't say anything.'

John showed him the survey, which made no mention of the markings. 'Has anybody been up in this loft since you bought the house?'

John and Susan looked at each other. 'An engineer from Telecom,' she said.

'No one else?'

'Other than the builder, I don't think so, no,' Susan said.

'Maybe the rest of the body's buried in the garden,' John said, then immediately regretted his joke. The detective was looking at him too seriously.

'We could dig it up for you, sir, if you like,' he said.

'No,' Susan said, quickly. 'No, I don't want that.'

Rice looked distastefully at the finger. 'I'll have Forensic check this out, see what we can find out about it.'

'Presumably it has some occult ritual significance,' John said. 'Cut off someone during some rite.'

'Or it might have been taken from a corpse in a graveyard – or a mortuary,' the policeman countered. Then, folding it carefully in the velvet, he asked, 'So, you don't know anything about the people you bought this house from?

'No,' John answered.

The detective nodded. 'Might be worth making some enquiries, see if they can throw any light on this.' Then he grimaced. 'That's the most likely scenario, that they were up to some occult practices.'

'Great,' John said. 'Maybe we should have the place exorcised.'

'If you believe in that sort of thing,' the detective replied, dismissively. His radio crackled, then Kündz heard a staccato voice come from it, something indecipherable. Rice wrote his name and phone number on a sheet of paper, which he tore from his notepad. 'If there's anything else you think of, you can reach me on this number.'

Then he left.

Susan closed the front door, then rounded on John. Her voice was quiet at first, and rapidly got louder. 'You knew about this. You're in with them, aren't you?'

'In with who?'

'This is the part of the deal you didn't tell me about. Don't lie to me John, *don't*.'

'Hon!'

'Don't lie to me.'

John raised his arms in the air. 'I'm not lying to you, hon. I don't know what you're talking about.'

'Oh, yes, you know. This has been planned, hasn't it? You're giving my baby to Mr Sarotzini so that he can sacrifice it – he and Van Rhoe – and you're in this with them.'

John tried to put his arms around her, but she stepped back from him, pressed herself against the wall, and shouted, 'Keep away from me!'

John stayed where he was. 'Hon, you got all this shit from Fergus Donleavy. I told you, from all the stuff he said, he must have had his wires crossed, and now he's dead from a drinking binge. I think the poor bastard must have been flipping out – had a nervous breakdown or a brainstorm or something. I'm really shocked that he's dead, I liked the guy a lot, but what he said to you on Monday, I mean, I'm sorry, but he'd lost it.'

Susan stared at John coldly. 'No, you're wrong. Fergus tried to warn me about Mr Sarotzini and Van Rhoe, and now they've killed him. You'll probably find they murdered Harvey Addison and your composer, Zak Danziger, as well.'

John moved away from her in despair. 'Come on! What did Harvey have to do with any of this?'

'You explain it!' she shouted at him. 'You tell me how come all that freaky stuff is right above my baby's bedroom! Tell me about that for a coincidence.'

John went through into the kitchen and sat down on a chair. He put his head in his hands. Susan came to the doorway and stood there, white as a ghost. 'Hon, you chose the bedroom,' he said quietly. 'You could have decorated any of the four spare rooms. You chose that one.'

She said nothing for a moment, and then, 'Why are you refusing to believe this? Or are you lying to me?'

'Don't do this to me, Susan,' John said, shakily. 'I love you, more than anything in the world.'

'You don't love my baby,' she replied. 'If you really loved me, you would love my baby. You're either lying to me about all this or you're an idiot, a blind idiot.'

John stood up, sharply, sending the chair crashing over backwards. Without saying another word, he stormed past her and took his coat from the rack. He opened the front door and went out, slamming it shut behind him.

Susan sat down, folded her arms around her abdomen and gave Bump a hug. She sensed the baby nuzzling her in return. She whispered, 'It doesn't matter. I love you, that's what matters. You and me, we love each other, right? I'll protect you, you're safe with me, I'll *never* let you go. And I'm gonna find out the truth about this. I'm gonna find out just what the hell is going on. But before I do anything, I'm gonna make sure you're safe.'

She heard John's car drive off.

Then she took the cordless phone off the cradle and dialled. Moments later, she said, 'Could you give me the number for British Airways, passenger reservations, please?'

Chapter Fifty

'Zilch,' said Archie.

'Nothing at all?' John stuck his squash bag down on the bench in the locker room. He didn't feel much like playing tonight but knew that the exercise would do him good. It might clear his brain a little and ease the tension that had been racking up inside him for several days now.

Archie took off his jacket. 'How's Susan?'

John drew breath, silently. 'Fine. And Pila?'

Archie grimaced and unbuttoned his shirt front. 'She's crazy, nearly bit off my nipple last night. Look, can you see? That's where she drew blood.'

Archie's body was not a pretty sight at the best of times, and the clearly visible scab did not improve it. All the same, John decided he'd prefer to have a nipple half chewed off by a wild Spanish beauty than have no sex at all.

No sex, and he had had to lie every night next to his wife who was both pregnant with another man's baby and freaked out of her mind that the baby was going to be used as a sacrifice. Nothing he said would calm her down, and it did not help that he, too, was feeling uneasy about it all.

He'd contacted the previous owners of the house, a retired architect and his wife – they'd gone to Australia to be closer to their children, who had emigrated years back. He had spoken to both the husband and the wife, and they had sounded charming, normal people. Of course, you couldn't be completely sure about anyone, but John was as certain as he could be that news of the occult drawings and the severed finger in the loft had come as a total surprise to them.

As they rightly pointed out, the house had been empty for almost a year before John and Susan had bought it: it was quite possible that there had been squatters who had done this, although Susan didn't buy the squatter theory. She seemed convinced that these symbols proved that Fergus Donleavy had been telling her the truth.

John wished Fergus had kept quiet: it had been crazy to worry Susan like

279

this, and the discovery of the symbols couldn't have come at a worse time. She had already been at a low ebb before Fergus's death – which had really rocked her – and this discovery had been the final straw.

And, no question, the symbols were disturbing. The sheer quality of the drawing was eerie: someone had gone to great trouble both to do them and hide them. And they had taken the same trouble over the compartment containing the gruesome finger. The squatter theory made some sense to him. But however much in his heart he wanted to dismiss the other theory, that Mr Sarotzini and Miles Van Rhoe were occult practitioners, the deaths of Zak Danziger, Harvey Addison and Fergus Donleavy preyed on his mind. There was a link, which might be only wild speculation but Donleavy was a respected academic – and Mr Sarotzini's obsession with secrecy had always bothered John.

He'd asked Archie to see whether he could find out anything about the Vörn Bank's connections that might yield any clues, in the hope that it would prove to Susan and himself that her fears were ungrounded.

It had been a horrendous weekend. Susan had been withdrawn, afraid of being in the house because of the symbols yet equally afraid to go out. And he had asked himself, many times, what choice he would have made if he could turn the clock back. What would their life have been like if they had rejected Mr Sarotzini's offer? And when this was all over, would their love for each other, their passion, ever get back to how it had been. Or had he, or Susan, or both of them changed for ever?

It was crazy. DigiTrak was doing so well, yet he found it hard to concentrate in the office and stay motivated. All the money they were making didn't mean anything. Sure, the bank balance was fine, Clake was sickly sweet whenever they spoke and had even asked John if he and Susan would like to come to Wimbledon this summer as guests of the bank.

John said, 'I don't understand how a company can be so – *invisible.*'

'Easy. Nominee directors, nominee shareholders. This Vörn Bank is probably a subsidiary of another bank, registered somewhere like the Cayman Isles, which is a subsidiary of another bank which is registered in Liechtenstein, which is a subsidiary of another one that's registered in the Dutch Antilles, and so on. If you have enough money you can be invisible, John. It would make a good on-line game for you for the Internet – hunt the real owners of fictitious companies.'

John removed his tie and slipped it over a peg. 'So, this cigarette lighter of yours that you reckon the guy from the bank stole. It could have gone half-way round the world by now?'

'Very witty.' Archie tugged on his squash shirt. 'Still pisses me off, that. I can't get over it. If I see that goon again – what's his name? Kündz.'

'No way to talk about a valued client, Archie.'

'Yup, well, maybe as he's a valued client I'll take him out on my boat one day in a force eight and ask him how he's enjoying my lighter while he honks over the side. Talking of which, this summer ...' He paused to pull on his sports socks. 'I thought, if the weather's half decent, of taking the boat over to France. We could take the girls, have a week cruising along the Normandy and Brittany coast, maybe go over to the Channel Islands. Fancy it?'

'Sounds good, I'd love to.' *Normality*, John thought. *That's the answer.* Plan things ahead. Get Susan to see there's life beyond the birth of the baby. Organise things for her to look forward to. Do the whole summer season this year, the Derby, Ascot, Wimbledon, Henley, Glyndebourne, the British Grand Prix, Cowes Week, Last Night of the Proms. Why not? She used to love all that. John pulled his shoes from his bag. 'Arch, you've never heard anything strange about the Vörn Bank, have you?'

'Strange?'

John nodded. 'A bank that employs someone who steals cigarette lighters doesn't sound like the usual image of the respectable Swiss banks we hear about.'

Archie looked at him. 'Something's really bothering you about this bank. What is it?'

John lowered his voice as someone came into the changing room. 'This probably sounds nuts. I'm just curious to know if they have any occult connections.'

'*Occult?*' Archie started tying one of his squash shoes. 'You mean black magic, witchcraft, that kind of occult?'

'Uh-huh.' John pulled a lace tight.

'Actually,' Archie said, standing up and stretching, 'it's quite interesting you should say that.'

John waited while Archie rummaged in his bag and produced a squash ball, which he squeezed as if he was testing the strength of his hand. 'Yup, that's quite interesting.'

'The suspense is killing me, Arch.'

Archie pocketed the ball, picked up his racquet and examined the strings. 'What are they called, those occult things?'

'What things?'

Archie struck the strings with his fingernails and they made a high-pitched ping. He seemed satisfied with the sound. 'You know, the symbols, mathematical thing, those five-pointed stars – there's a word for them.'

'Pentagrams?'

'Yup. Well, this guy I work with, next desk to mine, Oliver Walton.' He brought the racquet up to his ear and pinged the strings again. 'Last summer, on a hot day, the air-conditioning was down. He rolled up his sleeves, and I saw this thing on his arm. It was tiny, I thought it was a mole – then I looked closer and realised it was one of these things.'

'A pentagram?'

'Yup. I asked him why he had it, and he went very strange, quite huffy, rolled his sleeves back down, never really gave me a proper answer.'

'What *did* he say?' John was disturbed.

'Just mumbled about it being personal, some shit like that. Tell you the truth, it was a busy day and I forgot about it.'

'Do you get on with this guy, Oliver Walton?'

Archie grimaced. 'He's all right to work with. Don't see him socially, no idea what he does. He's a closed book, rarely talks.'

'He makes a lot of dough?'

'Serious dough.'

'Like you?'

'Yah, but I spend it. God knows what he does with it. Probably sticks it under the floorboards.'

'Wrapped in velvet?'

Archie didn't get this remark.

It was half past nine when John arrived home, and he was surprised that Susan's car wasn't outside the house. Just to make sure, he checked the street but there was no sign of it.

As he came in the front door leaden silence greeted him. Susan was not in. There was no note, and no supper had been prepared.

He dialled the answering service. There was just one message, from a Detective Sergeant Shawcross wanting to make an appointment to come and talk to Susan in connection with Fergus Donleavy's death. The message had been left at four fifty-five p.m.

Increasingly worried, he checked out each room, just in case she was lying unconscious somewhere, but when he checked their *en suite* bathroom, his stomach began to churn. Her toothbrush wasn't there. A few bottles were absent from the bathroom shelves. Her dressing gown, always hooked on the back of the door, was gone.

A cupboard door was ajar in the bedroom.

Her slippers had disappeared.

And, when he looked further, her large blue suitcase was gone.

Had it started? Prematurely? It was possible, particularly with the pains she'd been getting, that she'd gone into labour.

He thought this through. She could have called an ambulance – no, she'd have called Miles Van Rhoe. There was a number for him somewhere, an emergency number, day or night, and he was trying to remember where he had seen it. But if an ambulance had taken her, where was her car? Perhaps she'd driven herself. Why hadn't she rung him and left a message on his mobile? Surely she would have done that?

Then the phone rang. He dived for it, and was disappointed to hear Kate Fox's voice. John told her that Susan wasn't in, and she asked him to pass on the details for Fergus Donleavy's funeral. Next Tuesday, a crematorium in North London. He wrote it down on a slip of paper, and told Kate he'd give Susan the message as soon as she came in.

He put the note on the kitchen table and weighted it down with a pepper-mill. Then he hunted for Miles Van Rhoe's number, and finally, remembering, found it skewered on a hook on a shelf, along with the menus from the local takeaways.

He got the engaged tone and hung up. His brain was racing. Had she had an accident? Passed out shopping somewhere? He dialled Van Rhoe's number again and this time it started to ring. A gong sounded and a recorded voice told him that the call was being diverted. Then there was a ringing tone again, a different pitch, and almost immediately it was answered by a suave male voice saying, 'Miles Van Rhoe.' There was a din in the background, a babble of conversation

And John wondered whether he was making a fool of himself. Perhaps Susan was out with a girlfriend tonight and he'd forgotten. His confidence stripped by this thought, he said, 'Oh, hello, it's John Carter, Susan Carter's husband?'

The voice that came back was warm and friendly. 'Yes, good evening, how very nice to hear you. What can I do for you?'

He was so calm that John knew right away he'd made a mistake in calling him. 'I – I'm just a little concerned. I got home and Susan's not here, and there's no note or anything. I just thought, maybe something might have happened and you'd taken her into the clinic.'

Now Van Rhoe sounded worried. 'No, I haven't heard from her, not since I last saw her a couple of days ago.'

'Is it possible she could have passed out somewhere? Or gone into labour?'

In spite of the anxiety in his voice, Van Rhoe kept it calm. 'Well, yes, Mr Carter, these things are possible. I'm sure if she'd gone into labour she'd have rung me. She's a very level-headed young lady.'

John did not want to contradict him. 'Yes, of course, I'm sure too.'

'Have you tried the police? Or the hospitals?'

'No, not yet.'

'It would be worth ringing them. I'm afraid I'm at a medical dinner and I'm about to give a speech in a few minutes, otherwise I'd offer to help you.'

'No, don't worry, thank you, I can do that. I'm sure she's all right and I'm just panicking.'

'I'm sure she is, too. Will you call me later, in an hour or so, and let me know if everything is all right?'

John promised he would. Then he sat down at the table and asked directory enquiries for a list of the local police stations and hospitals. The *Daily Mail* newspaper lay on the table along with the morning post. There was an opened letter from Susan's mother, a couple of circulars addressed to him and an electricity bill.

He jotted down the numbers the operator reeled off, then rang each in turn. No police station had any report of Susan Carter, and no hospital had admitted her.

He wasn't sure whether to be relieved or even more concerned.

At eleven o'clock he rang Miles Van Rhoe again and told him Susan still had not appeared. There was a roar of talk going on in the background that made it hard to hear. The obstetrician sounded as if he'd had a few drinks, which annoyed John. He thanked John for keeping him informed, and suggested he tried another circuit of the hospitals and police.

John tried again, still with no success. Then he began ringing round all her friends, even Caroline Addison whom he woke up, but without success.

Susan had vanished.

Chapter Fifty-one

It was here, leaving the Customs hall, that the biggest danger lurked. Susan was feeling leadenly tired as she pushed the baggage cart out into Arrivals, the exertion making her perspire.

She scanned the crowds, the nameboards and placards that were being held up. She was looking for a face, she didn't know whose face, maybe Mr Sarotzini's, more likely one she wouldn't recognise but which would recognise her.

Although she was five thousand miles away, she wasn't dropping her defences, not for a moment. Her eyes peeled the faces, and she bit her lip, glancing behind her, all around her, picking up people she recognised from the plane, letting them go again. There had been five possibilities on the flight: five men travelling alone who could have been following her. She had deliberately hung back in the baggage hall, watching them, letting them go ahead of her. She couldn't see any of them now.

She knew that she'd been lucky that no one had queried her condition when she'd checked in; in advanced pregnancy, without a doctor's letter, they could have refused to let her on the aeroplane. But she hadn't put on much weight in her face, and the bulky coat she wore concealed her bulge.

Bump had slept most of the way over but was awake now. He was troubled, too. Susan looked all around her again – she could feel Bump's anxiety, her throat was dry, she wanted to get out of here quickly.

It was a murky, wet afternoon. In the Alamo lot she couldn't see anyone to worry about. It was quiet, one group of tourists piling themselves into a people carrier and a couple who looked like they could be on honeymoon loading up a convertible. With perspiration guttering down her, Susan fumbled around with the seat-belt adjustment of her rental car, trying to let it out so that it would fit over her extended abdomen. Then she drove up to the checkout barrier.

'Welcome to LA, Bump,' she said, a few minutes later as she trod on the gas pedal and accelerated on to the freeway. Bump responded by turning and rolling over inside her. Bump was relaxed again, now that they were in the car and away, but Susan wasn't. She was watching every car behind her in her mirrors.

'They want you for their rituals, they want to do hideous things to you, Bump, I don't know what kind of things, but they're not getting a chance. You're going to be born here, in California, you'll be safe here. Your granny and grandpa are going to help me look after you. You'll like them. They never made a success but they found their own kind of peace in life – well, they would have done if this thing hadn't happened to Casey.'

Susan fell silent. The wipers swung backwards and forwards in front of her, a truck thundered past so close that she swerved away from it, and a four-track on her inside gave her an angry blast on its horn. Now she was watching a sedan that was right on her tail – it had been there for a couple of minutes. She accelerated and the sedan accelerated. She slowed, the sedan slowed.

She tensed. Just one man on his own driving. Then the sedan peeled away, heading for an exit ramp. Susan breathed out. She concentrated on her driving for a while, and then she said, 'You're going to like Casey, she's your auntie. I mean, she's not going to be like a normal auntie who takes you out, buys you presents, that kind of stuff, but that doesn't mean she won't love you any less. You understand?'

Bump turned and rolled again in acknowledgement. Bump was going to *adore* Casey.

Susan switched her mind to medics. She needed someone to recommend an obstetrician. That wasn't going to be a problem – she had plenty of friends here, and she knew this place. Within twenty-four hours she'd be deluged with more recommendations than she could handle.

She exited the freeway at Venice and it was only a couple of miles now. Just a couple of miles and she'd be home. London was a long way away, another planet. Maybe it had all been a bad dream, and London didn't really exist, or maybe it did, but in a parallel universe and, in another parallel universe, Fergus Donleavy was still alive.

This was her reality now, here. She wiped away a tear with the back of her hand. Bump was real. This was her one certainty. Bump was the most real thing ever, in her entire life.

And, in just a few minutes now, they'd be home and safe.

And now she had to figure out what she still had not yet figured out. Which was what the hell she was going to tell her parents.

Chapter Fifty-two

Computers talk to each other, they shake hands down telephone lines and across radio waves, they trade digital data.

This concept, excited Kündz, this world he could not see that went on inside boxes. It had the magic of telepathy, but it was more focused, so much more precise, so much easier to use.

He found it incredible.

Three computers were talking to each other now – it was like a conference call. One was a circuit board in a tiny metal box clipped to the underside of Archie Warren's Aston Martin; one was inside a satellite orbiting the Earth; and the third was located in the rack of computers that lined one wall of Kündz's windowless monitoring room in his attic flat.

This computer here, right in front of him, was not happy. It switched on a warning light and an audible alarm. Archie Warren's Aston Martin had deviated from its normal route after squash on a Tuesday night. It should be heading home, but it wasn't. It was going in the opposite direction. It was going back towards the offices of Loeb-Goldsmid-Saxon.

The tyres squealed as Archie pulled into the entrance of the underground car park. He did this deliberately, to impress the night-security man; with this Aston Archie was like a big kid showing off his toy.

The night-security man, whose badge bore the name Ron Wicks, nodded at him from behind his glass window. Ron Wicks saw a fat prick in a flashy motor. He didn't know it was an Aston Martin, he wasn't interested in cars, he couldn't tell an Aston Martin from a Toyota, he didn't give a shit about them.

The only thing Ron Wicks cared about was whether his wife, Min, whose breast cancer had spread, would live to see their first grandchild born in three months' time, because that was what Min desperately wanted. There was nothing unusual about an employee arriving at nine thirty p.m. This company traded around the clock with the world; people were coming and going all the time in their flash cars and their flash suits.

Archie, driven by curiosity and by a desire to help John, who had seemed genuinely worried, rode the twenty storeys in the bronze elevator. Something was going on with John Carter and this deal with the Vörn Bank that was chewing him to pieces. Archie had repeatedly questioned his friend, but John had not been forthcoming. The only thing Archie could come up with was that the bank might have links with organised crime, and that John might be under some pressure over repayments – or at least something like that. But why wouldn't John tell him *that*?

The elevator doors opened and he stepped out into a dark corridor. Almost instantly, the lights came on. They were on a sensor that worked off human body heat, switching on when people came into a room and off when they departed.

The dealing room where he worked was deserted. As he opened the door the lights came on with just the faintest click. The cleaning people had already been: the detritus of the day was gone, no half-empty coffee cups and soft-drink cans littered the desks, it all looked pristine and reeked, squeaky clean, of polish. Only the computers were awake, the screens glowing different colours. Flying toasters drifted across one, tropical goldfish swam across another.

Archie sat at his desk and, out of habit, because it was like a drug from which he could not break free, he logged on, and quickly looked at the US government bonds page to check there had been no drastic movements of the Dow Jones. He also checked the Japanese Futures in Chicago. No movements worth noting since he'd left the office, he was relieved to see, and he hoped it would stay that way until five tomorrow morning, when his trading day began.

Glancing furtively at the door, he slipped from his desk to the one alongside it, belonging to Oliver Walton. The chair, although the same as his own, felt quite different, and the keyboard, also identical, felt lighter. He entered the log-in command, and when asked for his user name, he typed, using the house style of the company, the man's initial followed by his surname: `owalton`.

The computer then requested his password, and Archie had no problem with this: he'd watched Oliver Walton's fingers countless times as he logged on, knew exactly which keys he touched and in which sequence. It had never occurred to him before that there was any point in knowing Oliver Walton's password, but now this little titbit came good.

He typed: `verity`.

And then he wondered, Why *verity*? But he didn't dwell on it. He was now into Oliver Walton's system. He studied the screen carefully, trying to orient himself with the layout, which was pretty much the same as on his own computer, the standard software package that all employees used. Vertical columns of icons. A row of analogue clock faces horizontally along the top of the screen, covering key time zones across the globe. An organiser on the left of the screen displaying a list of priorities for tomorrow.

He tried a quick scan through Walton's file headings then, after glancing warily around once more, typed in a search command for the name, Vörn Bank, and pressed the return key.

Moments later a list of what appeared to be file headings appeared but, to his surprise, they were in a language he could not identify, perhaps Greek, he thought, trying to recall any Greek texts he might have seen in his schooldays. He looked for familiar letters, Alpha, Beta, Gamma, Delta, Omega, but there were none. Maybe it was a code, except it didn't look like one.

He moved the egg-timer cursor to the top line and double-clicked on it. There was a brief pause and then the screen filled with data, a mass of numbers, letters, symbols, all completely unintelligible. He laboriously opened each of the other file headings in turn, which all appeared to be encrypted in this same code.

Glancing anxiously at his watch, he knew Pila was going to be livid with him for being so late, but he couldn't help that. He turned his attention back to the screen, clicking on each of the icons in turn, in the hope of discovering a program that would translate the code, but without luck.

Computers had never been his forte; there might be something simple that he needed to do, and maybe if he spoke to John and described the code, he'd be able to tell him what it was. He reached for the phone, then hesitated, thinking about the time again, and had a better idea.

He started a new file, then opened the first heading and saved the contents off into the new file. Then he copied this file across to one of his own private files, deleted all traces from Walton's screen of what he had done, and logged off.

Sitting back at his own desk, Archie hastily typed out an e-mail to John, attaching the file. He sent it, then logged off, and phoned Pila to tell her he'd be over to pick her up in twenty minutes. She yelled a torrent of abuse at him.

'Hey! Calm down.'

'Calm down? Me – why I calm down? You say half past eight you gone be home. I cook the dinner ready for half past eight – you know the time is now? Huh? Ten o'clock.'

'I've been in hospital. Emergency.'

''Ospital?' Her whole tone changed. 'No, oh, no, darling, what happened?'

'I had emergency surgery to have my nipple reattached.'

There was a moment of silence. For an instant she sounded shocked. 'No, you –' Then she cottoned on. 'You bassard! You make me all worried!'

'I'll be home in twenty minutes. Get your clothes off!'

'No sex!' she said. 'Food!'

As he walked back down the corridor to the elevators, with a big grin on his face, he didn't notice that the lights in the dealing room had stayed on. They should have switched off automatically but they hadn't, because someone else had entered the room, from another door.

Oliver Walton sat down at his desk, and typed a command on his keyboard for a log trace. It took him less than a minute to find what he was looking for. Then he punched out a number on his phone.

Kündz answered on the first ring. He said, 'Yes.' And then he said, 'Yes,' again. He flipped open the lid of the gold Dunhill cigarette lighter he was holding, heard the hiss of escaping gas, then closed the lid and replaced the receiver. He stared at the lighter. The gold casing had a gridded pattern so it was not smooth, it was like frosted glass. The reflection was just shadow, a blur. He flicked open the lid, then closed it again. He liked this action: it was so well engineered, this lighter, it was a real pleasure to open and close the lid.

He telephoned Mr Sarotzini at his home number in Switzerland. 'I need your energy for a communication,' he said.

'This is early, Stefan. I was not expecting your call until tomorrow morning.'

'This is a different situation, an emergency.'

'You need my energy now and you need it again tomorrow morning? You are not leaving me much time to recover my strength.'

'This is necessary,' Kündz said.

'You have in your hand a personal object?'

'Yes.'

'Good. I am with you now. Can you feel me?'

'I can feel you.'

And he could, he really could. Kündz concentrated hard and, after only a few moments, he felt the connection between the two of them increasing, getting stronger and stronger until it felt as if Mr Sarotzini had slipped out of his own body and into Kündz's.

'Now tune in the object, be gentle with it, let it speak,' Mr Sarotzini said.

Kündz did as he was told. He held the lighter gently, cradling it in the palm of his massive hand, and allowed the feelings, the imprint, the vibrations, the memories of this lighter's owner to pour out into his hand. He felt the tiny pulses spread out and upwards through his body. He was a modem now. He was shaking hands with this lighter's owner across the airwaves, they were finding a matching vibration level between them ... now they were connecting ... they were exchanging signals. Yes ... good ... this was good ... the image was forming.

Kündz saw an underground car park. A man who needed to lose weight was walking across it. He could smell cigarettes on this man. The car park was almost empty, just six cars. One was a red convertible, and this man had almost reached it.

Kündz opened the lid of the cigarette lighter with a sharp flick, and heard the click. He shut it again, click. Then he opened it again. Shut it again. Each time a satisfying click. Mechanical excellence.

He could feel every atom in its owner's body.

Archie opened the door of his Aston Martin, clambered in, closed it. It shut with a solid thud. It was a hand-made door, hand-fitted, it was beautifully engineered. As he turned the ignition key, there was a click as the electrics came on. And there was another click as the CD powered up. And there was another click, but this was distant, faint, so faint, so deep inside his head that Archie barely noticed it.

The engine rumbled into life, and it sounded like an orchestra. Archie, the conductor, blipped the accelerator. The tremor of power rocked the Aston Martin and the music of the exhausts filled the car park.

Archie pressed his left foot down on the clutch, but nothing happened. Puzzled, he tried again. The signal travelled from his brain to his foot, but his foot did not respond. He tried a third time, and still no success.

Gone to sleep, he thought. It's gone numb.

He tried to shift position in his seat, but now his arms wouldn't do what he told them either. This was freaky. He saw the rev counter hovering around the thousand mark, dipping and rising. He could hear the rumble of the engine, the boom of the exhaust, and he had his sense of smell, no problem with that, he could smell the rich aroma of the Connolly hide leather interior.

He heard another strange click inside his head, much louder than before.

Someone was tapping on the window. Archie wanted to look round, he knew he must look round, but he couldn't, his head wouldn't rotate.

A voice – Archie didn't recognise it, it might be the car park attendant. The voice was shouting, 'Oi? Oi? Hello in there, hello?'

Archie wondered if the man wanted a light.

At half past eleven, the phone rang. John, sitting downstairs in front of the television, snatched up the receiver, hoping it was Susan – it must be Susan, *please be Susan*.

It was Pila. She sounded worried, angry, hurt, and a little drunk.

'Hello, John,' she said. 'Look I's worried, I sorry it's late but I's really worried. Archie say he was playing squash with you tonight.'

'Uh-huh.'

'He telephone me, I don' know, hour and half ago, he was gone be here in twenty minutes. I try ringing him, no answer his home, his mobile, his office. Where he gone?'

John told her the truth, that he had left Archie at the club at nine o'clock. But he wasn't going to tell her that Archie had half a dozen girlfriends on the side at any one time, and might well have stopped off for a quick bonk on the way home.

And he decided not to tell her that Susan wasn't here, because he didn't want this crazy Spanish wildcat jumping to conclusions about Archie and Susan having run off together. He told her not to worry, Archie would turn up, and that if she was really worried she could try the police stations and the hospitals, just in case he'd had an accident.

After he'd hung up, he poured himself a brandy and finally broke open the pack of cigarettes he'd had in his briefcase for two months.

Susan had packed and gone somewhere. Now Archie had disappeared.

For a wild moment his brain connected the two of them, but he instantly dismissed it. If they were running off together tonight, Archie would hardly have played squash with him first. In any case, Archie was genuinely fond of Pila, far more fond of her than John could remember him being of any previous girlfriend.

And Susan, nearly eight months pregnant, was not about to run off with anyone. Except Mr Sarotzini.

Never.

Was Archie helping Susan to hide?

No way. He lit the cigarette and the first puff made him giddy. He took a second and that felt better: the taste was sweet, intoxicating, comforting; he felt as if he'd had a rush of adrenaline to his chest.

Archie was not involved in this. He wasn't devious. If Susan had asked Archie to help her, Archie would have told him. Archie was *his* friend, *his* chum, not Susan's. Archie was off bonking somewhere, simple as that. But Susan?

Where the hell was Susan?

As he drew on his cigarette and drank his brandy, he ran through the list of possibilities for the hundredth time tonight.

It was a pitifully short list.

Chapter Fifty-three

'He's been like that for an hour,' Ron Wicks said.

He stood beside Archie's Aston Martin with the two uniformed police officers, who had just arrived. The car's engine was still running and the air was thick with exhaust fumes.

One officer opened the door and tapped Archie on the shoulder. 'Sir,' he said. 'Good evening, sir?'

Archie didn't react. He sat, eyes open under the brightness of the dome light, staring ahead.

'He's not said anything?' the second policeman asked.

'Not a word.'

'Catatonic,' the first policeman said. 'I've seen someone go like that with shock, a father at a car accident when his daughter was decapitated.'

'He might have had a stroke,' the other said. 'Have you called an ambulance?'

'No,' Ron Wicks replied. 'I didn't know what I ought to do.'

'I'll call one.' The officer spoke into his radio.

Archie made a strange upward flicking motion with his thumb.

'You say he keeps doing this? With his thumb?' the second policeman asked.

'Yes,' Wicks said. 'Think he's trying to signal to us?'

'Dunno,' the man said, frowning. 'It's odd. Looks more like he's trying to light a cigarette.'

The house sat six blocks back from Venice Beach, but it was more than just a few hundred yards of distance that separated it from the million-dollar homes hunched along the promenade.

It was small, a humble single storey with a dormer and the warped clapboard was badly in need of the same lick of paint it had been needing for a decade. Once it had been white, now it was the colour of nicotine.

Beneath the corrugated iron mail-box was a peeling strip of lettering spelling the name Corrigan.

The vehicles parked outside were in a similar condition. Her father's pick-up had a list to starboard, and her mother's Corolla just looked plain sad. Anyone walking their dog along this neighbourhood could have been forgiven for thinking that a couple of hillbillies lived in here. But they'd have been wrong.

They'd have been surprised by the back yard, with its immaculate flower-beds and its carefully pruned fruit trees, and they'd have been even more surprised by the interior, elegantly crammed with antiques, books and paintings, many of which – all those of boats and seascapes – were by Susan's father.

Susan lugged her blue suitcase up to the front porch, then stood, tense, and with a lump in her throat. It felt strange arriving like this, unannounced, a child fleeing home to its parents. Was she coming back to Los Angeles for good? Had her life with John been just a seven-year interlude? Her emotions were in turmoil, and she was exhausted from the flight and the time difference. It was six p.m. here in Los Angeles, two a.m. London time. The pain in her abdomen was terrible, just solid, endless, red-hot-knife pain now and all the time it felt like it was getting steadily worse.

She still had a key in her purse, but she decided not to use it. This was not the occasion to waltz in, like some great happy surprise. Instead she pulled open the fly-screen, stepped inside the porch out of the rain, and rang the doorbell.

Her mother, Gayle, answered it and stood there for several seconds, jaw open. Susan stared back at her, lamely. Her mother was wearing jeans, a sweatshirt and slippers, and she'd put on a little more weight since Susan had last seen her, over a year ago. Otherwise she seemed little changed. Perhaps the lines in her face were etched even deeper, as if someone had just gone over them with a charcoal pencil, and her hair, shovelled up and clipped untidily, now had more grey than blonde in it. Her mother has been slim and strikingly beautiful, but since Casey's tragedy she'd put on weight, which had stayed, and she'd let herself go, right down to her red-varnished nails, which used to be neat and were now badly chipped.

A smell of cooking came out of the door. Her mother was always making casseroles, Susan could never remember a time when the house hadn't smelt of something good cooking, and this now stirred so many memories.

A whole raft of questions was flooding into those wide blue eyes of her mother's. Your pregnant daughter did not suddenly pitch up on your doorstep with a suitcase, thousands of miles from home, if everything was fine. No way.

'Hon, what's –?'

Susan swallowed, managed a smile, then before she could say anything, she started to cry. The next moment she was in her mother's arms and she was a kid again, just a kid who'd fallen over and hurt her knee, and her mom was hugging her, holding her hard in spite of that big bump between them, and everything was going to be better in a minute, it was all going to be better.

Everything was going to be fine.

Susan had a shower and a short rest. Then they sat in the family room, Susan on the antique settle, her parents in battered armchairs either side of her. She could remember the day her mother had bought the settle, years back, in a garage sale in Santa Monica. Her father, Dick, with his thin, craggy face, furry eyebrows, alert eyes, wistful Henry Fonda smile, and faded denim overalls that reeked of turpentine, stared at the bottle of beer he was holding in his rough, paint-stained hand, and listened.

Susan, who had thought she'd become so much stronger than her parents, was feeling even more like the child she'd left behind, oh-so-many years back. She felt as though she was being interrogated over a misdemeanour. 'John's in league with them,' she said, registering the horror in their faces – except that she wasn't sure whether it was horror or just plain disbelief.

Her mother said, 'Tell us more about what you found in the attic.'

'The *loft*,' Susan corrected. She described the symbols that she could remember, and then the finger. The finger disturbed them.

'This deal that John did with the bank, what kind of say did you have in it?' her father asked.

'It was my choice.' Susan shrugged. 'I went along with it because –' She hesitated.

'Because you trusted John?' her mother prompted. 'Sure you did.'

'I always liked John,' her father said, 'but he's a hustler. I always felt he put ambition above everything else.'

Susan winced as the pain suddenly became acute. It might have been the baby moving.

'I think we should get you to a doctor tonight,' her mother said, anxiously.

Susan shook her head. 'I'm just very tired. It'll be better tomorrow, after I've had some sleep.'

'I'm getting you seen by a doctor tomorrow. We'll go down to the medical center, get you in to see Dr Goodman, you'll like him, he's just the nicest doctor you could ever meet.'

Susan sipped her apple juice. The air in the room felt sluggish, and she wondered whether she was dreaming all this. It just seemed so bizarre to be here, sitting alone with her parents like this. The silver clock on the mantelpiece had come out of an old Packard car and ran off a battery tucked away behind it. The clock said seven twenty-five, and she did a calculation. It was three twenty-five a.m. in England.

She suddenly felt guilty that she hadn't left a note for John and wondered if she should call him to let him know she was all right, and that she was going to stay over here until the baby was born and until it had the protection of the courts.

But then he would know where she was, and he'd tell Mr Sarotzini or Van Rhoe.

And they would come and get her.

Kündz, sitting in his flat in Earl's Court, listened to Susan saying, 'I can't let my baby go. I can't let it go and be killed.'

Then he heard her mother say: 'If this man Sarotzini shows up here ...'

Susan's father, Dick Corrigan, said, 'We have to be practical, Gayle. Susan's tired and she's pretty emotional right now. She's had a bad shock and she's had a long flight. These flights knock the hell out of you even when you're strong – remember how we felt when we got back from Europe that time?'

Her father continued, 'I don't think we ought to make any decisions right now. I think Susan needs a bite to eat, a good night's rest and then we'll talk about this in the morning.'

'I'm telling you one thing, Dick,' her mother said. 'There's no way she's handing over that baby, not to anyone.'

'Gayle, I don't think we ought to rush to any conclusions right now. We're here for you, Susan, and we're gonna take care of you, but I think we're gonna find there's some other explanation for all this,' her father said.

'There's been a lot in the news about surrogate babies just recently,' her mother said. 'There was a documentary on Channel Nine last week. Maybe we should find a help group for Susan, get some advice?'

Dick Corrigan raised his voice. 'But if John doesn't *want* this baby, how's Susan gonna make him change his mind? Tell me that.'

'He will,' Susan said, with quiet determination. 'When my baby's born, he'll change his mind, won't he?'

Kündz smiled. This was all working out so well. *Oh, Susan, I'm so proud of you.*

Shortly after half past seven in the morning, John arrived in his office, drained and fraught with worry.

He hadn't slept. The one time he had started to nod off, around half past three, Pila had rung him, totally hysterical, from a pay phone at St Thomas's Hospital, to tell him that Archie was in intensive care.

He'd driven straight there and promptly had a row with the ward sister, who wasn't going to let him or Pila see Archie because they weren't relatives. When he got to Archie's bedside, it was a distressing sight. His friend stared blankly ahead, neither responding nor reacting to anything John said, occasionally making an odd flicking motion with his thumb.

A bolshie junior houseman pumped John for information, then lectured him. He told John that Archie was grossly overweight for his height and age, a heavy smoker, doing a crazily stressed-out job. He had played a hard game of squash, immediately followed by alcohol, and had then gone back to work in the office. That made him a pretty good candidate for a whole raft of problems, and a stroke was one of the possibilities high on the list. They wouldn't know more until they got the test results back in the morning.

John sat at his desk, his whole life apparently in tatters. He was beside himself with anxiety about Susan, and deeply upset about Archie – hell, he and his friend were the same age, and he'd always considered Archie indestructible. OK, so *he* wasn't overweight and he didn't really smoke any more, but he was just as stressed as Archie. If something could happen to Archie, it could equally easily happen to him.

He closed his eyes. *Where are you, Susan, darling, hon? Oh, Jesus, where the hell are you?*

He tried hard to put himself in her position. She was pregnant, she was terrified that Sarotzini and Van Rhoe were planning to sacrifice the baby, she was freaked out by the occult shit up in the attic, she was gutted by Fergus Donleavy's death, and now she didn't even trust him.

Everything, in her mind, was a conspiracy against her or, more particularly, against her baby.

Somehow, he had to talk sense to her.

Although he wasn't sure what *sense* was any more. His tired brain was thinking about all that weird shit up in the attic. About Archie's colleague with the pentagram tattoo and the Vörn Bank as a client. He was thinking about how Zak Danziger had conveniently died soon after the Vörn Bank had become involved. About Harvey Addison dying after they'd gone for a second opinion. Fergus Donleavy dying after warning Susan. Now Archie, down with a stroke or whatever.

But how the hell could all that tie together? It couldn't. It was easy to get spooked and jump to conclusions; being calm and rational was much harder. It could be just a chain of coincidences, and Susan, with her hang-up about coincidences, could have got herself into a state over nothing. But however much he told himself that, he couldn't convince himself. Not totally. Worry burrowed away at his confidence, undermining it further all the time.

Susan, where are you?

She wasn't at any of their friends', so where might she have gone? Where would he have gone in her shoes? What was the natural instinct of anyone in trouble? To head for the comfort of home, of parents?

California?

She couldn't have gone to LA, surely. And, anyway, you weren't permitted to fly if you were heavily pregnant.

Jesus, Van Rhoe would do his tank if Susan had left the country – he didn't even want her to leave London, not even for a few hours. He checked his watch. Seven forty-five. That made it eleven forty-five p.m. in Los Angeles; late, but that couldn't be helped. He looked up Susan's parents' phone number in his address file, and dialled it.

His father-in-law answered, sounding as if he had just woken up. His tone was more formal and cooler than normal. Probably because it was late, John reasoned.

'Dick, look, I'm sorry to bother you, and I don't know how to explain this very well – but I think Susan might have had some kind of breakdown. I arrived home last night and there was no sign of her. She seems to have packed a bag and left. I wondered if by chance you or Gayle had heard from her, or whether she'd come over to you?'

There was a brief silence, then Dick Corrigan said, 'No, I – Gayle and I – we didn't hear from her for a couple of weeks – er, Sunday last she called. Sounded fine, a little tired but fine.'

John asked him to call if they heard from her. He promised he would, asking John to do likewise, then hung up.

John sank his head into his hands. Just in case Susan had sent him an e-mail he switched on his computer, and logged on. The usual twenty or so awaited him. Then, scanning through them, he saw that one was from Archie Warren, sent at nine forty-seven p.m. last night, with an attachment. He double-clicked on the message and read it:

> john, all the stuff on vörn bank here seems to be encrypted.
> loads of files. if you can decode this file, let me know and i'll
> copy the rest over to you. read then eat this. arch.

John stared at it, thinking. Archie hadn't mentioned this at squash – and, from the time it had been sent, he must have gone back to the office afterwards. Archie had found the files on the Vörn Bank, and then he had had a stroke?

Could there be a connection? Was he crazy to try to make one?

Or crazy to dismiss it?

He double-clicked on the attachment, to open it, and seconds later his screen was filled with a jumble of letters, numbers and symbols, meaningless to him. He called Gareth and asked his partner to come into his office.

A few minutes later, looking more hung-over than usual and dressed in clothes that appeared to have been retrieved from a laundry basket, Gareth was staring at his screen. 'PGP,' he announced.

'Pretty Good Privacy?' John said. It was one of the Internet's standard encryption systems.

'Yup.'

'Can you decode it?'

Gareth looked at him as if he were addressing a child of three. 'Sure, no problem. Give me a Cray supercomputer and four years off and I'd be in with a sporting chance.'

'Shit. You serious?'

Gareth turned back to the screen. 'What's the provenance of this?'

'How do you mean?'

'Does it come from someone who knows what they're doing?'

'Yes, I would think so.'

Gareth lit a cigarette. 'So it's probably an NP-complete problem.'

'Uh?'

'Nondeterministic polynomial.'

'Want to give it to me in English?'

'Sure. You're fucked.'

'Great, that's really helpful, Gareth.'

'To read this, you need to have the encryption phrase – the sender would have it, and the recipient. When you encrypt something in this system, you provide a key, 8-bit, 16-bit, 24-bit, or even higher, depending on how sophisticated you are. It works on a doubling principle, like the grain of rice on the chessboard.'

'What grain of rice?'

'You stick one grain of rice on the first square, two on the second, four on the third, eight on the fourth, sixteen on the fifth and so on. By the time you reach the sixty-fourth square you have three times the entire world annual production of rice, or something like that. That's the same principle on which this works.'

John stared at him with a feeling of helplessness. 'So? There's no way we can read this?'

Gareth looked round for an ashtray, then flicked ash into the waste-paper basket. 'How urgent is it?'

'Seriously urgent.'

Gareth paced up and down the office and windmilled his arms. 'Um, right, OK, um, I have a friend, right?' He moved towards John and lowered his voice, looking around, nervously. 'We were at Sussex together – he's now at GCHQ, you know, the top-security government listening place. They have a Cray there, and he's told me this, strictly off the record, that they have the keys to most Internet encryption systems. He's into real ale. I could try to have a drink with him at the weekend.'

John shook his head. 'This is really urgent, Gareth. Couldn't you do anything quicker than that?'

His partner looked at the screen again, and said, resignedly, 'Oh, all right, do me a copy. I'll give it a go, no guarantees.'

And Kündz, in a club-class seat, was eating a breakfast of omelette, chipolata sausage and mushrooms, on an early-morning British Airways flight to Geneva.

Chapter Fifty-four

His room looked out on to the vineyards and olive groves on the southern slopes of the Ligurian hills. Down below, on the ribbon of road that mirrored the river's tortuous path across the floor of the valley, lay the burnt-out remains of one of Mussolini's last convoys.

He was thirteen. The war had been over for two years. Local kids, garages and scrap dealers had long ago picked the carcasses of the trucks and half-tracks clean of anything that could be flogged as a souvenir, or carted away on the back of a van, and now just the hulks remained. They had started to rust.

This was his life, this room with its low, slanted ceiling and narrow slit of a window, and its dull little paintings of flowers, and its views out over the valley, which was lush in winter and arid in summer, and up towards the firmament. This room and his books were his life. It was the rear of the attic, and there was a sheer drop of several hundred feet below; no one could see in. No one in the village, apart from the couple beneath him who owned the house, fed him, and slaked his thirst for knowledge with a constant supply of books, knew that he was here. Only a tiny handful of people in the whole world even knew that he existed.

Which was why, when they came for him, he was not expecting it.

He never saw those people who burst into his room that night. It happened in a rush of darkness. He was asleep and then he was awake, with a blindfold over his eyes and a foul-tasting gag forced into his mouth.

Whispered voices around him, he did not know how many, he knew only that he was frightened, and that they were mostly women's. They dragged him from the bed and on to the floor, then hoisted him on to the table that was also his desk. All the time they repeated, over and over and over, 'Ĕll Diavolo ... Ĕll Diavolo ... Ĕll Diavolo.'

He heard the woman who looked after him, Signora Vellucci, screaming for them to leave him alone, warning them of terrible vengeance, but they ignored her.

302

His nightshirt was ripped off him, and then he was being prodded, poked, examined like a calf at market. A woman's voice said, in a pause between the chanting, 'Ce l'ha il padre, deve averlo anche lui.' *It is on his father, it must be on him also.*

Another woman, who was pushing the hairs on his head apart, examining the scalp beneath, murmured that Emil Sarotzini's son even had the devil's hair.

Then a finger probed his anus, pushed hard, coarsely up inside, making him cry with pain into his gag. The finger was retracted, just as harshly, a remark was made that he did not catch and there was a roar of laughter.

Then silence.

Fifty years later, he could still remember this silence.

He could remember the hands that gripped his wrists, his ankles, his thighs, like a vice. One arm went round his neck, pulling his head so tightly down on to the table that he could hardly breathe.

He could remember the fingers seizing his penis and pulling it sharply upwards. And he could remember the panic as he felt the fingers close around his scrotum and another woman's voice saying: 'We are not allowed to kill him, but we can make sure the Sarotzini line ends with this boy. He will be the last.'

And then the pain, oh, yes, the pain between his legs from the blade of the knife. And all the loss that followed from it.

And the words of the Tenth Truth, 'A man who feels no thirst for vengeance feels no pain.' These words he remembered every time he thought back to that night.

No one from that village had ever given birth since 1947. Ajane d'Annunzzi was dying, it was known as the Village of the Damned. No one understood what it was about this place, whether it was something in the water from the chemical plant upwind or the high fungi diet the locals ate. Doctors and scientists, concerned about growing infertility around the world, had done many studies, and Ajane d'Annunzzi had achieved fame in medical papers, but no conclusions had been reached.

Mr Sarotzini was thinking about this now as he stared across his desk at Kündz.

It was necessary to think about this.

'How was your life before I found you, Stefan?' Mr Sarotzini asked.

'It was nothing.'

'And how did I find you?'

'The Voice,' Kündz said. 'It was the Voice that came to you.'

'And what did this Voice tell me?'

303

'It told you where I was living, where it was possible that you would find me, in a village, in Tanzania in Africa. I was five years old.'

'And what were you doing in this village?'

'I was learning to track game.'

'And?'

'That was all.'

'And where did you come from, Stefan?'

'I don't know.'

'A missionary nun who was raped by a game warden?'

'I don't know.'

'Why did the game warden rape the nun?'

'I don't know.'

'What do you know, Stefan?'

'That you came for me.'

'And why did I come for you?'

'The Voice guided you.'

'And why did it guide me?

Kündz gazed down at the thick Persian carpet. 'Because you had need of me. Especially you had need of a gene I carry. A rare gene.'

'And does this Voice guide you, Stefan?'

'You guide me.'

'And what are you, Stefan?'

'"An infant crying in the night: An infant crying for the light: And with no language but a cry."'

'Who wrote that, Stefan?'

'Tennyson.'

'And who is your light, Stefan?'

'You are.'

'So why do you disobey me? Why have you turned weak? Because you are in love? The pleasures of the flesh? These pleasures are a distraction, they are there in your mind every waking moment, they drive you, rule you, obsess you, yes?'

Kündz had no answer.

'Why did you allow Susan Carter to go to America, Stefan?'

'Because you instructed me to.'

'And you always obey me? Are you my Pavlovian dog? Do you salivate when I ring bells?'

Kündz hesitated, and he knew this was a dangerous thing to do. 'Yes.'

'Do you salivate when you think of Susan Carter?'

Again Kündz hesitated.

'I gave you Susan Carter, Stefan, and you let her go to America.'

'My powers are limited,' Kündz replied. 'I do not have the authority to restrict her.'

There was a flash of anger in Mr Sarotzini's face. 'One telephone call to the airport, Stefan, to inform them how many weeks pregnant she was, and they would not have permitted her to fly. That was all you needed to do.'

Kündz lowered his head in shame.

'Look at me, Stefan. You are weakened by your love.'

Kündz raised his head and stared back at Mr Sarotzini, but had no answer. Mr Sarotzini might have congratulated him for having the presence of mind to ensure Miles Van Rhoe was flown over to America immediately, to be there even before Susan Carter landed, but this was not a moment for praise.

'You understand this baby is going to need a father, Stefan?'

Kündz swallowed, nervously. 'Yes.'

'Did I honour my pledge to you, Stefan?'

'Yes.'

'And it was good?'

'It was good.'

'As good as you had dreamed?'

Kündz replied: 'Virgil said there are two gates of Sleep. One is said to be of horn, through which the spirits of Truth find an easy passage. The other made of ivory, through which the gods send up false dreams to the upper world.'

'And through which gate did you enter Susan Carter?'

Kündz thought for a moment because, with Mr Sarotzini, all questions were traps. 'The horn,' he said.

Mr Sarotzini smiled. 'You remember, Stefan, the Fifteenth Truth?'

Kündz replied, '"To achieve your dream is strength. To repeat your dream is weakness."'

And now from a drawer in his desk, Mr Sarotzini produced a barber's razor and handed it to Kündz. 'Is this sharp?'

Kündz tested the keenness of the blade with his finger. He told Mr Sarotzini that it was sharp.

Mr Sarotzini took a cigar from a box on his desk but did not light it. 'Only you and I will ever know the truth, and this baby is the truth.' He examined the band on the cigar, then stared at Kündz. 'I kept my part of our bargain and now you must keep yours. Are you ready to purify yourself, Stefan? To protect yourself against future temptation? To show me that I am wrong and you are not weakened by your love, but strengthened by it?'

Kündz stifled a fleeting surge of panic. He did not want to do this, he really did not, but he could not disobey. And he must demonstrate to Mr Sarotzini that he was not weakened by his love. He tried to calm himself. It would be for the best. He trusted Mr Sarotzini absolutely, and Mr Sarotzini would not make him do this unless it was for the best. It was going to be painful now, but it would be for the best. And he had made his pledge.

He drew a breath and said, 'I am ready.'

Mr Sarotzini went to the cabinet and opened the door. Then he turned on the videotape player and Kündz shuddered. He knew what was coming next and he did not want to watch this, but Mr Sarotzini was presenting him with no alternative.

He had to watch.

Claudie appeared on the screen. She was naked. The left side of her body was a milky white colour, those flesh tones that had so excited Kündz once, that he had found so sensuous. But the right side was a pinky colour and the texture was quite different, and the nipple was missing from the breast.

She was held by chains, one around her neck that rose tightly to the ceiling, one around each ankle, securing them to the floor, and one around each arm, holding them out in the crucifixion position. She was staring at the camera and there was such horror in that face, such terror, and she was screaming, pleading, her eyes bulging with fear.

On the tape, Kündz watched himself enter the frame now and go up close to her. He was holding a knife in his hand, a small boning knife that was as sharp as a razor, and he had no choice, he had to continue with the job he had begun days before.

He remembered that when he had been close up to Claudie, he had tried to communicate that he was sorry, that he really did not want to do this. And Kündz, watching this now, was pleased that this attempt to communicate with her did not show.

He observed himself make a small horizontal incision below her left shoulder blade, being careful not to cut into the flesh itself, and then – even he flinched as he watched what followed – he continued his task of skinning her alive.

After a few minutes, Mr Sarotzini stopped the tape and said to Kündz, 'You would not want to hear Susan Carter scream like this?'

Kündz said that he wouldn't, and he meant it, he really wouldn't.

Mr Sarotzini said, 'When you have done your duty, Kündz, I will keep my second pledge. Susan Carter will be yours for ever.'

Kündz stared back at Mr Sarotzini, stared hard into his eyes, and felt the same trust he always had in the man. It was the right thing, it must be done.

Taking the barber's razor, he went through into the washroom behind Mr Sarotzini's office and closed the door. Swiftly, he unbuckled his trousers, let them fall to the floor and then he dropped his cotton boxer shorts.

Claudie was now, finally, mercifully, dead. But Susan Carter was alive. And if Susan Carter tempted him again, tried to seduce him again, or even just tried to run away again, he understood that Mr Sarotzini would make him punish her the same way he'd had to punish Claudie. And he could not bear to do this, because he loved Susan. He had to save Susan from this.

He tested the blade of the razor again, then fought off his nerves, his hesitation, his doubts, by reminding himself that Mr Sarotzini had experienced this same pain himself, and that he was saving Susan Carter's life. And perhaps some of Mr Sarotzini's powers were so strong because of the way he was. And that if he wanted to become as strong as Mr Sarotzini, he must become like him.

Yes, now he understood, this was Mr Sarotzini's way of telling him, of making him understand. And he did, and it was beautiful.

And he was saving Susan Carter's life.

Flooded with gratitude to Mr Sarotzini, he gripped his scrotum, and his testicles hurt as he squeezed them, as he pulled them tight against the sac, searching for the base of his penis. But this pain was nothing compared to the pain that now followed as he sliced the blade of the razor through the skin and then through the gristle, blood spurting over his hand and dripping in an increasing trickle on to the tiled floor.

He bit his lip, stifling a cry of pain through clenched teeth. He was shaking, his eyes narrowed. He tried desperately to keep his hand steady, fighting the pain, perspiration torrenting down him. There was more, a long way to go, he tried to keep up the concentration, to keep going. *I'm saving your life, Susan.* Tiny grunts, moans, hisses escaped from his mouth: he clenched his teeth even tighter, his body contorting, twisting, bending then straightening.

He must not scream.

A dagger shot right up into his guts, skewering the base of his skull, exploding into needles that ripped through his brain, then down through his body again. He doubled over, let out a roar of pain, followed by a terrible, shocked groan; and then, unexpectedly, the bloodied sac was free in his hand. Near delirious with agony, he dropped it into the lavatory bowl and pulled the chain. Blood sprayed into the bowl. He looked down at the blood streaming on to his thighs and the floor, grabbed a handful of lavatory paper, balled it and pressed it up between his legs.

Then, unable to stand the pain any longer, he knelt, pressed his red-hot forehead against the cool tiles of the lavatory wall and retched. He retched again. He was being weak, he knew, and this scared him. Mr Sarotzini would not approve of this, he had to be strong, had to find strength, had to draw on reserves. Mr Sarotzini was waiting for him, he had already taken enough time, he must show strength.

He retched again, and then he vomited. Afterwards his head felt a little clearer. Staggering to his feet, he took the gold Dunhill lighter from his pocket, and opened the lid. Then, silently reciting each of the Truths in turn, he removed the bloodied paper, and applied the flame to the ragged skin. He felt the pain, the smell of singeing flesh filled his nostrils, but the Truths gave him strength. He continued to repeat them over and over, one after another, until they became like a mantra, and he went on saying them until the wound was cauterised and he had somehow forced the pain into retreat, reduced it to a numb throbbing.

He washed the bloodstains off his shirt-tails, cleaned his hands, straightened his tie, then returned, walking slowly because it hurt terribly to walk, to Mr Sarotzini's office. He informed Mr Sarotzini that he had honoured his pledge.

But this, still, was not enough. Mr Sarotzini nodded, but he was not looking pleased. He told Kündz, 'Now you must explain to me, Stefan, why you have not yet punished Susan Carter for going to the obstetrician Harvey Addison?'

Kündz was unable to give this explanation. His brain was burning, the terrible pain was returning, but he dared not let it show.

'There is a weakness you have, Stefan, which is so dangerous. Do you understand the danger?'

Kündz swallowed, then nodded.

'And you are angry, Stefan?'

Kündz nodded again. He wanted to sit down, to lie down, to grip his crotch, to double up, to vomit again, but he could do none of these things in the presence of Mr Sarotzini.

'You are angry at your weakness? At Susan Carter? You must direct your anger, Kündz, you must focus it. You have brought with you the photograph?'

Kündz pulled the photograph of Casey from his pocket.

Mr Sarotzini nodded at him. Kündz took out the Dunhill lighter and, with it, set fire to the photograph. The banker held out his hand, took the burning photograph, and brought the flame to the end of his cigar. Then he dropped the burning photograph into the glass ashtray on his desk and they both watched as the last corner of it burned. 'You have something personal from Susan Carter, Stefan?'

Kündz produced the tiny handkerchief, embroidered with a blue 'S' that he had taken from the laundry basket in Susan's bathroom. She had never missed it.

Mr Sarotzini looked at his watch; then, holding the cigar in the crook of his finger drew deeply on it. 'Are you grateful, Stefan? Do you now feel gratitude for all I have done for you?'

Kündz dared not open his mouth because he was afraid the pain would show in his voice. He had already shown Mr Sarotzini one weakness, it was unwise to show him another. And he knew that Mr Sarotzini was playing with him now, trying to trip him up. And from out of his terrible pain a warning screamed at him. The Twelfth Truth: 'Gratitude is weakness.'

'I am aware of being privileged, but that is through birth and not charity.'

Mr Sarotzini looked delighted. 'Good, Stefan, that is such a good answer! Now, we need energy. You must hold the handkerchief, the connection will be made better through you than me. Close your eyes. Tune in the handkerchief. Let it speak.'

Kündz saw a tiny room, a child's room, a row of fluffy toys on a shelf, a flamenco-dancer doll inside a cellophane tube. A woman was sleeping in this room. It was Susan Carter.

It was twelve thirty-five p.m., local time, three thirty-five a.m. in Los Angeles.

Chapter Fifty-five

Casey ran on ahead along the hiking trail, though the craggy crimson bluffs and towering boulders, her flaxen hair shimmering beneath the blazing Colorado sun. Susan and her parents lagged behind.

Then Casey stopped and turned, a great big grin on her face, and shouted, 'Hey, come on, you guys, you're gonna miss the show!'

She sprinted down the ramp alongside the auditorium steps, and on to the stage of the deserted amphitheatre. Then she stood, in her jeans, sneakers and Save the Whales sweatshirt, hands on her hips, and hollered to Susan, her parents, and six thousand empty seats: 'This is it, once in a lifetime, Casey Corrigan performing live at the Red Rocks. Yeeeaaaahhhhhhhh!'

Then, using a short stick she had picked up as a pretend mike, she burst into Cyndi Lauper's 'Time After Time', singing at the top of her voice, throwing herself wildly around the stage. Then she followed it with Tina Turner's, 'What's Love Got To Do With It?'. Half-way through she paused. 'C'mon, join in, Mom, Dad, Susan. C'mon ... Susan, Susaaannnnnnn. Susaaaaaannnnnnnnnn. Susaaaaaaaaaaannnnnnnnnnnnn.'

Susan woke in panic, disoriented. Casey's voice echoing in her mind. The bed was too small, the window was in the wrong position. Where was John?

Then she remembered. She was home, in her old bedroom, in her parents' house. She was drenched in perspiration, deeply afraid. Casey.

Casey was crying.

Something was wrong with Casey.

I flew over from London yesterday.

The pain in her abdomen was worse than last night. Her back was aching like hell – probably from the bed, which had been built for a child, not for a heavily pregnant woman. She turned on the light and her watch told her it was three thirty-five a.m.

The Red Rocks. She could remember that day clearly. It was ten – more like twelve – years ago, when they'd gone on a family hiking holiday in the Rockies. Casey, just turned fifteen, had been the greatest fun on that trip. To look at, she was blossoming into a stunning young woman, but inside she was still a playful child, full of confidence and no cares in the world.

Susan could remember standing up there in the vast, deserted auditorium, Denver and the plains way down below them, watching her and suddenly getting that feeling of dread. She'd hardly been able to sing the words because of the foreshadowing she had that something bad was about to happen. It was almost as if she had realised that Casey was too kind, too big-hearted, too friendly for this mixed-up world to be able to leave her alone, and that somehow it was going to draw her in, corrupt her, change her, drag her down to its own level.

Three weeks later Casey took the tab and was changed for ever.

That hadn't been the first time she'd picked up feelings about Casey. Often when they had been kids, even when they were miles apart, she could tell how Casey was feeling. One afternoon she'd had a terrible pain in her right arm, and discovered when she got home that Casey had fallen off her bike and broken her right arm.

Susan knew that telepathy between twins was common, and although it was rarer among ordinary siblings, there were plenty of cases of it. Even during these past years when she'd been in England, there had been moments when she was certain she knew what Casey was thinking, or had felt that Casey was trying to get a message through to her.

She had that feeling now, intensely strongly. A feeling that Casey was frightened.

Bump was awake also – she could feel one of his feet pushing out the skin of her abdomen. He was thrashing around, agitated, as if he was trying to communicate something to her, as if he, too, could sense his aunt's distress.

Outside in the night a siren wailed. She swung herself out of bed, put her feet on the floor, stretched as far forward as she could over her swollen abdomen towards her toes, then straightened herself right up, trying to ease her back pain. She looked at the bed which, along with her suitcase on the floor, took up most of the space in this small, narrow room. It was sagging visibly in the middle.

A row of fluffy toys stared down at her from a shelf above the bed; a flamenco-dancer doll, with jet black hair and an inane smile, sat inside the cellophane tube in which it had been given to her, brought back years ago from some relative's travels.

She padded across to the window, parted the thin curtains and looked out. There was a full moon and this, together with the background glow of the streetlights, made it so bright she could have read a book in the back yard. A creature leapt over the fence, she didn't see what it was – a cat, or maybe a coyote or a raccoon.

Then, without warning, she was hit by a giddying wave of nausea. Unable to move, she gripped the window-sill, hung on to it, trying to keep upright, trying not to fall on the floor and pass out. She leant forward, pushing her head out of the window, so at least she would vomit into the garden, and closed her eyes.

After a few moments the cool night air began to revive her, and the nausea faded. But she stayed longer, breathing in the salty ocean tang, until the dizziness had passed. Then, wide awake now, she eased herself down on the edge of the bed. Her watch said three forty. She did a calculation. Three forty a.m. here made it eleven forty a.m. in London. It was hardly surprising she felt so wide awake: it was the middle of the morning for her.

What was John doing?

In his office, phoning around everyone they knew, trying to find her? For an instant she weakened, wanted to feel his arms around her, to hear his voice, to hear him tell her that he wasn't in league with Mr Sarotzini and Miles Van Rhoe. She wanted so badly to hear it from him now, she wanted him to say it to her face. To *swear* it.

But he couldn't do that because he was in league with them. She thought back to that first night she met Mr Sarotzini, in his club. It was so transparent a set-up. Had the dinner at the Guildhall, where John had met Mr Sarotzini, or *purported* to have met him, been a set-up too, just to fool her?

How far back did John's links with Mr Sarotzini go? She started thinking about the myriad nights when John had arrived home late, or even stayed away somewhere on business. Had those nights been when the coven, or whatever it was they called it, met?

Then she tried to think through it more rationally. Could John really have been a satanist long before she'd married him? If so, why had he never talked about it, never tried to convert her? Perhaps it was connected to DigiTrak's problems, a last resort for John. And he hadn't had the courage to tell her.

Zak Danziger, who had been a threat to DigiTrak, had died weeks after Mr Sarotzini had become involved. But why had Harvey Addison died? That made no sense, and she could see no connection. Fergus had been delving, that's why he had died. She had told John what Fergus had said, and John had reported this to Mr Sarotzini, who had had him killed. And ever since Mr Sarotzini had put in the money, the business had been booming: John had said they'd got almost every contract they'd bid for.

Susan knew from the book she had edited on the occult, and the one she had read on the flight, and from movies she had seen, that occultists, black magicians, satanists, whatever, could influence people. They could manipulate them, hurt them, paralyse them, blind them and even kill them just by concentrating their thoughts on them, just by *thinking* of them. It was like the voodoo doll into which people stuck pins, no different.

Was John in league with them, or had he simply offered them a deal? A baby for sacrifice, no questions asked, in exchange for money and for them using their powers to help his business.

And he hadn't had the guts to tell her.

She thought again of that dream (hallucination? reality?) in the clinic. The man from Telecom. The masked people. What if it *had* been real and not a dream or a hallucination? Had John been there as well, one of the masked people, and she hadn't recognised him?

Fergus had said that Emil Sarotzini was the devil incarnate.

But Emil Sarotzini would be a hundred and ten years old, at least.

If he *was* the Devil incarnate, there was no reason why he couldn't be a hundred and ten years old. Or older.

Then she had an even wilder thought. Was Archer Warren one of them too? Their Tuesday night squash games: did they really play squash?

What about all their other friends? She'd never met any of John's relatives – he had cut himself off from what fragments of family he had. What if all his friends were members of the coven and he'd brought her over, unsuspecting and naïve, from America? *Delivered* her to his coven. And all this crap of his about not wanting children – this had been simply to buy time, to preserve her intact for her true intended role as a brood mare.

Oh, God, Susan, what the hell are you thinking?

'Susaaaaaannnnnnnnnnn.'

She shivered. The cry sounded so close, as if Casey was here in the room with her. Bump thrashed again as if he'd heard it too. *Casey needs you*, he was trying to tell her, urgently.

She pulled on her dressing-gown, quietly opened her bedroom door and, like a child again, tiptoed past her parents' bedroom and downstairs. Using the phone in the kitchen she dialled the clinic's number. After four rings, she got a recorded voice saying the switchboard was closed until seven a.m.

Her anxiety deepening, she dialled directories and asked if there was a night emergency number for the Cypress Palisades Clinic in Orange County. The operator told her there wasn't.

The nausea was returning. Susan looked at the kitchen clock, which said three forty-five, and checked it against her watch, which said three forty-two. Three and a quarter hours before anyone would be at the clinic to answer the phone.

As she hung up, another wave of nausea swept through her. It was followed by another and now she was going to be sick. She just made it across to the sink and threw up violently. The pain inside her felt like a red-hot poker that was being twisted. Then she threw up again, tears streaming from her eyes. She wished her parents would wake, that her mother would come down here and hold her forehead the way she used to whenever she'd been sick as a child. But since Casey's tragedy both her parents had been on medication at night, and slept in drugged comas.

She threw up again, her legs buckling with exhaustion, barely able to support her. There was no more food to come up, she was vomiting foul-tasting, acrid bile now. She coughed, her lungs aching, her eyes blurred, waiting for it to pass now, and for the pain in her guts to subside.

Finally she rinsed out her mouth, and then the sink and began to feel a little better, except now she had a raging thirst. She poured herself a glass of iced water from the fridge and drank it straight down. Then she made her way upstairs again. It was like climbing a mountain. At the top she stopped, doubled up in pain, and had to wait until the attack passed before she was able to move. She made it back to her bedroom, and sat down on the edge of the bed.

Her forehead was burning, and she knew she had a temperature. Something was seriously wrong inside her, she was certain – and scared. It wasn't smart being all this distance away from Van Rhoe. Even if he was a satanist and was going to sacrifice her baby, he was a good doctor, the best. He would know what the pain was and do something about it.

Maybe I'm going into labour.

She had none of the early-warning symptoms Van Rhoe had told her to look out for, no contractions – unless these new pains were contractions. No blood. No mucus plug.

She lay back and closed her eyes, but her brain was whirring too much to sleep. Casey, Casey, Casey.

Casey was calling out to her.

She wondered if she could make it if she drove. She could call a taxi. But the nausea was coming back and she felt too ill to move anywhere right now. She looked at her watch: five after four. Three hours, I can call you. I'll get Mom or Dad to bring me over first thing, you can relax, I'm here in LA, I'm near you, I'll see you in a few hours. I love you.

There was a book at the bottom of her suitcase somewhere. She knelt down, rooted around through her badly packed belongings, and finally found it. Exhausted by even this exertion, she clambered back into bed with it.

It was the second of two reference books she had bought in an occult shop in Covent Garden. She'd read the other on the flight, but this one appeared to go into more detail in the areas that interested her.

She stopped scanning when she reached the section headed 'Amulets and Talismans', and started reading carefully.

According to Sir E. H. Wallis Budd, the egyptologist, the essential difference between an amulet and talisman is that an amulet exercises its protective powers continuously and in general around its owner whereas a talisman is called on to perform some isolated task of protection. Possession of items –

She stopped reading. The finger in velvet in the attic: had that been an amulet or a talisman? Then, as she read on, the egyptologist confirmed that bones, teeth, hair, spittle, blood and body parts all made powerful amulets and talismans.

Bump's hands pushed sharply outwards. Then he rolled, and pushed again, and suddenly into her head came an image of the man from Telecom.

'What do you want?' she shouted at him. And then she bit her lip: she'd shouted aloud.

I'm delirious.

'Susaaaaaaaaaaaaannnnnnnnnnnnnnnnnnnnnnn.'

Bump rolled again.

'Susaaaaaaaaaaaaannnnnnnnnnnnnnnnnnnnnnn.'

Casey was desperate and she wasn't imagining it. 'It's OK,' she whispered. 'I'm coming.'

She swung herself out of bed, pulled on the leggings and sweatshirt in which she'd travelled, stuck her feet into her flat shoes, pulled on her camel coat and grabbed her handbag.

'I'm coming, Casey,' she whispered again. 'Calm down, I'll be with you as quickly as I can.'

She let herself out of her bedroom, tiptoed past her parents' door and down the stairs. They creaked but no one stirred in the house, and she was relieved. She didn't want to have to explain to her parents what she was doing – she could tell from their expressions last night that they hadn't been sure whether to believe her or whether she was cracking up.

She'd made them promise not to tell John she was here if he called, and just after they'd all gone to bed, shortly before midnight, the phone had rung and she had hurried from her room, stood outside her parents' door, and had heard her father say, *No, I – Gayle and I – we didn't hear from her for a couple of weeks – er, Sunday last she called. Sounded fine, a little tired but fine.*

She closed the front door, using her key to soften the click of the latch, then climbed into her rental car.

It was a forty-minute drive in daytime but, in the pre-dawn quiet, Susan was in Orange County and heading towards the canyon in less than a quarter of an hour. It had stopped raining, but the road still had a glossy sheen from the water.

She suddenly saw flashing lights in her rear-view mirror, a whole broad band of them; it looked like a spacecraft was coming up the freeway behind her, and nervously, she moved across to the exit lane and slowed right down.

A convoy of fire trucks hurtled past, followed by two police patrol cars. Then not just one ambulance, but a whole fleet.

And, *oh Christ, no*, she could see where they were heading. She could see the red glow that was too thick, too concentrated to be street lighting.

Her distress deepening, she stamped on the gas pedal, pushed the needle up past ninety m.p.h. then a hundred m.p.h., chasing them, and two miles on, steadily gaining on their tail-lights, she followed them down the exit ramp and along the four-lane road that went through the small village. More emergency vehicles howled past her and crashed the stop light ahead. Susan crashed it too, beyond caring, a tight knot of fear in her gullet. This road had changed since she was last here, a year back, she thought. More flashing lights appeared in her mirror. She drove past a new development and she wondered – she *hoped* – whether some miracle had happened and they were all on the wrong road.

And then, to her disbelief, the convoy started to turn left. Braking hard, she shouted at them, through the windshield, 'Wrong way, you're taking the wrong –'

And then she stopped shouting.

They hadn't.

They weren't going to Casey's nursing home.

They were going to a different part of the canyon. And, she remembered now, there was a big lumber warehouse a mile or so up there. That's where they were going!

She lowered her window and felt a welcome blast of air on her face as she accelerated again. It was OK, there was no fire at the clinic. Casey was safe. The sirens screamed on up there above her like mad animals, and perspiration sloughed off her. 'I'll be right with you, Casey,' she said. 'Just coming up to the entrance now.'

The imposing white Doric pillars, each engraved with the words CYPRESS PALISADES CLINIC, were right ahead. She put on her right-turn signal, then halted to let a car out, one of the night staff or a doctor, she presumed, the headlights momentarily dazzling her. Then she accelerated hard up the long, tree-lined driveway, braking sharply every fifty yards to crash over the sleeping policemen.

The clinic was a handsome modern building, three storeys high, spread out along the ridge of the canyon with fine views in daylight out towards the ocean and inland across the desert. It was a medium-sized, luxury private hospital, with a high reputation both for cosmetic surgery and for its facilities for long-term care patients like Casey.

Most of the building was in darkness, but lights were on in the downstairs hall and in a few upstairs windows. Whenever she'd been here in the past, the parking lot had been full; now there was only a handful of vehicles parked outside.

Susan pulled into a bay, then got out of the car and looked anxiously up at Casey's room. It was on the second storey, with a row of window-boxes full of flowers that her mother kept up all year round, but she couldn't see these now. There was a faint tinge of burning wood in the air, and the distant wail of sirens pricked the silence of the night.

She walked as fast as she could towards the main entrance, but the automatic glass doors remained shut as she approached them. A sign on them read, AFTER 10 P.M. PLEASE USE BELL.

She pressed the button. Then, when nothing happened, she pressed it again. After an eternity, a uniformed security guard, who must have weighed a good three hundred pounds, ambled into view, gave Susan a cursory inspection, nodded at her then ambled away again. A full minute later, the doors slid open.

317

As she went inside, the guard was sitting behind the front desk with a National Rifle Association magazine open in front of him. 'Help you?'

'All right to go see my sister?'

He raised his eyebrows as if to say, At this hour? 'You know where she is?'

'Room 214 in the Laguna wing.'

He tapped his computer keyboard. 'Name?'

'Hers or mine?'

He gave her a weary look. 'Hers.'

'Casey Corrigan.'

'And yours?'

'Susan Carter.'

He studied the screen, then tapped some more keys. There was a sharp whir and a pass card printed out on a machine beside him. He pushed it into a plastic holder and handed it to her. 'Know your way?'

'Yes.' She pinned the card to her coat lapel. 'Thank you.'

'No problem. Have a good one.' He returned to his magazine.

The place reminded her of the Vörn Bank's clinic in London. The designers had done their best to make it look more like the foyer of a hotel than a hospital lobby. The walls were panelled in light cedarwood, hung with huge tapestries, and groups of comfortable chairs, separated by plants and vases of fresh flowers, were spread around the perimeter of the marble floor. But, again like the bank's clinic in London, the sterile smell was the giveaway.

The swift surge of the elevator car brought on another bout of nausea and dizziness. As she stepped out into the blue-carpeted corridor she had to lean against the wall and close her eyes. *Don't black out*, she thought. *Not now, please, not now.*

The elevator doors shut behind her with a hiss and the only sound in the corridor was the thudding of her own heart, the flat hum of the air-conditioning fans and a beeping sound, a steady, beep ... beep ... beep ... beep.

She opened her eyes and stared down the long corridor, each of the doors labelled with a typed name in a small metal holder. This was the long-stay floor. All the patients, like Casey, were in a persistent vegetative state, and most of the names on the doors were familiar to her as she stumbled past them. D. Perlmutter. Sally Shulman. Bob Tanner. Casey Corrigan.

A red light was flashing above Casey's door.

Her heart in her mouth, Susan ran, stumbling, down to it, and pushed

318

open the door. The room was in darkness; just a faint haze of green and orange light from the dials of the machines that kept Casey alive and monitored her every breath, heartbeat and brain signal. Three small red lights were flashing, and another audible warning was sounding, a shrill pip-pip-pip-pip.

Susan fumbled for the light switch and snapped it on. The brilliant overhead light dazzled her momentarily, and then she saw Casey lying in bed, just like she always was. Except Casey was motionless. The ventilator was still clunk-puffing away, but Casey's chest wasn't rising and falling, like it should, like it always did.

It wasn't moving at all.

And the colour of Casey's face behind that naso-gastric tube, did not look right. Her cheeks were usually rosy, as if this great long rest she was having was doing her good. But they weren't rosy now, they were the colour of spent chewing gum.

Susan's eyes swung up to the monitors then jumped along the dials to the ECG. Normally there would be steady spikes. But now instead of any spikes there was an unflickering green line, and on another monitor next to it, three words were flashing on and off: AIR SUPPLY DOWN!

Her eyes sprang to the ventilator, and she saw immediately what was wrong: the connector dock, linking Casey's breathing appliance to the rubber output tube from the ventilator, had come apart. The oxygen was being pumped uselessly out into the room.

Shouting for help, Susan tried to jam the two parts of the line together. She felt the hard blast of air, got them together but they sprang apart the moment she released them. They needed a clip, or tape, something.

'HELP!' she screamed. 'Help, someone, help, please help me!'

She ran out into the corridor. 'Help! Please help!'

There was no sign of anyone. Her brain raced, as she tried to think what to do. Someone must come along, there had to be someone on duty, it was more important to try to keep the air flowing. Christ, how long had Casey been like this?

She went back into the room, grabbed the two lines and forced them back together. A moment later, Casey's chest rose and fell faintly; at least some air was now going into her again. Susan stared at her, that beautiful face, framed by her long golden hair – a much prettier colour than her own, Susan had always thought – and that terrible grey colour of her face.

She stretched forward and touched Casey's face. It was cold, like putty. She'd never felt human skin as cold as this.

Grabbing the two halves of the air line, she forced them back together.

319

'HEELLLLLLP!' she screamed again. 'Please, please, someone help! Oh God, please help!'

Then the pain came. It felt like a steel band being tightened around her, crushing her, crushing everything inside her. Unable to help it, she cried out, doubling up. But somehow she managed to cling to the line, trying desperately to concentrate on holding the two halves together. And then it felt as if some huge steel blade was twisting inside her, ripping through her internal organs, and the pain was unbearable. Her head felt as if it was separating from the rest of her body, there was an unbearable pressure on her ears, they were imploding.

She screamed in pain, screamed for help for Casey. The floor suddenly tilted, rising steeply past her face, and she was struggling to stay on her feet now, they were losing their hold. The walls swung beneath her.

The carpet smacked her in the face.

She lay, unable to move, her nostrils pressed against the carpet. She could smell the cleaning fluid that had been used on it.

The pain was coming again, that blade twisted around inside her, ripping upwards through her guts. Bile was rising up her throat, she wanted to throw up and she was fighting against it with all her concentration.

She mumbled, unable to speak because she was swallowing back the vomit, *'Help me, someone, please, help me.'*

Somehow she was still holding the two pieces of line together, clutching them as if they were the only thing she had in the world.

Hang in there, Casey, don't die on me, please don't die on me.

And then the pain went off inside her like a detonation, and the ferocity of it this time sucked everything out of her, all the light out of her eyes and out of her brain. Everything was swallowed by a vast, unbearable vacuum of agony.

When she next saw something, it was very dim. A face she didn't recognise, a woman, in a white nursing gown, sleek black hair, a lapel badge right close up to her face which read, PAT CAULK, SNR NIGHT NURSE.

'Casey,' Susan whispered, urgently.

The nurse was holding her wrist – maybe she was taking her pulse, Susan wasn't sure. The nurse's arm was right across her face and the sleeve of the gown was pushed almost into Susan's mouth, muffling her voice.

'Casey,' she whispered again. 'Please –' Then her words slipped, along with consciousness, from her grasp.

Chapter Fifty-six

John cancelled a lunch meeting with clients because he was too worried about Susan to concentrate, and stayed closeted in his office, dialling home every half-hour or so in the hope that Susan might be back, or at least had left a message on the answering service.

But the only messages all morning were just a rambling one from Joe, the builder, about materials he needed to buy, one from Liz Harrison asking Susan to lunch next week, then an incomprehensible, hysterical one from Pila.

John immediately rang the hospital, and got himself put through to the intensive care nursing station. He lied to the nurse who answered that he was Archie Warren's brother, and asked how he was doing.

To his dismay, Archie was not doing well. He was still unconscious, on life support, and as yet they'd still not been able to diagnose what was wrong. The only positive news was that there appeared to be no damage consistent with a stroke, which left a mystery virus as the most likely explanation. But until they found out what it was – *if* they found out – they had no way of treating him. It was literally wait and see. He would either improve, remain as he was or deteriorate.

Deeply depressed, John hung up. If Harvey Addison were alive he could have rung him, asked the name of the best neurologist in the country and pulled strings for him to see Archie. He stared gloomily at his coffee. Everything was beyond his control. He was feeling frighteningly isolated, and helpless.

Susan was not with any of her friends or her parents. Either she'd had a breakdown and was wandering the streets somewhere, or she had gone into hiding in a hotel, or – he hesitated about this, although he knew it was a real possibility – perhaps Mr Sarotzini had abducted or kidnapped her.

At half past five in the afternoon, John was just putting down the receiver after yet another fruitless call home and debating whether to phone the police and report Susan missing, when Gareth Noyce came into his office with a wodge of computer printout. 'You never asked me to do this for you, right?' he said, excitedly.

'Do what?' John asked, then realised what he was talking about. 'You've decoded it?'

'Not me, exactly. You now owe a big favour to a *real ale* expert in Gloucester. My friend could go to jail for this – we're talking about the Official Secrets Act, right? Actually I promised him a pre-production copy of Dr Doomandgloom for his kids and he seemed pretty happy with that.'

John seized the printout, then immediately felt disappointed as he scanned the pages. On each were just columns of trades; this was a ledger record of the Vörn Bank's transactions, dating back about seven months. On each row was the name of a company, some of which he recognised but many he didn't, followed by a date, the number of shares held, the total number of shares issued, the percentage of total held, the current trading price and the twelve-month high and low prices. 'Thanks, Gareth,' he said, trying to sound enthusiastic. 'This is great.'

'Good, see you,' his partner responded, and was gone.

John rubbed his eyes, then, starting with the first of fifteen sheets, began to read carefully through the names, wondering if he might pick up any clues about the Vörn Bank. Crédit Suisse. First Boston. IBM. P&O. Glaxo Wellcome. Dai Ichy Kan Y. Espirito Santo. AOL.

By the time he was half-way down the twelfth page, he had begun to skim and almost missed the name: CYPRESS PALISADES CLINIC.

His eyes jumped back to it in surprise, and he read it again to make sure he wasn't mistaken. The ledger showed that the Vörn Bank had acquired one hundred per cent of the shares in the Cypress Palisades Clinic on 7 September last year.

He read it through yet again, then thought, carefully, trying to make double sure he wasn't getting this wrong. CYPRESS PALISADES CLINIC. No, he wasn't mistaken, he knew the name too well, he'd been there himself, many times. Nerves began to stir uneasily inside him.

It was the clinic that Susan's kid sister, Casey, was in.

Chapter Fifty-seven

Unsmiling faces. Rows of eyes. A massive, dazzling light.

The pain.

It felt like two people were trying to tear her in half by twisting her. The twisting hardened, the pain roared like a furnace inside her and she rose up, crying out pitifully, thrashing, delirious, trying to get away from it. Firm but gentle hands pushed her down. Drool ran out of the corner of her mouth.

Then another wave of this pain smashed through her, and with a sudden burst of energy, she screamed out for help, for anything. She didn't care if she died, anything, *anything* would be better than this pain.

And suddenly she heard a voice she recognised. 'Try to relax, Susan. We're going to give you an anaesthetic that will put you out, and when you come round, the pain will have gone.'

English, she thought, clawing ragged bundles of thoughts out of her memory. English. An English accent. She found the face where the voice had come from, locked on to it, thinking. Large eyes. Calm, suave voice. *I know you.* And then it came back. *Of course.* She recognised these large eyes now, and finally, with a squirm of terror, she connected the face to the voice.

Miles Van Rhoe.

No no no no no no no.

Miles Van Rhoe.

Noooooooooooooooo.

The obstetrician was standing over her, as if it was perfectly normal for him to be seeing her in California.

She shook her head, yammering with fear, pleading with her eyes at the other faces. *Help me. You have to help me.*

Then another surge of pain, and with it a gagging bout of nausea, and all she could do was wait until it passed.

'*Please!*' she gasped. 'Someone must listen to me! This man is going to take my baby, he's going to sacrifice it, he's going to use it for one of his rituals, he does black magic, satanism, please, someone believe me! He has a record with the police, with Scotland Yard in England, phone them, someone, *please*, phone them, you must believe me!'

Van Rhoe smiled at her, with a hurt expression. 'Susan, you're a little delirious and you really don't know what you're saying. We're not going to *harm* your baby. Your baby is special. It's going to be the most special baby that has ever been born and you're going to be such a proud mother!'

'Don't believe him!' she said, avoiding his stare. 'Please, someone,' she said, looking at each of the other faces in turn. 'Call the police, don't let him!'

They all stared back, watching her with concern, like medical students grouped around some freak case. One of the faces belonged to a woman she had seen recently, but she could not work out how recently or where. A badge. This woman had been wearing a lapel badge, she remembered suddenly, and now she could attach a name to the face. Pat Caulk. Yes, the badge on her lapel, standing over her in Casey's room, PAT CAULK. SNR NIGHT NURSE.

'Where am I?' Susan said.

'You are in the Cypress Palisades Clinic, Susan,' Van Rhoe told her. 'You're in a very fine place, you're a fortunate young woman. If you'd collapsed somewhere else, you might not still be with us now.'

'Casey? How – how is –?' Then another wave of pain drowned everything.

Through the haze of agony she saw a needle. Felt a prick in her wrist, then saw sticking plaster. She was being cannulated. She heard Van Rhoe say, quietly, 'We must wait for him, he doesn't want to miss this.'

John? Was it John they were waiting for?

The pain was subsiding, and her terror grew. She tried again, looking at everyone except Van Rhoe. 'Please, someone believe me! He's going to hand my baby over to Mr Sarotzini. They're all in league. They're satanists, they really are, I know it sounds incredible, but they really do do these things. *They sacrifice babies.*'

They were looking at her, but they weren't reacting. Didn't they hear her? Didn't they hear what she had just said?

Something was going into her arm, she could feel the pressure of the fluid.

What are you all? Shop-window dummies? Hello? Hello?

Then, suddenly, she felt calmer. Tiredness was seeping through her. She fixed each of them in turn with her eyes. You don't care? OK, fine. You don't have a problem with what Mr Sarotzini wants to do with my baby? OK, that's fine by me, do it, have it on your conscience, 's not my problem. It isn't.

She smiled at them but they didn't smile back.

Morons, she thought. Stuffed dummies. Do you know how sh- sh-shilly you all, you –

A voice asked quietly, 'How much longer will she survive?'

Another, also quietly, said, 'We have to keep her alive, somehow, until he gets here.'

Then silence.

John arrived home in mental turmoil. The Vörn Bank had bought the Cypress Palisades Clinic in September. Why?

Why?

What the hell did they want with a clinic in California? There was only one possible reason – and that was that they wanted the clinic because Casey was there. To think it was merely chance that she was there would be stretching coincidence way beyond the bounds that he was prepared to accept.

But why did they want or need to own the clinic where Casey was? It made no sense to him, and yet he knew there must be a reason. Mr Sarotzini would do nothing without a reason.

He checked the phone for messages and also scrutinized the house, looking for some sign that Susan had been back, if only to collect something, but could see nothing.

He poured himself a whisky, sat down in the kitchen and lit a cigarette. Either Susan had gone into hiding somewhere, maybe with a friend who wasn't telling him. Or ...

Then he had a thought. Hurriedly, he changed into his grubbiest jeans and an old sweatshirt, took the step-ladder and a torch out of the garage and carried them upstairs. He set up the ladder beneath the ceiling hatch, then clambered into the loft.

Using the flashlight and the meagre throw of the loft light for guidance, he squeezed past the chimney breast and into the right-hand side of the roof space where Susan had brought him just a couple of days ago, and where he in turn had brought the policeman, Detective Sergeant Rice. Some creature, a mouse, probably, scurried away into the shadows.

The beam struck the strips of roofing felt that hung down like sleeping bats, and he eyed again, with revulsion, the occult symbols painted on each exposed panel. He lowered the beam to the joists, and it illuminated more of the symbols that lay exposed where the insulation had been lifted away.

He checked out the small metal box, that Susan had thought was a ringing converter. It was about four inches long, with Telecom markings, and a cluster of wires ran out of it. They were thin and looked, to his untrained eyes, like telephone wires. He followed them across to the eaves where they entered a plastic junction box of a kind he had seen many times before.

Ignoring it, he returned to the area where the joists had been exposed, knelt, set down the torch carefully, and began, methodically, to rip away more of the insulation.

After five minutes of exertion, his hands prickling with fibreglass splinters, he nearly missed the wire. It was pressed down neatly, covered in black tape, which itself was camouflaged by a coating of mastic to make it look like an innocent sealant.

He tried to lift it, but it would not budge. It had been laid expertly, nestling into a tiny channel that had been cut for it and held firm by staples. Someone had gone to enormous trouble to lay this wire, he realised, as he tracked its course through meticulously drilled holes in each joist, until he reached its destination, a small plastic-cased object, recessed into the ceiling, directly above, he calculated, their bedroom.

He went downstairs and returned with a set of screwdrivers, a pair of insulated pliers, and insulating tape. First he cut through the wire, and wound insulating tape around the ends. Then he set about unscrewing the fixing plate that held the plastic object and, finally, after some moments of struggling, he eased out the dome-shaped object.

It was heavy for its size, no more than a couple of inches across, and from the tiny glass lens, less than a quarter of a millimetre wide, its function was immediately evident. He stared at it in shock. He'd reckoned on finding a bugging device up here but not a video camera.

He went down into their bedroom, switched on the light and stared up at the ceiling. It was easy to see why he had never noticed it: the hole above the bed was scarcely larger than a pin prick, and concealed within what appeared to be a natural crack.

Back up in the loft, he traced the wire along in the opposite direction, pulling away the loft insulation as he went, and after a few minutes, arrived at its destination: a shiny black metal casing, about a foot long, eight inches wide and four inches deep, recessed snugly between the joists and carefully camouflaged by two pieces of grubby hardwood bonded around it.

There were no clues as to what it was, although he had a good idea. Ignoring it for now, he began the laborious task of tracing the end of each of the other eleven wires than ran off the device. He found a second camera above the room that Susan had decorated for the baby, and further cameras above each of the other spare rooms, then all but one of the rest of the wires disappeared into a wall channel that appeared to drop down towards the next floor. No doubt there were cameras watching every downstairs room also.

The last remaining wire was more heavily insulated than the rest and connected, he discovered, into the house's mains electricity supply.

When John climbed down onto the landing, holding the heavy metal box under one arm, he was shaking with anger, outraged at this invasion of his privacy but at the same time deeply disturbed. He rang Gareth Noyce's home number and got his answering machine. Then he tried his mobile, figuring he would probably be in his local pub in Camden Town.

From the background hubbub when Gareth answered, John knew he'd guessed right. 'Gareth, where are you? In the Duke's?'

Gareth sounded giggly. 'They're having a regional ales night. I'm just drinking something called *Dead Pig*. It's *eight* per cent proof, for Chrissake!'

'Listen, drink it slowly. I need you to look at something for me – wait till I get to you before you get pissed, OK?'

'Well, you'd better hurry,' his partner said.

John got in his car, and started the arduous journey to North London, hoping, desperately, Gareth would still be *compos mentis* when he got there.

Focusing with some difficulty, Gareth removed one panel of the outer casing of the box with a screwdriver purloined from the publican.

He squinted at the innards, screwing up his eyes against the trail of smoke from his cigarette, then beamed with delight. 'Yes. Wow! Gosh, there's an 851, I'm surprised about that. Oh, this is interesting,' he said. 'Yes, brilliant, that's really clever!'

John waited. Gareth continued his examination and running commentary. 'This is powerful, I mean, like, there's more power than you're going to need here. Know how these work?'

'No, that's why I'm here,' John said patiently. He sipped the pint of Dead Pig real ale his partner had insisted on buying him even though he was driving.

'It's the first generation that doesn't need a wok,' Gareth said.

'A *wok*?'

'A satellite dish. This is an Iridium, right? So it doesn't need a satellite dish!'

John frowned.

'It sends signals digitally up to one of seventeen low-orbit satellites.'

'What kind of signals?'

'Anything – audio, video, e-mail. They can be picked up by anyone who has a base station, anywhere in the world. The system's brilliant! I've been reading about them but this is the first one I've seen. I was going to suggest to you that we ought to have these ourselves – they're really just very sophisticated mobile phones.'

Gareth probed around further with his screwdriver, like a child with a new toy, scarcely aware of his partner's silence.

An hour and a half later, when John arrived home, the protective haze of alcohol was wearing off, and he was now very frightened. If Mr Sarotzini was behind this bugging of their house he would have known everything that was going on. Had Harvey noticed something in his examination of Susan that he wasn't supposed to have seen? But what? And if he had noticed anything untoward, why hadn't he told them then and there?

Fergus had died the night after he had been to see Susan and had put all the occult thoughts in her head. Why? Had he angered Mr Sarotzini – or frightened him? And now Susan had disappeared. Maybe she had gone into hiding. Or, which was more likely considering what he now knew, Mr Sarotzini had become concerned and kidnapped her.

The sheet of paper on which Detective Sergeant Rice had written his phone number hung from a hook on the dresser. He pulled it down, then removed the cordless phone from its cradle. As he switched it on, the tone indicated that a message was waiting. With unsteady fingers he stabbed out the number to retrieve it.

It was from his father-in-law in Los Angeles, and he was sounding very distressed.

Chapter Fifty-eight

Susan opened her eyes and the room was empty. There had been people all around her and now they'd gone. Or had she imagined them?

No, they had been real. She panicked. *The baby? Have I had the baby? Have they taken –?*

Bump's hands pressed hard against the inside of her abdomen and her anxiety subsided. 'I'm not going to let them,' she whispered. 'I've promised you, they won't take you, Bump, I'm not going –'

The wave of pain caught her unawares – it happened so fast she didn't even feel it coming. *Oh, sweet Jesus.* She gritted her teeth, determined not to shriek. She was going to ride this one out, oh, Christ, oh, you bastard, oh, you, shitcreepfuckyoufuckyoufuckyou pain, oh, no, please, please, please stop.

NOW!

STOP!

She was gasping for air; she could taste amalgam in her mouth, and blood; tears were streaming down her face. But the pain had STOPPED!

And the room was empty. There was no one in it. Nothing! Just medical apparatus, shelves stacked with boxes of hypodermics, vials, surgical gloves, disposable wipes.

She tried to swing herself off this bed – this thing, this trolley – she was on, but her legs wouldn't work, the signals from her brain didn't seem to be reaching them. She pulled at the edge of the trolley with her hands, hauled herself painfully over to her left. For an instant she was aware of air beneath her, then she was toppling, head first. She flung out one arm to brace herself and the other she curled protectively around her abdomen as she crashed, with a cry of shock, on to the hard terrazzo-tiled floor.

Her left arm was suspended awkwardly in the air above her face, and she thought for a moment she had broken it. Then she realised that the drip line was holding her like a foul-hooked fish.

She ripped the line out of the cannula, then put both her hands on her abdomen to check on the baby. Bump was moving around, he was fine. Relieved, she crawled on to her knees and, holding the edge of the trolley, hauled herself up. But as soon as she let go, her legs gave way and she crashed back to the floor. 'Sorry,' she whispered to Bump. 'I'm sorry.' Desperately, she started crawling on her hands and knees towards the door. 'Get you out of here, Bump, going to get you out of here, somehow going to get you out of here.'

The door was closed. She grabbed the handle, pulled, and it swung open. Outside was a corridor, and a sign on the far side saying THEATER 6. People were approaching. She could hear rapid footsteps and a trundling sound. Before she had time to close the door, two orderlies wheeled someone past on a gurney but they didn't see her.

She made a determined effort once more to get up. This time her legs held, just. She gripped the side of the trolley for several seconds, until she felt confident enough to let go. Her heart was thrashing, or maybe it was the baby's heart, she didn't know. She was only thinking about one thing, and that was getting out of here.

Then she saw that all she was wearing was a hospital gown, and that she was barefoot.

How long have I been here?

She looked at her wrist, but her watch had been removed. Across the corridor was an observation window into Theater 6. Checking the corridor both ways, she padded unsteadily over to it, praying for her legs to hold. The clock on the wall said two twenty.

Confused, her brain leapt between time zones, trying to figure it out. It had been around four in the morning that she'd got here, and now it was two twenty? It must be afternoon now, she reasoned, unless she'd been here even longer than that.

Another wave of pain was starting. And voices were approaching. She looked, frantically, for an escape route. The corridor stretched into the distance in both directions with operating theatres all the way down. She ran, stumbling and swaying, in the opposite direction to the voices. The pain was worsening, but she didn't care, she *had* to fight it. She ran past a window where an operation was in progress, glimpsed a sea of green cloth, bright yellow light, a patch of bare human flesh.

Crossing a junction, she saw a door marked CHANGING ROOM, and burst in through it. To her relief it was empty. There were racks of surgical gowns, open lockers filled with white clogs, and several suit jackets hanging on pegs. Then, before she could do anything, a blowtorch fired up inside her.

Stifling a cry, Susan sank, doubled up and drooling, on to a bench. *Don'tscreamnotgoingtoscream.* Teeth grinding, eyes bulging, nails digging into her palms, she fought back. Her insides were on fire, and the flame of the blowtorch was being turned up stronger and stronger. The pain was going to win this bout, she was swaying, she was going to black out.

Got to keep conscious.

The floor rose towards her.

She pushed it back.

Her head was spinning, trying to detach itself, to free itself from this agony. She clung to a gown hanging from a peg, held on to it grimly with all the strength that remained to her and somehow, she didn't know how, but *somehow* she rode this beast out until it sank back into its lair, the flame flickered, receded, went out.

Susan staggered to her feet, feeling giddy as hell. Going to faint. Not going to faint.

A rack of gowns came towards her and she pushed herself away. *Head between legs to stop fainting*, she remembered, and she tried to do it but the baby was in the way. She took several more deep breaths, which helped. She was going to be all right, she was getting stronger again.

She grabbed a gown, pulled it on, tied the tapes, then pushed her feet into a pair of white clogs. They were too big but it didn't matter. She took a mask out of a dispenser, pulled it over her nose and mouth, fumbled with the tapes. Then, from another dispenser, she took a hat that was like an elasticised J-cloth, and dragged it over her hair.

She looked in the mirror, and a sickly-looking nurse stared back. Good. Throwing a nervous glance at the door, she checked through the jackets that were hanging up, patting them for bulges. In the breast pocket of the fourth she found what she was looking for: a cellular phone.

The power button lit up when she pressed it, and there was a reassuring beep. And the door opened.

Susan froze.

Two men in suits came in, doctors, she presumed. They were deep in conversation; one gave her a cursory nod, the other didn't even glance at her. She slipped out past them into the corridor, and as she did so she saw a group of people walking towards the room from which she had fled.

She turned and hurried away in the opposite direction, her feet slipping around clumsily inside the clogs. There was a FIRE EXIT sign ahead, down at the far end. She broke into a stumbling run, reached the door, pushed down the bar. It opened.

She was outside.

It was daylight, and a light drizzle was falling. She was at the back of the clinic somewhere, in a service area. Steam rose from a vent in a low, one-storey building ahead that looked like an annex.

There were windows above her, and Susan pressed herself hard against the wall so that she couldn't be seen from them. Then, holding up the phone, she tried to dial 911. But her fingers were shaking too much, and the wrong digits appeared on the display. She lost valuable seconds finding the Clear button, wiping the display and redialling.

As she was about to hit the Send button, out of the corner of her eyes she saw someone emerge from a door at the far side of the courtyard. It was a nurse in uniform. She looked across at Susan, smiled, then took something from her pocket, and Susan relaxed as she saw what it was: cigarettes. The nurse lit up.

Susan turned and walked away, trying to look nonchalant, as if she'd just finished a cigarette herself, and skirted around the side of the building, trying to remember, from all her previous visits to Casey, the geography around here. The terrain. There was the long driveway down to the main road, a quarter of a mile or so. No other road, just the shrubbery of the canyon, and miles of arid scrubland beyond.

She pulled at the two-inch base of the aerial, trying to extend it, but the top was broken and it wouldn't come out any further; then she pressed the Send button, brought the phone to her ear, and moments later heard the voice of the emergency operator.

'Police,' Susan said. 'Quickly, please.'

There were shouts right behind her, and she turned in alarm to see two men sprinting towards her. A third person, this one dressed in surgical scrubs, burst out of a door behind them, and stared venomously straight at her, before racing after the others, towards her.

Susan kicked her feet out of the clogs and stumbled into a run. After only a few paces, the pain started coming at her again, but she ignored it, increasing her speed, trampling through a flower-bed, then tripping, stubbing her toe and almost losing her balance as she blundered through a low hedge and into a rockery. Somehow she kept on her feet, put on more speed, sprinting now in spite of her huge burden, running as fast as she'd ever run in her life across prickly grass that was damp and slippery from the drizzle.

Then she reached the tarmac of the driveway, and the footing was better. A faint voice somewhere was saying, 'Hello? Hello? Hello, caller, are you all right?' For a moment she couldn't figure out where it was coming from.

She turned her head to look behind her. The two men in suits and the one in surgical scrubs were only yards away and gaining on her. Then she yelled, breathlessly, into the receiver, 'Please – help me, I'm, I'm at – Palisades Cypress Clinic, Orange County. Please – come – they – murder my baby.'

She didn't see the sleeping policeman that tripped her. She just felt an agonised jarring in her foot and then she was flying forward, helplessly, and flung her arms around her baby as she smacked face down on to the tarmac, the phone skittering out of her hand.

She could hear the footsteps of the men behind her and, near crazed with panic, she scrambled forward, grabbed the phone and somehow got back on her feet all in one motion. The men were yards away now, at full sprint, the one in surgical scrubs out in front was going to catch her. She heard him calling out to her, his familiar, smooth, urbane voice.

'Susan, stop, you must stop!'

As Miles Van Rhoe reached her, grabbing at her shoulder, she lashed out wildly with her arm at his face and, to her shock, the aerial of the cellular phone plunged into his right eye.

Everything seemed to go into slow motion, as if she was seeing a video in freeze-frame. Blood gouted out around her fingers, which were still gripping the phone. Van Rhoe's surgical face mask fell away to reveal his mouth hideously twisted. Then his body began to fold in on itself, sinking to the ground. The cellular phone, grotesquely wedged in his eye socket, slipped from Susan's grip.

Whimpering with terror, she tried to turn but, as if she were in a nightmare, her feet would not move. She lashed out with her left fist at a second man who was trying to grab her, and punched him on the jaw. He snatched at her gown and she punched him again, sank her teeth into his wrist then twisted free. Now her legs were working – but he had her gown once more. She pulled with such force that she ripped free of it, stumbled forward and broke into a run again. There was a line of trees ahead, and then the road beyond that. She could see the road.

It wasn't far.

It really wasn't far.

She didn't look left or right, she just ran straight out through the white pillars, flailing her arms, screaming for help, the image of Miles Van Rhoe sinking to the ground, with the cellular phone sticking out of his eye and blood trickling down his face, blinding her to almost everything else. The road was empty. Without pausing, she turned left and started running downhill. She could hear the footsteps inches behind her; a hand grabbed her shoulder; she found another spurt of speed; the hand grabbed her shoulder again.

She could hear a siren.

A glint of metal appeared ahead.

Then the most beautiful sight she had ever seen: a police patrol car rounded the bend in front of her. It screeched to a halt and before the policeman even had a chance to open his door, Susan was there, at his window, and he was smiling at her, a tubby man, with great chubby cheeks.

It felt as if a huge lever had been pulled inside her, and everything started to shut down. She clutched the window frame as the door swung open, and then he was holding her, had his big comforting arms wrapped round her.

And now the pain was coming again.

She looked into the policeman's eyes. 'Please help me,' she whispered. 'Don't let them take me back in there.'

And then the pain erupted. She doubled up, closed her eyes and just heard the voices. They sounded faint, so faint, they could be miles away, she didn't care, she was safe now, the baby was safe, they were both safe, she was with the police and she just had to deal with this pain, that's all, her baby was safe, just the pain to deal with now.

One voice said, 'I'm sorry, Officer, this patient's sister died last night and she's flipped.'

Another voice said, 'She has a delusional personality. She's imagining we're going to take her baby away and use it for some kind of devil worship.'

Then the first voice, said, calmly, 'She's dangerously sick – the poor young woman has a gangrenous cyst, which is giving her peritonitis, and this is causing her to hallucinate. If we don't operate immediately we are going to lose her.'

Then a third voice, kindly but firm, said, 'Lady, you hear that? Can you hear me? Can you hear what I'm saying to you? You're not at all well, and you've cut your hand. These kind people are going to take you back inside now. This is the best place for you to be, you just relax now, OK? If you have to be sick, this is the best place in the whole of Orange County! They're gonna take good care of you. Real good care of you and your baby!'

Chapter Fifty-nine

'John? I appreciate you returning the call,' Dick Corrigan said. 'It's –' There was a long pause. John waited, impatiently. 'It's – John, I don't – know how to put this –' he broke down in tears.

John felt a stab of panic. 'Dick, what is it? What's happened?' He looked at his watch. Ten forty. A quick calculation told him it was two forty p.m. in Los Angeles. The cushion against reality from his two pints of Dead Pig an hour or so earlier was fast wearing off.

'John – ah – we've –' His father-in-law was fighting to control his voice.

John, waited, trying to give him space. He had always liked the man, partly because he reminded him of one of his early screen idols, Henry Fonda. Dick Corrigan had the same build, the same quiet dignity, and John felt genuinely sad that success had never happened for him.

'I'm afraid something real bad's happened, John. I – I – oh God ...' Dick Corrigan began to sob.

John went cold. Oh, Christ, what the hell was it? Nothing to Susan, please not, please don't let anything have happened to her. 'Dick, what? What's happened?' he asked, urgently.

'I – I'm sorry, this is –' There was another long silence. 'Casey –' Dick said, getting her name out with difficulty. 'Casey's died.'

It took a moment to sink in. The room seemed to darken around him. 'Casey?' It was the last thing he had expected to hear. 'Oh, God,' John said. 'I'm sorry, Dick, I'm really sorry.' But inwardly, although shocked, he felt an enormous sense of relief – that it wasn't bad news about Susan. He tried to mask this in his voice. 'What happened?'

There was another long silence. Then Dick Corrigan said, 'Susan killed her.'

John almost dropped the cordless phone. There was a terrifying baldness in the statement that sent a slick of goosebumps coursing up his spine. 'What? What did you say, Dick? What do you mean?'

'It – was her air line. Susan – did something – a connector – she separated a connector – I – oh, God, John, what's happening?'

He was sobbing again.

A maelstrom of thoughts swirled through John's head. The Vörn Bank owned the clinic. Was this something to do with Mr Sarotzini? Some trick? 'Susan was in England. She couldn't –'

His father-in-law composed himself. 'John, I wasn't straight with you – last night when you rang. I told you Susan wasn't here. Well, she was here. She – ah – she'd begged me and Gayle not to –'

'She's with you? Susan's with you? She's in LA?' John paced restlessly around the room. He sat on the edge of the kitchen table, stood up again, crossed the room, leant against the sink, then turned, stared at the window, at his stricken, ghostly reflection. 'You say she's with you?'

Through his father-in-law's grief, John thought he detected a sudden edginess to his voice. 'She's – she's at the clinic right now. They – they're being good about it, John. They understand that she's having some kind of a breakdown.'

'Breakdown?' John could hear his mother-in-law saying something in the background.

'She arrived here last night in a – real bad state. I – Gayle and I –' He fell silent again. 'John – look, here's Gayle. She'll tell you.'

John heard the scraping sound of the receiver being manhandled, then his mother-in-law's voice. She sounded deeply distressed, but less distraught than her husband. 'Hello, John,' she said. 'What's going on? Please tell us what's going on.'

'Gayle, I'm sorry about Casey, I'm desperately sorry.'

There was another silence. Then, stiffly, she said, 'Thank you. You can imagine how we're feeling.'

John fumbled in his pocket for a cigarette. 'Gayle, did I hear Dick right? Susan disconnected Casey's air-line?'

'She killed her sister. I can't believe she did this, John, she loved Casey, she loved her more than –' She drew breath, as if struggling for self-control.

John waited some moments, then said, 'Have you spoken to Susan?'

'She's unconscious.'

'Where?'

'In the clinic. Seems that there might be complications. I had to sign a consent form – allowing them to operate. They're going to have to do an emergency Caesarean.'

336

John tried to make sense of what he was hearing. 'She's still in the clinic? What – about –'

'The police?'

'Yes?'

John sensed the same edginess in her voice that he had noticed in her husband's. 'The clinic are being very good about it, John. They – the director had a talk with us. They don't want a scandal – I guess – I guess any more than we do.'

A moment ago his mother-in-law had asked him what was going on; he was beginning to feel it was his turn now to ask that same question. Susan had gone to LA and had killed Casey? No way, *no way in hell* would Susan have harmed Casey. This was all wrong, seriously wrong.

'Gayle,' he said, 'listen to me very carefully. You have to get Susan out of that clinic now, right now. I can't explain why over the phone and you wouldn't believe me if I tried. Just do it for Susan. Get her to any other hospital, doesn't matter which one. Will you do that, please?'

There was another long silence, then his mother-in-law said, 'John, she's in the finest clinic in California and they have the best maternity facilities of anywhere there. We have to deal with this, we can't solve anything by taking her away. We need them real bad right now.'

'Look,' John said, with growing desperation, 'I'm coming over on the first flight in the morning. Get her out of there now, right now. Gayle, please believe me. They're going to *kill her too*.'

There was a click. He stared at the phone with incredulity.

She had hung up on him.

Chapter Sixty

The butcher hefted the slab of meat on the block, then raised his long-bladed knife. And Susan saw what he was going to cut. It wasn't meat at all.

She threw herself forward, screaming, 'No! That's my baby, please, please don't! Please, oh my God, *pleeeease.*'

The knife struck the flesh, skewering the baby on to the board beneath. A tiny geyser of blood bubbled up around the glinting steel, and the baby screamed, a hideous, curdling scream.

The scream calmed into a sobbing cry. And then a gurgle. And then the gurgle changed into a choking, rattling sound.

Susan heard the clunk-puff-clunk-puff of a ventilator. Someone was choking, gasping for air.

Casey.

Casey writhing on her bed.

Susan reached out towards her, but the image was fading. Casey turned, smiled as she faded. She looked so happy, so incredibly happy.

The image dimmed further, then dissolved into the darkness that was rising around her. Susan tried to hold on to the image, but a pain was intruding, a stinging sensation in her abdomen that was growing increasingly sharper. It was different from the pain she had had before. It was bearable, it wasn't comfortable, but it was bearable.

And then a shiver ripped through her.

She saw an image of Miles Van Rhoe sinking to the ground with a cellular phone sticking out of his eye socket, blood gouting from it, his mouth distorted with shock.

She broke into a sweat of fear.

Running. She had been running.

Christ, how badly had she hurt him?

And how had he found her? How had he known she was here? John. It must have been John who had told him. John must have phoned her parents and somehow gotten out of them where she was and he'd told Van Rhoe. So now Mr Sarotzini would know she was here.

And now through the darkness she felt the red glow of light against her eyelids. She opened her eyes and she was flat on her back staring up at a white ceiling and a sprinkler system. A face filled her line of vision, a stranger, a woman in a white gown, a nurse, with high cheekbones, a pretty face with short blonde hair, and she was smiling. Susan stared groggily at her.

'Congratulations, Susan, you've had a little girl!'

Susan looked at her blankly.

'Your baby,' the nurse said. 'You've had a girl!'

And Susan connected with this word *baby*. Baby.

'Girl?' Susan said, confused. Bump was a boy, she was sure Bump was a boy. 'Where – where is – she? Can I –?' And then she was gripped by a sudden deep anxiety as the memory returned. 'Casey? How's Casey?'

The flicker of a hesitation. 'Casey?'

'My sister. Where am I?'

'You're in the Pacific Palisades Clinic.'

'My sister, Casey, how is she?'

All smiles now. 'Casey Corrigan?'

Susan nodded.

'In the Laguna wing? She's your sister? What a lovely girl!'

Susan felt relieved. Casey was fine, she could see it in the smile.

'How are you feeling?'

How was Van Rhoe? Had that been a dream? Why wasn't the woman saying anything about him? It must have been a dream.

'Are you a little tender?'

She had to think about this for a minute. Her brain was woozy, still a little confused. She felt uncomfortable lying flat, it was hurting her stomach. She told the nurse this.

'I'm afraid you will be a little tender. I'm going to give you something for the pain.'

'My baby – I – I was having a boy.'

'A lot of women get surprised, Susan. Lots of women think they're having a boy and then they have a girl. She's a beautiful little girl.'

They were lying to her. She'd had a boy and they were taking him away. 'Can I sit up?'

'Just rest a while longer until you're fully round from the anaesthetic, and then I'll take you through to your room and bring your daughter in.'

Daughter. Susan liked the word: it gave her a feeling of pride. She felt a light prick in her thigh, and then the pain subsided, but did not entirely go away. And the hazy thought rode through it: *Daughter*.

You've had a baby.

A girl.

Bump was a boy.

As her thoughts became clearer, her fear deepened. What if this wasn't her baby but someone else's that they were going to show her? To trick her? How would she know? How did she know Mr Sarotzini hadn't already taken her baby away? They might be going to sacrifice it today, they might be doing it at this moment. One of her books had told her that new-born babies add great power to rituals because of their innocence.

She had tried to run. They had come after her. She had stabbed Van Rhoe through the eye.

Good. He was one of them. He deserved it.

She tried to sit up and immediately slumped down, crying out in shock at the acute pain. It felt like her stomach was ripping open. She turned her head to the left, then right. All she could see was a drip stand, monitoring equipment, bare walls. And a clock that said seven ten. She looked for a bell, a phone, but there was nothing in reach.

She lay still, her thoughts becoming clearer, fretting, thinking about the baby, thinking about Casey last night. About Van Rhoe. Casey's disconnected air line. What had happened? Casey's air line. How? How could it? Had the pressure blown it apart? Why hadn't anyone been there? What would have happened if she hadn't come and – and –?

She tried to remember what had happened. The pain. The nurse. Van Rhoe. She'd been running away. A policeman had come. It felt real and unreal at the same time.

I must have dreamt it.

Finally, after what seemed an eternity later although the clock told her only another twenty minutes had passed, the nurse returned with two orderlies. They wheeled her along a corridor into a room and lifted her into the bed.

She was allowed to sit up. They propped her with pillows. All kinds of medical paraphernalia surrounded her, machines, stands, pumps, a battery of blinking, flickering, winking dials and gauges; she had a drip in her wrist, a groin drain from her abdomen, and she was catheterised.

The nurse's lapel badge identified her as Greta Dufors. All smiles (Susan wondered whether she had any other expression), she told Susan she was going to bring her daughter now.

There was a cot beside the bed, with pink sheets and a pink cotton blanket. The room had a window with a view out over the canyon, an opened door on to an *en suite* bathroom, a large television, two armchairs, a vase of flowers, bright modern paintings on the walls. But no telephone.

Susan heard crying, and then, making soothing noises, Nurse Dufors brought in a tiny baby in a pink vest and diaper, its face scrunched up like a rubber ball as it howled.

'Here she is!' Nurse Dufors said. 'Here's your mummy!'

As Susan stared at this little creature, its tiny arms and legs stretching and contracting, her suspicions evaporated. It looked so helpless, so frightened, so confused.

So utterly beautiful.

She reached out instinctively and took the tiny bundle, and that was all she needed. As she held it and marvelled at how incredibly beautifully formed it was, and felt its movements, she knew, straight away, that this was Bump, this was the baby she'd been carrying inside her. She kissed her head and said, 'Hello, my darling, it's OK, it's OK!'

And the baby stopped crying and made a contented gurgle.

'There, that's better,' Nurse Dufors said. 'See what an instant effect you have!'

'She's beautiful,' Susan said. 'I've never seen a baby so beautiful. You are, aren't you? You're so beautiful!'

Nurse Dufors opened the front of Susan's gown and Susan put the baby's mouth to her nipple. There was a tiny stinging sensation, then she felt the baby's gums gripping her and the milk being sucked out. She was close to tears. This feeling, this tiny creature, her child – *she was breast-feeding her child*. It was so incredible she could barely believe it.

'She's drinking!' she exclaimed. 'She's feeding!'

Nurse Dufors nodded back, beaming. 'Isn't she beautiful?'

'She is,' Susan said. 'She's the most beautiful baby I've ever seen.' She cradled the little bundle that was her child with her left arm, and smelled baby powder and soap, and stared down at the wrinkled face, the tiny hands that were waving around, and she noticed the hair. There was a surprising amount of it, sleek, flame-red hair.

'Yes, you are gorgeous! My darling, you're incredible, you know that? You're just incredible!'

She wanted her parents to see her, and John, and Kate Fox and Liz Harrison and all her other friends, and she couldn't stop looking at her, looking at her hands, her face. *My baby*, she was thinking. *My baby!* You *are* my baby, you *are*! *You really are! And I don't care about all the pain you caused me, it was worth it, it was worth every second!*

341

She kissed her forehead, and then she kissed her again, and when she next glanced up, Nurse Dufors had slipped away. She was alone in the room with her baby. And suddenly, she had no idea why, she said, 'Verity.'

As if in acknowledgement, the baby glanced up, and Susan felt an instant communion with her. 'Like that name, do you? I like it too, it's a nice name. *Verity*. Know what Verity means?'

Verity sucked even harder on the nipple, as if to say she didn't know, it wasn't important, this nipple was the thing that *was* important.

'It means The Truth,' Susan said.

Susan carried on watching her – she couldn't take her eyes off that tiny mouth, those hands, that little nose, this little incredible miracle she was holding. And when, finally, she did take her eyes off her and looked up again, Mr Sarotzini was standing in front of the bed.

A chill blast of fear guttered through her.

She held Verity even tighter. She was not going to let go of her, no way.

Mr Sarotzini was smiling. 'Good. Excellent, Susan! How are we doing?'

Susan didn't return the smile. 'Fine.'

He stepped closer to the bed. 'She's a very beautiful little girl. I am informed that, considering she's a month premature, she's a good weight. And she's fit as a fiddle, she's really a terrific baby.'

'She is,' Susan said, holding her even tighter, as tight as she dared, and looked down at her again. 'You are, aren't you? Yes, yes, you are. You're terrific! And you know it, don't you?'

Susan looked up and saw the smile on Mr Sarotzini's face, and it sent another shiver through her. Now he was going to say something to her about Van Rhoe, she thought. But he didn't. He just kept on smiling.

'I'll come and see you again in the morning,' he said.

And then he was gone.

Susan switched Verity to her right breast, and after a while Nurse Dufors returned and showed her how to burp the baby, changed the diaper for her, and tucked Verity up in her cot.

Then Susan was alone again. She listened to the sound of her baby breathing, and played Mr Sarotzini's words over and over in her mind. *I'll come and see you again in the morning.*

That meant Mr Sarotzini wasn't going to try to take Verity tonight, didn't it?

And he had said nothing about Van Rhoe. If she had really stabbed Van Rhoe through the eye someone would have said something. It had been a dream, a bad dream, a nightmare.

Then she thought that *maybe that was how she felt about Van Rhoe*. Freud had said that the emotions you repressed in the daytime were released in your dreams. Perhaps the anger at the pain she had felt for so many months, or the deception, or a combination of everything had made her want to kill him.

And she could kill him, she knew, that was the frightening thing. She could, she really could, kill anyone who tried to take Verity away.

She looked down at the contented sleeping face, so tiny, so frail, so innocent. 'I won't,' she said. 'I won't let them. I won't let them take you, I promise you.'

Chapter Sixty-one

Susan was woken by footsteps. And by the faint sound of a musical instrument playing. A flute.

Her eyes sprang open. The door was ajar and light spilled into the room from the corridor. A shadowy figure was moving towards her, then stopped in front of the cot. The light caught the left side of its face. It was Mr Sarotzini.

The door swung closed, reducing him to a silhouette.

She watched him, throbbing with fear, afraid to move, not wanting to signal to him that she was awake, silently bracing herself, ready to spring if he tried to lift Verity from the cot. As her brain raced she tried to work out the time. Verity had had a feed just after midnight. The nurse had changed her and lifted her into the cot.

Mr Sarotzini leant over the cot and began chanting, quietly and intently. His voice was low, and Susan could barely hear him. As she strained to make out what he was saying, she realised the language was one she had never heard. It sounded like Latin, but it wasn't – she knew a little Latin, having done a course at school.

What the hell was he doing? What was he saying? The sight was so surreal she wondered whether she was asleep and dreaming this. Then she felt indignant at the intrusion, and at the stupidity of disturbing a sleeping baby.

Plucking up the courage, she said, 'What are you doing?'

Mr Sarotzini ignored her and continued his chanting. Then, still without looking at Susan, he turned away, and melted back into the darkness. The door opened; she could see him clearly for an instant in the light now and, in the background, she could hear the flute more clearly. He bowed respectfully to Verity, then closed the door and Susan was in darkness again.

But not alone.

She heard the rustle of clothes: another shadowy figure was moving towards the cot. Susan swallowed, her mouth dry. Was this some kind of ritual – or preparation?

Louder than before, her voice trembling, Susan said, 'Who's that? What are you doing?'

The door opened again, and in the throw of light she could see a woman standing over the cot, a stern, middle-aged woman with a heavily lined Slavic face. She was wearing a black polo-neck jersey, large, ugly jewellery, and exuded a heavy, aromatic scent that reminded Susan of incense. Behind her another person entered the room and the door closed again.

'What are you doing?' Susan said, increasingly frightened.

Like Mr Sarotzini before her, the woman ignored Susan and began to chant in a low intonation, in that same unfamiliar language. Then she, too, turned away, opened the door, bowed and was gone.

Another person moved towards the cot, and as he reached it, the door opened once more and the light struck his face. Susan became convinced that she was dreaming. He looked like the man from Telecom who had come to her house, and like the man in the strange dream – or hallucination – she'd had in the WestOne Clinic during her insemination operation.

He seemed to chant for longer than the previous two, and when he had finished, instead of turning away, Susan saw him move closer towards her, and lean over the bed, lowering his face until it was inches from her own. She could feel his breath, warm and minty, as if he had recently brushed his teeth, and his skin smelt freshly washed or scrubbed with a bland soap, and she could hear his breathing, which was slow, long, deep sniffs, as if he was inhaling some substance – almost, she thought, as if he were snorting coke straight from her skin.

She stared back at the face she could not see, petrified, trying to shrink away, but the bedding beneath her would not yield. *I'm dreaming this, I must be dreaming this. Please, God, let me be dreaming this.*

Her whole body was quivering, and the pulse in her wrist was jigging. Was this the start of the sacrifice ritual she'd been reading about? The Great Rite?

Could she take them by surprise, grab Verity and run?

She didn't even know where her clothes were. Run where? Barefoot and in her hospital gown? Straight back into the arms of the same policeman?

Thankfully the man moved away. He opened the door then lingered, staring at her, giving her a long, strange look. He seemed to be smiling. Then he was gone.

And now the door opened again, and an old man appeared in a

wheelchair, being pushed by a nurse she recognised. Nurse Caulk. The man was elderly, his eyes half closed as if he was blind, and he had a rug around his shoulders. The door closed and they were in darkness again.

Susan could hear Nurse Caulk wheeling him over to the cot, and then heard his voice which, although frail and faltering, had a quality that sent slicks of fear down Susan's spine. There was something about it, hatred, bitterness, spite, malevolence, conceit, all these things underpinning the intonations, and delivered with an authority, a mesmeric, oratorical style in spite of his ailing body that reminded her of the shrill evil in Hitler's voice at a Nuremberg rally, and penetrated deep into her soul.

She wanted him out of here; she did not want him in this room with her baby, did not want him speaking to Verity, did not want him communing with her. She tried to tell him to go, now, at once, but her mouth would not work, no sound would come out. She just stared at his silhouette, juddering helplessly.

Then the door opened. Someone else was coming in. And in the burst of light she saw to her shock just quite how old this man in the wheelchair really was. A centenarian, at least. His skin, gridded with creases and mottled with liver spots, hung shapelessly from his cheekbones, and his eyes, heavy-lidded, remained closed, like those of a basking reptile. Only his hair retained any vestiges of youth, carefully tended and brushed immaculately in a way that reminded her of Mr Sarotzini.

His gums had shrunk, like a corpse's, and his lips glistened with spittle. It was like a rotting skull chanting to Verity.

Go, please go, get out, please go, go, GO AWAY!

But the words yammered silently inside her head. He continued on, a litany of evil pouring from his drooling mouth and his crumbling teeth.

Go away, please, go away, please, go away.

Then the man turned towards her. The reptilian lids quivered, as if they were about to open, and Susan shrank back in terror. She did not want to see his eyes, did not want to meet his gaze. And at that moment, the light faded again and the terror surging inside her, erupted into a volcano of fear, and then she was falling, tumbling, being swept helplessly by a breaking roller of molten lava into a searing turmoil of darkness.

Chapter Sixty-two

Verity was crying.

Susan opened her eyes. The curtains were opaque. It was still dark, but not as dark as it had been. The blackness of the night had turned to pre-dawn shades of grey.

Verity was still here, thank God, thank God, *thank God*.

Fear, formless and indefinable, swirled through her veins. Had she dreamed of the people in her room? She reached out, found the light switch, pressed it, then blinked hard against the glare. Verity's crying strengthened.

'It's OK, hon, darling, Mom's here.' Susan sat up, oblivious to the pain in her abdomen and looked lovingly at Verity. The wall clock said four twenty. She reached over and lifted the baby from her cot. 'It's OK,' she whispered, tiredly. 'You're just a little hungry, that's all. It's OK. You and me, we're OK.'

When Susan next woke, the room was flooded with daylight. Something was wrong.

She couldn't hear Verity.

In panic, she sat up, wincing against the pull of her stitches and the stinging pain from the incision in her abdomen, which seemed much worse this morning, and looked anxiously into the cot.

Verity, wide awake, was staring back at her with her beautiful eyes. Round black pupils in orbs of shining lapis-lazuli.

Relief that she was still here burst through Susan. She reached over, ignoring the pain, and kissed her lovingly on the head. Immediately Verity started crying.

'Hungry again? You are one greedy little baby, you know that? Well, I think you're greedy, but I don't have much experience in these matters, you know. I mean, I haven't been a mother before and I guess you haven't been a baby before, so we're both new to this, right?'

Susan glanced at the clock on the wall. Eight ten a.m. 'Seem to be setting ourselves a regular four-hour pattern.'

Verity responded by crying even more loudly. Holding her breath against the pain of the movement, Susan hauled her out of the cot, hugged her, then rocked her gently. 'It's OK, it's OK! I'm not criticising you,' she said soothingly. Then, opening the front of her gown, she guided Verity's mouth to her left nipple.

Verity gripped hard and Susan cried out in surprise. 'Owww! Hey! Steady as you go, OK? Have a little care here, I'm fragile too!'

Verity settled down, sucking contentedly. Susan watched her. Then suddenly her throat felt tight, constricted with fear. She studied the concentration on Verity's tiny pink face, loving her and fearing for her more desperately every second.

There's no way I could ever let you go, not to anyone, she thought.

After Verity had finished feeding, Susan put her back in the cot, and watched her curl up contentedly and go back to sleep.

Then she lay thinking. Although she was able to move a little, every movement hurt like hell, and she was severely restricted right now – she was still catheterised and cannulated and still had the groin drain. She opened the front of her gown wider and examined the stitches. It was a grisly sight, and she wondered, but didn't care right now, how bad a scar she would have.

She had to phone someone who would believe her. *Her parents*. She had to find a phone and call them, get them to come over with a lawyer. They needed to get on to the surrogate helpline, get advice, find out where they stood, contact the lawyer she'd been to see in England, Elizabeth Frazer – she'd have an associate over here, she'd be bound to.

A phone.

She looked around the room and could see where it ought to be, but it wasn't here, it had been removed.

Her eyes watered and she clenched her hands with silent rage. She felt so utterly, utterly helpless.

A while later Nurse Dufors, all smiles as usual, came into Susan's room with a breakfast tray. She removed the catheter and the cannula and the groin drain, and helped Susan hobble painfully the few steps to the bathroom.

'Were you here last night?' Susan asked. 'All night?'

'No, I went off duty after your baby's midnight feed. Did you come up with a name yet?'

Susan hesitated. She didn't want anyone to know, she decided, not yet, she wanted to share as little as possible of her baby with anyone here. 'I – haven't got that far. I was expecting a boy.'

'That's very common, you know. A lot of mothers expect a boy and then get surprised.'

'I can understand that. I don't know why I was expecting a boy.'

'Girls are less trouble,' Nurse Dufors replied, breezily.

As Susan sat down on the lavatory seat, she said, 'I don't have a phone in the room. Could you do me a favour and bring me one?' Immediately she caught the sudden stiffening in the nurse's face.

'No problem,' she replied.

'And could we do something else – some time. I'd like – I'd like to show the baby to my sister, Casey. Could you help me up to her room?'

Nurse Dufors turned away. 'Sure, I – I'll take you up – when you're stronger. I don't think today.'

She helped Susan wash and get back into bed, then went out of the room. Susan reminded her about the phone and she promised she would look into it right away.

Susan forced down a little dry toast, although she wasn't hungry, and drank some tea and apple juice. Nurse Dufors did not reappear with a phone. Susan rang the bell above her bed then, exhausted, lapsed into a doze.

When she next opened her eyes, her father was sitting beside the bed, watching her, and her mother was standing over the cot, looking at Verity with a strange intensity. Susan smiled, feeling an immense sense of relief. 'Thank God,' she said.

'She has your grandmama's eyes,' her mother said, barely glancing at her.

Suddenly her relief at seeing them was tinged with unease. Susan wasn't sure if it was her imagination, but her parents looked awkward, as if they were posing for a Jan van Eyck tableau, and her mother's voice sounded stilted.

'She's beautiful, isn't she?' Susan said. The wall clock said ten twenty-five. A while yet before Verity's next feed. Good. Lowering her voice almost to a whisper, she said, 'They're here, the people I told you about, they've found me, they're gonna take the baby, you have to get me – us – out of here.'

Her father stared at her with an expression she could not read, his Adam's apple bobbing inside his open-necked checked shirt. He was unshaven and, although he always dressed in casual, working men's clothes, he never normally left the house without shaving. He looked gaunt and haggard, his skin drawn. Once, when she had been a kid, he had seemed so strong; now he looked weak, helpless – and old. Susan wondered, suddenly, whether he was sick.

Then she saw that her mother, too, was looking pale and drained, as if she had been up all night. And frightened.

'Has your father's nose,' her mother said, in that stilted voice again, as if she were trying to change the subject. 'A real Corrigan nose that one. See the way it turns up at the tip?' She moved away from Verity and paced up and down the room, wringing her hands and looking at Susan's father as if for help.

'We – we have to go. You have to get me out of here,' Susan said, even more urgently than before. 'The people I told you about, don't you remember? The staff here – I think they're in league with them. You've got to get me – us – Verity and me, and I think maybe Casey, too, away from here –'

She stopped as she saw the fleeting eye contact between her parents, and her mind shot back again to the beeping warning signal, Casey's terrible complexion, the disconnected air line. 'Is Casey OK?' she said, suspiciously.

Her father looked at her again and she saw his Adam's apple bobbing again, the way it always did when he was nervous about something. 'Casey's fine,' he said. 'She – she's good.'

Gayle Corrigan walked out of the room and closed the door behind her. Her father sat still in silence. It seemed to Susan that there was something he wanted to say, but he stood up and went over to the window. 'Grand view,' he said.

Susan couldn't believe this. Shaking with terror now, she said, 'Dad! They're gonna take Verity! Don't you believe me?' She raised her voice, until she was shouting, not caring whether she woke Verity. 'Dad! For God's sake you have to get me out of here! Daaaddddddd! *Listen!* Oh, God, *please* LISTEN to me!'

The door opened and Nurse Dufors came in, followed by Susan's mother, who was red-eyed, as if she'd been crying.

Nurse Dufors turned to the Corrigans and said, 'I'm afraid she's finding everything rather distressing at the moment. Why don't you let her get some rest today and come back tomorrow?'

Susan's father nodded.

'No!' Susan pleaded. 'Dad, Mom! No, don't leave me, you have to take me away – you –'

She couldn't believe her eyes. They were just walking obediently out of the room. Her father stopped in the doorway, fixed her with another stare that seemed to be a mixture of bewilderment, pity and reproach, and then they were gone.

Nurse Dufors raised a finger to her lips and said, as brightly as ever, 'Susan, please, calm down! You're going to wake your daughter!'

'Look, you don't understand, please –' Susan tried to get out of bed. The nurse placed a firm but gentle restraining hand on her shoulder.

'You and your daughter both need rest right now.'

Susan stared up at her: a pleasant face, handsome rather than pretty, with dark hair pulled back a tad severely, in her mid-thirties Susan guessed. Could this woman help her? 'I – I need to talk to you, in confidence.'

The nurse suddenly produced two pills and tiny paper cup of water. 'Take these, Susan, and you'll feel much better.'

Susan looked at her warily. 'What are they?'

'Mild painkillers.'

Mistrustful, Susan feigned swallowing them, dropping them from one hand into the other. Then she said, 'I don't want to stay here, I want to go to another clinic – or hospital – or home.'

The nurse frowned. 'You are in the best place in the whole of California. Why do you want to move, Susan?'

Susan hesitated. Would she believe her if she told her the whole story? Maybe that's why her parents were acting so strangely – because they didn't believe her, because they thought she was nuts. Or had John gotten to them and convinced them she was nuts? 'So why won't anyone bring me a phone?' she asked.

Nurse Dufors smiled again. 'The phone! I'll go get it sorted for you right away!'

Susan waited until she was out of the room, then pushed the two pills between the mattress and the covering slip. She looked at Verity again, still sound asleep, then lay back, exhausted, and closed her eyes, listening for the return of Nurse Dufors' footsteps.

Chapter Sixty-three

To John's relief the flight took off on time, and landed early, twenty minutes ahead of schedule, at twelve forty-five; but it was another hour and a quarter before he was in a rental car and heading out on the freeway towards Orange County.

Throughout the entire eleven hours of the flight he'd been churning over and over the same territory, trying to work out what best to do when he arrived, a steady fuse of anger burning inside him. Whether he should first try to convince Susan's parents of the danger Susan was in or go straight to the clinic and deal with the situation as he found it.

Given what Dick Corrigan had told him over the phone about the air line, the police were not an option. Finally he ruled out his parents-in-law, also. He needed to speak to Susan, and hear her version of what had happened with Casey. He just could not believe Susan had harmed her kid sister. Unless ...

The thought hung like a vapour trail. Unless ... unless in some twisted-up thought spiral Susan figured that by killing Casey she was freeing herself of the financial obligation to support her and that, therefore, keeping the baby and breaking the deal with Mr Sarotzini would be fine.

Breakdown?

He found that hard to accept. He knew Susan too well. She was strong, she was a coper. Yes, she had been deeply upset by Fergus Donleavy and Harvey Addison's deaths. She had been spooked by what Donleavy had told her about Van Rhoe and Sarotzini's occult connections. But enough to have pushed her over the brink and sent her to America to kill her sister? He didn't think so.

It was a fine afternoon, warm enough to turn on the air-conditioning in the car. John slowed as he approached the white Doric pillars at the entrance to the Cypress Palisades Clinic, then deliberately drove on past, checking out the place. The gates were open and there was no sign that any additional security had been introduced by its new owners. A long line of sprinklers threw spray across the lawns, and a Hispanic gardener was pushing a barrow laden with cuttings along a woodchip path.

Beyond the grounds, the road wound up into a canyon. He pulled up a quarter of a mile on, turned the blue Chevrolet round, then killed the engine and lit a cigarette, gathering his thoughts once more as he smoked it. He felt surprisingly alert after the long flight, the payoff from sticking to soft drinks and eating little.

The Vörn Bank had bought the clinic six months back.

They had told Dick and Gayle Corrigan that Susan had murdered Casey, but they were going to keep it under wraps.

The clinic are being very good about it, John. They – the director had a talk with us. They don't want a scandal – I guess – I guess any more than we do.

Maybe they didn't want a scandal. But Sarotzini had been watching them, and listening to them ever since – how long? Since before they had moved in? He would know that Susan was having doubts about handing over the baby. Maybe Sarotzini had decided to frame her, as a precaution. She could hardly fight a custody battle if she had a murder charge hanging over her head.

He wondered if he was being too far-fetched. But he was beginning to realise that, so far as Mr Sarotzini went, nothing was too incredible.

When Susan next opened her eyes, Mr Sarotzini was in the room, sitting beside the bed, staring into the cot in a rather detached way. He looked more like a man admiring an exhibit in a museum, than a father adoring his child. She had no idea how long he'd been there.

'Good morning, Susan. How are you feeling?'

She took some time to consider this question. Her abdomen felt as if it had just been used as a target in a knife-throwing competition, her backside had gone to sleep, she had pins and needles in her thighs, as well as a raging thirst and a headache. 'Fine,' she said, guardedly and unsmiling. Then she remembered, and said, petulantly, 'I'd be even more fine if someone brought me a telephone.'

Mr Sarotzini pointed to the bedside table, and she saw a phone sitting on it, plugged into the socket.

'We removed it for your own protection, Susan,' he said, good-humouredly.

'What do you mean?'

'Perhaps it is better that you do not remember. Your behaviour was – shall we say? – a little erratic yesterday.'

'What do you mean, erratic?'

353

He raised a hand, as if to signal the subject was closed. 'And how is Verity this morning?'

Startled, she asked, 'How do you – know – her name?'

'It's a pretty name, so appropriate.'

'How do you know it?' she asked again, more insistently.

He raised his eyebrows. 'Perhaps I know you too well, Susan.'

She shook her head. 'No, I don't think you do, I don't think you know me at all.' She glanced anxiously at Verity, who was sleeping peacefully.

Mr Sarotzini continued to smile at Susan. 'I am so very proud of you. You are going to make a wonderful mother, I always knew you would.'

'What went on last night?' she asked, sternly. 'Who were all those people, and what did they think they were doing – you, and all of them – coming into my room? And who was playing the music? The flute?'

He folded his hands neatly together and gazed at Verity, with a strangely distant look in his eyes. 'It was a little blessing ceremony for the new-born child.'

'A *blessing*?' she retorted, scathingly.

He turned his head and stared at Susan. 'My dear Susan, there is so much you are going to have to learn. There really is such a very great amount.'

Susan stared icily back at him. 'Mr Sarotzini, Verity is my baby. I am her mother and you need to understand that what I say counts. If you ever again want to bring your weirdo friends to a party in my room in the middle of the night, I don't care what your reason is, you ask me first, OK?'

Mr Sarotzini moved his focus from Susan to Verity, then back. 'Susan, I know you've been dredging up the law on surrogacy and taking advice, but you don't have to worry.' He smiled again. 'You really do not have to worry. I just wanted to see proof for myself that you could love this child as much as if she were a child of your very own. And you have given me that proof.'

Susan's thoughts went haywire. He knew? He knew that she'd been to a lawyer? How? Had John told him?

Of course he had. John was in on this. John had told him.

'I – I don't quite know what you mean,' she replied.

'I think we can do business together, Susan, that's what I mean. We made one deal for you to have this baby, I think we can come to another arrangement that will enable you to keep her.'

She stared back at the aristocratic face, the silver-flecked hair, the finely

354

tailored suit, the elegant tie, feeling astonishment – and a strong tinge of suspicion. 'I can – keep – Verity? You're going to let me? Keep her?'

'A baby belongs with its mother, Susan.'

'What about your wife?'

He ignored the question. 'Tell me, how much do you love Verity?'

She gave a nervous half-laugh. 'I – I don't know, I can't measure it. I love her with all my heart.'

'Si parva licet componere magnis,' Mr Sarotzini replied. '"If one may measure small things by great." Virgil.' He looked at Verity fondly, yet with a certain distance, a remoteness. 'Your husband? How will you deal with this problem?'

Susan looked at him suspiciously. What exactly had he and John agreed? 'When John sees Verity, I'm sure ...' She hesitated.

Mr Sarotzini said, 'If you can imagine something, then it exists.'

She frowned, still on guard, then said, a little cynically, 'So if I can imagine John loving Verity, he will? Just like that?'

'Indeed.'

Suddenly, Susan understood what was going on. Of course. 'When we met in London, you told us how much you and your wife wanted a child, and that you couldn't have one because she had had a cancer operation. Was it a *boy* you wanted? A son and heir? Is that why you don't want Verity?'

There was a long silence. She watched his face like a hawk, but instead of shiftiness, all she registered was sadness.

'Susan,' he said finally, 'I told you a small white lie when we met.' He fell silent again. Then he said, 'I have no wife. I have never married.'

The words hung in the air. They didn't dissolve but they weren't absorbed into Susan's brain for a long time. She just heard them repeating, echoing, endlessly going round and round. The banker's face was rigid, as if he were trying to shield himself from his own emotions. His eyes had become two wells of sadness.

'Not married?' she says. 'You – you don't – you have no wife?'

And as she looked at him, she couldn't help feeling sorrow for the man in spite of her shock. But with it came the growing, angry realisation that she had been conned. And confusion.

'A *small* white lie?' she said.

He seemed to be ageing as they spoke. His shoulders sagged, he clenched his hands, and creases like fault lines were breaking out along his forehead. When he spoke, it was no longer the voice of a powerful, man-of-the-world international banker, but the voice of a lonely old man.

'Susan, I – I cannot explain this easily. This is not something that will take just a few minutes.'

'I'm very confused, I don't understand what you want. What's going on?'

'Let me try to explain. You see, I am the last in the line of a very old family. We can trace our ancestry back in direct lineage for twenty-five thousand years before the birth of Jesus Christ, the Great Impostor. I have a duty to pass on the baton. I cannot be the one to let this die out, to end this line, Susan. Not now, not at this time in history.' He looked again at Verity. 'Not when our greatest dream has finally come true.'

'What baton? What dream?'

He was quiet for a moment, and then he answered, 'My religion.'

Susan felt the hairs rise on the back of her neck. Fergus's words came back to her. Was it possible? *The devil incarnate.* Was she was sitting here with the *devil incarnate* and his baby?

Her baby.

Fathered by the man who had murdered Fergus?

Had she conceived the *devil incarnate*'s child, carried it in her womb, given birth to it?

She looked at Verity and then at Mr Sarotzini, feeling a prickle like a current running through her. And there was a power coming from his man, she could feel it. Her skin was crawling as if it was alive with static electricity. But the *devil incarnate*? What did it mean? What had Fergus meant? What *was* the devil incarnate? A madman? An obscenely rich dilettante with delusions of grandeur?

Someone who had the power to kill Zak Danziger, Harvey Addison, Fergus Donleavy?

She looked at her innocent baby, then at Mr Sarotzini again. 'What religion?' she asked. 'You're a devil worshipper, is that it?'

He smiled. His confidence seemed to be returning and, with it, his stature and assurance. 'And you worship the Great Impostor, Susan, who teaches us that we are all cursed with Original Sin. That we are born evil and corrupt and we can only obtain salvation through divine grace. Through pouring money into a church collection box.' His face regained its normal good-humoured expression. 'Look at your daughter, look at her – look at Verity. Is she evil? Is she corrupt? Is that how she has been born? Is that how you view her when you look at her, hold her, suckle her? An evil, corrupt monster? Is it, Susan?'

'It's not that simple.'

'No, you are right,' he said wistfully. 'It is not that simple and we have

356

much to talk about. It will take many days, Susan. Perhaps at the end you will still not agree with me, but you will understand the validity of my reasoning. And you will agree to bring up Verity in my customs and in my family's religion.'

Susan shook her head. 'I'm sorry. I'll bring up my child in *my* customs and in *my* religion. You can't just walk into my life and think you can buy my beliefs. They're not for sale, I'm sorry. End of story.'

Mr Sarotzini nodded, and sat in silence. Verity rolled her head and opened her eyes. He touched the baby's hand with his finger, then stood over her and made faces at her, trying to get her to smile. Just watching this intimacy made Susan angry and possessive.

Then, lowering his voice, as if he didn't want the baby to hear, Mr Sarotzini said, 'I can ruin your life, Susan. It will take just one phone call.'

It wasn't the words he'd said, or the way he said them. It was something in his face as he spoke that truly frightened Susan. She saw, for the first time, the power, an immense, dark power. And it stripped away all her new-found confidence. Mesmerised, she said, 'I – I don't understand?'

'You have been told that your sister, Casey, is dead?'

She stared at him in disbelief, as if convinced he was playing a game and had said this to shok her. 'What? What did you –?'

Her voice fell away. 'Casey?' she said, her scalp tightening. He was not playing a game. Black, icy water swirled in her guts. Mr Sarotzini went out of focus. 'Casey. Dead?' *There was a mistake here, there had to be. Please God let there be.*

'You have not been told?'

She looked for some sign in his blur of a face, something she could reach out to that could give her hope, that would tell her perhaps that he had made a mistake. Her voice came out as a squeak. 'Dead?' It wasn't possible, 'Casey was fine, she was alive, she –'

'I am aware how much you loved her, Susan.'

He was so calm, so matter-of-fact. Casey was dead and Mr Sarotzini was being calm. She wanted to lash out at him, scream at him. Instead she spoke quietly, her voice stretched tight, at its outer limits, on the verge of breaking up altogether. 'What – what do you mean, Casey's *dead*?'

He returned her stare, saying nothing.

Something was all wrong about this. Casey wasn't dead, she'd been in her room, the air line – something – disconnected – Her grip on reality seemed to be shrinking away from her. She sniffed, her eyes filling with tears. 'The nurse said – she said Casey was OK, she –'

'She's dead, Susan,' he said, with a sudden coldness. 'Would you like to see her corpse?'

She covered her mouth with her hand, closed her eyes, shaking terribly. 'It isn't true, please tell me it isn't true.'

'She's dead.'

'Wh – when? When did – did she – die?'

'You know the answer to that, Susan. You were in her room at four o'clock yesterday morning, holding her severed air line.'

And as she looked at him she saw what he was implying. Tears streaming down, she shook her head, barely able to believe this. 'Oh no,' she said. 'No, no, no, no, you've got this wrong.'

He stared resolutely back at her.

'I loved Casey.' She broke down, sobbing, and it was some moments before she was composed enough to speak again. 'I loved her so much. I agreed to have Verity to help Casey, to pay for Casey to stay here, that's why I agreed.' She fumbled for a tissue to staunch the tears. 'I loved her, Mr Sarotzini, I couldn't harm – her, I –' Now she was crying too much to talk.

Verity, picking up on her distress, began to cry too. Mr Sarotzini lifted her from the cot and placed her in Susan's arms. Almost instantly Verity quietened, and the effect of holding her baby calmed Susan a little also. She looked at him imploringly. 'Please tell me it isn't true?'

Mr Sarotzini said, 'Susan, I believe you did not intend to harm her, that what you did was caused by the emotional state you were in, and I am sure that in your mind at the time you did it with the best intentions.'

'I didn't – I didn't do it, I did not kill her. The air line was broken when I got there. Nurse – the nurse – Caulk, Nurse Caulk, ask her –'

Mr Sarotzini looked at her with an expression of deep compassion. 'Susan, do you think I would entrust you with my child if I thought you had really intended to harm Casey? I believe it was a temporary state of mind, a moment of madness borne from despair. But would a judge and jury believe you?' Suddenly, his tone hardened again. 'All I have to do is pick up the phone and call the police and give them the affidavit I have from Nurse Caulk, and you'll be spending the next ten years of your life in and out of prison, fighting court battles.'

Susan was unable to believe what she was hearing, and barely able, through her grief, to comprehend. 'You think I did it? You really think I did it?'

'Do you recall what you did yesterday afternoon, Susan? It was hardly the behaviour of someone in their normal frame of mind.'

Running. She remembered running. Lunging out. Miles Van Rhoe sinking to the ground with a cellular phone jammed in his eye. Was that what he meant? *Yesterday afternoon?*

It wasn't a dream?

'And please think about this, Susan. If I make that call, you will never see Verity again. I will be given immediate custody, no argument. And, Susan, this is important for the future. There is no statute of limitations for murder in the state of California. I can pick up the phone right now, or in ten years' time, or in twenty years' time. Perhaps at the end of it you'll get the death penalty, perhaps you'll get life, perhaps you'll be committed to an institute for the criminally insane. Possibly you'll go free.'

'Please, please stop.' She was shivering terribly, trying to think straight, to think back to when she arrived, to reconstruct those moments. Could she have done it?

Casey is dead.

Could she have done it? Could she? Could Mr Sarotzini be right?

Had she hurt Miles Van Rhoe, too? Why hadn't he been in to see her? Had she killed him, too?

Van Rhoe hadn't been in to see her because he'd gone back to England, that was why ... if he had ever really been here at all ... *yesterday afternoon* ... Reality was slipping away ... *Do you recall what you did yesterday afternoon, Susan?*

A tremor rocked through her. She hugged Verity even harder, as if the baby was all the reality left to her in the world. Her brain was screaming at her *no*, no way did she harm Casey.

But it was also reminding her of all the discussions she'd had with her parents and the doctors over the years, about not giving Casey medication if she got sick and letting her slip away. It was her mother who had fought for the ventilator. Susan had studied all the literature available on people in persistent vegetative states, and believed that Casey shouldn't have been given a ventilator. If she could breathe on her own, fine, but with almost zero brain activity, if she couldn't breathe on her own, then was there any point in keeping her alive?

Oh, God, how she'd wanted her to slip away, wanted it so much. In those early days, she and her father had even talked about finding a way to do it themselves. Except neither of them ever could have done, they loved her too much. Didn't they?

Hadn't she?

And they had been hoping for a miracle, or a breakthrough in neurosurgery. It was possible: so long as Casey was still alive, it was possible that one day she might smile and laugh again, and stand on the stage at the Red Rocks and sing her heart out.

Do you recall what you did yesterday afternoon, Susan?

Mr Sarotzini leant forward and stroked Verity's head lightly with his index finger. 'Susan, I can't tell you how much it would hurt me to put you through all this. Not, of course, to mention the trouble I would have in finding another mother as wonderful as yourself, but you must believe that if you make me, I will do it, you will leave me no alternative.'

'Then go ahead, do it.' She nodded at the phone. 'Do it.'

He looked at her seriously. 'You need to think this through, Susan.'

'Do it,' she said, bitterly.

'They will come here and arrest you, Susan. I have the legal documentation with me, establishing myself to be Verity's father. I will fly to Switzerland with her today and you will never see her again.' He continued to stroke Verity's head; she was fast asleep now.

Casey was dead. Nothing mattered any more. She didn't care what happened any more. She felt drained, her batteries were flat. They could kill her too. As if in protest, Verity suddenly opened her eyes, stared, blinking at Susan, then went back to sleep. *Me,* she seemed to be saying. *Me, I matter.*

Susan held her closer, tighter, suddenly jolted back to sense, and lowered her voice. 'I won't bring her up under your terms, Mr Sarotzini. I will not bring up my child to be a devil worshipper, or any other loony things you might want her to do, I won't, so you'd better make that call, just do it, do it now.'

He lifted the receiver and calmly asked the operator to put him through to the Orange County Police Headquarters. Susan watched him, as if he were some figure in a distant landscape, her thoughts in turmoil, see-sawing wildly. Casey was dead. Verity was connected to that, somehow. Casey, the air line, the dark room, the broken air line – she could picture it so vividly.

Or could she?

Mr Sarotzini said into the phone, 'Homicide division, please.'

She closed her eyes and heard him say, 'Yes, good morning. I am a director of the Cypress Palisades Clinic, and I wish to report the suspected murder of one of our patients.' There was a pause, and then Mr Sarotzini said, 'Of course, certainly.' There was another pause. 'Yes, of course ... the patient's name ... it is *Casey Corrigan.*' He started to spell it out.

Something snapped inside her and Susan screamed at him, 'Stop! Please, no, no, no.'

Verity's eyes opened in alarm. Susan was sobbing uncontrollably. 'Please don't, please, please, I didn't do it, I didn't, please. Please don't take Verity, too.' She held her even more tightly. 'Please, please, let me keep her, I'll be a good mother, I promise I will!' She closed her eyes again, sobbing and hugging her baby.

There was silence.

The silence continued. She opened her eyes. Mr Sarotzini was holding out the receiver to her. She took it and listened, unsure what she was expected to say. And then she realised.

There was no connection.

Mr Sarotzini had an icy smile. He took back the receiver and hung up. 'I think it is so wise that this was only a rehearsal, Susan. Don't you?'

She said nothing.

And Mr Sarotzini said, more kindly now, 'It is the Nineteenth Truth that tells us that only in the vortex of our deepest fear can we see with true clarity.'

Chapter Sixty-four

John slowed for a sleeping policeman, then accelerated on down the drive. As he came round to the front of the clinic, he saw that the visitors' car park was almost empty, which was normal. The clinic had never seemed busy – he could barely remember seeing anyone other than staff on all the previous occasions that he'd been here.

Maybe that feeling of privacy and seclusion was the reason for its success, he speculated, as he locked the Chevrolet and walked, under the watchful eye of a closed-circuit camera, through the automatic doors of the main entrance, into the plush cool of the wood-panelled lobby. Today the quietness made him uneasy.

'Help you, sir?' The man on duty at the desk was black, about forty, and an honours graduate in courtesy.

'I've come to see my wife, Susan Carter.'

'And your first name, Mr Carter?'

John told him, he entered it on his keyboard and, seconds later, the computer printed out his name, time of entry and pass number. The guard tore it off, slipped it into a plastic lapel holder and handed it to John. Then he picked up his telephone, stabbed a button, and said, breezily, 'I have Mr John Carter to see Mrs Susan Carter, two zero one, Monterey Wing.'

He replaced the receiver and gave John a beamer of a smile. 'Someone be right with you to take you up.' He pointed towards the cluster of low chairs. 'Have yourself a seat.'

'It's OK, I know my way around. Tell me where she is and I'll find her.'

The guard gave him an apologetic look. 'I'm sorry, Mr Carter, everybody has to be accompanied – security policy.'

'Wasn't last time I was here,' John said, testily, and remained standing, pacing around distractedly. He picked up a brochure on the clinic and flicked through it, glancing at pictures of the rooms, operating theatres, views, the grounds. But he could find no mention of the new owners.

'Mr John Carter?'

The voice was tinged with a guttural mid-European accent. John turned to see a tall, unsmiling man with close-cropped hair and massive shoulders, staring at him. Dressed in a dark, shiny suit, plain black tie and shiny black loafers, he didn't fit here. He looked like a minder, not a medical orderly.

Guardedly, John said, 'Yes.'

'This way, please, you will follow me.'

In contrast to his powerful appearance, the man walked lamely, in a hobbling gait, as if he were in pain. John followed him across to the elevator, and as they stood waiting for it to arrive, he was aware that the man was studying him intently.

'How is my wife?' he asked, awkwardly, feeling as if he was undergoing some physical inspection.

The man bristled, as if John had asked a forbidden question, then replied, stiffly, 'She is satisfactory.'

The double doors opened and John stepped into the car, which was wide enough to accommodate a gurney. Continuing to stare at him, the man pressed a button for the third floor.

The doors closed slowly and a little jerkily, then the elevator began to ascend. *Satisfactory*. Susan was *satisfactory*. Whatever that meant. Was Susan under guard? Presumably. To protect other patients from her? Or, more likely, to prevent her from going anywhere.

'Slow elevator,' John said, disconcerted by the scrutiny what was still going on, and trying to break the awkward silence. But the response was a narrowing of the man's eyes and an even more intense stare. Then John noticed that the man's fists were clenched tight, his knuckles white. His whole face was taut and he was quivering, as if struggling to contain some private rage.

Alarmed, John eased himself back, away from him, but within a few inches he was pressing against the wall. The light on the panel indicated 3 and the car stopped with a jerk. But the doors remained closed.

The man looked at them, glanced at the panel, then stabbed a button. Nothing happened. He tried again, with the same result. Then, with a sudden burst of fury, he punched one of the doors with his fist Then he punched the door again, even harder.

John watched the display of temper, saying nothing. He had a feeling that if he opened his mouth, the man might switch his aggression to him – he looked nuts, a psycho, well on the edge of losing it.

Without uttering a sound, the man took another swing, and this time he struck the door with such force that John could see it bulge and light

363

appeared down the centre. He hit it again, then again, then again, then again, setting up a reverberating metallic drumming sound, and shaking the car so violently that John became apprehensive that they were in danger of plummeting downwards.

Then he stopped, and again tried a button on the panel. The car jerked up a couple of inches, halted, and the doors, mercifully, opened.

With the drumming sound still in his ears, and his temper worsening, John followed the man out, down a corridor and into a small room occupied by a secretary, who was concentrating on her keyboard and barely glanced at them. There was an open door behind her and the man gestured for him to go through.

John entered a large, well-furnished office that smelled faintly of cigar smoke, then stopped in his tracks. Seated behind the desk, framed by Venetian blinds behind him and a workstation to his right, was Emil Sarotzini.

John stared at the banker, surprised. It had not occurred to him that he might be here. The door closed behind him with a quiet click.

The banker stood up, smiling courteously, and extended a rigid hand. 'Mr Carter, how very pleasant to see you here in the United States. Please sit down.'

John shook his hand coldly, and remained standing. 'I asked to be taken to Susan, not to you.'

'In good time,' the banker said.

'I want to see her *now*. How is she?'

'I have just been with her. She is fine.'

'That's not what I've heard.'

'She is fine, Mr Carter, I can assure you.'

'I'm not interested in your assurances.'

Remaining calm, Mr Sarotzini replied, 'Perhaps I should remind you that you were interested a year ago, Mr Carter, when I was all you had.'

'Yes. I must have been a bloody fool. I had no idea quite how ubiquitous you were.'

The banker looked at him quizzically.

'What a *coincidence* that your bank should acquire the one clinic in the world in which Susan's sister is a patient,' he said sarcastically. Then, digging in his jacket pocket, he produced a tiny dome-shaped video camera, and thrust it across the desk. 'I think this belongs to you.'

Mr Sarotzini cradled it in his bony fingers, examining it for some moments. 'No, Mr Carter, I regret I am not familiar with this object. It is a lamp of some kind, perhaps?'

'Let's cut the crap. I found twelve of these concealed in the ceilings of my house and a satellite transmitter. You've been bugging Susan and me. You've been spying on us. Is this how you get your rocks off? Watching us in bed? This is outrageous, grotesque.'

The banker sat down and made a gesture for John to sit also, which he ignored. After studying John solemnly for some moments, seemingly deep in thought, he said, 'Events have proven the surveillance to have been a wise precaution, Mr Carter, would you not agree?'

'I didn't think voyeurism was your style, Mr Sarotzini. For some foolish reason, I thought you were a gentleman. You're not even going to apologise?'

'On the contrary, Mr Carter, you should thank my colleague, Mr Kündz, for his foresight.' Mr Sarotzini inclined his head, and John suddenly realised that someone else was in the room. He spun round and saw that it was the man who had brought him up here. He was standing behind him, squarely blocking the door, and acknowledged John's glance with a hint of mockery in his eyes.

Mr Sarotzini's tone became icy. 'Perhaps you would care to explain, Mr Carter, why your wife disobeyed Mr Van Rhoe's explicit instructions not to leave London and instead, recklessly, with no thought of the baby's well-being, flew out here?'

Angrily, John replied, 'I'd have thought you knew the reason, since you've been able to hear everything in our house for God knows how long. She was scared, OK? Zak Danziger died, then Harvey Addison, then Fergus Donleavy. The one connection between all three was *you*. And she was informed that her wonderful obstetrician, whom you insisted on, Mr Miles Van Rhoe, has a Scotland Yard file as a devil worshipper. And now my friend Archie Warren's in a coma, and guess what? He was trying to find out information about you when it happened. Then I find that the Vörn Bank has bought this clinic – and suddenly Susan's sister is dead. And –' John checked himself from saying something about Emil Sarotzini the war criminal, who had died in 1947.

Mr Sarotzini looked at him impassively. 'These are serious accusations, Mr Carter. I think perhaps you are experiencing some of the stress that your wife has been under. You must be tired after your flight. Would you care for some refreshment? Coffee, perhaps?'

'I want to see Susan. I want to hear her side of what's happened, before I hear from anyone else, OK?'

'Of course.' The banker raised his hands expansively. 'In a few moments. We need to talk first, to understand each other a little more.'

John shook his head. 'No, I want to see her *now*. I want to see my wife right *now*. Then I'll come back and talk to you, if I'm happy – and if I'm not happy, I'm calling the police.'

Mr Sarotzini examined his keyboard tapped out a command, then swivelled the monitor towards John. It showed in colour, Susan lying at a lopsided angle in a bed, breastfeeding a baby. The clock on the wall, clearly visible above her, showed the time as being now. This wasn't a recording, it was live.

Relief burst through him. *She was all right.* Susan was all right, alive. Thank God for that.

He leaned forward, closer, watching in a swirl of emotions. 'When did she have the baby?'

'Last night, Mr Carter. She's a very healthy little girl. They are both doing excellently. I can understand your wish to speak with her, but there are important things that you should know first. Please sit. This is going to take a little time.'

John hesitated, then looked over his shoulder: the flunkey was still resolutely blocking the door. The sight of Susan had defused some of his anger, and he sat down in front of Mr Sarotzini, then watched Susan again. She was looking at the baby and there was a tenderness in her face, such incredible tenderness. It moved him and, at the same time, gave him a pang of anguish. It was going to devastate her to let this baby go.

'You have been informed, I believe, about the death of Susan's sister, Mr Carter.'

He looked at the banker. 'I had a phone call from Susan's father telling me something totally crazy – that Susan had killed Casey. There's no way, absolutely no way, that Susan would have harmed her.'

Mr Sarotzini nodded, apparently sympathising with his view, then he said, 'I'm afraid it is much worse than that, Mr Carter. Your wife has killed her sister, Casey, and she maimed Mr Van Rhoe. He has lost an eye and he has irreparable frontal-lobe brain damage. He is paralysed down the entire length of one side of his body, and he will never work again.'

'Van Rhoe? *Miles Van Rhoe?*' John stared back at him in disbelief. 'Her obstetrician? Susan was responsible?'

'I regret so.'

This was absurd, totally ludicrous. Some bizarre practical joke was going on, some test he was being put through. His eyes went back to Susan, who was transferring the baby to her left breast. He laughed, thinly. 'Come on!'

But there was no humour in the banker's face. 'It is not something I would have thought your gentle wife capable of, Mr Carter. But how often do we really know anyone?'

The banker tapped out another command. The image on the screen changed from Susan breastfeeding, to the exterior of a building. It was the clinic, John presumed from the style of architecture, although he didn't recognise this part. A figure emerged from a door, dressed in green scrubs, wearing a surgical face mask and cap, and holding a cellular phone. The camera zoomed in tightly on its face.

For a moment it was too difficult to make out just from the eyes, who it was, but it seemed to be a woman. Susan? Then, as she dialled the phone, she tugged the mask down from her face, and John could see clearly that it was Susan. Suddenly, she looked over her shoulder, then began to run.

Other cameras picked her up from different angles as she raced across a flower-bed, a lawn, then down the drive, three men appearing behind her now, chasing her, two in suits, one in surgical scrubs.

John watched in horror. Susan tripped over a sleeping policeman and sprawled headlong onto the tarmac drive. She scrambled forward on her hands and knees, grabbed the cellular phone, which had fallen from her grip, and stood up. The man in surgical scrubs had caught up with her and put a restraining hand on shoulder. In a reverse camera angle John could see the man's face: he was about sixty and puffing with exertion. In that same split second, John saw Susan strike out and stab him in the eye with the pointed aerial end of the phone.

Blanching in shock, John watched the man, whom he presumed must be the obstetrician, sink to his knees with the phone jammed in his eye, then fall sideways. The camera zoomed in on his face. Blood rolled out around the phone; the man lay still.

Mr Sarotzini switched off the replay, then slowly, as if he had all the time in the world, formed a bridge with his fingers, and studied John across the top of it.

John stared back at the banker, feeling sick, the image burning through his mind, replaying itself over and over. There was a tremor in his voice. 'Wh – what was he trying to do to her?'

'Mr Van Rhoe was going to deliver the baby, Mr Carter, that was all. She was his patient. She ignored his instructions to remain in London, and did a very foolish thing, getting on an aeroplane and flying out here. He very kindly agreed to come out himself, to be available for her.'

'How fortunate she came to a clinic you owned.'

Mr Sarotzini ignored the barb. 'I'm afraid Susan has been suffering some form of breakdown, Mr Carter. Her behaviour has been most erratic.'

John leant forward. 'Do you blame her? If I was pregnant and discovered my obstetrician was on a police file for devil worship, I'd run too, Mr Sarotzini.' He watched the banker's face very closely. 'Perhaps you knew all about that. Perhaps that was the reason you insisted Susan go to him in the first place.'

Mr Sarotzini sat up straight, and looked deeply hurt. He sounded hurt, too. 'I think, Mr Carter, you misjudge me. I admit I have kept your wife under surveillance although, as you may be aware, this is not against the law in your country. But have I, in any other respect, behaved in an untoward manner to either of you?'

John stared back at him in silence. He was trying hard to think his way through what was happening, and had no immediate answer. Was he making a serious misjudgment in accusing the man?

'Mr Carter, I have saved your business and your home, and I have tried not to interfere with your lives. We made an agreement and I have stuck strictly to my end of it. Regrettably, your wife has not. She has sought help from surrogacy groups on the Internet, she has consulted lawyers, she has disobeyed her doctor's instructions, she has shown every intention of breaking our agreement and keeping the baby, which is why she is here, and it is why, as you have seen in that regrettable video footage, in an act of total madness she fled from the clinic and savagely attacked Mr Van Rhoe.'

Mr Sarotzini's face tightened with anger. 'And now you have the effrontery to come here, making insinuations to me about the deaths of a composer and two other people, and about someone else who is in a coma, and to imply that in some way our acquisition of this clinic is connected to the death of your wife's sister.' He pointed to the phone on the desk. 'Go ahead, Mr Carter, phone the police, please. It will make us both more comfortable. Ask them to come here. Tell them you wish to make a statement.' He lowered his eyes. When he looked up at John again, he said, 'And inform them that the directors of the clinic wish to make a statement also.' He pushed the phone towards John. 'Please, just lift the receiver, ask the switchboard to connect you.'

John pressed his hands tightly together. They felt clammy; his whole body felt clammy. He swallowed. Mr Sarotzini pushed the phone even closer towards them, and then, in a sharp jerk, even closer still. John fixed his eyes on it. There were two rows of memory buttons, each with a small plastic window containing a typed name. With a sharp screech on the polished desktop, the telephone moved closer still towards him.

His eyes remained rooted to it. He was unable to lift them, unable to look Mr Sarotzini in the face. The hideous image of Van Rhoe collapsing to the ground seemed to reflect at him straight from its grey plastic casing.

'Would you prefer that I make the telephone call for you?'

John looked up, bleakly. Susan had been trying to escape, Christ she must have been desperate. But a confrontation here with Mr Sarotzini wasn't going to get them anywhere. She had – allegedly – killed Casey and the police had not been informed. She had stabbed Van Rhoe, and again no one had called the police.

Was Sarotzini trying to protect Susan?

Or hide something?

'I'm going to talk to Susan before I make any decision,' John said.

Mr Sarotzini gestured with his hand. 'Mr Kündz will take you to her room – but a word of warning first, Mr Carter. I think you need to be careful about what you tell your wife. She is in a state of considerable mental distress. She knows, although she is reluctant to believe it, that she was responsible for her sister's death by disconnecting her air line. But she seems to have blotted from her mind her attack on Mr Van Rhoe. It is fortunate that there were no witnesses to this incident other than our own staff.' He inclined his head, giving John a knowing look.

'Fortunate or convenient?'

'I don't think Susan would cope very well with the duress of a police interrogation at this moment. Would you care to see her indicted on a homicide charge? And, possibly, an attempted homicide charge as well? She is in a mental state where she is unable to separate reality from what is in her imagination. In time, with gentle treatment and care, she will come out of this. To inform her of Mr Van Rhoe's condition might, I fear, push her over the brink.'

John considered this. Susan's behaviour in recent weeks at home had given him concern, however much he did not want to admit it to himself now or to Mr Sarotzini. 'She's been in constant pain for months. It's not surprising that –' He checked himself.

Mr Sarotzini opened out the palms of his hands to John. 'Who knows? Perhaps it was the combination of pain and stress – almost certainly, I would say. The emotional turmoil of all she is going through. It is harder than people realise to give birth to a baby and then hand it over, never to see it again. Much harder.'

'Yes,' John said. 'I've learned that.'

Mr Sarotzini was looking at him strangely now. 'Susan loves that baby with all her heart.'

'I know,' John said quietly. 'I think it would be best if you were to take it

– her – now. Every minute that Susan spends with her is going to make it harder. Please take the baby, give me back my business and our home – that's all I want. Just take her and let us have our life back.'

For what seemed an eternity Mr Sarotzini studied John in silence. He pressed his fingertips lightly together, forming a bridge once again with his two hands, and continued to study John over the top of them, his eyes never leaving John's, as if he was reading something written inside them.

Then he said, 'I think now it is time for you to go and see Susan.'

Chapter Sixty-five

Susan looked up in alarm as John opened the door, shrinking away from him against the headboard and flinging a protective arm around her baby, which continued suckling her exposed breast, obliviously.

He smiled and received a silent, wary stare in return. She was pale and drawn.

'Hi,' he said, hesitantly, closing the door behind him, aware that almost certainly Mr Sarotzini was watching him, and avoiding looking up to where the camera might be, not wanting to alarm her further. He shrugged at her and smiled again. 'How you doing?'

The room had a sickly sweet smell of baby powder, fresh laundry, and something else that John couldn't identify but always associated with new-born babies.

He looked, curiously, at the infant, at its tiny face and minute hands. It's nose was a miniature replica of Susan's, he thought, and its flame-red hair was Susan's too, and this surprised him because – perhaps the situation would have been easier to accept that way – he had imagined the baby would have only Mr Sarotzini's features.

Feeling a heave of emotion, he walked across to the bed, sent down and kissed Susan lightly on the forehead. She did not respond.

'She's lovely,' he said. 'Looks like you. Has your hair and your nose.' He wanted to touch the baby. There was so much of Susan in her – it was even more evident now that he was closer – but a warning gong in his mind made him hold back, told him to keep his emotional distance.

She dropped her eyes. 'Her name's Verity,' she said, in a flat, detached voice. And then in the same tone, almost matter-of-fact, she said, 'Casey's dead.'

'I heard.' Then he hesitated. 'I'm sorry, darling, I'm –' He wasn't sure what he felt or what to say. 'I'm really sorry,' he said, lamely. He reached out with his hands to touch her, to comfort her, but still she did not look

371

at him, keeping her eyes fixed on the baby. He stroked her shoulder lightly, then laid a finger against her cheek but there was still no response.

'He said I killed her.'

John waited a beat, then said, 'Who said that?'

'He said I killed Casey. That I disconnected the air line.'

John watched a solitary tear roll jerkily down her cheek; it was followed by another, then another. He pulled out his handkerchief and dabbed them. It felt like being in a room with a total stranger, not his wife.

'Who said so?' he asked.

'The nurse. Nurse Caulk. Mr Sarotzini said Nurse Caulk had told him.' Still without looking up at him she said, 'It wasn't like that, I didn't – I –'

He dabbed away more tears.

'My parents think I killed her, too. I didn't, John. People can say what they want, think what they want, but they can't take away the truth from you, can they?'

'No,' he replied.

'She was my reason for living.'

There were a couple of hard chairs in the room. John pulled one up to the bed and sat down, ignoring his hurt feelings at the remark. 'I know. You did everything you could for her. She was lucky to have had you.' He looked at the baby again, at the tiny puckered mouth sucking greedily, and at the hair, the flame-red Susan hair and the tiny turned-up nose.

He searched for traces of Mr Sarotzini in its face, but could see none. It was all Susan, just a miniature clone of her. Or perhaps that was wishful thinking.

'You were a wonderful sister to her,' he said. 'You did everything you could for her. You made her life a lot nicer than –' He fell silent, thinking of the video he had seen of Susan plunging the aerial of the mobile phone into Van Rhoe's eye, and shuddered. Mr Sarotzini had been right not to tell her: she was in a bad enough state of shock as it was.

Then he leant forward and whispered in her ear, not caring whether he could be overheard or not, 'I don't believe you killed her. And I love you more than anything on earth.'

She looked up at him, a fleeting, uncertain glance, then silently back down at the baby.

He watched her with a heavy heart. What a mess he'd got her into. Suddenly he found himself hating his bank manager, Mr Clake. Mr Clake with his Bible on his desk was to blame. If he'd only let things be, the business would have turned round and none of this, *none*, would have happened.

And now his wife was lying in a hospital bed, accused of murdering her sister and maiming another man, and a stranger's baby was suckling her breasts.

Oh, God, how had he ever let himself agree to Sarotzini's crazy demands? Why hadn't he been strong enough to say no, forget it? They could have coped – OK, they'd have lost the business and the house, but they would have had each other. Instead, they had this nightmare that was destroying them both.

Susan glanced up at him, watched him for some moments, then gazed down at her baby again. She said, very quietly, 'Mr Sarotzini is going to let me keep her.'

John looked at her in amazement.

And then, peering nervously up at John again, she asked, 'Are you?'

Chapter Sixty-six

The first visitors came at two fifteen the following afternoon. An elderly, rather shabby couple, dressed in clothes of good quality but which should have been given to a jumble sale years ago – or perhaps had come from one, John thought.

The woman's badge read *Mrs M. Lebovic*. She had blue-rinsed hair, ruby lipstick, gaudy jewellery and wore a velvet cloche hat. *Mr S. Lebovic* carried a trilby in his hand, wore a drab, frayed tie and looked meek. They might have been Hungarian, John thought. Or Polish or Rumanian, somewhere like that.

'She's beautiful,' the woman said, in a thick Brooklyn accent, ignoring both Susan and John and stepping right up to the sleeping cot. The man followed her, approaching Verity with an air of humility and awe. Then both of them stood still, as if the cot were an altar, closed their eyes and mouthed a silent prayer.

It reminded Susan eerily of the night that Mr Sarotzini and the other people, including the old man in the wheelchair, had come into her room.

'Are you friends of Mr Sarotzini?' John asked, taking an instant dislike to them.

The man carefully levered a package wrapped in old newspaper from his raincoat pocket and, ignoring John, held it out to Susan, who was watching him warily. 'Please,' he said. 'For the new-born.'

The object was surprisingly heavy, and Susan nearly dropped it. She pulled off an elastic band, then unfurled the paper to reveal a dark green figurine. It was neither human nor animal, probably some mythological creature, she assumed, not caring for it very much. 'Thank you,' she said, uncertainly.

'It is her heritage,' the man said, then turned to follow the woman, who was already at the doorway.

'Wait,' Susan said. 'I don't know your connection with –'

They were gone, leaving more quickly than they had arrived as if anxious that they had outstayed their welcome.

She gave John a who-were-they? look.

'Mr and Mrs *Lebovic*.' He took the statuette from her. 'Friends – Christ, this is heavy – friends of Mr Sarotzini? Relatives? What did he say? *It is her heritage*? What the fuck does that mean?'

Susan looked at Verity, who was sleeping peacefully. 'Maybe it's some family heirloom they've been keeping.'

John turned the statuette over, searching for some clue as to its provenance. He knew little about antiques; this felt old, its texture smooth, like glass on a beach polished by the sea and sand, and he guessed it was malachite. It had graceful legs, like a racehorse, a male human torso and a scaly head that reminded him of a gryphon. It did not repulse him, but it was unattractive, rather sinister-feeling. 'Don't think I'd mind too much giving this away if it was in my family,' he said.

'It is, now,' she replied.

Their eyes met, for an instant, then John looked away. Susan's emotions were a minefield and he needed to pick every word he said with care. He examined the statue again, wondering if it had some occult significance, but said nothing.

Last night, he'd slept in a room adjoining Susan's. He'd had only one further conversation with Mr Sarotzini after his confrontation with him yesterday afternoon, in which the banker had informed him that he had to return to Europe on business, and would leave him and Susan to consider their position. Mr Sarotzini told him he could stay at the clinic for as long as he wanted, and strongly advised him to remain with Susan until she was fit enough to return to England. John had no intention of doing anything else.

Susan had been seen this morning by her new obstetrician, a courteous Swiss of few words named Dr Verlag. Under John's questioning he told them he had removed a small ovarian cyst after the Caesarean and that Susan was fine, she would be able to mother as many more children as she wanted.

No mention was made of Miles Van Rhoe, and John thought that that was for the best, for now. Just let her keep it blotted out until she was in a stronger mental state.

This morning, Susan had again told John exactly what had happened when she'd arrived in Casey's room. He wanted to believe her, and what she said had that indefinable ring of authenticity about it. And yet there was a question mark that hung like a gallows across his mind.

If Susan was able to blot from her mind her attack on Van Rhoe, then was it possible that she had killed Casey and was blotting that out, too?

Could Sarotzini possibly have been telling the truth?

She had a motive: with Casey dead, she had no financial obligations to prevent her absconding with Verity. But would Susan really have put her love for her unborn baby higher than her sister's life? Not if she was normal. But if she was having a breakdown ... if the balance of her mind was disturbed ... then what?

And he had a feeling that Susan was holding back from telling him everything. She wasn't sure about him, she wasn't sure at all.

Ten minutes after the Lebovics had departed, the second visitors arrived. Mr and Mrs Stone, a decade younger than the Lebovics and much better dressed and, John guessed, also of middle European origin. Like the Lebovics, they, too, were interested only in Verity, virtually ignoring Susan and John, except to hand them a gift, this time in a box tied with ribbon, a magnificent gold chalice that John boggled at and reckoned must be worth thousands.

Visitors continued to arrive in an intermittent trickle throughout the afternoon. Concerned at the stress on Susan, John spoke to the obstetrician, asking if he could put either a restriction or a total ban on visitors, at least until she was stronger, and Dr Verlag's curt response was that these people admired the great man, Emil Sarotzini, and had come, many of them right across America, to pay respects to his child. It would be an insult to reject them.

There was no let-up each afternoon for the next three weeks. The visitors were invariably polite, but mostly reticent, normally addressing Susan and ignoring John. All brought a gift. Some of the women also dispensed advice for care of the baby, about nutrition, sleeping positions, room and bath temperatures. Susan was given remedies for colds, herbs for Verity's bones, and advice on vitamins to add to the baby's milk once she moved from breast to bottle feeds.

The visitors were invariably middle-aged to elderly, some more affluent-looking than others, and although just about every race was eventually represented, mostly they were white and predominantly of central European extraction, John judged from their appearance, their names and sometimes their voices.

The first few afternoons he stayed in the room, watching them carefully, and exchanging comical glances with Susan as some departed. Although she was tired, Susan was, at least, showing signs of regaining her sense of humour.

Many of the gifts were antiques, and dark green or black were the favoured colours, malachite, wood or marble, and often wrapped with black silk ribbon. But there were also some in brass and gold. The largest gift was an ornately carved black lacquered crib. A couple delivered it with great pride and said it had been in their family for centuries. After they had gone, John and Susan exchanged a look of horror. Susan said it gave her the creeps having it in the room and John removed it, putting it in the trunk of his car, and donated it to a startled couple he found in an LA suburb preparing for a garage sale.

There were censers, crucibles and other jars and vessels, and a large amount of old jewellery, some beautiful, but much of it vulgar and showy with huge stones. The gifts Susan liked best were the linen, which several people brought with pride, the finest Susan had ever seen or touched. She had John remove all the overtly occult gifts and store them away, not wanting her parents, who came every morning, to see them.

John did some work for DigiTrak, visiting existing clients on the West Coast and trying to drum up new business, although his heart wasn't really in it. Mostly he bided his time, thinking, trying to understand what was happening, watching Susan, talking to her and trying to coax back into their relationship the closeness they had once had. But always Verity lay between them, like a brick lying in the shattered glass that had been their love.

Susan continued to insist that Mr Sarotzini had said she could keep Verity. John did not contradict her, presuming that the banker had his reasons. Perhaps he, too, was concerned about Susan's sanity, and was allowing her to keep the baby until she was strong enough mentally to cope with parting from her. Although John suspected that the man was too ruthless to let feelings of that kind cloud his judgement, and that he must have some other agenda.

And he felt also that it was a bad decision. The longer Susan spent with Verity, the harder she was going to find parting with her. He was even finding his own emotions getting tangled the more time he spent with the baby, holding her at Susan's insistence, talking to her, teasing her. He wasn't sure that he was getting closer to Verity but it was getting harder, as the baby showed signs of recognising him and as he watched Susan's intense love for her, to remember that this was another man's child. And he no longer saw Verity as some distant, disconnected object, but as a frail infant, a fellow human being, helpless and trusting in these two fallible people, Susan and himself, who were her world.

He called Pila in England every couple of days and the bulletins she gave him on Archie remained unchanged. He was deeply distressed by the condition of his friend, and thought constantly about his confrontation with Mr Sarotzini, and how aggrieved the banker had been when he had suggested a connection between Archie's illness and the deaths of Harvey Addison, Zak Danziger and Fergus Donleavy.

He replayed over and over the banker's reaction, trying to gauge how a genuinely innocent man might have responded, and concluded every time that Mr Sarotzini's evasive reply, his reaffirmation of his so-called honourable behaviour, followed by his bald challenge to John to call the police, were those of a man who had something to hide.

A million questions boiled in his mind. Susan had gone to Harvey Addison for a second opinion and that night he had died. It had been, ostensibly, an overdose of cocaine – but perhaps his death had been set up to look that way? Then Fergus had told Susan what he knew about Sarotzini and Miles Van Rhoe, and that night he had choked on his vomit in a drunken stupor. Again that could have been a set-up. Zak Danziger had died of a drug overdose in a hotel in New York. Again a set-up?

Archie Warren had gone to his office and e-mailed him files about Sarotzini's company, and that night he had had a stroke and was still in a coma, with a poor prognosis. It was a common belief that occult practitioners could harm victims merely by thinking about them, or by sticking pins in wax effigies of them. Was that what had happened to Archie?

Was such a thing really possible?

And why had these things happened? The motive for Zak Danziger's death had been clear enough: to get him off DigiTrak's back. But Harvey Addison? Just because Susan had been to him for a second opinion? Was there something about the baby that Harvey had not been supposed to see or know?

John knew that Harvey had been a womaniser, and that he took cocaine. It was possible that his death had been a genuine accident. It was possible that Fergus Donleavy's death had been an accident also – Susan had told him that Fergus was a heavy drinker. It was possible that Archie's obesity and incessant smoking had finally taken its toll.

And just supposing that Sarotzini was prepared to kill people and get involved in illegal cover-ups, then how safe was Susan? Or himself?

What did Sarotzini really want from them?

Susan had told him that Sarotzini had lied about his wife and wasn't married. And she told him that he'd talked about his religion and had said that Jesus Christ was an impostor, but she was unclear what his religion was, and urged John to read the books on the occult that she'd left in the bottom of a suitcase at her parents' house.

He had read them. Some of the chapters that enabled him to understand the significance of the occult symbols in their house and of new-born babies disturbed him deeply. And the daily visitors, with their occult gifts, disturbed him as deeply, as if by the sheer weight of their numbers they lent credibility to his consternation.

OK, Susan's fears that the baby would be taken and sacrificed the moment it was born had been groundless, but only *so far*. Perhaps it didn't need to be a new-born baby. Perhaps Sarotzini was keeping Verity for one of the specific dates listed in his book. Walpurgis Night was coming up: 30 April. Or the Summer Solstice on 21 June. Or Lammas, the great Sabbat festival, on 31 July. Or the Autumn Equinox. Or Samhain. There were any number of festivals ahead.

How deeply were they into something they did not understand?

And what was their exit? Handing over Verity? That was no longer an option for him, not without tremendous reassurances, backed by hard evidence, that her future safety would be assured. And, even with that, he doubted Susan would ever consent, not now.

He said nothing of his fears to her or to her parents. Dick and Gayle Corrigan were having a tough time coping with their grief over Casey, and he knew the room was bugged, probably being watched, and maybe their house and their cars and God only knew what else.

That feeling of helplessness he'd experienced a year ago in Mr Clake's office had returned with a vengeance. But then he'd had at least some idea of what to do and where to turn.

Now he had none.

Chapter Sixty-seven

As the private jet accelerated Susan felt the joins in the runway bumping beneath them. Verity's mouth opened in alarm, and Susan cuddled her, making soothing noises. The roar of the engines deepened, the plane shook, and then it was riding a cushion of air and Los Angeles was tumbling steeply away beneath them.

Her ears popped. She held her nose and blew, then Verity started to cry. Susan wondered if her little ears were hurting too – they must be, she decided, and she didn't know how to deal with this.

She turned to John. 'Hon, does it say anything in your CD about how we get Verity to pop her ears?'

He hauled his briefcase on to his lap and opened it. All the papers in it slid forward from the angle of the climb. Rummaging inside, he pulled out his laptop, powered it up and inserted one of DigiTrak's recent CD releases, which he'd had sent over, titled *Dr Harvey Addison's 1001 Useful Things to Know About Your Baby*. He searched through it. Ears popping on an aeroplane was not among them.

Verity's crying worsened. Mr Sarotzini, sitting opposite in one of the rearward-facing seats, said, 'If you feed Verity, the sucking and swallowing will ease the pressure in her ears, Susan.'

She looked back at him resentfully. With every day that passed she found it harder to accept that Mr Sarotzini was Verity's father, and regarded even this piece of advice as an intrusion. So what did he expect now? That she was going to expose a breast right here, in front of him, and start suckling Verity?

And then, she wondered, suspiciously, How did he know what to do? Had he had other babies, like Verity? From other brood-mare mothers, like herself?

'She'll be OK,' she replied. 'She'll settle down. It's just the noise of the take-off that unsettled her.'

Verity bawled even more loudly, her tiny mouth contorting, her face puce. As soon as the jet began to level out, Susan unclipped her seat belt and, a little unsteadily, carried Verity down to one of a cluster of chairs around a small boardroom table at the rear of the cabin.

There, in privacy, she slipped out her left breast and held Verity's face to it. Within seconds, the baby's screaming faltered, and she began to nuzzle the nipple. Susan watched her contented expression, and felt a glow of warmth, which almost immediately gave way to a feeling of anger that Mr Sarotzini had been right. 'We're going to England,' she whispered. 'You're coming home with me. Are you looking forward to it?'

John peered round to check if Susan was OK, but couldn't see her, then looked back at his laptop and clicked on the *Introduction* icon, which was a small avatar of Harvey Addison.

A second later, Harvey filled the screen, oily smooth and silky-voiced, welcoming every new mother in the world to his essential guide. John's emotions churned at the sight of his friend. He'd been in the studio to oversee the filming of this intro, less than a year ago, and could remember it clearly.

He looked up and saw Mr Sarotzini watching him. The banker had returned to accompany them personally to England. John had been wary of accepting his invitation to fly them home in his private jet. If Sarotzini wanted to get rid of him and Susan, a thousand miles out over the Atlantic would have been as good a place as any. But then so would the clinic have been, he reasoned. If Sarotzini's people could cover up Casey's death, then his own and Susan's would not have posed a problem either.

Mr Sarotzini had told him that commercial airliners were breeding grounds for bugs; it was in the best interests of Verity's health that they accepted. And, John had to admit, he was enjoying the novelty: this plane was the size of a commercial airliner, and had proper beds. And he'd got a certain thrill of power going through a separate section at Los Angeles airport; being, however fleetingly, in the realm of the super-rich was seductive. But not seductive enough to dull his wits.

Mr Sarotzini said, quietly, 'So, Mr Carter, the two of you have had three weeks in which to consider my terms. You have arrived at an answer?'

'I haven't had any terms from you,' John said fractiously.

The banker looked at him reproachfully. 'I conveyed them to Susan. I would have thought, perhaps, during the past three weeks you would have discussed them?'

'Susan's in a state of shock. She needs counselling, therapy, probably a long haul with a psychiatrist. She doesn't trust you or me or anyone right now. She believes you and I are in cahoots and that we have a hidden agenda. How can you expect her to think rationally? She's a strong girl, she's doing her best, she's coping, but that's all she's doing. She's coping, she's trying to be a good mother, OK? If you have terms you want to discuss, you discuss them with me.'

'I am permitting Susan to keep the baby. She has told you this?'

'She's under that impression. Presumably my feelings don't count.'

'You are her husband, Mr Carter. You are at perfect liberty to say no. I would understand.'

John stared at the banker, at his coldly arrogant face, his immaculate suit, his shiny loafers, his expensive tie, reclining but alert, like a basking reptile, in his wide seat. 'Would you?' John said, cynically. 'Would you really?' He looked back at his computer screen, at Harvey Addison's face frozen now, still, motionless.

Dead.

'Exactly how long does Susan get to keep her for?'

Mr Sarotzini raised his hands. 'Susan is Verity's mother. How long does a mother keep any child?' He leant forward and, unhurriedly, pressed his fingertips together forming the familiar bridge. 'Of course, Mr Carter, I understand. It is not easy for you.'

'That's something I will have to discuss with Susan when she's fit and ready. I also have a number of conditions for you.'

The banker looked at him quizzically, as if amused by his presumption. 'Yes? Please tell me.'

'The first is that I want Susan under doctors of our own choosing from now on.'

There was no reaction. 'And the second?'

'I don't want any more surveillance. No more bugging of my house, no more cameras.'

'Give me no cause for alarm, Mr Carter, and further surveillance will not be necessary.'

'Susan ran because she was scared you were going to take the baby away.'

'That is no longer an issue.'

'So there will be no more surveillance?'

'No more, Mr Carter.'

Their eyes met and John tried to gauge the sincerity of this statement. But he couldn't. 'Third thing, I don't want anyone else coming to harm.' John watched the man's face carefully, but there was no visible reaction.

'You require a bodyguard? Someone to protect Susan and Verity – and yourself?'

'That's not what I meant,' John said. This time he saw a definite tightening around the man's mouth and eyes. 'And I want phone numbers where I can get hold of you. I want to know how often you expect to see Verity, what she will be told about who her father is, and who will pay for her upkeep.' He hesitated. 'And I want to understand what's going on. Why did you want to have this baby so much? Why are you willing to give her up? This is not making any sense to me.'

'In your Bible, Mr Carter, there is an eloquent line in, I believe, St Paul's letter to the Corinthians. '"Now we see through a glass darkly. Then, we shall see clearly."' You are familiar with this line?'

'I'm familiar with the quotation, but it's not *my* Bible, I'm not religious.'

'I don't require you to be religious, Mr Carter. I am simply explaining that although at present you do not understand my decision to leave Verity with her mother, one day you will. It is not necessary to understand everything. Man has lived on this planet for four hundred thousand years without understanding the universe around him. That is a far more vexing problem than why a baby girl should be allowed to remain with her natural mother, is it not?'

'You might have a reason that's rather less cosmic,' John replied. 'Perhaps you were hoping for a boy, and a girl doesn't suit your purposes. Or does she have some rare genetic disorder that's going to kill or cripple her and you don't want to be landed with an invalid?'

Mr Sarotzini gave John a look of profound sadness, as if John had wounded him deeply. 'And there is no place in your heart, Mr Carter, for simple compassion? You would not entertain in your harsh judgement of me the possibility that I, too, am a human being, and am capable of simple human emotions? Perhaps because you perceive me as wealthy, this puts me on a pedestal where I cannot be touched by the kinds of feelings and responses common to other people?'

The distress in the banker's voice took John by surprise. The man sounded genuinely close to tears. John was not sure what to say. Then the banker continued. 'I have done everything in my power for you and Susan. I saved your business and your home, and I have risked disgrace and prison to save Susan from a possible murder charge. Can you not understand how fond I have grown of dear Susan? How much it would hurt me to see her unhappy? If I take Verity away, it will unhinge her further. And what purpose would it serve? Just to satisfy the whim of an old man.'

'What about your wife?' John said, softening a little, moved by the man but not sure he was telling the whole truth. 'You told Susan that you have no wife.'

Mr Sarotzini lowered his eyes. 'Would Susan ever have agreed if she'd known that? I don't think so. I'm just an old man, Mr Carter, old and lonely, who wanted to leave something of himself behind on this planet when he died.' He nodded a few times, still looking down. 'And, thanks to you and Susan, I have done that. Susan will make a better mother than any nurse or nanny I could hire. You – you and Susan will make better parents, give Verity a happier upbringing than I could ever hope to do. That's all, that is my only agenda, that is the truth, Mr Carter.' He looked up at John abjectly.

John's emotions were in disarray. Had he misjudged this man? Had he been swept along by Fergus's wild stories of satanism? Jumping to conclusions about the occult drawings in the loft? Maybe Mr Sarotzini did practise the occult in some form – the religion he'd told Susan about, which she hadn't understood – but the occult wasn't necessarily bad, was it? There were plenty of good occultists, *white* witches, weren't they called?

Was that how Sarotzini had amassed his wealth? Through the occult? Through casting spells?

The thought was absurd. Yet it was absurd also to be sitting in this private jet, absurd that his gentle wife had killed her sister and maimed her obstetrician, absurd that they were taking home a baby that he hadn't even fathered, and that they would have to live a lie that he was the father for –?

For how long?

Until Mr Sarotzini came to claim her?

'I presume,' John said, 'that you are going to release the shares in my business and the deeds to our house?'

The question seemed to take Mr Sarotzini by surprise. 'Our arrangement, Mr Carter, was that you would hand over the baby to me on the day it was born, and I would then return the deeds and shares to you. This has not happened. You and Susan have not yet earned my trust. How do I know that you will not decide, when you return to England, to put Verity out – for instance – for adoption by strangers?'

John exploded, 'That's ludicrous!'

'Yes,' he said quietly. 'I would like to hope so. But Susan, as you have admitted, is unbalanced. Who knows what is going through her mind?'

'Susan intends to keep Verity. She loves her more than anything in the world – far more than she loves me.'

Mr Sarotzini smiled. 'All is well, then. You need not fear for the shares or deeds.'

'So when do I get them back?'

'When I am convinced.' He smiled again and settled back in his seat. Then he pointed to John's laptop. 'Please, you have work to do. Don't let me interrupt you any longer.'

John stared back at him, seething with rage, all feelings that he might have misjudged the man swept aside. It was all he could do to restrain himself from getting out of his seat and grabbing the banker by the throat. There was nothing to be gained by an outburst.

He stared back at his computer screen, at the motionless face of Harvey Addison, and tapped a few keys, clearing the screen, trying to clear his mind, his rage turning slowly to despondency. He was tired of being Mr Sarotzini's puppet, tired of having his life controlled by this man. When they had gone into this, he had been able to see a clear exit at the far end. And just a month ago he had thought that when the baby was born, it would all be over.

Now, it seemed, that had been only the beginning.

They would be landing soon. Susan was dreaming, and Verity, curled in her arms, her tummy full of milk, was sleeping soundly. In the dream she was in a room she did not recognise: it was a large room and she was alone with Mr Sarotzini and another man who was in the shadows at the back; a very old man in a wheelchair.

Mr Sarotzini said, 'Susan, dear Susan, it is time now for you to understand what I am.'

'What are you?' she asked.

'I am an instrument, that is all. I am merely an instrument for a Higher Power, Susan, just a humble servant of this Power, that is all, a messenger, a link in a chain, given a duty to carry a baton and to pass it on. This baton is a genetic code that contains knowledge from far back in history, a knowledge of all the Truths. It is a knowledge, Susan, whose time has come.'

Then with a trace of bitterness, he said, 'Regrettably I am not physically capable of passing it on. The Power has made me search for two others who carry this gene, and there are few on earth who have it, a mere handful of people. It has not been easy. The first success was twenty-five years ago, when the grave of an old man in Bavaria led me to the male, a small boy who was living in Africa.'

Susan asked him, 'Is this boy, the carrier of this gene, is he Verity's father? Is he the man from Telecom?' She felt lost, like a small child, like Alice in Wonderland. Her voice echoed around this chamber as if she was in a cave. 'Is he the man who was in the room – when – when I was being fertilised? Are you Verity's father, or is this man? This boy you found?'

'It's not important.'

'It is. It is important. It's everything. I want to know the truth. Tell me the truth.'

'You, dear Susan, are Verity's mother, that is what counts.'

'And the father? Who is the father? Is it the man from Telecom? The man who was in the room in the WestOne Clinic?'

'There are some things it is better never to know.'

'I want the truth.'

'There are many Truths.'

'Please, Mr Sarotzini, don't play games with me.'

'The Twenty-eighth Truth states that sometimes it is better to believe than to know. The Thirty-fourth Truth states that reality is what you believe, not what you *want* to believe.' He smiled. 'So similar and yet so different. It is beholden on all of us to find those Truths with which we are comfortable, and live by those. And it is more beholden on you, than on anyone else. Because one day, Susan, your baby will change the world.'

'Why me? Why my baby?'

'Because you also carry this gene. You must never be afraid, you must only be proud.'

'What is this gene? How do you know I carry it?'

'We searched for twenty-five years for a female who carried it, Susan. Last year, finally, we were successful. We found the grave in Los Angeles of a lady called Hannah Rosewell.'

'Hannah Rosewell? My grandmother?' Susan replied in astonishment.

'We performed DNA tests on her remains.'

'My grandmother?'

'There are a mere handful of people in the entire world who carry this gene, Susan, and forces beyond nature have kept them far apart. The Apo-E-AA. This is the gene of my tribe.'

'Your coven?'

Mr Sarotzini ignored the remark. 'If you have this gene you will live for at least a century, and probably longer. It is the strongest, most resistant gene in our species. We identified it in your family through a search through longevity records. Your grandmother, Hannah Rosewell, lived to a hundred and one. It a privilege to carry this gene, Susan, and when two people who carry this gene meet and produce a child, they are producing a human of a strength that has not been seen in thousands of years.'

'Why not?'

Now Mr Sarotzini's face was close to her own, so close, and he was smiling, smiling so fervently. 'Because, Susan, the Great Impostor's followers have prevented it. For two millennia the world has been in the grip of a conspiracy of evil. My people have been labelled gnostics, witches, heretics. They have been hunted, persecuted, tortured, butchered.'

The jolt of the wheels on the runway woke Susan and woke Verity also. Mr Sarotzini was staring hard at her. Susan looked away, and when she looked back, Mr Sarotzini was still staring at her. She felt strange and disoriented.

Outside it was a fine Sunday morning. London was in bloom. It was spring, and it felt like summer here in the jet as the engines died and the air-conditioning was switched off.

But then the stewardess opened the exit door, and a wind blew in, a harsh, savage wind that felt as if it had come from somewhere else, some distant place, carrying to Susan in its icy blast all the depths of an Arctic winter.

Chapter Sixty-eight

In contrast to the grand, post-modernist reception area of the law firm, Elizabeth Frazer's office was small and sparsely decorated. A framed drawing of the Bridge of Sighs hung on the otherwise bare walls. There was a photograph on the desk of a man and two small children on skis posing in front of a chairlift. A vase of flowers on the desk. Two shelves of law books. Otherwise it was just stacks of files, some piled on the floor behind her desk, others on the window-sill, obscuring the view of another office block across the Aldwych, and a computer terminal.

Susan had told him that Elizabeth Frazer was the country's leading specialist in child law, and his own lawyer had agreed.

She was in her late thirties. A tall, wiry woman, with curly brown hair and steel-rimmed granny glasses, dressed in a denim blouse and black trousers, she had the air of a radical student revolutionary who had never mellowed. She was not unpleasant, but there was a brittleness about her with which John did not feel comfortable.

Coffee arrived, and the solicitor dealt him a cup. 'This is all very different from when your wife came to see me in March,' she said.

'You told her that she had a strong case.'

'You've given me a lot of new information, Mr Carter. Under the Human Fertility and Embryology Act, the donor has complicated rights when he is not anonymous. When Mrs Carter came to see me, I advised her that our best chance would be to take out a Prohibitive Steps Order, which can taken against either a parent or someone who tries to act as a parent.'

'But Mr Sarotzini would actually have to be served with this?'

'Yes.'

'That could be difficult – I mean, embarrassing. I would rather he didn't know.'

Scathingly, she said, 'If he doesn't know he's not allowed to take your daughter away, what is to stop him?'

John had no immediate answer.

She glanced at her scrawled notes on a large pad. 'Your wife's mental state is the biggest problem here. You won't tell me exactly what she's done – and you will have to before we go to court. But you say this Mr Sarotzini has sufficient evidence to enable serious criminal charges to be brought against her?'

'Yes.'

'And is she guilty?'

'No, of course not ...' He hesitated. 'No. And one of these I don't believe at all. The other –' He thought about the video of Susan stabbing Van Rhoe. 'I mean – it would be a question of interpretation. She did something in self-defence and, I think in her mental state, she over-reacted.'

'What's your opinion of your wife's mental state?'

John grimaced. 'I think she's in a bad way. She was close to a breakdown – if not actually having one – in the last couple of weeks of her pregnancy. Our family doctor saw her yesterday and his diagnosis is that she's suffering post-natal depression.'

'Which kind?'

'Puerperal psychosis.'

'That's the worst kind.'

'Yes.'

'So she has delusions? Hallucinations? Suicidal tendencies? And she's very tired?'

'Yes, all of those. He's prescribed antidepressants and he's arranging for the community psychiatric nurse to visit her. He's also suggested I should think about a residential nursery nurse for a period of time – either that or have her admitted to hospital.'

The solicitor glanced at her notes again. 'Verity was born three weeks and three days ago.'

'Yes.'

'We're going to have problems if we try going the Prohibitive Steps Order route. If Susan starts telling a judge all this stuff you've been telling me about satanism and black magic, she's not going to get a sympathetic hearing, unless you can come up with some convincing evidence. All judges are aware that this occult activity really does go on, but most of the time it's a bunch of perverts using the trappings as an excuse for ritual abuse. And do we have enough to convince anyone here? Tell me honestly, Mr Carter, do you believe that Verity is in danger from the occult?'

389

'I don't know,' John said. 'I really don't know.'

'You've found weird stuff in your attic, but you have no idea how long it's been there. Anything else?'

'No,' he said. 'Not tangible.'

'Your wife's fears could be connected to her mental state. Hallucinatory in nature?'

'I have a lot of respect for Susan, but she's in a bad way. Yes, they could be connected, I just don't know.'

She pulled a plastic dispenser from a drawer in her desk and, with a daintiness that surprised John, clicked two artificial sweeteners into her coffee. 'I think a better option for us would be to apply to have Verity made a ward of court, on the grounds of your wife's mental state.'

'What does that mean?'

'It means effectively that the court would have custody of Verity, it would act *in loco parentis*. It would decide everything to do with Verity and monitor her future. No one could remove her from England without the court's permission.'

'And I would have to testify that Susan was not in a fit mental state to look after her?'

'No, we'd have a psychiatrist do that.'

'Would Mr Sarotzini have to be notified?'

'As the biological father, yes.'

John shook his head. 'That's the problem. I'm scared of what he would do.'

'Surely that's the point of why you are here, because you're scared of what he might do, or try to do?'

John nodded gloomily. 'Yes. But it's not that simple.'

'You realise you might have another problem if we go to court? The court might decide that Mr Sarotzini is a better parent to bring up the child than your wife.'

Chapter Sixty-nine

The Venerable Doctor Euan Freer walked through the fine May sunshine. It was a Saturday and normally this would be his quiet day, but this was not a normal day.

He was wearing a suit, which was unusual for him: he habitually wore clerical robes, and when not in robes then a dog collar, at least. But today there was nothing outwardly to identify him as a priest, he looked like an overweight, middle-aged businessman with an imposing presence and greying hair, pessimistically carrying a raincoat over his arm on such a fine day.

He was perspiring heavily, but this wasn't from the heat of the afternoon sun, it was from his nerves. He was shaking inside. On his face there was a grim mask of determination but inside the mask there was fear.

And inside the raincoat there was a Sabatier kitchen carving knife.

He had to do this. There was no choice, it *had* to be done, and quickly. With every day that passed, the news of this infant, this monster, this beast, gave strength and confidence to its people.

There were channels he should have gone through, sanctions he should have sought, but their bureaucracy alarmed him. It could take years and, in any case, there would be informers inside the Church. And besides, in the end, what could the Church do? Make a feeble condemnation? Issue a public warning? Increase the prayers? What *teeth* did the Church have?

This was a decision he had had to take by himself, and at least he knew, from the guidance he had sought in his own prayers, that for this deed he had the highest sanction of them all.

It was the only one he needed.

A swirl of leaves rose up from the verge and rattled past his face with the fury of a striking serpent. The wind plucked at the roots of his short-cropped hair, a deep, icy wind full of hatred, that had slid inside his skin and was blowing though his veins. He could feel it shaking his sinews, he could hear it screaming in his ears, he could feel it freezing the sweat on his skin.

But he walked determinedly on, down to the end of the street. He did not know this part of London well. He'd never been in this tree-lined street before, but he knew it was the right street – he knew that, without even having to look at the sign bearing its name. He could feel the presence here.

He walked on, until he reached the house with the turret.

The temperature was in the early seventies. It was too hot in the garden for Verity: she was asleep in her room, in her cot, after her noon feed.

Susan lay, with her eyes closed, in a recliner in the garden. Caroline Hughes, the nanny sent by the agency, who had been with them for three days now, sat at the barbecue table assembling a farmyard-animals mobile that Kate Fox had brought round this morning.

Caroline was a pleasant girl in her late twenties, solidly built with short brown hair cut like a page boy, and dressed in a cream blouse and a pleated navy skirt. Clipped to her belt was the radio intercom, relaying the sounds from Verity's room. All was quiet there, just the strong, steady, reassuring noise of her breathing.

Across the fence, Susan heard the swishing of a lawn sprinkler. Both the old people had died, within a couple of days of each other apparently, and someone had rented the house, so Lom Kotok at the Thai restaurant, who knew everything, had told her – although he'd heard it was in a pretty grim state. Susan had not yet caught a glimpse of her new neighbours.

She was exhausted. Dr Patterson had given her some capsules, and yesterday they'd turned her into a zombie. Despite all John's entreaties, she had refused to take them today. She wanted to be able to think clearly, but it didn't seem to make any difference. The same confused thoughts and fears haunted her brain. Casey. The air line. The broken connector. She had got out of her car, gone into Casey's room and found the air line separated. Surely she would remember if – if she had –?

She shivered. It was as though there was a compartment in her mind that she could not reach. She had been in her car and then she had been on the floor in Casey's room holding the two separated bits of air line. Some space in between was locked in that compartment. The same compartment that contained something that had happened with Miles Van Rhoe. She had been running and then Miles Van Rhoe was sinking to the ground with a cellular phone sticking out of his eye. *And still no one had said a word about him.* Every time she mentioned his name to John, he blanched and changed the subject. Yesterday she had rung Van Rhoe's office and spoken to his ice-queen secretary, who told her that Miles Van Rhoe was *out of the country.*

If he was away, abroad, he must be all right, mustn't he?

But she still felt that John was trying to protect her from something – or, as she suspected more strongly, was trying to hide something from her. The truth?

What truth?

Was John playing for time, just keeping her sweet? Helping Mr Sarotzini? Were they going to come for Verity today, tomorrow? Next week? When?

John had met with the lawyer, Elizabeth Frazer, on Tuesday. When he'd come home, he said there was nothing they could do because any action they took would involving serving papers on Mr Sarotzini. Elizabeth Frazer hadn't said anything about that to her.

Had John been lying?

Maybe her parents were in on this too? On all their visits to the clinic, she'd repeatedly told them exactly what had happened that pre-dawn morning in Casey's room – at least, as much as she could recall – and although they had nodded convincingly, she had caught those glances between them, those furtive, fleeting moments of eye contact.

And, sometimes, in her darker moments, Susan wondered if there had been another reason why they glanced at each other. *Did I do it?* Had I flipped?

Am I insane?

Her mouth was parched. Her lemonade stood on the grass beside her, but she was too tired even to reach down for it.

The constant stream of visitors was wearying. For the past three days it had been just like in California; and it was much the same mix of people, mostly middle Europeans but others too. All were unfailingly polite: they came to pay their respects, left their gifts and departed. Even so, mistrustful, Susan sat in vigilant guard by the cot throughout every visit.

Verity had received so many gifts that they were starting to have problems over where to put them. Two of the spare rooms were already at capacity. She heard the doorbell ring. Must be after two: the visitors never came before then, as if observing the courtesy of allowing her the mornings to herself. John could deal with them, or the nanny. She drifted into a troubled doze.

John had the entire contents of his golf bag spread out on the hall floor in an endeavour to find his swipe card for the clubhouse locker room. Late for his game, and in a filthy mood, he opened the front door and saw an overweight but distinguished-looking man in a business suit with a raincoat over his arm, perspiring heavily. He reminded John of someone, and then he realised who: the actor Robert de Niro.

'Good afternoon,' the man said, in a gentle, cultured voice. 'My name is Doctor Freer. I was a friend of Fergus Donleavy.'

'Ah,' John said. The man didn't look like a medic. 'Yes. Very sad, that. Terrible.'

'It was, it was quite terrible,' Freer said. 'Tragic. He was a fine man, remarkable intellect. Formidable.'

John wasn't in the mood right now for eulogies. And he'd always thought Susan had been a bit *too* fond of Fergus Donleavy. 'Is my wife expecting you?'

'No, no, I just called, on the off-chance. I hope it's not –?'

'Susan's resting at the moment. She's very tired.'

Freer tried not to show that he was pleased by this news.

'Would you like to come in? You're welcome to wait, but I don't want to wake her.'

'Well, if it's no trouble?'

John glanced at his watch. One twenty. He had to get going. He went through to the garden and signalled for the nanny. 'Caroline,' he said as she came hurrying in, 'Doctor Freer's come to see Susan. He'll wait until she's woken up. Could you look after him?'

'Yes, of course, Mr Carter.' She turned to the priest. 'Would you like to sit out in the garden?'

Freer mopped his brow with his handkerchief. 'Thank you. If it's no trouble, I would prefer to sit inside in the shade.'

'Of course.' She looked at John for instructions.

'It's cool in the drawing room,' John said.

She led him through. John knelt down again and began hastily to repack his golf bag. He heard the nanny ask the priest if he would like a drink, and the priest, politely, requested a glass of water.

Euan Freer sat down on a large, comfortable sofa. The young woman came in with a tumbler of iced water. 'Can I hang that up for you?' she asked.

He placed a protective arm over his raincoat, which lay carefully folded beside him. 'No, thank you, it's fine.' He smiled at her.

'I'll be outside,' she said. 'I'll let Mrs Carter know you're here as soon as she wakes.'

He thanked her and sipped his water. He heard the front door open then close and a few moments later the sound of a car starting and driving off. Then silence.

He stood up and walked over to the window. A woman in a cotton dress lay sleeping in a lounger – Susan Carter, he presumed. The young woman who had brought his drink was seated at table near her, absorbed in threading cotton through an object, a mobile of some sort. No sign of the baby: it must be in its room.

Good.

Scooping up his raincoat he walked quickly into the hallway, then stood still, holding his breath, listening. Trying to be quiet, he climbed the stairs, panting from the exertion as he reached the top and perspiring even more heavily now, his nerves in shreds.

He stopped and listened. His heart was tugging inside his chest and his throat felt tight. He looked down at the empty hall, then turned and stared along the landing. It was cold here and the air felt sluggish, as if all the energy was being drained from it. A door was ajar at the far end.

A voice inside his head told him to forget this crazy idea, to go back downstairs, to leave this house, to make an appointment with the bishop and deal with this via the proper channels.

And yes, yes, that would be much easier. Walk away. Forget about this. Yesterday, when the plan had been forming in his mind, it had seemed so simple. He had slept remarkably well and had woken this morning with his conviction strengthened and his courage high. But now that he was actually here, he felt daunted.

And taking a life, any life –

It was sanctioned, yes, in the Bible, but –

Closing his eyes, he prayed, 'Oh, God, give me strength.' Then, as quietly as he could, he tiptoed down the landing, entered the room and closed the door behind him.

The cold air made him gasp. A vapour trail rose from his mouth. His eyes jumped around, looking for an air-conditioning unit, but could see none. The curtains were drawn and it was dim in the room, but not dark. There to his right, against the wall, was a plain, simple cot, prettily draped in white, embroidered linen, with a small rug in front of it on the otherwise bare floorboards.

He tiptoed across and peered in, trembling terribly. The baby was asleep, a thin trail of vapour rising from its mouth. How could any baby survive in this cold?

His heart whipping the walls of his chest, he stared for some moments at the tiny scrunched-up face, so pink against the white sheets. The flame-red hair, the eyes closed, the tiny lips pursed together, the minute fingers of one hand entwined in the loose weave of the cotton blanket.

It was hard to believe that this was it, this little creature, so sweet and innocent-looking. Except that he could feel the presence radiating from it. He could feel its raw, hideous energy, and he knew he mustn't falter, must not be deflected by any emotion, must not allow doubt to enter his mind.

His teeth chattering with cold and fear, he started to whisper the words of the Lord's Prayer, so quietly they were barely audible. And as he reached the end of the prayer, he let the raincoat slip to the ground and raised the blade of the stainless-steel knife above his head, gripping the handle in both of his sweating, slippery hands.

And suddenly he could hear a terrifying hissing. It was the sound of his own blood coursing through his veins.

It was as if all the valves in his body had been opened, all the taps turned on, and the blood was hurtling through his system. His heart was throbbing, vibrating, shaking on its mountings, sending pains shooting down his chest, his arms, his legs. There was a terrible pain inside his head. His vision blurred. Then, with a clatter, the knife fell to the floor.

He let out a small, stifled croak.

Susan, startled awake by the nanny's shout, scrambled out of her recliner. Panic-stricken, the girl was already running in through the patio doors. Susan followed her upstairs, shouting for John.

The sight of the closed door deepened her alarm. The nanny sprinted ahead down the landing, hurled it open, then stopped in the doorway. Susan crowded in behind her.

A man she had never seen before, one of the damned visitors, she guessed, was on one knee, a raincoat spread out on the floor beside him, looking up at them, his face clammy and pallid. Heart in her mouth, she dashed to the cot and stared down. To her relief, Verity was sleeping peacefully.

She heard the nanny say, in a scolding tone, 'What are you doing up here?'

The stranger, sounding short of breath, gasped, 'I – I'm – so – so sorry – I –'

Susan knelt beside the man, trawling her brain for the first-aid protocols she had learnt, years back. He might be having a heart attack. She seized his wrist, searching for the pulse, and shivered. The room felt cold – maybe it was just shock.

The man grimaced at her apologetically, and then up at the nanny. 'I – just wanted – to see the baby. The heat – it – I –'

Susan found the pulse and looked at her watch. The pulse was high, racing.

'I'm all right,' he said, glancing anxiously at his raincoat. 'The heat. I'm all right, thank you very much, I'm sorry.'

Releasing his wrist, Susan turned to the nanny, who had the back of her hand pressed to his forehead, testing his temperature. 'I think you'd better call an ambulance, he doesn't look right.'

He shook his head. 'No, thank you, I –' He scooped up his raincoat clumsily from the floor, folded it several times, like a bundle of laundry, jammed it under his arm and stood up. 'The heat,' he said. 'Outside – I made a mistake, didn't realise how warm it was.'

'You feel very cold,' the nanny said. 'Do you have a heart condition? Blood pressure problems?'

'No, no problems, nothing important.'

'You'd better come downstairs and sit down for a few minutes,' Susan said. 'Are you OK to walk?'

'Yes, yes, thank you, yes, I'm fine.'

Susan led the way along the landing, the nanny flanking behind, and stayed close to him on the stairs, ready to grab him if he looked like falling. She led him through to the drawing room and he perched on the edge of the sofa, holding the raincoat on his lap.

'Can I get you anything?' Susan asked.

'No, I –' He glanced round. 'I still have my glass of water, thank you.' He picked it up with a hand that shook so much, water slopped over the top.

'Your husband asked me to show him in here,' the nanny said to Susan by way of an explanation.

'Who are you?' Susan asked.

'Euan – er – Doctor Freer. Did Fergus Donleavy ever mention my name to you?'

'Fergus?' she said in surprise.

'He was a very good friend.'

'Fergus Donleavy?'

'Yes.' He drank some water, the glass clattering against his teeth. 'A good man. He's left a very big hole behind him.'

'Are you the professor of theology? And Archdeacon Emeritus of …?'

He nodded.

'Yes, he has talked about you.' Her expression softened. 'I wanted to go to his funeral, but I – I was away. I was very shocked by his death. It was just so ...'.

Freer glanced warily at the nanny, then asked Susan, 'This young lady?'

'Caroline Hughes, our nanny.'

'Would it be possible, Mrs Carter, just for a few minutes, that you and I might speak in private?'

'I'll go up and check Verity,' the nanny said, and slipped out of the room, closing the door behind her.

The clergyman looked up at the ceiling and lowered his voice, as if nervous of being overheard. 'Mrs Carter, how much did Fergus tell you about your baby?'

She sat down in an armchair opposite him. 'He came round on the afternoon of the night he – he died.' She was silent collecting her thoughts, feeling very lucid, suddenly, far more clear-headed than she had for days. It was comforting to be in the presence of a priest.

'He was tense, but he wasn't very clear. He told me there was a file on my obstetrician, Miles Van Rhoe, at Scotland Yard – that Van Rhoe was involved in the ritual sacrifice of babies. And that a man with the same name as my baby's surrogate father, Mr Sarotzini, was a notorious occultist before the war – the devil incarnate, he called him.'

The priest nodded.

Then she remembered something else. 'Oh, yes, it was strange. We were having lunch one day last year, and he suddenly asked me if I was planning to get pregnant – that thought really seemed to worry him.'

'And what did you tell him?'

'I lied – I said no, and that calmed him down. It was a surrogate baby – I don't know if –?'

'Yes, I know.' Freer glanced up at the ceiling again, his mind in turmoil. Should he try again to kill the thing – and then himself? Did he have the courage? He could go back up there, before they realised what he was doing. He could go into the room, sweep past the nanny, and do it.

He should do it.

Except. He had already failed once. Perhaps that was God's hand restraining him, trying to show him there was another way, a better way. Or perhaps he just lacked the courage. He took a breath and in a voice that was barely above a whisper, said 'Susan, did Fergus explain to you what you have here in your house?'

She frowned, not comprehending.

'Your baby must have the protection of the Church. And you and your husband.'

'Protection?'

'We are going to have to work very hard, you, your husband and I. And we will need the help of others. Is your husband a churchgoer?'

'No. What do you mean "work hard"?'

Still shaking badly, he drank some more water. 'Everything Fergus told you is true, but this is not about protecting the baby from being taken for sacrifice, this is something else altogether.'

'What is it?'

'I don't think we should talk here. You must bring the baby to me, you and your husband, I want to start by baptising her. We must do it quickly. You have been baptised?'

'Yes. Please tell me what it is – what's going to happen to her.'

Again his eyes went up to the ceiling. 'I don't know how much the baby can hear. It would be better if you and your husband come to see me. Then we can talk in safety.'

Susan began to wonder about the man's sanity. His eyes were looking wild. 'Verity's only three and a half weeks old,' she said. 'She can't hear you.'

'Never underestimate her, Mrs Carter. Never make that mistake. Please, always remember that in the years ahead.' A few beads of perspiration ran down Freer's face and he dabbed his brow with his handkerchief. 'Your husband is playing golf?'

'Yes.'

'He will be back this evening?'

Susan nodded.

'I want the two of you to come and see me tonight, alone. Can you do that? Leave the baby here with the nanny. It is very important that we start our work as soon as possible. The baby will be getting stronger every day. She will find it progressively easier to resist.' Then, clutching the raincoat to his chest, he stood up.

There were questions Susan desperately wanted to fire at him. 'Please,' she said, 'Can you –?'

'I should go,' he said, interrupting her. 'I don't think my presence here is good. I will help you, but you and your husband must trust me. I – is – is it all right if I call a taxi?'

'Where are you going?'

'Central London – the Brompton Road.'

'There's a local minicab firm who're good, and cheaper than a black cab. Shall I call them for you?'

'Thank you,' he said.

Susan walked through to the kitchen, and dialled the number off the card on the wall. She felt so sick with fear she could barely give her address when the taxi firm answered. Euan Freer was someone of whom Fergus had spoken highly. Far too highly for her to dismiss him as a crank.

When she returned to the drawing room he was seated once more on the sofa, his hands together in front of his face, eyes closed, and he was mouthing a prayer. She stood in the doorway, not wanting to intrude, waiting for him to finish, remembering Fergus's disturbed expression at lunch last year, his agitation when she had seen him last.

The bell rang. Was that the taxi already? So quickly? She went to the front door and opened it. A blue Ford saloon with a roof aerial was sitting outside with the engine running. She turned to fetch the priest, but Euan Freer was already in the hallway, raincoat clutched untidily to his chest.

'My taxi?'

'Yes, I think so.'

He handed her a card, and looked at her imploringly. 'This is my home address and phone number. You and your husband will come tonight to see me?'

She hoped she would be able to persuade John. 'I'm not sure what time he'll be back.' Then she remembered something. 'The nanny – she's going to a concert tonight with a friend. I told her it would be all right.'

'Come afterwards, it doesn't matter. As late as you like. You will come?'

She nodded. 'I'll talk to her. Maybe we can get a relief nanny for a few hours.'

'Good.'

She glanced at the card. 'Please, Doctor Freer, tell me what you meant when you said that Verity will find it progressively easier to resist. Resist what?'

'Let me explain tonight, in private,' he said. Then, casting an anxious glance at the upstairs landing he hurried out, down the porch steps and over to the taxi.

Susan stood watching as he opened the rear door and clambered in. Then she caught a glimpse of the driver's face as he turned to greet the priest with a broad smile.

Her mouth fell open in shock. 'No,' she whispered. 'No. No. No.'

Even before the priest's door had closed, the car was accelerating fiercely away, the tyres squealing on the road.

Racked by shivers she tripped down the steps and broke into a run. 'Stop!' she screamed. 'Stop! Get out! Doctor! Doctor Freer! Get out! *Oh, please get out!*'

She sprinted helplessly after the car, watching it draw further and further away. The brake lights came on, but it barely stopped at the junction at the far end before turning right and disappearing.

'Stop!' she yelled, futilely. 'Please stop! For God's sake get out!' She sank to her knees in the middle of the road, sobbing. The driver's face burned in her mind. The smile.

That same smile she had seen before when he had come to fix the telephones. That smile as he had come towards her in the clinic. It was him. She was certain beyond any doubt.

The driver was the man from Telecom.

Chapter Seventy

John played well.

For the first time in many weeks he felt relaxed. He'd had a couple of beers, heard some new jokes. For a few precious hours, his troubles with Susan and Sarotzini had been pushed into the background. As he turned into his street, he was replaying in his mind his chip out of the trees on the fourteenth, which had struck the pin and gone down for an eagle, winning him the game. Still revelling in the memory, he pulled up outside the house.

Something was wrong.

Susan's car was gone.

His immediate reaction was that the car had been stolen – she hadn't driven since they had come back from the States. The little VW had been standing on the patch of concrete outside the house for weeks.

John ran into the house and was greeted by the nanny, who came hurriedly downstairs, dolled up with make-up and smartly dressed in white trousers and a jacket. He could tell from her expression that something was wrong. 'Oh, I thought it might be Mrs Carter coming back,' she said.

'She's gone out? In the car?'

'With Verity,' she said, nervously.

'Where?'

'I don't know, Mr Carter.'

'What do you mean *you don't know*?' he said, snapping at her and then immediately regretting it. 'Sorry.'

She smiled understandingly. 'Mrs Carter sent me out to the shops to get some groceries shortly after the gentleman – the priest – left. When I got back she and Verity had gone.'

'What time was that?'

'About two o'clock.'

'She didn't tell you she was going out?'

402

'No.'

John looked at his watch; it was seven twenty.

'I've been worried – perhaps something was wrong with Verity and she took her to the doctor or the hospital,' the nanny said. Then, sounding more reassuring than she looked, she added, 'I'm sure she'll be back soon.'

'Five hours? What did the priest want?'

'I don't know,' she said, openly.

'This was the man who arrived as I was leaving?'

'Yes.'

'You didn't hear anything he said to my wife?'

'No, he wanted to talk to her in private.'

John looked at her distractedly. 'He didn't say anything to you?'

'No.'

'And there's been no call, no message?'

'No, nothing. There were several visitors to see Mrs Carter and the baby – I told them they'd have to come back.' She swallowed nervously. 'There is one thing – I don't know if it's significant – but as the priest was leaving, Mrs Carter ran after the car. I don't know if he'd forgotten something, but she came back looking extremely distressed.'

John frowned, then thought for a moment. 'Freer. Doctor *Freer*. Was that his name?'

'I – I think that's how you introduced him.'

Out in the street a car hooted. The nanny made a move towards the door, but John got there first and saw a dilapidated Citroën 2CV outside, with the engine running. There was a young man in the driver's seat.

'Oh, that's my friend,' the nanny said. 'I'll just go and tell him I have to cancel tonight – I've been trying to phone him but he's been at a cricket match all day.'

'You're going to a concert, aren't you?'

'I'll cancel it, Mr Carter. I was going to tell him when he arrived. I didn't want to go until Mrs Carter got back.'

'Go,' John said. 'No point ruining your evening.'

She looked hesitant. 'Don't you think I –?'

'Go,' he said. 'Have a good time!'

'You're really sure?'

'Yes.'

She looked delighted. 'Thanks!' She waved cheerily at the driver of the car, then darted back inside to fetch her bag. She told John she'd be home early, and then she was gone.

John lugged in his golf bag and trolley from the car, and stored them away in the cupboard under the stairs, his brain racing. Sarotzini hadn't taken her. If she and Verity had been snatched she wouldn't have driven in her car. Where was she?

Had she gone back to America?

No, surely not.

Then where?

He went into the kitchen, picked up the phone and dialled directory enquiries. When they answered, he asked if there was a Canon Freer listed, and gave them a variety of spelling options.

He was given two numbers. One was a flat in the Brompton Road. The other was at University College, London. He tried the flat first and got an answering machine. He left a message, asking for Canon Freer to call him back, urgently. Then he tried the university number.

There was no answer.

The double glazing made the room eerily quiet. It was a fine evening outside: the London skyline, streaked with crimson, had a pink hue.

Verity was feeding hungrily. Behind her, the television was on, mute. Susan surfed the channels with the remote, barely noticing anything. Inside her head she surfed her brain in the same detached way.

She was crying. She had been crying all afternoon. She was thinking about Euan Freer. What had happened to him? The same thing that had happened to Fergus, Harvey, Zak Danziger and maybe even Archie Warren? She had phoned the numbers on his card repeatedly, every half-hour, desperate to hear that he was unharmed, that he was home, that she had only imagined the man from Telecom's face in the minicab.

And she was crying for her loss of Fergus. He had been trying so hard to tell her something and she hadn't listened – not in the way that he'd needed her to listen.

Susan, did Fergus explain to you what you have here in your house?

Your baby must have the protection of the Church. And you and your husband.

Verity's tiny hand was stroking her breast as she fed. Susan stared down, feeling an immense closeness and love for her. It was incredible: this was her baby, she had carried this creature inside her body and now her body was feeding her.

Never underestimate her, Mrs Carter, never make that mistake. Please, always remember that in the years ahead.

She looked so pretty, so innocent, so adorable, in her white cotton all-in-one sailor outfit. How could she ever change?

The man from Telecom. Would he come along one day and change her?

Her mind was drifting. The pink hue outside was deepening.

Fergus had tried to warn her and she hadn't listened. He had tried to tell her what she might be bringing into the world and she hadn't wanted to hear.

'I'm not going to let them,' she whispered. 'They think they can come and take you one day and use you in their rituals. But they can't. I will never let them, never. I promised you that when you were just li'l ole Bump inside me. Remember that?'

When Verity finished feeding, Susan opened her handbag and took out the number Mr Sarotzini had given her, where he had assured her he could be reached day and night. She dialled it.

He answered on the second ring.

'Mr Sarotzini,' she said. 'It's Susan Carter.'

There was a pause and then he said, pleasantly, 'Hello, Susan, how are you?'

'I want you to listen to me very carefully. I'm on the fourteenth floor of the London Hilton and I have Verity in my arms. If you don't do exactly what I tell you, I'm taking her with me out of the window.'

Chapter Seventy-one

Kündz said, 'Let me talk to her.'

He had driven the Mercedes limousine to Heathrow because he wanted to be with Mr Sarotzini when he went to Susan.

'Just take me to the London Hilton in Park Lane, Stefan. You are familiar with this hotel?'

Mr Sarotzini was sitting in the rear of the car. It was dark and Kündz could not see Mr Sarotzini's face in the mirror, and this made him uncomfortable. Mr Sarotzini was in a bad mood and this made him uncomfortable also. Kündz wanted him to be in a good mood when he met Susan, because he was afraid for her. She was behaving foolishly; he needed to speak to her, to warn her of the dangers of angering Mr Sarotzini.

Oh, Susan, Susan, my darling Susan, why have you done this?

It was Saturday night, and the traffic was heavy. The drive in from the airport took forty-five minutes, and it was nearly eleven when they pulled up outside the hotel entrance. A boisterous group of people in evening dress came out through the revolving doors.

Mr Sarotzini had said nothing on the journey, and only broke his silence now to say, 'Wait here.'

The rear door opened. Kündz heard the rustle of a bank-note, and then the doorman was in front of him, waving him forward into a space on the packed forecourt. Anxiously he watched Mr Sarotzini enter the hotel. Then he peered up. Susan was in a room: her light might be any of the ones he could see.

Please be sensible, Susan, oh, please be a sensible girl. I don't want to have to punish you.

Every day Kündz tried to avoid thinking about the baby, but he couldn't help it. Mr Sarotzini had promised him that one day he would be together with Susan. He, Susan and Verity, the three of them together, a family, a unit, a trinity. He longed to hold the baby in his arms, the tiny creature with Susan's red hair that was his daughter, to have her look into his eyes and reach out her arms towards him, and to hear her say, *Daddy!*

Instead it was John Carter's eyes that she looked into.

For the past four weeks he had been experiencing new and confusing emotions. He saw the world in a different light, a world that no longer centred around himself but around his tiny child. How he wished he could sweep Susan up in his arms and kiss her tenderly and tell her that it was he, not Mr Sarotzini, who was the father and that they were going to be together for ever, that he would protect her and Verity. No one would ever harm either of them. And how he wished he could tell her that Mr Sarotzini sanctioned their love!

Oh, Susan, will you ever know quite how much I love you? Will your child – our child? Will she? Please, you must be sensible, my darling, you must not play games with Mr Sarotzini.

You must not jeopardize our future happiness.

Emil Sarotzini got out of the elevator at the fourteenth floor, oriented himself with the room numbers, then turned left, walked down the corridor and stopped outside room 1401. A DO NOT DISTURB sign hung on the door. He rang the bell.

There was no answer.

He rang the bell again, for longer. Then waited. Then he rang the bell again.

At last he heard the sound of a safety chain being removed. It was followed by the clunk of a lock. Then the door opened and he was confronted by a large, bearded man, in a white towelling dressing-gown. A blonde girl was sitting up in the bed and leather clothing was strewn on the floor.

'Who the fuck are you?' the man asked, in a thick, Irish accent.

Holding his ground and his icy calm, Mr Sarotzini replied, 'I've come to see Susan Carter.'

'Who?' The man's surprise was clearly genuine.

'Susan Carter,' he repeated.

'You've got the wrong fucking room.' He slammed the door.

Through the spyhole of room 1402, opposite, Susan watched Mr Sarotzini turn and walk away. Verity, who had enjoyed her eight p.m. feed, was sleeping peacefully.

'Why did you not check, Stefan? Why did you not confirm for me that Susan Carter was where she said she was?'

'There are other Hiltons in London,' Kundz replied. 'it is possible that –'

'No.' Mr Sarotzini cut him short. 'It is not possible. She was most specific. Room 1401 of the London Hilton in Park Lane. They have no Susan Carter registered. They are not aware of any woman with a baby staying in this hotel.'

Kündz felt a burst of happiness that Susan had not been there. He had been scared for her; there was no knowing what Mr Sarotzini might do when he was angry, but now there was a paradox. Susan was not there, so Mr Sarotzini had not been able to harm her. So Susan was safe. But this had inflamed Mr Sarotzini's anger more. So now she was in even greater danger.

Oh, Susan, I'm so proud of you. Stay free, run, hide, stay free, you and my baby, our baby, our daughter!

And, suddenly, Kündz had a plan forming in his mind. If he could find her, he could help her to hide. He could keep Mr Sarotzini away from her.

But that would be disloyal to Mr Sarotzini. He had never been disloyal to Mr Sarotzini in his life. He was not even sure he could be disloyal, however much he wanted to. Even the idea made him afraid.

Then the thought of what Mr Sarotzini might make him do to Susan, to punish her, made him even more afraid. He could still hear Claudie's screams sometimes, when he closed his eyes, and that was difficult. He did not know how he would cope with Susan screaming – he was afraid that perhaps he might not be able to handle that.

'I will find her,' he said, as he pulled up the Mercedes outside Mr Sarotzini's club.

'That will not be necessary, Stefan. Susan will contact me again. She is unbalanced. When people are unbalanced they have to be treated very carefully, you need to understand that. You will now return to your flat in Earl's Court. I will call you in the morning.'

For the first time ever, Kündz disobeyed Mr Sarotzini's instructions. He did not drive home, but instead to South London, to the Carters' street, where he parked the Mercedes a safe distance away from the Carters' house.

He could see John Carter's BMW, but there was no sign of Susan's Volkswagen. As he switched off the engine he felt a sudden deep swirl of fear. Did Mr Sarotzini know he was here? What would he do to him if he found out?

Kündz knew the answer to that. But he knew also that Mr Sarotzini could not know that he was here. Unless, and now he was worried again, *unless* he could pick up Kündz's fear. But he doubted that tonight. Mr

Sarotzini was weary from the journey, it was late, he would be going to sleep.

It was worth the risk. It was worth everything.

He stayed in the Mercedes, watching, listening. The nanny was a loose cannon. She could return home at any time, she might already be back now, although he didn't think so, there had been no voice-print activity from her in the house since seven thirty this evening. Just to make sure, he dialled in on his mobile phone and activated the remote playback. Nothing there of consequence. Just a series of phone calls from John to friends asking if they had seen Susan. Now he was calling the police, telling them his wife had had a breakdown and gone off with their baby.

Maybe John Carter really did not know where she was. Or maybe it was just a great act.

Kündz had wanted to arrange a special nanny for Susan but he had not been permitted to do so. Mr Sarotzini was insistent that Verity should be brought up in a normal environment. He had reminded Kündz of the words of the Twenty-third Truth, which stated, 'I hear and I forget; I see and I remember; I do and I understand.'

Mr Sarotzini wanted Verity to do and to understand. To live in the ordinary world and, by doing so, to understand it better. When she was older, that was when they would begin their work on her. Until then, it was necessary to protect her but nothing more.

It had been useful having Susan and John Carter away from the house for three weeks. This had enabled Kündz to conceal the monitoring equipment so well that no one would ever find it, not unless they demolished the house brick by brick – and, he prided himself, unlikely even then.

He let himself in through the front door, using his own key, closed it carefully and moved swiftly to the bottom of the stairs, where he would be out of sight of anyone emerging either from the kitchen or the drawing room. He could hear John's voice on the telephone: it was coming from the drawing room.

Then he stood still for a few moments, breathing in Susan's scents, savouring them. It was so good to smell her again this strongly. The house needed this, needed her smells – it had been such a lonely place without them while she was away in America. Now she was everywhere again, she was all around him, and this made him deliriously happy.

He felt he had come home.

Whisky and cigarette smoke came to him strongly. Reluctantly, he tuned out Susan's scents and began to concentrate on his task here. He moved stealthily up to the drawing-room door, which was ajar, and peered in.

The television was on, the sound muted. John Carter was sitting on a sofa with his back towards him, talking, it sounded, to a hospital.

Kündz waited, the hatred he felt for this man powering up inside him, increasing with every second that he watched him, until, like a demon possessing him, it took control and moved him forward, closer, silently covering the few yards of carpet until he was right behind John. On the television, two men were sitting by a campfire, smoking cigarettes and, although he could not hear them now, Kündz knew they talking about the meaning of life. He had seen this film also: the men were talking crap, it had angered him then and it added to his anger now.

He waited until John finished his call and hung up the receiver, and then he said, 'Good evening, Mr Carter.'

John spun his head round, and Kündz hit him, three inches beneath the chin, with a karate chop that knocked him off the sofa and on to the floor but was not heavy enough to break his neck. Kündz did not want to kill him too quickly.

John lay there, winded and gagging, his ears numb, spikes of pain shooting through his skull, looking up in shock at the huge man towering over him. Then, gathering his wits, he pushed down with the palms of his hands on the floor, trying to lever himself up. Kïndz kicked him hard underneath his chin, a single kick that shattered his jaw and several teeth, and pitched him violently on to his back.

Dazed, but numb to the pain, John stared, unfocusing, at Kündz. Slowly he began to gather his thoughts. Who was he? A madman? Burglar? What the hell did he –? Then, as his vision improved, something in his brain connected. The face. In the clinic in California. He looked like the man, the flunkey, who had taken him up to Mr Sarotzini's office that afternoon when he had arrived.

Kündz stood over John, with his hands in his pockets, and said, 'Mr Carter, I need you to tell me where Susan has gone.'

John tried to speak, but the movement of his jaw hurt so much he cried out in pain. Gripping his chin with his hands, and dribbling blood, he mumbled, 'Don't – don't know.'

He was trying to think clearly. Had Sarotzini sent this man?

The hatred was so strong now as he stared down at John that it was almost tearing Kündz apart. *Are you enjoying this, Mr Carter?* he wanted to ask. *How does this compare to screwing your wife?*

There were so many things Kündz would like to do to him right now

410

that he was finding it hard to decide where to start. 'I'm going to hurt you, Mr Carter, I'm going to hurt you so very much. You are aware of the reasons I have?'

John looked back at him, bewildered. 'I don't – she – this afternoon – she went – didn't say –'

'You are not understanding me very well, Mr Carter.' Kündz smiled at him. He wanted John Carter to relax, to calm down, to *listen*. He wanted him to know why he was being punished. He wanted John to be *grateful*. The Thirteenth Truth stated that all true gratitude is borne from punishment. And John would be grateful if he could understand, *really* understand the importance of this child his wife had given birth to.

Then, before Kündz knew it, John Carter had his hand around a small, solid table and was swinging it with all his strength into his shin.

With a cry of shock, Kündz staggered backwards and fell heavily across the arm of the sofa. John Carter was up on his feet, running through the doorway and out into the hall. Even more enraged by pain, Kündz threw himself, hobbling, after him.

John reached the front door, and pulled the handle of the Banham latch, but it did not move. *Oh, Christ.* The lock pin was down. With fingers trembling so much they would barely work he pushed it up, tried again. The door swung open then stopped with a jerk and a loud clank after a few inches, as the safety chain was yanked taut.

In desperation he slammed the door shut. How the hell had the safety chain got on? How? How? How? He tore at it with his fingers, then he was being yanked back fiercely by his hair, his legs were kicked out from beneath him and he crashed backwards on to the floor with a sob of despair.

In fury, Kündz stamped on John's right kneecap, with all his force, shattering it.

The pain and the shock jerked John upright up like a marionette. He bellowed in agony, fell back, writhing, rolling his head, thrashing, pummelling the floor with his fists. He rolled left, right, moaning terribly, white-hot knives of pain shooting out through him in every direction. *Oh, God, let me die,* he thought. *Let me die. Anything, please, just stop this pain, kill me, please kill me.* He clutched at the rug with his fingers, bit into a tuft with his teeth, yammering, crying, the pain exploding through his eyes, ears, his scalp.

Then he was pulled over on to his back and his neck was pinioned to the floor by the man's shoe.

John's eyeballs were rolling, sweat was pouring down his face and he was gagging, struggling for breath, choking on his own blood. Kündz smiled at him. 'The First Truth, Mr Carter, states that from pain comes real love. I would like you to think about that. I would like also for you to understand that I am doing this to help Susan. If you knew what I am risking to help her then you would love me, Mr Carter, you really would. Please think very hard and tell me, where is she?'

He pressed down hard with his foot. Too hard. There was a crunch of bone, John Carter's eyes bulged and he made a gurgling sound. Kündz released the pressure, a fraction.

'Sssshon't know,' John groaned, '*don't* know. I *shon't* know. Pleeassssh believe me.'

Kündz pulled from his pocket a small penknife and opened the blade. 'I don't like it when you make love to your wife, Mr Carter. I'm going to make it hard for you to do that in future.'

Still keeping his foot firmly on John's neck, Kündz began to bend his legs, lowering himself down, his left leg hurting badly. Then he gripped the belt of John's trousers, and jerked it open.

John let out a terrible cry; his body shook, his arms flailing.

Then Kündz heard a noise behind him.

He turned. The front door was open, the safety chain pulled tight. A woman called out, 'Hello? Mr Carter? Hello?' It was the nanny, Kündz recognised her voice and clamped his hand over John's mouth.

'Coming!' Kündz called out. 'Close the door so I can take the chain from it.'

The door closed. Kündz, thinking quickly, grabbed John's right wrist and made a deep slash across the vein and in a fraction of a second did the same to the left wrist. Then he hurried through into the kitchen, pausing to rinse his knife under the tap and dry it.

Then he unbolted the rear door, let himself out into the garden and slipped away, over the fence and into the darkness of the park, and made his way swiftly back to the Mercedes.

He had parked sufficiently far back that the nanny, whom he could see clearly in the porch light, would barely even have heard him start the car. And, besides, all her concentration was on the front door. He could see her unlocking it again now, and pushing it open, just a few inches until the chain ran out of slack.

When Kündz arrived home, twenty minutes later, a message awaited him from Mr Sarotzini: 'I have an appointment with Susan at 10 a.m.

tomorrow. You will collect me from the club at 9 a.m. This time she will not let me down.'

Chapter Seventy-two

It was a wet Sunday morning: heavy summer rain was pelting down. Kündz drove the huge Mercedes at a steady 70 m.p.h. along the fast, undulating road through Buckinghamshire countryside. The stretch they were currently on was three-lane, with a double white line that had alternating breaks for overtaking. The clock on the dashboard showed it was nine fifty.

There was little traffic going the same way; more was coming from the opposite direction, heading into London. A massive truck blattered past, blinding Kündz with spray and shaking the limousine with its slipstream. He increased the speed of the wipers.

Mr Sarotzini had said nothing about last night, and Kündz presumed that this meant that he did not know he'd disobeyed him. All the same he was nervous that Mr Sarotzini might say something.

He had woken feeling low this morning; and deeply uneasy. Instead of feeling elated about John Carter, he felt flat. He did not understand why. He felt dirty, as if he needed a bath, except that he had already had a shower. It would be different when he saw Susan again. Then he would feel fine.

But he was scared of Mr Sarotzini's mood today. It was bad, far worse than yesterday. He could not ever remember Mr Sarotzini in such a black mood. He was scared of what Mr Sarotzini might instruct him to do to Susan.

'Last night, Stefan,' Mr Sarotzini said.

Kündz stiffened, saying nothing.

'Last night, when Susan Carter telephoned me for the second time.' Kündz watched him in the mirror, nervous that Mr Sarotzini was going to question him about John. The banker was looking out of the window, stroking his chin, taking his time before he continued. 'She explained to me, Stefan, that she wanted to know she could trust me to come alone. That is why she put me to the test yesterday.'

The ominous tone in Mr Sarotzini's voice increased Kündz's anxiety.

'She saw your face, Stefan. As you were driving away the creepy little priest, Doctor Freer. *She saw your face.*'

Kündz knew this. He had seen hers too, he had seen that flash of recognition. 'Yes, it was a mistake,' he answered.

He could deal with it. When he saw Susan, he would be able to explain and she would understand. He was just a shitty little priest, vermin. He was history.

'Too many mistakes, Stefan. I think your love for this woman is clouding your judgement.'

The harsh, scolding tone of Mr Sarotzini's voice sent a chill through him. Before he could respond, Mr Sarotzini continued, 'You are making mistakes all the time, Stefan. I am losing count of the number you have made just recently. You allowed Susan Carter to flee to the United States. You allowed the priest, Doctor Freer, to be alone in that room with Verity. And now you have disobeyed my instructions. You did not go straight home to your flat in Earl's Court last night, you went to the Carters' house.'

Kündz froze. He connected with Mr Sarotzini's eyes in the mirror, then stared ahead once more at the road. How? How? How?

Then he realised, and another much deeper chill coursed through him. Of course. *The nanny.* Mr Sarotzini had not permitted him to select a nanny himself; he had told him that the choice of the nanny needed to be random. But there was nothing, *nothing* in Mr Sarotzini's world that was ever random.

Mr Sarotzini had put the nanny there not just to look after Verity. *She was there to spy on him.*

'Susan Carter is dangerously unstable, Stefan. She has reminded me over the telephone of the promises I made to her husband that there would be no more killing and that there would be no more bugging. She is making threats to harm the baby, to kill herself and the baby. She says that if she ever sees you again, she will kill Verity.'

'I will explain everything to her,' Kündz said, trembling. 'I will calm her down, she will understand.'

'I cannot take this risk, Stefan.' There was a terrible finality in Mr Sarotzini's voice.

Kündz drove on in silence.

'You have brought about this situation, Stefan, and I will give you the choice of how you deal with it. Either you will kill Susan Carter or you will have to stay away from her for ever.'

'I cannot kill her,' he said quietly.

They were approaching a slow-moving van Kündz pulled out to overtake, but a stream of cars was coming in the other direction. He pulled back in.

'Then you will stay away from her for ever.'

'My duty is to teach Verity the Truths,' Kündz said.

'Verity has been born with the knowledge of all the Truths, Stefan. This is what makes her special. This is what makes her unique. She will require no one to teach her these. As she grows older she will simply know them. They will be second nature to her. As will many other things.'

'You promised me I could have Susan for ever.'

'The Twenty-seventh Truth states that nothing lasts for ever. It is the law of entropy. Disorder naturally increases with the passage of time. Not even promises last for ever, Stefan.'

Kündz drove on in silence. He tried to imagine killing Susan and he could not. He tried to imagine living without ever seeing her again. He could not.

Without his protection, what would happen to Susan? She was too free-spirited, too strong-willed. One day she would anger Mr Sarotzini again.

And then?

Claudie's screams echoed inside his head.

He pulled out again to see beyond the van. In the distance a large truck was approaching. There was time, just time, if he accelerated hard.

But he swung back in again. Then, looking at Mr Sarotzini in the mirror, he said, 'I have failed you. I am impure. The Fifth Truth states that "The only purification is eradication."'

Kündz swung the steering wheel hard over to the right. The Mercedes veered out from behind the van straight across the oncoming lane.

Straight into the path of the oncoming truck.

Susan, my love, this is for you, this is how much I love you, so much more than you will ever know.

Kündz heard Claudie's screams once more. Then, for the first time in his life, he heard Mr Sarotzini's scream.

And that was worth everything.

The massive truck hit the limousine broadside, sheering off its roof then dragging the mangled wreckage along for two hundred yards beneath its wheels, before slithering off the road on to the verge and coming to a halt in a wide ditch.

Seconds after the driver jumped clear from his cab, the petrol from the

Mercedes' tank exploded in a ball of fire, taking the truck up in flames with it.

Epilogue

Ting ... ting ... ting ... ting ... ting ...

The noise was driving Susan nuts. She had a copy-edit deadline of the end of the following week for an anthology of Fergus Donleavy's writings, and she had been working all weekend on it. The book had been her idea and she'd persuaded Magellan Lowry to commission a bright science journalist – who, some years back, had coincidentally written a profile on Euan Freer – to put it together.

It had been a slow process, a five-year labour of love, but she felt she had done Fergus justice with it, and it would be a fitting tribute to the man.

Ting ... ting ... ting ... ting ... ting ...

She could hear it through the ceiling. That damned gerbil, Buzzy – they'd bought it for Verity as a fifth birthday present a fortnight ago. It was going round and round on the treadmill in its cage. And she could swear, sometimes, that Verity encouraged it. Every time Susan settled down to work, the gerbil started its goddamn aerobics.

She was wrestling with a difficult section of the book. One of Fergus's many thoughts on the theories of time. She remembered trying to get her head round this passage once before, when she'd been working on the manuscript of the last book Fergus had written, which had been published posthumously. It had had good reviews, but had not been the brilliant best-seller she'd hoped for. But she was consoled by the knowledge that Fergus would have preferred it that way: good reviews from his peers had always meant more to him than his sales figures.

Time is a curve, not a straight line. Linear time is an illusion; we exist in a space-time continuum.

Sometimes she hoped that was true, that time was an illusion, and that people did not simply die and cease to exist; that everyone who had ever existed still did exist. But that hope had its flaws. She wanted Fergus still to exist. And Harvey Addison. But not Mr Sarotzini.

She kept the newspaper cutting of Mr Sarotzini's death in a drawer of her desk: it was a constant reaffirmation to her that he really was dead. It was a small article, just a few column inches, stating that a Swiss banker, Emil Sarotzini, and his chauffeur, Stefan Kündz, had been killed when their Mercedes had collided with an articulated lorry on the A413 in Buckinghamshire.

She had been a little surprised, but not disappointed, that no obituary of Mr Sarotzini had appeared in any newspaper.

Ting ... ting ... ting ... ting ... ting ...

She looked at her watch. Four p.m. John would be back from golf in an hour, and they'd have to get going soon after that. He was playing with Archie Warren, who had now recovered fully from his stroke and was fine, although he'd been advised never to play squash again.

Ting ... ting ... ting ... ting ... ting ...

Exasperated she looked up at the ceiling and shouted, '*Verity! Shut that bloody thing up!*'

Almost immediately, the noise stopped. Silence! Sweet, precious silence!

Not that Verity was a noisy kid: on the contrary, she was almost worryingly quiet at times. A loner, she wasn't good at mixing with other children, preferring her own company sitting up in her room reading voraciously or playing on her computer. The teachers at her school said she was advanced for her age – probably, the head had explained, the advantage of being an only child with a literary mother.

She and John had been trying for three years now for another baby, but so far without success. They'd had all kinds of tests and there was nothing wrong. It just hadn't happened. Yet.

There was something Susan carried in her heart, which was that she wanted, more than anything, to believe that John was Verity's father. Sometimes, although John didn't like to talk about it, she sensed when she saw him talking to Verity, or playing with her, that he, too, believed it himself. And, as she had constantly told herself, *it was possible.*

Even though Verity had been born a month premature, she'd been a good-sized baby and had surprised everyone by how strong she was. Maybe she had been conceived a month earlier than everyone had thought, and John really was her father.

Every few months she had a strange recurring dream, in which Mr Sarotzini was sitting beside her bed. He would smile sadly at her and say, 'Susan, the Twenty-eighth Truth states that sometimes it is better to *believe* than to know.'

There was something else Susan carried in her heart. It was the memory of a conversation she'd had in her room in the clinic with Mr Sarotzini soon after Verity had been born. He had said to her, *Look at your daughter, look at her, look at Verity. Is she evil? Is she corrupt? Is that how she has been born? Is that how you view her when you look at her, hold her, suckle her? An evil, corrupt monster? Is it, Susan?*

She believed, fervently, that Verity *was* born pure and innocent, the way all babies were. How they grew up and changed was as much due to the moulding they received from their parents as from their genes. If she and John could show Verity enough love and care and warmth and humanity, then they could overcome whatever bad genes Verity might have inherited. They could destroy whatever it was Mr Sarotzini might have had planned for her.

That was why she had decided never to have a nanny and only to work freelance from home. She wanted to be there for Verity. She wanted to be the best mother it was possible to be.

Shortly after five, she heard the sound of the front door opening, the rattle of golf clubs, the thump of the bag being dumped on the hall floor. Then John came limping into her office, looking sunburned and gorgeous, and kissed her on the forehead. 'Hi,' he said.

His limp was permanent but, fortunately, his only legacy from the savage attack on him in the house. The doctors had said it was the quick action of the nanny that had saved his life. The police never found the assailant, neither did they ever come up with a motive for the attack. John's memory of the man was hazy but his description was enough for Susan to be pretty certain who he had been. She had told John she thought he was one of Mr Sarotzini's henchmen, but she never told him about her night in the WestOne Clinic.

'Hi, hon,' she said. 'How was the game?'

'Good, I played well.'

'Did you win?'

'Lost on the eighteenth – it was all on the last putt and Archie sank a blinder. I just want to have a quick shower. Are we going?'

'Yes, of course.' She looked at him testily.

'Sure, no problem, I'll get ready. Where's Verity?'

'Upstairs. She was playing with her computer, that new Endangered Species game of yours.'

'Is she enjoying it?'

'Uh-huh, I guess so.' Susan found it hard, sometimes, to know what Verity was thinking.

'She ought to be outside on a day like this.'

'So should I.' Susan smiled. 'Guess I'm not setting her a good example. I'll go get her ready.'

Susan went upstairs and along the corridor to Verity's room. The door was closed as usual. She went in, and saw Verity, in dungarees and a T-shirt, sitting in front of the computer screen. She was studying something intently, her face framed by her long red hair, her mouth puckered in concentration as she tapped the keyboard, then moved the mouse across the pad. Susan heard the trumpet of an elephant. 'How you doing, hon?'

Verity raised a hand, signalling her not to interrupt. 'I'm moving elephants to a new watering hole.'

Susan walked over to the gerbil's cage and peered in. 'Hi, Buzzy, you were a noisy little –'

The gerbil was lying motionless on its side on the floor of the cage.

Susan shot a glance at Verity. Christ, had she noticed? She opened the cage door warily, because Buzzy had sharp teeth and had bitten her nastily a week ago, and touched the little creature lightly with her finger.

It was rigid.

Verity was still absorbed in her game. Susan picked up the gerbil and held it in the palm of her hand, studying it. She frowned. The head was at a strange angle. When she touched it, it was loose, as if it was only attached by skin and not bone. Then she saw blood in its mouth and over its tiny incisors.

A cold slick travelled down her spine. 'Verity,' she said, her voice several octaves higher than normal. 'What's happened to Buzzy?'

'Buzzy's dead,' Verity said, nonchalantly, moving her mouse again and tapping more keys.

'How did this happen?'

'He was annoying you so I broke his neck. It's the best way to do it.' She leaned forward to peer more closely at something on the screen.

Susan was unsure how to handle this. 'You killed Buzzy? You killed your pet? I thought you liked Buzzy.'

Verity shook her hair away from her face. Then she stared at her mother levelly and said, 'The only true pain is to hurt the thing you love.'

'What?' Susan said, in amazement.

Verity turned back and resumed her game.

Susan walked over to her, and put an arm around her shoulder. 'What did you say, hon?'

Verity turned back towards her, breaking free of Susan's arm with a ferocity that startled her. 'Leave me alone!'

'It's nearly half past five, you have to get ready for church.'

421

'Not going to church. I don't want to go to church. We go every week and it's boring and I don't want to go any more.' She burst into tears and began screaming, 'Donwannago! Donwannago!'

John came into the room. 'What the hell –?'

He stopped as he saw the gerbil in Susan's hand. And the look of steel in Susan's eyes.

Susan knelt down and, with her free hand, pulled the computer's plug out of the wall socket. Then she stood up, grabbed Verity by the neck of her T-shirt and yanked her out of the chair.

'We're just getting ready for church,' Susan said, brightly.